Praise for Linda Green

'★★★★' *Sun*

'Smart, witty writing' *ELLE*

'One of the most touching books I think I
will ever read. A triumph' *Chicklit Reviews*

'Witty and funny' *Company Magazine*

'Laugh-out-loud funny' *Reveal Magazine*

'Utterly riveting' *Closer*

'Linda has a great writing style which is almost
effortless but be prepared to laugh and cry'
LoveReading.co.uk

Linda Green is an award-winning journalist and has written for the *Guardian*, the *Independent on Sunday* and the *Big Issue*. Linda lives in West Yorkshire. *The Mummyfesto* is her fifth novel.

The
MUMMYFESTO

Linda Green

*There's no better book
to celebrate International
Women's Day and
Mother's Day.
Enjoy!   Katerina*

Quercus

First published in 2013 by

Quercus
55 Baker Street
7th Floor, South Block
London W1U 8EW

A CIP catalogue record for this book is available
from the British Library

PB ISBN 978 1 78087 522 4
EBOOK 978 1 78087 523 1

10 9 8 7 6 5 4 3 2

Printed and bound in Great Britain by Clays Ltd, St Ives plc

Typeset by Ellipsis Digital Limited, Glasgow

For Rohan

'If you don't like the way the world is, you change it.
You have an obligation to change it.
You just do it one step at a time.'

Marian Wright Edelman

1

SAM

'Mummy, watch how fast I can go.'

I had this crazy, outlandish dream, well, more of a fantasy really, that one day we would arrive at school not just on time but actually early, maybe even by as much as five minutes. As I watched Oscar career along the canal towpath, totally oblivious to the mound of dog poo he was fast approaching, I realised that this was not going to be the day that happened.

'Oscar. Stop. Now.'

It was too late.

'Mummy,' called Zach, who was a few paces ahead of Oscar but had turned to see what all the commotion was about, 'Oscar's gone straight through that pile of dog poo.' He said it with an air of fascination and awe rather than any hint of trying to get his little brother into trouble.

Oscar looked down and wrinkled his nose. 'Urrgghh,' he said, 'I'm going to be the smelliest boy in school today.'

'No you're not, Oscar,' I said, at last catching up with them and surveying the wheels of his powerchair, 'because we're going to get you cleaned up right now.'

'Are you going to take me through the carwash, Mummy?' asked Oscar. 'Please, can you take me through the carwash?'

I smiled down at him, resisting the temptation to ruffle his hair in case he insisted on redoing the gel and prolonging the delay even further.

'No, love. I don't want you getting squished in the rollers. It's going to be good old-fashioned elbow-grease, I'm afraid.'

'Why are your elbows greasy?' asked Oscar. There was no time to try to explain.

'Zach, stay here with Oscar. Don't let him go anywhere or do anything he shouldn't do. Oscar, do what your brother says and I'll be straight back, OK?'

I ran back down the towpath. It was the sort of occasion when I was grateful I was not one of those pristine power-dressing mums who totter to school in their stilettos (not that we had many of those in Hebden Bridge). Say what you like about Doc Martens, they are bloody good for legging it down muddy towpaths during a school-run emergency.

It was not the first time I'd had to abandon my children and run home. Usually it was a forgotten book bag, packed lunch, PE kit or something for show and tell. But nor was the powerchair-meets-dog-poo situation entirely new to us. Which explained why there was a plastic container in the toolshed in the front yard marked 'poo' (as opposed to the one next to it marked 'punctures'), which contained a scrubbing brush and a mini-bottle of washing-up liquid.

I grabbed the watering can, which was half full with rainwater (one of the good things about living in the Pennines) and set off back down the towpath.

When I arrived, Oscar looked at the watering can and back to me, rolled his eyes and said, 'Mummy, I am not a sunflower, you can't water me to make me grow.'

Zach laughed obligingly, knowing full well, as I did, that Oscar understood precisely what the watering can was for and only said it to get a laugh. I winked at Zach, held the watering can over Oscar's head for a second to make him squeal before I sprinkled it on the wheels of his powerchair and attacked it with the scrubbing brush and washing-up liquid.

Miraculously, we still made it through town and up the hill in time to see the last few stragglers heading through the main doors into school.

'Come on, Mummy,' called Oscar over his shoulder as he whizzed up the road in front of me. I joked sometimes that the reason we chose this school in preference to the nearer one was that I knew the school run would keep me fit. It wasn't the real reason, of course. We chose it because we thought it was right for Zach and, very importantly, that it would also be right for Oscar. Everything always had to be right for Oscar.

Shirley the lollipop lady bent to talk to Oscar who threw his arms around her in his customary greeting. It was only when I finally caught up with them and Shirley stood up that I noticed the tears in her eyes.

'What's the matter?' I asked.

'I knew it,' she said. 'I managed to keep myself together for other kids but second I saw your Oscar that were it.' She sniffed and wiped her nose with her hand before managing a watery grin at Zach.

'What's happened?' I asked.

'Just been given me notice by council. Doing away with me they are. Me and half a dozen others.'

'But they can't. That's ridiculous. This is such a busy road.'

'Bean-counters in suits, that's all they are. Don't give a toss about kids, all they're bothered about is cutting budget.'

'What's Shirley saying?' asked Zach. 'Why is she crying?'

I crouched down to Zach's level and put an arm around him and Oscar.

'The council are trying to take Shirley's job away,' I told them. 'They're trying to save some money.'

'But we need Shirley,' said Zach. 'She keeps us safe.'

'She stops us getting run over by lorries and splatted flat on the ground,' added Oscar. Letting him renew *Flat Stanley* from the library twenty-four times had obviously been a bad idea.

'Council bigwigs don't know you kiddies, see,' said Shirley. 'They don't realise how important you all are.'

'We'll write to them and tell them,' said Zach.

'But we'll say please,' pointed out Oscar. 'So they don't think we're being rude.'

They both looked up at me. It scared me sometimes. How trusting they were that those in charge would always be fair and just. I wasn't sure when I would sit down with them and explain that it didn't always work like that in the big bad world out there. All I knew was that I wasn't ready to do it just yet.

'Yes and we'll start a petition,' I told them. 'Get all your friends and their mummies and daddies to sign it. To say we need Shirley to keep you all safe.'

'Can I write a bit about not wanting to get splatted flat by a lorry?' asked Oscar.

'You can if you like, love.' I smiled.

Shirley sniffed and held up her lollipop. A white transit van drew to a halt and she ushered us across.

'We're going to fight this,' I told her, squeezing the hand which wasn't holding the lollipop. 'We're not going to let them do this, don't you worry.'

We hurried across to the playground. I kissed Zach and Oscar, distributed the correct book bags and lunch bags and waved them off with instructions to apologise to their teachers for being late.

'Can I tell Mrs Carter about the dog poo?' asked Oscar.

'If you must,' I said, shaking my head and hoping the description wouldn't be too graphic, though the memory of his detailed account of the time another child was sick in the swimming pool led me to suspect otherwise.

*   *   *

I actually managed to leave work on time for a change that afternoon. I was keen to get back to school to talk to other parents before the children came out. Anna was the first one I saw. Anna was always early. She had a phone which beeped to remind her to leave for school in plenty of time. And she had the advantage of working from home on Mondays.

'Shirley's being made redundant,' I blurted out to Anna.

'Hello, Sam,' she said, reminding me that I had forgotten to do the pleasantries. 'Who's Shirley?'

'You know, Shirley. The lollipop lady.'

'Yes, of course,' Anna said. I took it she didn't know Shirley as well as we did, what with her living on the right side of the road. 'Well, that's outrageous.'

'I know. She told me this morning, in tears she was, poor thing. I said we'd do a petition. That we'd fight it all the way.'

'Of course we will. I'm surprised you didn't know about it, though. You'd think they'd consult the governors.'

'Obviously not. I spoke to Mrs Cuthbert on the phone and she only found out this morning. We're going to have a governors' meeting next week, but in the meantime I've run this off. Tell me what you think.'

I handed her the petition form I'd printed out.

Anna read it, nodding as she went. 'Seems fine to me.'

'Good. Because I've printed a couple of dozen off already. I thought we'd better get started as soon as possible. You don't mind do you?'

Anna looked at me, a slightly bewildered expression on

her face, as I produced a clipboard with several copies of the form attached from my shopping bag and handed it to her.

'You don't hang about do you?' She smiled.

'Well, no. The council are voting on this in a couple of weeks. We need to get started.'

'Started on what?' asked Jackie, collapsing on the wall beside us and immediately removing a pair of red platform shoes which were so unsuitable for walking up the hill, let alone being on your feet all day teaching, that they took my breath away.

'We're starting a petition,' I told her.

'Who's we?' she asked.

'Er, me, Anna, you, I guess.'

'Great, count me in. Where do I sign?'

'You haven't asked what it's against yet,' I pointed out.

'I guess I'm just a born rebel,' she said, taking a clipboard and pen from me and beginning to read. 'Jesus, they can't do this,' she said a moment later.

'I know. That's why we're doing a petition.'

'We need more than a petition. We need a meeting, letters to MPs, a protest march. Let's throw whole bloody works at them.'

'You'll be suggesting the children go on strike too, I suppose?' said Anna. She was trying to be funny, but the fact was however long the Islington brigade lived here, they never quite stopped being taken aback by the no-nonsense Yorkshire way of doing things.

'I don't think we should rule anything out,' said Jackie,

her feet back in her shoes now as if preparing herself for battle. 'Not if they're putting kids' lives at risk.'

I looked at Jackie's face, her jaw set, her forehead tensing. There was no way I could warn Anna to tread extremely carefully without making an awkward situation even worse.

'Yes, but we've got to be careful we don't sound over the top,' warned Anna.

'I am not waiting until a child gets killed trying to cross this road to get angry,' said Jackie, her finger jabbing the air in front of Anna's face. 'Because that will be too bloody late.' She took the clipboard and walked off across the playground to accost a group of Year One parents. I remembered once reading an article which said the most dangerous creature on earth was an angry hippopotamus mother who had been separated from its young. Right now, I thought the hippo would come a poor second.

'Did I say something wrong?' asked Anna.

'Er, yeah. Bit of a delicate one. It's all right, she's not mad at you. She's just mad.'

'Should I go and apologise?'

'No, just go and get some signatures on your petition. She'll appreciate that far more.' Anna nodded and set to work. I didn't feel it was my place to tell her. Jackie had taken a long time to confide in me. When she was ready, maybe she'd do the same with Anna.

I'd managed to collect a page full of signatures by the time the school doors opened and the children exploded into the playground like an uncorked bottle of champagne.

I spotted Zach straight away amongst the melee – it was one of the benefits of having a son with a mop of auburn curls. Fortunately he hadn't yet reached the age where he was bothered about standing out from the crowd. If I remembered rightly from my own childhood, he still had a couple of years to go before that kicked in. At least when the time came I would be able to regale him with stories about all the names I'd been called over mine. The weird thing was I liked them now. Maybe, at thirty-eight, I'd finally grown into them.

'Hi, love,' I said, letting Zach nuzzle his face into my tummy. 'Had a good day?'

'Yeah. What's that?' he asked, pointing to the clipboard.

'The petition. The one to say we don't think the council should get rid of Shirley.'

'Can I sign it?'

'Yes, of course you can.' I handed him the pen and watched as he carefully wrote his name and then attempted a spidery scrawl of a signature. It always made me smile, how difficult children found it to write messily when they set their minds to it.

'Can I get some more people to put their names on?'

'Yeah, that would be great. Just be polite when you ask them. Explain that it's to save Shirley's job.'

Zach looked around and headed straight up to the mum of one of his classmates, clipboard in hand, a determined look on his face. I smiled to myself, imagining what Rob would say if he could see him. As if he needed any more evidence that I had produced a mini-me. Still, he'd got his own back when Oscar had arrived. In a certain light there was an auburn tinge to his blonde hair but in every other respect he was straight out of the tin marked 'pint-sized version of his father'.

I glanced around the playground for Oscar. Not that there was any doubt about where he'd be. Somewhere in the middle of a cluster of children, most of them girls, who seemed to follow him wherever he went. Any worries we'd had about him not fitting in at mainstream school, about him not being accepted, had evaporated pretty much on his first day when he'd emerged Pied Piper-like from the classroom and informed me that he had a girl-friend and his teacher had told him off for being cheeky. I'd been worried that he would get special treatment because he was in a wheelchair. I don't think a parent has ever been so relieved to hear their child had been told off.

Esme ran up to me. 'Oscar's been telling rude jokes again,' she reported, bouncing up and down as she spoke.

'Rude like about bogeys and bottoms, or ruder than that?' I asked.

'Just bogeys and bottoms.'

'Thank you,' I replied. 'You just let me know if he gets too rude, OK?'

Esme nodded. 'They were very funny jokes.' she said.

'Well, I suppose that makes it OK then.' I smiled. Esme skipped off in Anna's direction, shrieking a greeting in a voice seemingly several decibels higher than the rest of the children in the playground put together. I watched

Anna recoil as she heard it. Esme was definitely not a mini-Anna.

Gradually, the cluster of children around Oscar dispersed to reveal him hand-in-hand with Alice, who was giving him a wide, gap-toothed grin.

'Hello,' I said, walking over to them. 'I hope you've been behaving yourself.'

The last comment was directed exclusively at Oscar. Alice wouldn't be capable of misbehaving if she tried.

'Can I go and see Alice's rabbit?' Oscar asked.

'Not tonight, love. You've got to go and see Katie for your exercises, remember? Maybe another day this week. Would that be OK, Alice?'

Alice nodded. That was generally as much as you could get out of her, unless you were Oscar, of course, in which case she would whisper sweet nothings in your ear all day long.

'Look, I've got loads of signatures,' Zach said, running back over to me brandishing his clipboard.

'Fantastic,' I said. 'Well done you.'

'I think Zach's going to be my shop steward,' said Jackie, coming over to join us and patting him on the back.

'What does that mean?' asked Zach.

'That you're very good at getting people to do what you want them to do.'

'Oh,' said Zach. 'That's good then.'

'Has Anna gone?' asked Jackie scanning the playground.

'No. Over there,' I said, pointing to the pavement outside where Anna was grabbing parents as they left.

'I really snapped at her, didn't I? I feel terrible. I just ...'

'I know. Look, she's getting signatures, isn't she? She can't have been that put out.'

'No,' said Jackie, visibly brightening. 'I guess you're right.'

'Mrs Carter said I didn't smell of dog poo at all,' chipped in Oscar.

Jackie looked at me quizzically.

'It was one of those mornings,' I explained.

'Fill me in later,' she said. It was my turn to look at her with a frown. 'First Monday of the month,' she went on. 'Don't tell me you'd forgotten.'

I mouthed a four-letter word at her to signify that I had. It had been a combined New Year's resolution, this night-out-once-a-month thing. January's had been good fun, but now it seemed I was in danger of failing spectacularly to make it to February.

'I'll ask Rob,' I said. 'It might still be OK.'

'Well, if it's not, let us know. We could always make it another night instead.' I nodded, although I could tell by her voice that she'd been looking forward to this. And I also knew that the logistics involved in getting three mums of six children out of their respective houses by eight o'clock on a particular night were immense.

'I'm sure it'll be fine,' I said. 'Shall I check that Anna's remembered?'

Jackie gave me a suitable look. In a competition between an electronic organiser and Anna, it would be foolish in the extreme to back the electronic organiser.

'Come on, Mummy,' said Zach, tugging at my hand. 'We're going to be late.'

'I'll see you there,' said Jackie. 'And don't worry about any wine, it's my turn.'

I nodded, hoping that were true and she wasn't just saying it because she knew how skint we were.

Mondays was physio. Other children had an action-packed after-school programme of football, street dance and Beavers. Oscar had physio, occupational therapy and swimming in a special hydrotherapy pool. Not that he complained about it. And Zach never complained about being dragged along to watch either. We did at least manage to leave an afternoon a week free for going to the Woodcraft Folk meetings (which Rob described as Boy Scouts for *Guardian* readers), but I felt bad about it all the same. It wasn't what you planned for your children.

I helped Katie lift Oscar into the standing support sling. I hadn't planned this either, of course. That the only way I would see my youngest son stand was with the help of what looked like an outsize baby bouncer. And the worst of it was that every time I saw him in it, his legs dangling to the floor, I was reminded of when he was little and I'd put him in a real baby bouncer, encouraging him to try to use his legs to help him bounce, blissfully unaware that my efforts would be in vain because Oscar's leg muscles would never be strong enough to support him. Because those were the days before he was diagnosed. Before our world was blown apart.

'That's great, Oscar,' said Katie. 'Fantastic movement there.'

She was lovely, Katie. Full of enthusiasm and praise. It must be hard for her because unlike some of the other children she saw, there was no chance of Oscar making any real improvement. This was simply about holding off the deterioration as long as possible. She never let on about that to Oscar though. Always made him come away feeling he had done something new.

'I want to be the birdman of Bognor,' said Oscar. Katie laughed and turned to me.

'I showed it to them on YouTube,' I explained. 'Zach was doing something at school about how things fly.'

'Humans can't fly really,' said Zach, 'it's just a silly game they play.'

'I'm going to fly,' said Oscar. 'I'm going to be the first person to fly to the moon.'

Katie smiled at him. We all did. Because that was the effect he had on you.

As we turned off the towpath into Fountain Street, a familiar tall figure wearing painting overalls and sporting sticky-up hair with tell-tale flecks of green paint, turned in from the other direction.

'Look!' Oscar laughed, pointing at him. 'It's Spencer.'

Most fine art graduates would probably baulk at being compared to a painter and decorator from *Balamory*. Rob, fortunately, was not one of them.

'Thank you, cheeky,' he said with a grin. 'So, what's the

story in Hebden Bridge today, or wouldn't I like to know?'

'I've been practising flapping my arms and taking my feet off the ground,' said Oscar.

'Have you now?' Rob said, stooping to give both him and Zach a hug. 'Well, at this rate I'll have to build a nest for you.'

Oscar started giggling. He had a brilliant giggle. Entirely infectious.

'Orang-utans build nests in trees,' said Zach. 'And they're one of our closest relatives.'

'So they are,' said Rob. 'In fact, I do believe that's where Mummy got her red hair from.'

Oscar and Zach collapsed in a fit of giggles. I raised my eyebrows at Rob but couldn't stop myself smiling.

'And welcome home to you too,' I said. Oscar started singing 'I Wanna Be Like You' from *Jungle Book*. Rob joined in, doing some kind of ape dance. If any of our neighbours had not already come to the conclusion that our whole family was nuts (and that was probably unlikely), then they certainly would now.

'Come on, mancubs,' I said, shaking my head. 'Time to get you some tea.'

I turned to go inside. The usual assortment of pond-dipping nets, Zach's scooter and various bats and balls was strewn across the front yard. To be fair to the boys, most of the bats and balls weren't even ours. While it was lovely that the children in our little street were permanently in and out of each others' front yards, it had somehow resulted in ours becoming the communal toy-dumping ground.

I opened the front door, Fleabag, our cat (that is what happens when you let your children name a pet, although I've always suspected that Rob put them up to it) offered a plaintive miaow and ran out. I shrugged and shook my head; you could lead a cat to the cat flap a hundred times, but getting it to use it when you were out was clearly another matter.

Oscar followed me in, commentating on his progress up the ramp as if he were Evil Knievel about to jump over thirty-two London buses.

'Can we have spaghetti?' he asked, once he had safely 'landed'.

'Yep,' I said, smiling down at him. 'And the good news for you,' I added, turning to Zach, 'is that it's carrot sticks for starters.'

Zach grinned. Everything he ate had to involve carrots. This was, as Anna had pointed out to me, not exactly a bad thing when compared to the children she saw who would only eat chocolate-spread sandwiches or chip butties. But I guess if your children do anything to excess you tend to worry. Even carrots.

'Right, you boys go and wash your hands,' I said. 'I'll get the table laid.'

'Everything OK?' asked Rob as they left the room.

'Yeah. Oscar did really well. Katie said his scoliosis hasn't got any worse.'

'Good.'

'Oh and Zach's still got his homework to do after tea. We didn't get a chance while we were there. It's something you need a mirror for.'

'Right.'

'Nice colour,' I said, gesturing towards his hair as I reached past him to the cutlery drawer.

'Fern-green. Always a good one for bathrooms.'

I was quite sure he had meant for it to come out in a light-hearted, jovial way. And maybe it would have sounded like that to the untrained ear. Maybe it was only me who picked up that hint of something else buried several layers beneath. Something which made what I was about to ask even harder.

'Look, I'm really sorry but I completely forgot that it's supposed to be our girls'-night-out thing this evening. I know you were planning to go to the studio and I really don't mind not going if you want to go tonight.'

'Don't be daft, you go.'

'Are you sure?'

'No, so don't ask me again in case I change my mind.'

He said it with a smile on his face. And followed it up by putting his arms around my waist and pulling me closer.

'Thanks,' I replied, kissing him on the lips. He'd made a lot of sacrifices for our family. I knew that. But sometimes I wondered it he knew how much I appreciated it.

'We're only going to the Olive Branch and we won't do starters and Jackie's insisted on taking the wine even though she won't be drinking.'

'Stop apologising,' said Rob. 'It's not as if you're out gadding about every night. And don't you dare go for the cheapest thing on the menu.'

'OK,' I said. 'I might even get some olives as a side.'

'Hey,' said Rob. 'Who said anything about olives?'

I smiled at him as Oscar hurtled back into the kitchen.

'Zach wouldn't let me squirt the soap by myself,' complained Oscar.

'Well, that's probably because the last time you did it you decided to squirt a picture all over the tiles.'

'Oh yeah,' said Oscar. To be fair, he always acknow-ledged when he'd done something wrong, never tried to squirm his way out of it. I smiled at Zach as he quietly took his seat at the table. Just occasionally I wished he would do something naughty too. Anything which would make him seem more like a normal seven-year-old boy.

Rob had spaghetti with the boys, which made me feel even worse about going out. I sat down with them as they ate, Rob and I taking it in turns to remind Oscar not to speak with his mouth full.

'Do you remember that time,' said Zach, 'when you said "don't eat with your mouth full" by mistake.' Oscar giggled and immediately snapped his mouth shut, doing a hamster impression with his cheeks.

'Thank you, Oscar,' said Rob. 'But you may carry on eating.'

Oscar groaned and went back to sucking up the spaghetti from his bowl. It was the strange thing about mealtimes. Sometimes I could kid myself that we were a normal family, sitting around our kitchen table like this. Mucking about, reminding our children of their table manners. It was only the head support of Oscar's powerchair which gave the game away.

It was stupid really. I hated the word 'normal'. Had fought against it all my life. Always wanting to be different, never wanting to conform. And it annoyed the hell out of me that of all the things I found myself craving now, it should be normality.

I sat with Oscar later, the Cough Assist machine mask pressed over his mouth and nose, trying not to flinch each time he did. There were some things you never got used to. This was one of them. It was also the reason Zach went to bed before his brother. He couldn't bear watching it, even though he knew that it was helping Oscar. Keeping his chest and airways clear to try to prevent him getting an infection, ending up in hospital, all the things we dreaded.

At last, when the machine was finished, I took the mask off and suctioned around Oscar's mouth, removing the last of the mucous.

'There,' I said. 'All done.'

He snuggled into me, the way he always did afterwards, feeling small and vulnerable in my arms.

'Love you loads,' I said, rocking him to and fro, delaying the moment I had to put his night-time ventilator mask on as long as possible. The house was still around us. Zach asleep – or, more likely, reading one of his astronomy books with a torch under the covers. Rob downstairs, doing the washing-up, no doubt wondering when he'd next get the chance to go back to his painting at the studio instead of painting bathrooms. And me, holding my little boy close to me.

Normal. Our kind of normal, at least.

'Sorry,' I said, hurrying into the Olive Branch at quarter past eight and plonking myself down in the seat next to Jackie.

'That's OK,' said Anna. 'We're just glad you made it. We were beginning to think it might be the two of us.'

'No, Oscar was a bit clingy, that's all. Or maybe I was a bit clingy actually. We've got a little girl in at the hospice at the moment, who has only got a day or so left.'

Jackie nodded and poured me a glass of wine.

'I still don't know how you do it,' she said. 'I'd be in bits every time.'

'It does get to me sometimes, especially when I go straight to school to pick up the boys after something's happened. But most of the time I'm squirrelled away in the office writing press releases or whatever. It's far harder for the nurses and the family support workers. I think if I was involved with the children as much as them I'd probably be a jibbering wreck by now.'

'Well, you're still a braver woman than me,' said Jackie.

'Says she who has to keep order in a class of thirty teenagers every day,' chipped in Anna.

'Oh God, that's nothing. At least I'm not teaching them maths, or owt important. If they get a bit rowdy I can always get them to pretend to be having a riot or summat.'

'I couldn't do that,' I said. 'I always hated that improvisation stuff in drama. I'd be frozen to the spot in terror.'

'You were never shy at school, surely?' said Anna.

'I was. Painfully so.'

'So what happened?' asked Jackie.

'Started going to protest meetings and marches with my mum when I was a teenager. Realised that you didn't get anywhere in life by keeping your mouth shut. That you had to shout loud enough to make yourself heard.'

'What about you?' asked Anna, turning to Jackie.

'Oh, I've always been gobby. Runs in the family. Maybe that's why I'm good at getting kids to shout up. But there again I couldn't sit and listen to some teenager who's taking drugs or cutting themselves and not tell a soul about it.'

Anna looked down at the table and fiddled with the napkin which was already on her lap.

'I didn't mean it as a criticism,' said Jackie, quickly. 'I know you have to do that. I just don't know how you manage it, that's all.'

Anna smiled and shrugged. 'They need to be able to confide in someone. It's an honour, really, that they trust me enough to do it.'

'So basically,' I said, 'we're all bloody brilliant at our jobs but none of us likes to shout about it. And that's exactly why men get away with screwing up the country.'

'Yeah, but there's a difference between being good at what we do and being able to run the country,' said Anna.

'Is there? Look at the qualities we've got between us: compassion, empathy, an ability to communicate our ideas and inspire people. Don't tell me the country couldn't do with some of that.'

'Yeah, but it's that old power corrupts thing, in't it?' said Jackie. 'Put us in Downing Street and within a few months I'd be cutting education funding and saying drama were a waste of resources, Anna would be withdrawing counselling services and telling kids to pull themselves together and you'd be talking about closing hospices and introducing a pay-as-you-die policy.'

Anna smiled.

'We wouldn't though, would we?' I said. 'Women don't do things like that.'

'Was Thatcher not a woman then?' asked Jackie.

'Course she wasn't,' I replied. 'Don't you remember the *Spitting Image* puppet of her in a pin-stripe suit?'

'Well what about rest of them?' asked Jackie. 'Blair's babes and all that.'

'It was window-dressing, wasn't it? How many of them had any real power to change things? Country was still being run by Blair and all his cronies.'

'Sorry to interrupt,' said Anna, 'but are we actually going to eat tonight or just put the world to rights and go home hungry?'

'Hey, aren't you forgetting my resolution to make a difference this year?'

'Hard luck,' said Jackie. 'You'll just have to wait until next time. Given the choice between plotting a revolution and having time for dessert, the tiramisu wins every time.'

'OK,' I said with a smile. 'I'll go with the majority and we'll order. But some day they'll write about this meal, it'll be up there with Blair and Brown's meal at the Granita. Only in our case it will be the political coup that was thwarted by the lure of tiramisu.'

'Are you wanting cream or ice cream with that?' asked Jackie.

'Soya cream actually,' I replied with a grin. 'Because in Hebden Bridge there's always a third way, you see.'

2

JACKIE

When I got there, she was still on the pavement outside her house, brandishing the secateurs.

'Hello, Mum. It's me, Jackie.'

'I'm doing roses.'

'You don't have any roses out here, Mum. They're all in back garden.'

'Well I can't see them.'

'That's because you're out front, Mum. Anyway, love, you've done them already. Quite a few times in fact.'

I took Mum by the arm and guided her steadily towards the front door, waving an acknowledgement to Pauline across the road as I did so. The phone calls were becoming more frequent. At least six since Mum had come out of hospital a month ago. I was lucky this time that it was a Sunday, that Pauline could get hold of me and I could come straight away. Christ knows what I was going to do if it happened in the middle of a lesson. It wasn't fair to expect Pauline to intervene. She was getting on a bit herself. The last thing she wanted to be doing was trying to wrestle a pair of secateurs from my mother. A tough old bird, that's what Mum had always called herself. Which had been great when I was growing up, but it didn't make things so easy now.

We went through into the front room. It was like a museum exhibit labelled 'my childhood'. Nothing appeared to have been touched or moved and yet it had been lived in all that time. I swore even the carpet was the same one I remembered from my teens. Waste not, want not. Another one of her mantras. A rug covered the bare patch near the fireplace, while a smaller one concealed the area in front of the other armchair which my father's feet had worn away over the years. The armrest covers remained on his chair too – although he was no longer around to make anything dirty. And the bureau in the corner was still covered with school photographs: Deborah and I smiling out from under a selection of wonky fringes. And later ones of me sporting a flick the like of which Halifax, mercifully, will never see again.

I sat Mum down in her armchair and took the secateurs from her without her seeming to register the fact. Her shrivelled hands lay meekly on the armrests. Sometimes I could still see the outline of Mum's plump body surrounding her, a ghost-like image of her former self. It was ironic really. All those years she'd spent battling her weight and now, finally, she was positively skeletal. Only she didn't have the mental faculties to appreciate it.

'I'll put kettle on,' I said. There was no reply. I wasn't even sure if it had registered. But I left the room and filled the kettle anyway, letting the whooshing sound of the water wash over me, blocking out the noise of the silence. I thought of her as two different people now. The mum I had grown up with: strong, funny, feisty. And the one who sat in the front room: someone completely unrelated. Someone who'd taken her place, not overnight but by stealth over the past few years. And now refused to leave.

I didn't bother with the teapot. There was a time, not too long ago, when I couldn't get away with it. When she'd have pottered out here after me to make sure I'd put the cosy on. Checked the bin for tell-tale signs of teabags. Or taken one sip and accused me of crimes against loose-leaf tea. These days she drank what she was given without a whimper of complaint. How I'd love now to be able to use the word cantankerous against her.

I went back into the front room, placed her cup of tea down on the occasional table next to her chair and put my own coffee mug on the mantelpiece. She didn't appear to have moved a millimetre since I'd left her.

'How's your arm feeling? Has it been giving you any trouble?'

'Why? What's wrong with it?'

'You broke it, remember? When you fell. That's why you were in hospital.'

'No. I've never broken a bone in me life. You must be thinking of Deborah. She broke both arms, she did. Not at same time, mind.'

I hesitated, unsure whether to put her right or let it go.

'It's been mild today, hasn't it?' I said.

'Roses will need pruning soon.'

'They're fine, Mum. You've done them already.'

I had a feeling that there would be no rose bushes left at this rate. She made Edward Scissorhands look positively slovenly in the pruning department.

I waited for something which didn't come. An opening gambit of conversation, a comment on something she'd heard on the news. So instead I filled the space. Telling her about what Alice was up to, how her animal hospital of cuddly toys was threatening to engulf her entire bedroom, how Paul's school was having an Ofsted inspection the next day (although I didn't mention how I shouldn't really be there because Paul had a stack of work to get through). How the council were planning to get rid of the lollipop lady outside Alice's school and how we were going to fight it.

'Your school had a lollipop lady,' Mum said. 'Do you remember her? Deborah always used to call her Mrs Tiggywinkle. Her name was Mrs Tingle really.'

She always did this. Just when you thought there was no one at home, that all the lights had gone out.

'Yeah. I do remember her,' I said. 'Short, skinny woman with silver hair.'

'You'll have to ask Deborah if she can remember what she used to call her.'

I looked down at the carpet. The lights may have flickered for a moment, but they were clearly off again now.

'I'll put the television on for you before I go,' I said. 'Might be something nice on a Sunday afternoon.'

I wondered if Alice would have to do this for me one day. And if she would feel as bad as I did. More than anything, I hoped she would not have to cope with it on her own.

'I'm sorry, love. I know you're up to your eyes in it tonight. But it's . . . er, that time again.'

Paul looked up from the pile of papers on his desk in the spare room. It took a second for his eyes to focus on me, a few more for the penny to drop and a moment longer for the smile to creep across his face.

'Jeez, you work a bloke hard. Do you think inspectors will let me include that in my mitigation? "Sorry my assessment sheets weren't fully completed only my wife needed me for procreation purposes."'

I smiled. Any romance or spontaneity had so long ago disappeared from the process that I couldn't help but see the funny side. At least I had stopped short of leaving my positive ovulation sticks in obvious places where he would see them. I knew of several women on the fertility website forums who admitted to doing just that.

'Well, you'll be glad to hear that unlike Ofsted I will not be grading your performance or publishing it on a website for public scrutiny.'

'Bloody glad to hear it.'

'Hey,' I said, sidling up to Paul and putting my arms around him. 'I wouldn't be so quick to dismiss the idea. I might have given you an outstanding.'

'I could say summat,' said Paul. 'But I'm not going to. I don't want to be accused of lowering tone.'

'Good. I'll give you five minutes to finish off then.'

Paul smiled and kissed me on the forehead. If he did resent my persistence, he was very good at not letting it show.

We lay there afterwards, Paul's body, warm and sticky next to mine, me with a couple of pillows shoved under my hips, attempting to look as sexy and laid back as is possible while trying to stop sperm spilling out of you.

'Well, I think your effort and application to duty were outstanding,' I said.

Paul shook his head. 'I just hope Ofsted inspectors are equally fulsome in their praise.'

'But not that they'll be wearing a lacy camisole and hot pants, obviously.'

'Oh, I don't know,' said Paul. 'Might make it more interesting.'

I stroked his arm, well aware of the reason he had gone into comedian mode.

'I don't know what you're worried about. It's a bloody good school,' I said. 'Everyone knows that. That's why you took the job, remember?'

Paul had only been there two years. His first job in a special school after years at a mainstream primary.

'I know. I just can't bear the thought of letting those kids down.' I turned to look at him. The emotion clearly bubbling up behind his normally smiling blue eyes.

'You're a soft bugger for a Yorkshireman, Paul Crabtree. Probably why I married you, mind. The kids adore you. The parents do too. I can't see how you could possibly have put any more into that job than you have done.'

'Thanks, love,' he said stroking my hair. 'I'll just be glad when it's all over. When I can get back to teaching instead of worrying about bloody form-filling.' Paul smiled at me and wiped his eyes. Took a moment or two to compose himself.

'How was your mum? I haven't had a chance to ask.'

'Oh. You know.' Paul nodded and squeezed my shoulder.

'Look, I know you don't want to, but maybe it's time you did look into a home. You can't keep going over and getting her back in house. And you can't lock her in either.'

'Sometimes I wish I could tether her like a goat,' I said. 'Just enough slack to let her get the food she needs, but not enough for her to sample the grass on the other side of the fence.'

'Is it worth getting on to the council again? See if they can do another review of her care?'

'I will do. I think I know what their answer will be, though. It's not long since last one.'

It was simply a matter of putting off the inevitable, I knew that. Maybe the truth was that I didn't want to be the one who took that decision, I wanted someone else to do it for me. After all Mum had been through, I couldn't bear to be the one who took something away from her. Something she held so dear.

'The thing is, you've got to look after yourself as well, love. This can't be helping you.'

I knew exactly what he was getting at. I'd read enough how-to-get-pregnant books to know they all had a chapter on reducing stress. None of them, however, had a subsequent chapter on how you were supposed to achieve this if your mother had Alzheimer's and refused to go into a home.

'It's probably something else that's stopping it happening. At least when we go for tests we'll find out.'

Paul went to say something, then stopped himself. It had been my idea to finally go for the tests. Paul had put me off, citing various reasons over the years: that there was no need to rush, that he wanted to enjoy Alice first, that these things took time, that we were probably trying too hard. Until eventually he'd run out of reasons why he didn't think we should go. Apart from the obvious one that had been there all along. The one that neither of us spoke about.

'It might not be that straightforward, remember. They can't always give a reason for these things.'

'Apart from us being on the wrong side of forty, you mean?'

Paul smiled. Squeezed my hand.

'Look, if you still want to us go through with it, I will. Just as long as you know it's not too late to change your mind.'

I smiled back at him. I loved that he wanted to protect me from the hurt. But I also knew that sometimes you couldn't just put your fingers in your ears and sing 'la, la, la, la' at the top of your voice to block out something you needed to hear. Even if you didn't have a bloody clue how you were going to react when you heard it.

The other side of the bed was empty when the alarm woke me the next morning. I knew exactly where Paul would be, though. I showered quickly, hurried downstairs and made coffee before taking a mug into him in the study.

'Thank you, you're a star,' he said, looking up briefly from his paperwork and smiling.

'So are you, remember?' I said.

'Are you OK getting Alice ready? I want to go in early.' By early he meant even earlier than usual. He was always at school way before he needed to be.

'Of course. Have you had any breakfast?'

'No. I haven't really got time.' I handed him the banana I'd just put in my dressing-gown pocket.

'Thought as much,' I said. Paul shook his head, smiled at me and unpeeled it.

I crept into Alice's room. I loved it that she wasn't one of those children who woke at the crack of dawn every morning; mainly because I liked my sleep and couldn't have hacked it, but also because it gave me a chance to have these first few quiet moments of the day with her.

I pulled up the blind, although the dreary February morning outside didn't seem to want to come in. I lay down on the bed next to Alice, managing to squeeze myself in between the menagerie of soft toys. I used to watch her sleep all the time when she was a baby. Marvelling at her nose, her lips, her fine blonde hair. Having to pinch myself that she was mine. That something so perfect could have come from me.

Alice stirred a little, turning over and stretching her arm across me. Her warm fingers touched my neck. A few seconds later she opened her eyes, saw that I was there and promptly shut them again.

'Morning, sweetheart,' I whispered.

'Have you fed Betsy yet?' she asked, her eyes still closed. Betsy was her pet rabbit. It was actually a male rabbit, but Alice had said she didn't like any boys' names. Paul had suggested calling it Roger, but she'd been too young to see the film and she didn't get the joke.

'No, not yet.'

'Good,' she said, opening her eyes, 'I'll do it with you then.' A second later she was up and starting to get dressed. Wherever she had got that ability to go from fast asleep to wide awake in ten seconds from, it certainly wasn't me.

'Where's Daddy?' she asked when we got to the empty kitchen.

'He's gone to work early. Remember I told you his school is having an inspection today? It's like a little test.'

'Has he learnt his spellings?' she asked.

'Yes,' I smiled, 'I expect he'll come top of the class.'.

She nodded and picked up the compost box in which we kept leftovers for Betsy. 'I think for Christmas,' she said, 'I'd really like a donkey.'

Drama teachers had it made. To be honest, I sometimes wondered why anyone would want to teach any other subject. You got to take kids out of the classroom environment, free them from the confines of textbooks and whiteboards. It was like that moment when Angela Rippon kicked up her legs and emerged from behind the newsdesk on *Morecambe and Wise*. You got to see what the kids were really capable of. The surprising talents which no one else knew existed. And for much of the time you got to do it without anyone else bothering you. The Head was far too busy bearing down on the English and maths departments to interfere in what I was up to. As long as the kids put on impressive shows at Christmas and summer, I was left pretty much to my own devices. No doubt at some point Michael Gove would decide that drama teachers were surplus to requirements or would introduce minimum standards in improvisation and mime. But until that point I was simply going to keep my head down and get on with it.

Sheila, on the other hand, appeared to have the words 'sacrificial lamb' tattooed on her forehead. It was hard to imagine a more stressed-looking person than the one who sat opposite me in the staffroom, sipping her coffee as if she were scared a sea monster might leap out of the mug and gobble her up at any moment.

'What's Frodo said now?' I asked. The Head's name was actually Nathan Freeman. But ever since Sheila and I had both watched a BBC2 natural history programme where the dominant bonobo chimpanzee, named Frodo, had bullied the other members of the troupe into submission, he had been referred to by his ape name.

'He hasn't said anything. That's the problem. He came into my classroom this morning, unannounced, stood at the back and watched for ten minutes and then left.'

'Jeez, that's scarier than the shower scene in *Psycho*.'

'What am I going to do?'

'Make sure you check behind the door before taking a shower?'

'I'm serious, Jack.' Sheila spoke in hushed tones although the other members of staff within earshot were all fellow victims.

'I've told you. You need to get out of this place before he turns you into a jibbering wreck.'

'But it's wrong, isn't it? The person being bullied shouldn't be the one who has to go.'

'Of course not. But who said life was fair?'

'Besides, I'd miss the kids too much. I owe it to them to stand my ground. If I go, he'll hire some joyless smart arse who drills them in grammar until they never want to pick up their pens and write again.'

'So defy him. Teach the way you want to teach. Dare him to take you on.'

'And what if he does?' Sheila asked, pushing her glasses back up her nose.

'Who do you think the kids would back if he took any action against you? They'd have a sit-in at least. Probably start up some kind of campaign. They're the children of *Guardian*-reading radicals and revolutionaries, remember. They're hardly going to stand by while you're thrown to the slaughter.'

'Yes, you're right. Of course you're right.' Sheila's voice had acquired a steely quality not heard for some time. She put her mug down and stood up, straightening her back and jutting out her chin as she did so. 'Thank you.'

'That's OK. Although obviously if it goes horribly wrong, I'll put my official NUT rep hat on and deny all knowledge of this conversation.'

She smiled and walked out of the staffroom, head held high. I finished my coffee, imagining myself sitting in the Head's office writing 'I must not encourage staff mutiny' two hundred times.

'Parents' meeting in the hall in five minutes,' I shouted across the playground. 'Come and help us save our lollipop lady. The kids can be looked after in class two. There are no excuses.'

A steady stream of parents started making their way through to the hall. Sam turned and grinned at me, in serious danger of tripping over her long skirt in her excitement.

'Wow, this is great,' she said, 'you're making them all come.'

'I guess it's my persuasive charm.'

'No. It's because you're bloody scary. All you need now is a loudhailer.'

I laughed. Though the truth was I did secretly hanker after one. It wasn't that I couldn't project my voice – when you spent your days trying to make yourself heard above thirty teenagers, that clearly wasn't an issue. It was simply that loudhailers appeared to be de rigueur in those archived news reels of industrial unrest in the seventies and eighties. If they'd had a rabble-rousing badge in the Girl Guides, that would have been the picture on it.

'Get me one for my birthday,' I said, winking at her. I stood square in the middle of the gates. Anyone who wanted to escape would have to get past me first. I guessed it was a kind of reverse picket line.

'I'd better go and check on the boys before we start,' said Sam. 'Make sure Oscar's behaving himself.'

'Can you make sure the DVD they're showing's not a scary one. Alice is still recovering from *One Hundred and One Dalmations*. I suspect I am Cruella de Vil in her nightmares.'

Sam smiled. 'Will do.'

I walked through into the packed hall. Anna was already working the room, her dark hair sleek and stylish as ever. Her face animated as she talked to people, engaged them, put them at ease then passed them the pen and pointed to where to sign. It appeared effortless. At least on the surface.

She looked up as I walked over. 'What a fantastic turnout,' she said. 'People obviously feel really strongly about this.'

I nodded, not wanting to admit that actually they hadn't had any choice in the matter. I got the impression Anna might not agree with my 'resistance is futile' tactics.

'How many signatures have we got?' I asked.

'Over a thousand so far. The ones we put in the shops

and the library have done really well. We got a hundred signatures in the Co-op alone.'

'Brilliant. Well done.' Anna was also a bit of a whizz at sweet-talking business types. I guess I was John Prescott to her Tony Blair.

Sam squeezed through the doorway and struggled to the front. 'The kids are all fine,' she said. 'They're watching the *Jungle Book* and Zach's under instructions to keep an eye on Alice when Kaa comes on. Right. Are we ready to start?' Anna and I nodded. I looked at the assembled group of parents before us: mostly mums, the usual mixture of middle-class professional types and the more alternative brigade, and a spattering of those very handy right-on dads which Hebden Bridge possessed. All of them ready for battle. I had a sense that we actually stood a chance.

'Thank you so much for coming everyone,' said Sam. 'For anyone who doesn't know me I'm Sam Farnell, one of the parent governors and mum to Zach and Oscar. Jackie here, who's Alice's mum, is chair of the PTFA and Anna, Esme's mum, is secretary of the PTFA.'

We stood there tall (well, obviously not in Anna's case) and proud, brandishing piles of petition forms. The three musketeers had nothing on us.

'As you all know, we've started a petition against the council's plan to get rid of Shirley, our school lollipop lady. The good news is, we've got over a thousand signatures so far. The reason we've got you all here today is to discuss what our next step in this campaign should be. We only have two weeks to go until the council's budget meeting so we need to do something to make them sit up and take notice.'

Sam looked around, waiting for suggestions.

'We could write to our local councillors,' one of the reception mums suggested. 'Maybe even to our MP.'

'Great idea, so great we've already done it.' Sam smiled. 'The governors have written a letter and the PTFA has too. But if any of you could send individual letters that would be great. The more they get, the harder it will be for them to ignore us. I've got addresses and a draft letter if anyone wants them.'

The room went quiet again. I'd been planning to let other people go first, but if no one else was going to say anything I didn't see any reason to hold back.

'How about a stop-the-traffic protest outside school?' I suggested. 'The point being that if Shirley is made redundant, there will be no one to stop the traffic for our children.'

'But we can't actually stand in the road, can we?' one of the dads said. 'It's illegal, isn't it? Obstructing the highway.'

'He's got a point,' said Anna. 'It wouldn't exactly help the cause if we got ourselves arrested.'

'We won't technically be obstructing anything,' I said. 'The protest will be on the other side of the road from school and we'll just take an exceptionally long time getting all the children across the road one by one. With Shirley's help, of course. It doesn't take much to cause traffic chaos in Hebden Bridge. I think it'll do the job for us.'

There were positive murmurings from around the hall. Anna still looked a bit uncomfortable about the idea.

'We'll invite the local media,' I continued. 'Have big SAVE OUR SHIRLEY placards. Get the kids to join in too. We need to do something that'll get on the local news. It's the only way to get them to take notice.'

A lot of heads nodded, including Sam's. I looked at Anna.

'Perhaps we should take a vote on it,' she said. That was the only trouble with Liberal Democrats: they were always so bloody democratic.

'OK,' said Sam. 'All those in favour . . .'

A mass of hands went up.

'Against . . .'

Nothing.

'I think we'll take that as a yes then,' she said. 'Thank you all for coming and we'll let you know the date of the protest next week.'

Sam turned to smile at Anna and me as the other parents began to file out of the hall.

'Great. I guess we need to get a placard production line going then.' She grinned.

'Can Rob give us a hand?' I asked. 'I think these placards should be objects of beauty. This is Hebden Bridge, after all. People will be expecting something arty-farty.'

Sam laughed. 'I'm sure he can be roped in. The kids can make their own though. It'll make it more personal.'

'Do you think we need to notify anyone?' asked Anna.

'The police or the council. I wouldn't want Shirley getting into trouble.'

'I don't see why,' I said. 'We're really not doing anything wrong and the last thing we want to do is get this stopped before it happens.'

Anna still looked concerned.

'Shirley won't get into trouble. She'll simply be doing her job. And all we'll be doing is helping our children safely across the road. No one can possibly complain about that.'

Anna nodded, her jaw appeared to soften a little too. Or maybe I was just imagining it. We stacked the remaining chairs and made our way down to class two. As we entered Oscar was twirling around in his powerchair singing 'I wanna be like you hoo-hoo,' at the top of his voice.

'Sorry,' said Sam to Mrs Cooper who had been trying to hold the fort. 'Has he been like this all the way through?'

'Yes, but we've all enjoyed the performance.' She smiled.

'Are we going to save Shirley's job, Mummy?' asked Zach, running up to Sam.

'Do you know what, love?' she said. 'I think with all your help, we just might.'

3

ANNA

'Look, Esme. The first snowdrops are almost out.'

Esme stopped leaping along the stepping stones between the roses in our front garden for a nano-second to glance down to where I was pointing.

'Oh yeah,' she said, with the casual indifference of one who has better things to do. I smiled to myself. It was one of the things you didn't get told in parenting manuals. That one of your children may be so different to you that you sometimes wonder if she is really yours at all. Not just different to me, mind. Different to her entire family. I used to spend hours in the garden with Charlotte when she was this age. She wanted to know what every flower was called. The names of the roses, the variety of tulips. She would help with pruning and planting bulbs. Sit for hours on the front step writing notes and drawing leaf shapes in her exercise book. Even Will, although he'd been less studious in his interest, still used to join me out here and help with the weeding and planting. Although maybe the novelty factor had played a part there. We hadn't had a front garden in Islington. Or a back one come to that.

Esme attempted to leap over two stepping stones. She landed in between them. Right on top of the snowdrops I'd just pointed out to her.

'Oops,' she said, looking up at me and pulling a face. 'Will they boing back up again?'

'Probably not, love,' I said, surveying the flattened stems and trying to keep my voice calm and measured. 'Tell you what. Why don't we go and play indoors for a bit?'

'OK,' said Esme, turning on her heel and bounding up to the front door which I'd left ajar. 'Are there any muffins left?'

They were savoury ones. I'd got the recipe from the woman who made them at Organic House. It was an ingenious way to get children to eat asparagus and broccoli without them realising it. And they had pesto in them. Esme would quite happily eat anything that involved pesto.

'Yes, but wash your hands first please,' I called after her. There was a seven-year-old girl equivalent of a screech of brakes and a handbrake turn as I heard her crash through into the downstairs bathroom.

I busied myself in the kitchen as Esme sat at the table and in between mouthfuls of muffin regaled me with stories of what she'd been up to at school.

'And Mrs Johnson said I wasn't to do handstands up the wall in the playground any more because of that thing with Amy yesterday.'

'That thing' was her way of glossing over the incident in which she had accidentally whacked a classmate in the face with her foot because she'd had the temerity to walk past as Esme had been coming down from her attempt at the world's longest handstand. Fortunately the girl's mother had been very good about it when I'd apologised profusely in the playground at home time. Said the tooth had been wobbly for weeks anyway.

'I think that's only fair, sweetheart. You wouldn't want anyone else to get hurt. Save your handstands for gym club. That's the safest place to do them.'

Esme shrugged and said 'OK' in a mock disgruntled teenager voice that I presumed she'd picked up from her brother, then reached across to grab a magazine, knocking over her glass of juice in the process. It was the one moment of insight David had had on the parenting front. That perhaps Grace would make a better middle name than first name for our third child.

Charlotte and Will arrived home together. It didn't always happen, of course. On Mondays Charlotte went straight to her piano lesson and on Wednesdays she had choir practice. Tuesdays and Fridays Will went to a youth-theatre group, but on Thursdays, for some reason, Hebden Bridge was momentarily a cultural desert.

'Hi, you two. Good day?'

Will grunted and pulled a face as he yanked his tie off

and tossed it on the floor. Charlotte said nothing. Just slipped her coat off, hung it up neatly and sat down opposite Esme at the table.

'The thing is,' said Will, 'if we didn't vote for that poxy new uniform I don't see why we have to wear it.'

'It's called democracy,' I replied. 'Nobody voted for a coalition government, but we've still got one and we still have to live with what they do.'

'Yeah, but you and Dad voted Lib Dem. The government thing is at least half your fault. I voted for the polo-shirt and sweatshirt. It was all the other stupid parents and staff who voted for the tie-and-blazer crap.'

'Will,' I said, sternly, nodding towards Esme.

'Sorry,' he said. 'I bet she'll kick off about wearing it too, though, when it's her turn.'

I suspected he was right. I also knew this was not the time to tell him that his own father had voted for 'the tie-and-blazer crap'. There again his own father had wanted him to go to grammar school. I was the one who'd argued that Will's happiness was more important than his exam grades, and if all his mates were going to the local comprehensive and they had a good drama department which was what he really loved doing, then that was fine by me.

'Well, all you can do is try to get them to change the system. Give more weight to the pupils' votes next time.'

'Yeah, but it won't be in time for me, will it? It's all right for you. You can change the government in a couple of months.'

'Not if the majority disagrees with me I can't.'

'You know what I mean. At least you'll get to have your say.'

I wasn't about to admit to him that I was actually dreading the general election. We'd always made it a family thing, going down to the polling station together. David was very keen on showing the children democracy in action. I guess as a local councillor he had to be. Quite how I was going to hide the fact that I couldn't bring myself to vote for his party this time, I hadn't yet worked out. Nor had I worked out who I was going to vote for instead, come to that. It was all looking decidedly awkward.

'Anyway. Would you like something to eat, love?'

'Yeah, but nothing you've got.'

'You don't know what I've got.'

'The muffins are yummy,' said Esme.

'If you like eating green vegetables dressed up as cake, which I don't.'

'Will!'

'Well, come on. She's going to work it out sometime.'

'They're aren't any vegetables in my muffin are there, Mummy?'

Will and Charlotte both looked up at me, keen to see how I'd talk my way out of this one.

'Only little bits, love.'

'Where?' asked Esme, picking up another muffin from the plate and starting to dissect it.

I gave Will a look.

'What? I was simply broadening her education,' he replied with a grin, before disappearing upstairs.

'Charlotte, love. Would you like something?' I asked.

'No thanks.'

'I can do you a cheese-and-tomato sandwich, if you like.'

'No, really. I'm not hungry.'

Charlotte never usually turned down a cheese-and-tomato sandwich.

'Is everything all right, love?'

'Yeah. I'm fine. I'm just not hungry.' Charlotte pushed her chair back, poured herself a glass of smoothie from the fridge and took it up to her room.

She wasn't fine. I knew that. But clearly she didn't feel inclined to tell me what was bothering her. The irony of the professional counsellor who specialised in adolescent behaviour not being able to talk to her teenagers was not lost on me. I consoled myself with the thought that it would be different with Esme. I couldn't imagine Esme ever being quiet long enough to bottle something up.

David arrived home at 6.01 p.m. He did so every night, just like Mr Banks in *Mary Poppins*. To be fair, it wasn't his fault. It was simply that if he walked at his usual pace up the hill from the station, that was the time he arrived. And at least he didn't expect his slippers to be waiting for him or the heirs to his dominium to be scrubbed and tubbed by 6.03. It was simply that it put the thought of an Edwardian banker in my head, which was never a good start to the evening.

'Hello, love,' he said, placing his hands lightly on my

shoulders from behind and giving me a peck on the cheek. 'Smells good.'

'Roasted red pepper, cannellini bean and sweet potato stew.'

'Oh, great.'

It was said with only a modicum of enthusiasm. David was a meat, potatoes and two-veg man. When he cooked at weekends that is what we tended to have. On weekdays I got to do my thing.

David hovered in the kitchen for a moment. 'Remember I'll need to leave about quarter to seven for the meeting.'

I hadn't forgotten. Hebden Royd town council meetings were one of the many things listed on the family-organ-iser calendar which hung on the kitchen door. Esme had called it a family-planning calendar once, causing David to mutter under his breath that it was a bit late for that. It was a joke, of course. The sort which appealed to his dry Scottish sense of humour.

'That's fine. It'll be ready in a couple of minutes if you want to give the others a shout.'

Esme was the first to respond, managing to drag herself away from the lounge where she'd been watching CBBC. While I was cooking was the only time she was allowed to watch television. Fortunately it coincided with the one point during the day when her energy levels took a momen-tary dip. Half an hour of recharging her batteries on the sofa while watching *Blue Peter* and she'd got her second wind.

'Daddy,' she said, throwing her arms around his waist.

'Hello, Esme,' he said, bending to kiss her. 'What have you been up to at school today? Not knocked anyone else's teeth out I hope.'

'No. I'm not allowed to do handstands any more. They didn't say anything about cartwheels, though. Maybe I can still do them.'

'Gym club, Esme,' I called out over my shoulder. 'I told you to save all that for gym club. Or the park when it's nice weather.'

I put David's dinner on the table and went to the bottom of the stairs to call out again to Charlotte and Will. A few moments later Charlotte descended the stairs and silently entered the kitchen.

'Hello, Lotte,' said David. He'd called her that since she was tiny. It was quite endearing really. Although I suspected she didn't think of it that way. 'How's the homework going?'

'Fine, thanks,' she replied. I wondered whether to warn David that was the answer he'd get to anything he cared to ask this evening, but didn't want to embarrass Charlotte by doing so.

I watched as she picked at her food, taking an eternity to chase one chunk of sweet potato around her bowl. Next to her, David appeared to be eating in indecent haste. I waited for him to notice. To catch my eye, mouth across the table asking what was wrong. He kept on eating, eyes fixed firmly to the front while Esme chattered on about what stunts and daredevil challenges she would do if she were a *Blue Peter* presenter.

I heard Will's footsteps galloping down the stairs and got up to take his bowl out of the simmer oven. It was only as I carried it over to the table that I caught sight of him in the hall putting his jacket on.

'Where are you off to?' I asked.

'Out.'

'I was hoping for something a bit more specific than that.'

'With Jack and Troy.'

I tried really hard not to roll my eyes. And to resist the temptation to point out that he was still not answering the question about where.

'What about your tea?'

'We're gonna get some chips.'

'That's not what I mean.'

'Sorry, Mum. I just haven't got time.'

'Well, if that's going to be the case can you at least tell me next time so we don't waste the food?'

'OK.'

David called out from the kitchen.

'Have you done your homework, son?'

'Yeah.'

'OK then.'

That was it. Permission had been granted. There was nothing else I could say.

'Home by ten then,' I said, doing my best to raise a smile.

'Yeah. Laters.'

Will grinned at me, knowing how much I hated the

expression and pulled the door shut behind him. I walked back through to the kitchen. Esme was still describing how she would hang-glide off Mount Everest for Sport Relief. Charlotte remained silent and had barely eaten a thing. David stood up, rinsed his bowl before putting it in the dishwasher and turned to me.

'Thanks, love,' he said. 'I'd better be off.'

I nodded and walked out into the hall with him, closing the kitchen door behind me.

'He's gone to the park,' I said. 'I know he has.'

David shrugged. 'We can't stop him going out. You know that.'

'Yeah, but you've seen the kids who hang out there. It's Special Brew corner.'

'He could at least drink a Scottish brew.'

'David, I'm being serious.'

'He's sensible enough to keep himself out of trouble.'

'It's the company he's keeping that bothers me.'

'Why doesn't he see Sol any more?'

'He's got a girlfriend. Pretty serious from the sound of it.'

'Maybe that's what Will needs. Keep him out of trouble.'

'You wouldn't be saying that if he had a girlfriend.'

David put his scarf on, adjusted his glasses in the mirror and picked up his briefcase.

'Charlotte's really quiet tonight,' I said.

'She's always quiet.'

'She's hardly eaten. I'm worried the whole thing's started up again at school.'

'Your job,' said David, 'makes you worry too much. You read too much into things.'

I let out a long sigh.

David kissed me briefly on the lips. 'Don't wait up. It could be a long one, tonight.'

'OK. You will remember to ask them about the protest on Monday, won't you?'

David looked at me blankly.

'The lollipop lady thing. You said you'd try to make it. Get some of the other councillors along.'

'Yes. Yes, of course. I'll ask tonight.'

I nodded and opened the door for him. Watched him walk briskly down the short path and close the gate behind him.

I walked back into the kitchen. Charlotte had still barely touched her food.

'Actually, Mummy,' said Esme. 'I think I might try and cartwheel to the Arctic Circle instead.'

I nodded. At least I wouldn't have to worry about that one for a few years yet.

It was only when I arrived outside school on Monday afternoon and caught sight of Jackie that I realised my placards might be a little on the small side. They had looked fine on the kitchen table and there was no question that the lettering was neat and clear on the sheets of A4 card but I'd obviously failed to think about the impact factor. While Jackie's banner (it appeared to be written on what looked like an old bed-sheet) may have had slightly wonky lettering, it could probably have been seen by the NASA space station.

'I suppose they are rather on the small side,' I said, as Jackie squinted to make out the words on the placards I was holding.

'Small but perfectly formed.' She grinned. 'And anyway, we all know that size isn't important.' She was saying it to make me feel better, I knew that.

'I take it you've done this sort of thing before then,' I said nodding towards the banner and the big pile of placards on the grass verge.

'A long time ago, in my student days. You can't really do much as a teacher. The Head doesn't take kindly to his teachers doing anything political.'

'But surely this isn't political? All we're doing is fighting for our children to be safe.'

'Everything's political in his eyes.'

'So might you get into trouble?'

'Don't know. Depends if anyone sees me, I guess.'

'But you know Sam's invited the papers and Calendar and Look North.'

'Yep.'

'And it doesn't bother you?'

Jackie shrugs. 'Some things are worth taking a risk for.'

I nodded. It was funny how you could be friends with mums at school for years, but still not really know them. Not know what makes them tick. What they lie in bed at night worrying about.

I spotted Sam struggling up the hill with an armful of placards and went to help her.

'These are amazing,' I said, smiling at the brightly coloured designs in vivid shades of greens and blue.

'The boys have been busy. Rob included.' She dumped them on the grass verge, brushed her hands together and looked up at Jackie's SAVE OUR SHIRLEY banner which was tied between two trees. 'So, it's a low-key approach, is it?' She grinned.

'No one ever got heard by keeping quiet,' said Jackie.

'Which is why I got you this.' Sam handed her a large shopping bag. Jackie opened it and started laughing as she pulled out a loudhailer.

'But it's not even my birthday,' she said.

'I've borrowed it from one of Rob's mates. I'm afraid you'll have to give it back later. But I figured it might come in handy.'

Jackie looked like a kid who had just been given a Christmas present she'd put on her list but had never really expected to get. She held it up to her lips.

'Testing. Testing. What do we want? George Clooney. When do we want him? Now.'

'Oh God,' groaned Sam. 'I can see I'm going to regret this.'

'I'm just glad you didn't bring her an AK47 and live ammunition,' I said.

'Take no notice of Anna,' said Jackie. 'She's sulking because she went for the minimalist approach with her placards.'

Sam looked at the apology of a placard in my hand and cracked up laughing.

'Are they that bad?' I asked.

'Is that peasticks they're mounted on?'

'Er, yes. But what they lack in size they make up for in sentiment.'

'I'm sure they do,' she said. 'Is David coming?'

'I hope so. It just depends if he can get away from work in time.'

Sam nodded. I didn't want to admit that David hadn't sounded very hopeful when I'd reminded him about it that morning. Actually that wasn't true either. It wasn't that he hadn't sounded hopeful, more not that he hadn't sounded unduly bothered, to be honest.

A steady stream of parents came up the hill to join us, some carrying their own placards, others choosing one from our pile. Mostly Sam's and Jackie's though, it had to be said. Mine were clearly going to be the consolation prize for anyone who arrived late. I spotted the Calendar TV van drive past us and park further up the hill.

'Look,' I said, grabbing Sam's arm. 'Calendar are here.'

Sam jumped up and down next to me. 'Fantastic. We might just make the evening news.'

A swish-looking woman with ironed-flat hair and a microphone made her way down to us, followed by an older man with the camera.

'Hi. Thanks for coming,' said Sam, offering her hand. 'I'm Sam Farnell. I sent in the press release.'

'Good to meet you, Sam,' said the reporter. 'I'm Georgina

Lupton and this is our cameraman Bob Jukes. Where's the lollipop lady?'

'She's just coming up the hill now,' Sam said pointing.

'And what about the children?'

'They'll be out in about ten minutes.'

'Great. I know you said your own boys gave you the idea for the campaign. We'd like to interview them if possible.'

'Yes, of course,' said Sam. 'They're not exactly backwards in coming forwards.'

'Fantastic. Well, we'll get set up and start filming as soon as the kids come out.'

Georgina and Bob crossed to the other side of the road. Shirley arrived, slightly breathless.

'You're going to be on telly, Shirl,' said Jackie.

'I wish you'd have told me, I'd have done me hair.'

'You look lovely as ever,' said Sam. 'They want to interview you for the local news.'

'I can't believe all this,' said Shirley, gesturing around her at what was by now a sea of placards.

'We don't do things by halves,' said Jackie.

'Well, I'm touched. I really am. You ladies haven't got any lippy I can borrow, have you?'

Jackie reached in to her capacious handbag and pulled out a bright red lipstick.

'Here,' she said, handing it to Shirley along with a mirror compact. 'Colour will suit you a treat.'

With all the parents now gathered, Jackie picked up the loudhailer and began to go through the plans for the protest.

'Please take your time crossing the road. Only one family will go across at a time and do make sure you have your placard with you. When you are safely across please gather on the grass verge where you can wave your placards and make as much noise as you like. Are we ready?'

The chorus of whoops and cheers which greeted Jackie suggested she had whipped the crowd into something approaching a frenzy. She was clearly loving it too: marshalling everyone into the correct positions, geeing them all up.

When the children streamed out of school a few minutes later they were already in a heightened state of excitement due to the prospect of being able to shout and wave some placards around. Seeing the television camera there as well sent them into the stratosphere.

'Mummy,' squealed Esme, cannoning into me, 'are we going to be on telly?'

'We might be, sweetie. They've come to film the protest about Shirley's job for the news.'

'Are the Prime Minister and the Queen coming?'

'No, love.' I smiled. 'I think they're a bit too busy.'

'Is Daddy coming?'

That was probably as ridiculous as the previous question, but I didn't want to tell her that. I wanted to appear hopeful, even if I didn't feel it inside.

'He's going to do his best to get here, love. He wants to help if he can.'

'Can't he stop them getting rid of Shirley. He is a friend of the Mayor.'

Trying to explain to Esme that being a friend of the Mayor of Hebden Royd town council was not the same as having the ear of the Prime Minister seemed too complex and fraught with the danger of further questions, the answers to which could well be relayed back to David along the lines of, 'Mummy says you're not very impor-tant at all, actually.' I decided on a diversionary tactic instead.

'Oooh, look. They've started filming, Esme. Would you like to go across the road now?'

'Yes, please.' Never had crossing a road appeared quite such an exciting prospect to a child. I handed Esme one of my placards.

She regarded it thoughtfully. 'I don't want a children's one, I want a grown-up one like Jackie's,' she said.

Clearly, I didn't make the grade as protest mum.

'Come on,' I said. 'It's our turn next.'

The traffic was already tailing back quite a way down the street. The drivers didn't appear too bothered at the moment and we were getting lots of toots of support, but I suspected that might change by the time thirty or forty more families had gone across. I was quite glad we were doing it while the going was good.

'Right, come along Esme,' said Shirely. She knew all the children's names, even ones whom she didn't often have to see across the road. Sam had told me once that she even remembered her boys' birthdays. Esme fairly bounced across the road shouting 'Save Our Shirley' at the top of her voice and brandishing the placard with rather alarming vigour. I surprised myself by shouting pretty loudly too. I could see how touched Shirley was by the whole thing. Realised that this was probably about the biggest thing that had ever happened to her. We were fighting for her job. We were all in this together. Much as I disliked the term 'the big society', this was it. Or at least what it should have been about.

When we reached the grass verge on the other side of the road we looked back and saw Sam coming over with Zach and Oscar, both of them shouting at the tops of their voices. Georgina, the TV reporter, came up to me. She appeared rather awkward.

'Er, Sam's son, the one in the wheelchair, is he going to be OK to be interviewed? Only we wouldn't want to ask him, if it was going to be difficult, I mean.'

'He'll be fine,' I said, feeling snappish on Sam's behalf. 'He's got spinal muscular atrophy type 2. It's a muscle-wasting disease. There's nothing wrong with his brain, if that's what you mean. He's an exceptionally bright child.'

'Great. Thanks. Sorry I had to ask. I didn't want to embarrass her, you see, by trying, if it wasn't going to be possible.'

I smiled and nodded. I didn't think she had meant it nastily. It simply rankled because I knew Sam got this all the time. And that it got to her – even if she pretended otherwise.

I watched as Georgina approached Oscar and Zach and the cameraman began filming.

'So, Oscar, can you tell me why you wanted to save Shirley's job?'

Oscar looked up at Shirley, who was standing next to him. 'Because she looks after us every day and stops us getting splatted by big lorries and cars. And she's smiley and squidgey when I give her a hug.'

I saw the tears well up in Shirley's eyes as the microphone was directed to Zach.

'I wanted to help because it's wrong. Children are important. More important than saving pennies.'

I swallowed hard, catching Sam's eye as I did so. And that was when I knew that we couldn't let this one go.

'Jackie,' I called over, when the interview was finished, 'could you pass me the loudhailer, please? I think it's my turn.'

'Daddy,' called out Esme later that evening when she heard his key in the door, 'come quickly, we're going to be on TV.'

David stuck his head around the living-room door as he slipped his shoes off. Saw us all squeezed on to the sofa waiting.

'Did Calendar come then?' he asked me.

'Yeah, they did.'

'Sorry I didn't make it,' he said, hovering in the doorway. 'I couldn't get away from work.'

I nodded, deciding not to say anything more in front of the children.

'The Mayor was there,' said Esme. 'And Mum shouted on a big microphone and there was a huge traffic jam and everything.'

David looked at me, a slight frown on his forehead.

'Ssshh,' I said, grabbing the remote and putting the sound up. 'We're coming on.'

David, Will and Charlotte watched in stunned silence as a cacophony of noise filled the room and a shot of me leading a chant of 'kids not cutbacks' flashed on to the screen.

'Cool,' said Will afterwards. 'My mum's a secret anarchist. Who knew?'

4

SAM

People's reactions when I told them where I worked tended to be entirely predictable. They would usually say I was brave – which couldn't have been further from the truth – and also that it must be very depressing. To which I would answer simply, 'Ah, you've never visited a children's hospice then.'

Most people hadn't, of course. That was the problem. If they had, they would understand that for the vast majority of the time, children's hospices were the least depressing places on earth. Nobody moaned you see. Most offices, shops or factories where you turned up on a Monday morning would be full of people moaning about the weather, the roadworks, the train being late, the boss being a bastard or one of their colleagues being a pain in the arse. That, as far as I was concerned, would be depressing.

Whereas turning up at the Sunbeams Children's Hospice on a Monday morning, you were met with smiles, laughter, tales of enormous courage and wall-to-wall love. Nobody moaned if someone had forgotten the milk for the tea. You couldn't. Because the child in the next room wasn't expected to see their third birthday. Perspective. That was what was needed to stop people moaning. And it was the one thing Sunbeams was never short of.

There was nothing depressing about seeing a child smile as they reached out to catch the dancing lights in the sensory room, or hearing a parent describe what it meant to be able to spend some time alone with their other child, knowing that the sick one was being expertly looked after. I was of the view that they ought to write prescriptions for visiting children's hospices on the NHS. It would be a damned sight more effective than antide-pressants.

'Morning, Sam,' Marie called over from her office as I passed.

'Morning,' I said, backtracking and sticking my head around her door.

'How's Bella?'

'She's hanging in there. She was comfortable last night, at least. I think her mum and dad managed some sleep.' I nodded. Bella had leukaemia. She'd been discharged from hospital a couple of days ago to come here. She wouldn't be leaving, we all knew that. But it was our job to make sure we did everything possible to ensure her last days were very special ones, for her and her family.

'Good. That's something. It's amazing what a decent night's sleep can do for you.'

It helped, of course. Having Oscar. Gave me a keyhole to look through into the world of the people we were caring for. Most of the time I didn't mention his condition to the parents who came here. It was like telling someone your child had gashed his knee when theirs had just had his whole leg amputated. That was one of the weird things about working here. It made me feel lucky. I spent so much time outside with people feeling sorry for me that it was quite refreshing to come here and feel lucky.

'By the way, there's a quick staff meeting in fifteen minutes,' Marie said.

'Oh. Do we know why?'

'Funding situation.'

'Ah. I take it Simon's heard, then.'

'Yeah. I don't think it's good news, though.'

'Right. I'd better go and stick the kettle on. I'll see you in there.'

We gathered in the committee room as requested at ten. Mugs of strong coffee at the ready on the table.

'I'll keep this brief,' said Simon. 'Suffice to say we've heard from the Department of Health, and it is as we feared. Our grant will be cut by 10 per cent from April.' The news was greeted with resigned nods from around the table. We'd been expecting it but it didn't make it any easier to stomach.

'And it's not to be replaced by any other pots of money from the government?' asked Marie.

'No.'

'That's outrageous,' I said. 'They only give us two hundred grand a year anyway. How the hell do they think we're going to make up the shortfall when there's a recession on?'

Simon looked at me. I was well aware that I was preaching to the converted. I was simply unable to contain my anger.

'I know,' he said. 'But we're going to have to find a way.'

'We should go to the media with this,' I said. 'We could get together with the other children's hospices. Make a big noise. Shame them into a U-turn. I'm sure the public would support us.'

There was an awkward silence around the table. I suspected they thought I was being wildly idealistic and far too confrontational. But they had also heard the catch in my voice so they didn't like to say so.

'I understand your frustration, Sam,' said Simon. 'And I'm not saying we shouldn't make our voice heard on the matter. But we've also got to be careful not to appear to be politically motivated, especially so close to a general election.'

I nodded, although I didn't see what was political about wanting the best for dying children.

'How much are we down on fundraising this year?' asked Chris, one of the nurses.

'We haven't got the exact figures yet, but it will be in the region of 5 to 10 per cent.'

Another silence. We'd broken all records on fundraising

the previous year. To come up with any increase on that was going to be difficult. Especially at a time when everyone was so stretched.

'I'll schedule a meeting next week to discuss the fundraising situation in more detail,' said Simon. 'I've asked Alice and Denise to present us with a report and some suggestions, but the more ideas anyone can bring to the table the better. Thank you all. And sorry to be the bearer of bad news.' Simon rose and left the room. He was as gutted as anyone, I knew that. He was simply a damned sight better than me at remaining dignified and composed in such situations.

I walked back along the corridor with Marie.

'Oh well, it could have been worse,' she said.

'Could it?'

'No, not really but I thought I'd better do the British stiff-upper-lip thing.'

I smiled at her. 'As opposed to my hysterical ranting, you mean?'

'I guess the rest of us are just resigned to the fact that there's nothing we can do about it.'

'I don't agree. There's always something you can do.'

Marie stopped outside her office. 'Were you like this as a teenager?' she asked, still smiling.

'Like what?'

'Believing you could make a difference. Make the world a better place.'

'Yeah. That's what comes of having hippy parents, I guess. I suppose it's why I wanted to be a journalist as well. Although it took a while for me to work out that the people running local newspapers weren't interested in challenging stuff like that. But look where I ended up working. Look at what goes on here. How you guys make such a difference.'

'In a small way, yes. But only in the lives of the people we touch. Outside that we can't change anything. We're the little guys who get kicked. We can't kick back.'

'That's why the politicians get away with all this crap. Because people don't understand the power they have.'

Marie shook her head. 'I guess the rest of us were brought up to toe the line.'

'Well I'll have to teach you how to kick ass sometime.'

'That,' said Marie, with her hand on my shoulder, 'might come in very useful.'

I carried on along the corridor, past the glass memory wall, each block engraved with the name of a child who was no longer with us, and on to my little office.

I switched on my computer, the screensaver photo of Zach and Oscar making me smile as it always did, but making me angry as well. People shouldn't have to fight for their children to have somewhere comfortable and dignified to die. They just shouldn't. I opened up the spring newsletter I'd been working on the previous week. That was the only trouble with working school hours, you never seemed to actually get anything finished in a day. Half past two had a habit of coming around very quickly indeed.

I'd been working on the fundraising page: tales of people sky-diving, shaving their heads, running half-marathons, all to raise some precious extra pounds for us. It suddenly struck me as ridiculous. People wouldn't have their operations cancelled because not enough people had shaved their heads to pay for it. And yet here we were, possibly having to reduce the amount of respite care we could offer for the very same reason. It was obscene. Actually obscene.

My mobile rang. I fumbled in my bag and pulled it out. I felt my body relax as I saw it wasn't the school's number. It wasn't a number in my address book.

'Hello. Sam Farnell.'

'Oh, hi. It's Georgina from Calendar. I just wanted to congratulate you on your victory.'

'Sorry?'

'Haven't you heard? The council backed down at their meeting last night. They voted to scrap the plans to make the school crossing patrol people redundant. Said they'd try to find savings from elsewhere instead.'

'But that's fantastic. I can't believe it.'

'Sounds like your protest had quite an impact. Everyone seemed to have seen it. And the petition too. Two thousand signatures was amazing.' I was glad Georgina couldn't see me as I danced a jig of delight around the office.

'Thanks for letting me know. And thank you so much for coming to film us.'

'Glad to have helped. Actually, the reason I called was to see if you could come on the programme tonight.'

'What, outside the school or something?'

'No, here in the studio. The producer would like Fiona

to interview you. You and your two friends who organised it all. And Shirley, of course. Would that be OK?'

'Yes,' I said, 'I mean I'll have to ask the others and we'll need to sort out childcare and everything. Well, obviously not Shirley, but . . .' I was aware from the silence on the other end of the phone that I was blithering like an idiot. 'I'm sure it will be fine. We'll make it.'

'Great. Can we send a cab to pick you all up for 4.30? Is outside the school OK?'

'Yes, that'll be fine. Thank you.'

'Brilliant. I'll see you later then.'

I put my mobile down, shut the door and did the 'woo-hoo' bit from Blur's 'Song 2' very loudly indeed.

It felt rather like an Olympic homecoming when I arrived at school that afternoon. Fortunately they had stopped short of laying on an open-top bus procession but there was a crowd of cheering parents and someone had hung a 'well done' banner across the school gates.

Shirley was the first person who came up to me. She took me by the hand and started patting it. Her mouth opened and closed, but no sound came out. So she threw her arms around me and gave me an enormous hug instead. I understood then why Oscar liked them so much. She was a particularly good hugger.

'I can't begin to thank you enough,' she said eventually, looking up, her eyes moist and glistening.

'Don't be daft. You keep our children safe. It was the least we could do.'

'Well, I'm touched. I really am. I never thought anyone would do owt for me like this.'

'And are you all set for your TV appearance tonight?'

'I went straight to hairdressers after school rang me. Do you like colour?' Shirley stroked her short wavy hair, which now had a golden tint to it.

'You'll knock them dead.' I smiled. 'Now I'd better let you get on with your job. Can't have you slacking after all this effort, can we?'

Shirley trotted off with her lollipop stick, accepting the congratulations and good wishes from other parents as she went. I turned around to see Anna standing next to me. The normally super-cool, demure Anna looked fit to burst.

'We did it,' she said, her voice at least an octave higher than usual.

'I know,' I said, giving her a hug. 'I still can't quite believe it.'

'Why not? You masterminded the whole thing.'

'Don't be silly. You're the one who got half of those signatures on the petition. It was teamwork, that's what it was.'

We were almost knocked off our feet as Jackie bowled into us.

'Group hug,' she shouted, attempting to bounce us up and down in some kind of football team-style celebration dance. Anna looked horrified for a second then appeared to decide to go with the flow.

'It was the loudhailer wot won it.' Jackie grinned.

'No. Mum power,' I said. 'Nothing as scary as a bunch of women fighting for their kids.'

I squeezed Jackie's shoulder, sensing how deeply she was feeling this.

'Are you sure Paul's OK to have the kids?'

'Absolutely no problem. He's going to be home by four at the latest.'

'Rob will come straight round to get the boys after work.'

'And Will's going to pick up Esme on his way home,' said Anna.

'Brilliant,' said Jackie. 'Sounds like we'll have time for a celebratory drink when we get back from Leeds.'

'Now that is being optimistic,' I said.

The main doors opened and the children streamed out into the playground. Judging by the looks on their faces, they'd already been told.

'You did it,' said Zach, running up to me and jumping up and down. 'You saved Shirley's job.'

'No,' I corrected, as Oscar zoomed up to us, 'you did. You and Oscar. It was your idea after all. And all the other children who took part in the protest and signed the petition. It was a team effort.'

'Is it because of what I said on TV about not wanting to get splatted like Flat Stanley?' Oscar asked.

'Yes, love. That helped. You all helped. You made the people in charge at the council realise that it wasn't a good idea at all.'

'Will we get medals?' asked Oscar.

'Yes, like in *The Railway Children*,' said Zach. 'They got medals for saving people's lives.'

'I'm afraid not,' I said. 'The council don't give out medals.'

'They could give us a Lego set instead,' said Oscar. 'I wouldn't mind.'

I smiled and shook my head. Thinking how much Rob would laugh when I told him later.

We sat in the green room at Yorkshire Television with a local businessman who was bucking the trend by doubling his workforce and a teenager who was going to be playing the ukulele on *Britain's Got Talent*. I guessed it was that kind of a news day.

'Ooh, it's right posh, in't it?' said Shirley, stroking the plush chair seats.

'Would you like a drink?' I asked her. 'They've got still and sparkling water.'

'I've never had sparkling water. I think I'll give it a whirl. Live it up a bit.' I smiled at Anna as she passed the bottle.

'I'm wishing I hadn't told people on Twitter and Facebook I was going to be on TV now,' Anna said. 'It's bad enough trying not to think about everyone at home watching, let alone all the mummybloggers as well.'

'You mean we're going to go viral?' asked Jackie.

'I don't know about that but I expect there'll be a fair few watching it online later and retweeting the link.'

'Oh God. Now I'm nervous,' I said. 'I'd been imagining Oscar and Zach as the only audience.'

A young woman poked her head around the door. 'OK, ladies,' she said. 'If you can follow me through to the studio. You're the lead item on the programme.'

'Lead?' whispered Anna. 'I thought we'd be the And Finally spot.'

'What do you think the ukulele kid's doing here?' I whispered back.

We took our seats on the sofas. Shirley waved at Fiona and Derek the presenters as if she were a lifelong friend. Derek, very sweetly, waved back. The bright studio lights glared down on us. I looked down at my DMs, aware they were not the normal attire for sofa-TV interviews. They looked even worse sandwiched between Jackie's trendy wedges and Anna's sleek courts. I glanced across at Jackie. I didn't think I'd ever seen her nervous before. As the countdown to air began, all I hoped was that we wouldn't make complete fools of ourselves.

'Hello everyone,' boomed Derek. 'Welcome to Calendar with Derek Masters and Fiona Gould. Here's what's making the headlines this Tuesday evening.'

'Saved from the axe,' said Fiona. 'The lollipop ladies across Calderdale whose jobs have been saved by parent power.'

I grinned at Jackie as Fiona and Derek continued with the rest of the headlines. We'd made a difference. We really had.

'Now,' said Fiona, sitting down on the sofa next to us

after they'd run a report showing clips of the stop the traffic protest and an interview with the council leader who insisted, of course, on talking about school-crossing-patrol personnel rather than lollipop ladies, 'we have with us in the studio the three women behind this campaign and the lollipop lady who inspired it. Shirley, had you any idea how much you meant to the pupils and parents at your school?'

'Not a jot,' replied Shirley. 'I mean they're all lovely to me and the children give me hugs and that but I were gobsmacked when they told me what they were planning to do. And when I saw the turnout on day of protest, well . . .' Shirley's voice trailed off. She turned to smile at us. I swallowed hard.

'So, Sam,' said Fiona, 'it was your sons who gave you the idea for this campaign, wasn't it?' I resisted the fleeting temptation to give one of those little mum waves to the children watching at home and attempted to sound über cool.

'That's right. As soon as Oscar and Zach found out about the plans to get rid of Shirley they said we had to do something, and they were right. You can't just stand by and watch things like this happen.'

'Now, Jackie, we saw you in the clip there marshalling the troops with your loudhailer. Had you done anything like this before?'

'Not really. I'd been on political protests as a student, but I'd never organised something as personal as this, something where children's lives and people's jobs were at stake.'

'And Anna, were you surprised that a bunch of angry mums could actually force the council to do a U-turn?'

'Not really, no. Hell hath no fury like a woman whose child is in danger. There's no greater motivation to do something and therefore there's no limit to what parents like us can achieve.'

Fiona appeared a little taken aback by Anna's assertion. She wasn't the only one.

'But you heard what the council leader said in our report. They're going to have to find the savings needed from elsewhere now.'

Jackie jumped in to answer before I could open my mouth to say anything.

'Unfortunately this has all been caused by the government cutbacks, but what we've got to ensure is that politicians of all parties have the right priorities when making difficult decisions. And I think we've shown them that no one puts children in danger without having an enormous fight on their hands.'

'So what next?' asked Fiona, turning back to me. 'Having won this battle do you fancy trying something a bit bigger? There's a general election coming up in a couple of months, do you fancy having a go at sorting the country's problems out as well?'

I glanced across at Anna and Jackie, still marvelling at how eloquently they'd put our case. They were fired up, I could see that. Almost as fired up as me.

'Why not?' I said. 'I think we could make a damn sight better job of it than some politicians.'

'There you go,' said Fiona, 'sounds like it's a case of watch this space. Well done, all of you. Back to you, Derek.'

The producer had already briefed us to stay seated on the sofa until they went to the next report. To be honest she needn't have bothered. I suspected I was not the only one who was incapable of moving.

Jackie stared at me with a questioning frown. Anna had the scared eyes of one of those passers-by who are caught up in some kind of political riot they never meant to get involved with. And here we were, effectively kettled on the Calendar sofa, everyone's brains whizzing a bit too much for their own liking. Only Shirley provided a picture of serenity as she gazed dreamily at Derek.

We were given our cue to make a swift exit and passed the businessman with the booming company in the corridor as he made his way to the studio.

'Great stuff,' he said, putting his thumb up in a rather awkward fashion. 'Really inspiring. I'd certainly vote for you.'

'Thank you.' I smiled, aware that the others were looking at me as if I'd finally lost the plot.

'Well you kept that quiet,' said Jackie with a smirk, as we waited while Shirley popped to the ladies.

'What?'

'The fact that you were planning to declare we were standing in the general election.'

'I didn't know she was going to ask the question, did I?'

'I take it you were joking,' said Anna.

I thought long and hard before I answered. 'No,' I said. 'I don't think I was.'

Zach and Oscar were both in bed by the time I got home. Oscar had apparently declared himself far too excited about seeing me on TV to possibly go to sleep, but had succumbed nonetheless. Zach was still awake though. He never went to sleep until I was home, not that I went out that much. It was like some strange role reversal of an anxious parent listening out for their teenager's key in the door.

His head lifted as soon as I opened his bedroom door a crack.

'Night-night, love,' I whispered, bending to kiss him softly on the forehead.

'You were brilliant, Mummy,' he said, his arms around my neck pulling me closer.

'Thank you, sweetheart.'

'Oscar was really happy that you said our names.'

'Good. I had to, didn't I? It was all your idea.'

'Are you going to sort out the country's problems now, like the lady said?'

I smiled. 'I don't know, sweetie. I'd love to but I don't want anything to get in the way of being mummy to you and Oscar. That's my most important job.'

'We don't mind. We'd share you for a bit. So you can help other people.'

'That's really kind of you, love,' I said, stroking his hair. 'I'm not sure I'll be able to do it, though. I'd have to stand for election and get lots of people to vote for me. Thousands of them.'

'I'd vote for you.'

'I know you would. Unfortunately you can't vote until you're eighteen, though.'

'Well, I'd get grown-ups to vote for you, then. I'd explain how you're good at helping people.'

'That would be great.'

'You should try, Mummy. You always tell us that we'll never know if we can do something unless we try.'

'You know, Zach, you talk a lot more sense than most of the grown-ups I know,' I kissed him again on the forehead. 'Now, you get some sleep. It's very late.'

'Love you, Mummy.'

'Love you too.'

I closed the door quietly and crept back down the stairs. Rob had a cup of tea waiting for me on the kitchen table.

'Thanks, love,' I said. He looked up at me from his copy of *NME*, his head propped up on his hands, an expression of bemusement on his face.

'You were being serious, weren't you?' he asked. 'About standing in the general election.'

I nodded. 'You think I'm crazy, don't you?'

'Yes, but I always knew that.'

I smiled. 'I don't quite know exactly how or what yet. All I know is that I can no longer just sit here and do nothing.'

'How far do you want to go, exactly? On the scale to world domination, I mean.'

'I don't want to dominate anything. I just want to try to make things better. To shout about all the things that are wrong and get them put right.'

Rob nodded slowly, ran his fingers through his mousey hair.

'And how are you going to find time for this? We hardly see each other as it is. You put in far more hours than you're paid for at the hospice and what with the governors' meetings at school, not to mention looking after Oscar. Jeez, there's going to be nothing left of you.'

I looked down at the quarry tiles, which were cracked and needed replacing. Not that we could afford it, of course. I wasn't used to Rob doing serious. I knew this was an enormous ask. He was right, we didn't spend enough time together as it was. And it had taken its toll on us over the past few years. It was probably only the fact that we'd been so bloody strong in the first place which had kept us going. And now here I was wanting to throw a huge bloody grenade into our already stressed lives and expecting Rob to be OK about it.

'I'm sorry,' I said. 'I know this is going to be really tough on you and I don't want Oscar or Zach to suffer in any way because of what I'm doing. But nor do I want them to grow up in a country where they're the soft targets. Where the government says, "Oh yeah, we'll cut services for kids because they can't complain or vote us out." I want to do something that will make this country a better place for them to grow up in. Them and every other child who lives here. And if I don't do it I'm not sure anyone else will.'

Rob stared at me as my eyes misted over. I thought I saw him swallow. He shook his head.

'What?' I asked.

'It still does my head in sometimes. How bloody brilliant you are.'

I grinned and threw my arms around him. 'You mean you don't mind if I give it a go?'

'No,' he said, kissing my shoulder. 'Just so long as I don't end up as Denis Thatcher.'

'That will never happen,' I said with a smile. 'You hate golf for a start. And I don't possess a handbag for you to carry.'

5

JACKIE

'Is Grandma going to talk to me today?' asked Alice.

We were on our way to see Mum. I hadn't taken Alice with me since Mum had come out of hospital. Mainly because she'd been so upset after she'd visited her there. But then yesterday Alice had asked why she never saw her any more. And the guilt had got me from the other direction.

'She was only quiet when she was in hospital, love. It was because of that medicine they gave to her to calm her down.'

The 'medicine' in question was actually an antipsychotic drug. I'd gone ballistic when I'd found out. There was no medical reason to put her on it. She was agitated because she was losing her mind and had been taken to a strange place. It was an entirely natural response. What she needed was love and familiarity and security. Not a bloody chemical cosh.

'So is she cross and bothered again?' asked Alice. 'You said they gave her the medicine because she was cross and bothered.'

I sighed. How did you even begin to explain this to a six-year-old?

'She was cross and bothered in hospital because she wasn't at home. She was confused. And when people are confused they can get a bit angry.'

'So isn't she confused now?'

I turned off the main road through Boothtown and began making my way left, right and left again through the narrow roads of terraces which I knew so well. I pulled up as near to number 52 as I could park and turned to reply to Alice.

'She is still confused, love. But not as badly as when she was in hospital. Just her normal confused because of the disease we talked about.'

Alice nodded. She didn't seem at all sure. I got out and went round to open her door.

'Tell you what, love,' I said as I helped her out. 'If you want to go at any time you just tap me on the knee and I'll know, OK?'

'OK,' said Alice.

I knocked twice and then let myself in with the key.

'It's only me, Mum,' I called out. Alice was holding on to my left hand very tightly. We slipped our shoes off on the mat and went through to the front room. Mum was sitting in her armchair. The first thing I noticed was that she had two skirts on; a beige pleated one poking out from under a mauve floral one. She had teamed them with a yellow, short-sleeved blouse. You could quite clearly see the goosebumps on her arms.

'Hello, Mum,' I said, bending to give her a kiss. 'I've brought Alice to see you.'

I waited, willing her to say something positive. Or at the very least not to ask who Alice was.

'Hello, dear,' she said, smiling in Alice's direction. I ushered Alice forward. She planted a kiss softly on Mum's cheek before retreating back to the sofa.

'Your arms feel cold, Mum,' I said. 'Where's your cardi?'

'It's dirty,' she said. 'It's in the wash. They're all in the wash.'

'Let me go and find you something to put on,' I said. 'Alice, why don't you tell Grandma what you did in swimming this morning?' Alice looked at me hesitantly, but started speaking when I nodded at her.

I went upstairs and into Mum's bedroom. Clothes were strewn all over the floor, it looked more like a fifteen-year-old's room than a seventy-two-year-old's. I opened the top drawer in the chest where she kept her cardigans and jumpers. It was empty. I hurried downstairs. I could hear Alice still trying to explain what a swimming noodle was as I passed the open door on my way to the kitchen. I checked the washing machine. Nothing in there. Or the laundry basket. I began opening cupboard doors, looking in the bin, anywhere I could think of. And then I came to the cooker. I could see the outline of something through the tinted glass in the door. I put the interior light on. Only I wasn't checking to see if a cake had risen. What I was really illuminating was the inside of Mum's head. It wasn't just the one cardigan. It was all of them. Bundled in there ready to be washed. The only saving grace was that she hadn't gone as far as turning it on. Because I suspected gas mark 4 might well have been translated as a 40-degree wash.

I opened the oven door and began unloading the clothes into the laundry basket, aware that my hands were shaking. I picked a blue cardigan out from the middle of the pile that hadn't touched the inside of the oven. I sniffed it. I could still smell the fabric conditioner from the last wash. I loaded the rest straight into the washing machine, added powder and put them on a quick cycle. I heard the water gush in, watched the clothes being tossed around the drum and the bubbles slowly creep up the glass. She was going under. I knew that. Not waving but drowning. She wouldn't even think to wave. She wouldn't recognise anyone to wave to. And it appeared I was the only lifeguard on the beach.

I went back through to the front room. Alice, bless her, was still talking. Telling Mum the names of all her cuddly toys. Clearly she was going to become skilled at an early age in the art of filling awkward silences.

I took Mum's left arm and eased it into the sleeve of the cardigan.

'You can put this on for now,' I said. 'The rest of them are being washed at the moment. I'll put them on the airer before I go.'

She nodded. 'I like this one,' she said. 'Bill always used to say it set me eyes off a treat.'

I smiled at her as I buttoned the cardigan up. 'I don't want you to do any more washing,' I said. 'Just leave it in the laundry basket in the bedroom and I'll do it for you when I come. Or ask Cath to do it. I take it she hasn't been today?'

'She'll be coming any minute to give me my breakfast.'

I looked at the clock. It was half past twelve.

'You haven't had anything to eat this morning?'

'No. I'm waiting for Cath.'

I nodded. 'I tell you what. We'll have something while we wait.'

I went into the hall and phoned the out-of-hours number for social services. Cath was off ill. Someone else was supposed to have come. Only quite clearly they hadn't.

'I want to speak to the care manager,' I said.

'She doesn't work weekends.'

'No, I bet she doesn't. Unfortunately my mother still eats at weekends. Or rather she should do.'

'Is there a message I can give her?'

'There is but you probably wouldn't like to repeat it to her face, in which case I'll save it until I speak to her tomorrow. She's not going to like it, mind.'

I put the phone down and strode back through to the kitchen. I started cooking scrambled egg on toast. I figured I may as well do enough for all of us. We were clearly going to be here some time. The sound of the egg sizzling must have covered up the noise of the kitchen door opening. The first indication I had that Alice was in the room was when I felt a gentle tapping on my knee.

'What's the matter, sweetheart?' I said, taking the pan off the hob for a second when I saw her solemn face looking up at me.

'I'm ready to go now,' she said. 'Grandma keeps calling me Deborah.'

'How you feeling?' asked Paul when we were lying in bed later.

'Worried, despairing. Mad as hell.'

'No, I meant about tomorrow.'

The one good thing about spending the day fretting about my mother was that it had at least taken my mind off the impending hospital visit.

'Oh, that. I just want to get it over with, to be honest. Just want to move things forward.'

Paul nodded. Though I suspected he didn't feel the same way.

'What about you?' I asked.

He hesitated. I heard him sigh deeply next to me. Watched his chest rise and fall before he spoke.

'Worried, despairing. Mad as hell.'

I propped myself up on my elbow and turned to look at him.

'Why?' I asked.

'I'm worried they're going to say it's my fault then I'll feel really bad for letting you down, I'm despairing of what we'll do if they say we can't have another baby because

I know how much it means to you and I'm mad as hell that you're having to go through all this when everyone else seems to be able to pop out another one without any problem. That's why.'

I shut my eyes and bit my lower lip. I had no idea he felt like this. I thought it was me who was wound up about it.

'Hey,' I said, squeezing his shoulder. 'It won't be anybody's fault, whatever they say. And if it's bad news, we'll deal with it. I don't know how, but we'll do it. OK?'

'Yeah,' he said, stroking my arm. 'You're right. I know you are. We need to be strong. Both of us. I'll stop being such a wuss.'

'Don't be daft,' I said. 'I'm glad you told me. Sometimes I get it into my head that it's only me going through this. It's actually good to know that you're in as big a state as me about it.'

'That's all right then,' said Paul with a smile. 'We'll be crap together.'

We sat in silence in the waiting room of the assisted conception unit. Paul held my hand and squeezed it intermittently. I felt a bit of a fraud, to be honest. Here I was attending the infertility clinic when I had a happy, healthy six-year-old. I wondered if the other women waiting could tell. If there was some tell-tale mumsy evidence which gave the game away. If they'd be talking about me to their partners afterwards. 'I don't know what she was doing there, she clearly already has one.'

Maybe I was being greedy. One was enough for lots of people, why wasn't it enough for me? I knew the answer to that, of course. And it was a perfectly valid one – at least to me. But it still left me feeling that my pain was not as great as other people's. That this was a sham and I should go home to my child, give thanks for what I had and let someone else have a turn.

Only child. The term still rankled with me. All the times I had been asked if I was one or people had simply presumed I was and I had suffered a fresh explosion of hurt inside. And already people were saying it about Alice. People assumed we'd made a lifestyle decision. That one was quite enough, thank you, and we didn't want our lives disrupted by the inconvenience of another. People who should keep their fucking noses out of our business.

A nurse came through to the waiting room. 'Paul Crabtree,' she called. Paul let go of my hand and stood up.

'Have fun,' I said. Paul managed a weak smile and followed the nurse out. He was embarrassed about it. He'd told me so last night. The fact was that while I was prodded and poked and subjected to all manner of indignities and discomfort, he'd get shown to a private room with a collection of 'adult' magazines and be told to amuse himself in a way which teenage boys up and down the land considered a pleasure not a chore. There were some things feminism simply couldn't change. The complexities and difficulty of access of the female reproductive system was one of them.

I picked up one of the celebrity magazines on the table.

Personally, I could have quite happily got off on looking at the photos of George Clooney getting arrested outside the Sudanese embassy. He didn't even have to take his clothes off. The handcuffs were enough for me.

But sadly it was not to be.

'Jackie Crabtree?' The young woman who called out my name smiled when I got to my feet. 'Have you come far?' she asked.

'Only Hebden Bridge.'

She nodded. I wondered if she was specially trained to make small talk to put people at ease before inserting a camera up their private parts. Perhaps she would continue by enquiring whether I had any holiday plans while trying to get a good shot of my ovaries.

I was told to undress, put on a delightful hospital gown and given a small paper towel as some kind of modesty blanket, which didn't really make sense as the only person it would screen my bits from was me and oddly enough I'd seen them before.

I leant back and opened my legs as requested and tried hard to cling on to the image of George Clooney in handcuffs. But it was difficult when the monitor next to me insisted on showing me pictures of what could have been some ropey seventies space movie but was actually the inside of my womb.

I remembered going for the scan when I was pregnant with Alice. Seeing the hazy image on the screen and needing Paul to point out to me where all her limbs were so I could try to make sense of what I was looking at.

And now here I was looking at what wasn't there. The space. The ache. The emptiness inside. I'd actually been worried this morning. Wondered about cancelling the appointment. Just in case I was actually pregnant and whatever they were planning to do was going to wrench this new life from me. I'd even thought about how ironic that would be if it happened. I felt stupid now, of course. Like some grown adult with an imaginary friend. Telling people to watch their step, not bump into him, be careful when they swung around. There was nothing there. There hadn't been for four years and to think there was now had clearly been fanciful at best, borderline insane at worst. The only positive thing I could think of was at least this time I wouldn't be disappointed when my period came. What you already knew couldn't hurt you.

I listened to the older woman, who was monitoring the screen, giving directions to the younger one: left a bit, go back slightly, let's go round again. It was akin to someone doing their cycling proficiency test inside me. I was trying to detect something in her voice – any note of concern, any hint that she found something untoward – but she was good at this, clearly an old pro at not giving anything away.

I asked in the end. I had to.

'Have you seen anything that gives you cause for concern?'

'Well, obviously you'll have to wait for your appointment with the consultant to get a full report, but I think it's safe to say there's no evidence of anything sinister.'

I nodded and thanked her. I don't know why. There's something about people in hospital uniforms that makes me feel compelled to be grateful for even the tiniest morsel of information.

'No evidence of anything sinister.' What the hell did that mean? That there weren't a gang of masked robbers lurking in my uterus. That she hadn't found an al-Qaeda cell trying to infiltrate my Fallopian tubes.

'OK, Mrs Crabtree,' said the younger woman. 'We're all done here. If you'd like to get yourself dressed I'll take you through for your blood tests.'

I nodded. Imagining Paul sitting back in the waiting room. And actually being quite pleased that he did feel guilty.

Paul was quiet on the way back to Hebden Bridge. He didn't really say anything much until we pulled up near Sam's road.

'I'm sorry if it's my fault,' he said.

'What do you mean?'

'Well, if they didn't find anything wrong with you it's probably me, shooting blanks or summat.'

'Don't be daft,' I said. 'We don't know it's not me, yet. They probably wouldn't have told me if it was. Anyway, we shouldn't be talking about fault. It's not intentional is it? On either part.'

'No, you're right.' Paul's shoulders straightened a little. 'I just want you to know I appreciate what you're putting yourself through.'

'Thank you. And I appreciate how difficult it must have been for you to look at those magazines.'

'Well, you know how it is,' said Paul with a grin. 'Sometimes you've just got to go through with summat, no matter how much it pains you.'

'Thank you for the sacrifice. And just so you know, you won't ever be allowed that excuse again, OK?'

'Wait till I tell the lads at rugby club. They'll all be queuing up for sperm tests.'

'And for what it's worth,' I said, holding his hand. 'I have a theory that Yorkshire sperm are particularly tenacious. Endurance above speed and all that.'

Paul grinned. 'That about sums me up.'

'It doesn't matter how long the journey takes, does it,' I said, 'as long as we get there in the end.'

'No,' said Paul. 'I guess not.'

We climbed up the steps and across the bridge to Fountain Street. It was virtually an island, bordered, as it was, on the other end by the canal. Sam sometimes referred to it as the People's Republic of Fountain Street. Eclectic was the kind word to describe its population. Paul was more inclined to use the word 'hippyville'. Not that he'd ever used it to Sam's face, of course. He wasn't that daft. A collection of various children's toys, pushalongs and playthings were strewn across the front gardens. Scooters that had seen better days, a plastic cooker with the oven door missing. There was even a rabbit hutch with a cuddly toy rabbit inside.

'Now that,' said Paul, 'is a smart idea. Think what they'll

save on vets' bills. And they won't have trauma of a kid in tears when it dies. Why didn't we think of that?'

'You see,' I said. 'Sam'll convert you to her way of living yet.'

Paul rapped on the door of number ten with his knuckles. Nobody seemed to have a doorbell or knocker, probably because they were in and out of each others' houses so much that most of the time their doors were open. The paint was peeling off the front door. Sam said that because Rob spent his days painting other people's houses it was the last thing he wanted to do when he got home. Sam finally opened the door and Fleabag bounded out and fled down the road, clearly not welcoming of visitors.

'Sorry,' she said. 'We were in the middle of a game of Sam Says. It's like Simon – sorry, I'm sure you worked that out. I'll shut up now. Come in.'

She stepped forward and gave me a huge hug. I'd been all right until that point.

'Are you OK?' she asked, seeing my trembling lower lip.

'Yeah. We're fine. No news is good news for now, eh?'

'Well, Alice has had a fab time with the boys.'

She was interrupted by shrieks of laughter from the front room.

'Sounds like she still is,' said Paul. 'I bet we'll never get her away.'

Oscar appeared in the doorway, wearing a pirate hat and with what appeared to be a stuffed parrot on his shoulder.

'Pieces of eight, pieces of eight,' he said.

'Amazing what you can find in the charity shops in Hebden,' Sam whispered to me.

Alice came running out behind him and hurtled into Paul and me in turn.

'Pirate Oscar and Pirate Alice are going on a treasure hunt,' Oscar said.

'Well, I'm afraid Pirate Alice needs to go home soon,' said Paul, ruffling her hair.

'Please, Daddy, just one treasure hunt.'

'OK,' said Paul. 'If it's quick.'

'Pirate Zach's hiding the treasure in the backyard,' Oscar informed him.

'Well, we'd better find it quick then, before any other pirates get there,' said Paul, shepherding them towards the back door.

'Fancy a cuppa?' asked Sam.

'I'd love one.'

I sat down at the kitchen table and smiled at the jumbled collection of photos, paintings and weird and wonderful creations camouflaging Sam's fridge.

'Can you actually still get in there?' I asked.

'With difficulty.' She smiled. 'Rob keeps telling me to throw the old stuff away to make some space but I can't bring myself to do it. It's like I'm throwing away their life histories.'

I nodded. As someone whose fridge still had the scan picture of Alice stuck on it, I couldn't do anything else.

Sam put a mug down in front of me. I liked having friends who knew me so well they always hit the exact colour shade of coffee I liked.

'So did they tell you anything?' Sam asked, sitting down opposite me with her tea.

'Only that there was nothing sinister there.'

'Well, that's good, isn't it?'

'I guess so. I won't get the blood-test results until we go back, mind. Or Paul's sperm results. And if everything's clear I still might have to have my tubes checked.'

'That sounds fun. How does Paul feel about it all?'

'Oh, you know. He tries to joke about it and stuff, but he's pretty stressed too. He doesn't want to go down the IVF route. I do know that much.'

'And what about you?'

I shrugged. 'I'd do anything. It's not for me, see. It's for Alice. I want her to have a brother or sister.'

Sam nodded and took a sip of her tea. She looked down at the table. 'If it does turn out to be bad news I want you to know that it's fine being an only child when you've never known anything different. I actually liked having my parents all to myself. Bit selfish I suppose, but there you go.' I smiled at her. 'The most important thing is that you don't forget what a brilliant mum you are to Alice.'

'Thank you,' I said. 'I just want what's best for her. I guess all mums do.'

'That's what makes us so strong,' she said. 'We're fuelled by love. It's much more powerful than money or ego.'

I put my mug down on the table. 'You're still serious about this election thing, aren't you?'

'I've never been more serious about anything in my life.'

'It's completely crazy; you do know that?'

'Not as crazy as the hospice having to beg people in the streets for money, or you having to chase up the council because they're not looking after your mum properly.'

She had a point. I knew that. And I also knew that Sam didn't know the meaning of the words 'can't' or 'won't'. That was what worried me.

'OK. Supposing I agree with you. What exactly do you propose we do about it?'

'I told you. We stand in the general election.'

'Who for?'

'Our own party. We start a new one.'

'Now you have lost it.'

'No. It's obvious. Everybody's fed up with politicians. How many people do you hear say "they're all as bad as each other"? How many people don't even vote because they're so hacked off with the whole thing?'

'So why would they vote for us? Apart from the fact that we're three hot young things, of course.'

Sam smiled. 'Because we're fighting for ordinary people. For kids, for grannies, for everyone who hasn't got a voice.'

'And you really think there are enough granny-huggers to vote for us? Beyond Hebden Bridge, I mean.'

'Of course there are. Look at the bloody alternatives. We'd be a breath of fresh air.'

I hesitated. Sam was a very hard person to say no to.

'You'll never get Anna on board.'

'Why not?'

'She oozes common sense for a start.'

'Well, I'll just have to convince her that doing this *is* common sense.'

'And how do you propose to do that?'

'I'm having a meeting. A week tomorrow. Eight o'clock. Here. At this very table. Me, you and Anna.'

'And what if we don't turn up?'

Sam looked at me as the shrieks from outside indicated that Oscar and Alice had found the treasure at last.

'You will,' she said. 'Because we only regret the things we don't do. Not the things we do.'

6

ANNA

'Why do you feel the need to cut yourself, Jodie?'

You shouldn't have to ask questions like that. Not to fifteen-year-old girls. No one at my school cut themselves. I would have seen the marks. We all would. The communal showers at Grove Park School allowed for neither modesty nor concealment.

I couldn't put an exact date on when girls started cutting. All I knew was that in the ten years I'd been doing this job, the numbers had grown every year. Girls barely into their teens feeling the need to slash and burn.

'Because I can like, see the hurt. Instead of it all being inside.' She looked down at her hands which poked out from under the long-sleeved shirt which covered the evidence of her self-harm. She reeked of pain. Pure, unadulterated sadness. Sure, I worried about things at her age but they were stupid things: spots, the size of my breasts, whether my breath smelt. The usual suspects. Beneath that, at the core of me, I'd been happy, surely? I certainly hadn't been *un*happy. Any pain I'd felt hadn't penetrated. It hadn't flowed through my veins.

'And does that make you feel better?'

'Yeah. For a while, at least.'

'Where does the hurt come from, Jodie?'

'From inside.'

'How does it get there, though? What causes it?'

'I dunno. Everything I guess.'

'Name some of the everythings.'

I knew her parents were divorced. I knew she hadn't got many friends at school. That she hadn't been doing very well academically. She'd told me all of this already. But I didn't want to put words into her mouth.

'Danny.'

'Who's Danny?'

'My boyfriend. Well, he were till he, like, dumped me.'

'Did he give you a reason? For breaking things off, I mean.'

'Yeah. Said I were a minger and that he were going with Serena because she were good at sucking his cock off.'

I nodded slowly, working hard at keeping my face expressionless. 'I see. That's not a very nice thing to say about someone who was your girlfriend, is it?'

Jodie shrugged. Her scraped-back hair gave her no place to hide the hurt on her face, though.

'Did he say nice things to you when you were with him? Did he make you feel good inside?'

Jodie shrugged again.

'How long were you with him?'

'About six months.'

'Can you name one nice thing he said about you or did for you during that time?'

There was a long silence. Jodie shifted in her chair.

'It weren't like that.'

'What was it like, then?'

'I dunno. Just normal stuff. Getting off with him and that.'

I nodded. 'Did he ever hurt you, or make you do things you didn't want to?'

Jodie looked down at her feet. 'Only a bit. He weren't as bad as a lot of them.'

'What do you mean by that?'

'He didn't post any photos of me on Facebook. Or text them to his mates. That's why I loved him, see. He weren't like the others.'

I nodded slowly, trying not to think about Charlotte, who was only two years younger than her.

'So when you said he was one of the people who hurt you, who made you want to cut yourself, what did you mean by that?'

'I'm hurt that he, like, dumped me. That he doesn't think I'm fit enough.'

'Have you talked to anyone about how you feel. Your mum, your friends?'

'It's not gonna change owt, is it?'

'How do you know that?'

'Well, me mam wouldn't take any notice for a start. She hasn't got time to listen to me.'

'Because of her work?'

'That and her boyfriend. And he slaps her about so she wouldn't think anything of it.'

'And what about your friends?'

'They can't do owt about it.'

'They could support you, though. Be a shoulder to cry on.'

'Not really. They've got their own crap to deal with.'

'What do you mean?'

'Keely were raped by her boyfriend and his mates and Shaz's dad knocks her mam about.'

'I see. So how have they coped with all of that?'

'They cut too.'

I nodded slowly again. I was used to hearing depressing things. I'd worked with a lot of troubled teenagers. But occasionally, I was still blown off my feet with the sheer awfulness of it all.

I blogged about it that evening. Not Jodie's case specifically, of course. I was careful never to compromise client confidentiality. But the kind of messages society as a whole conveyed to girls. A society where how you look is everything and girls are conditioned to believe that they somehow deserve to be hurt, physically or emotionally, if they don't measure up. A society where being beautiful inside counts for nothing and a word like minger even exists. A society where girls feel it necessary to harm themselves as a way of showing how much they are hurting inside.

I posted the blog, linked it to Twitter and Facebook and waited for the response. David said that was why I'd started the blog. That I needed to know other people out there felt like I did. That I wasn't, as I sometimes feared, a lone voice in the wilderness. Maybe he was right. But the one thing which had become abundantly clear in the five years since my Mothers' Talk blog had come into existence was that if I had ever been a lone voice, I certainly wasn't now. For some inexplicable reason I regularly made the top ten UK Mummy Bloggers list. Consequently, companies were queuing up to advertise on my blog. If I was honest, totally honest, I got a little kick out of how that made me feel. And an even bigger kick about how perplexed David was about it.

The comments started coming in. One from a mother whose daughter cut herself and who was plagued with guilt about it. A few from teachers who had seen the scars on their pupils and didn't know what to do. The majority from mothers who simply didn't want their daughters to grow up in a world where the best they could hope for was that their boyfriend didn't knock them about. And where the hurt inside could only be assuaged by a razor blade.

I replied to as many of them as I could, even if it was only to offer sympathy. I advised the teachers to do what Jodie's teacher had done – to speak to the girl, give her contact details of youth counselling services and hope like hell that somewhere beneath the scars she had a tiny shred of self-worth left – enough to prompt her to go and see someone.

And all the while I thought about Esme, fast asleep in her room, and Charlotte, probably still reading with that little purple book light I'd got her as a stocking-filler at Christmas. About the world which awaited them and how much I wanted it to change.

I glanced down at the clock in the corner of the computer screen: 10.20. That was the only trouble about being online; you had absolutely no idea where the time had gone. I logged out and shut down the computer. David was downstairs, an increasingly rare night when there wasn't some sort of council business to attend to. I hurried downstairs and went into the kitchen to make us both a mug of tea.

'Sorry,' I said, as I went through to the lounge and handed it to him, 'completely lost track of time.' David looked up from the comment page of the *Independent*.

'That's OK. Easily done.'

'I hope Will's got a better excuse.'

David looked at his watch. 'He's got two minutes to go yet. You know how he likes to scrape in just under the wire.'

'To be honest,' I said. 'I wouldn't mind him being a few minutes late if he was doing something worthwhile.'

'As opposed to being a public eyesore in the park, you mean?'

'It's not funny, David. I don't like where he is or who he's with or what he's doing.'

'You're not supposed to – you're his mother.'

'Well are you happy about it?'

'No. But unlike you I don't think there's anything we can do about it.'

'Since when did you subscribe to the laissez-faire method of parenting?'

'You chose to live in Hebden, Anna. What did you expect? Nine o'clock curfews and a drink and drug-free environment.'

His words stung me. The way he made out this had all been my doing. As if he'd merely been a passenger with no say in where we were going.

'You're the one who first suggested moving here.'

'Yeah. Because you were so keen to get the kids out of London.'

'So what are you saying, that you didn't want to come?'

'No. Just that I came with my eyes wide open. You may have thought this was some kind of utopia but I certainly didn't.'

I was trying to formulate some kind of reply when I heard Will's key in the door. I glanced up at the clock: 10.29. Will stuck his head around the living-room door with the cockiness of someone who knows they have not left forensics anything to go on.

'Thank you and goodnight,' he said.

'Hang on,' I said, hurrying out to the hall. 'We haven't even had a chance to ask how the history mock went.'

'It's OK, Mum,' he said. 'I wouldn't worry. It's all in the past.'

'Unfortunately,' I replied, pretending to tweak his ear, 'there aren't many openings for full-time comedians.'

'Shame.'

'So do I take it from your response that Simon Schama has nothing to worry about?'

'I don't know, you'll have to ask him.'

'If they did mocks in being too clever for your own good—'

'I know, I'd be an A-star student,' grinned Will, giving me a peck on the cheek.

'Love you,' I called after him as he headed up the stairs.

'Whatever.'

I shook my head. It was hard to know whether to laugh or cry sometimes. I suspected if I'd seen the people he'd been hanging out with tonight, it would be the latter.

I went back into the lounge. I wanted to talk to David about Will, but he was watching *Newsnight* now and appeared to be particularly engrossed in a studio discussion on the Greek economy. I sat down next to him on the sofa. My arm brushed his knee as I reached for my mug of coffee and I found myself apologising, actually apologising, for accidentally touching my own husband. He even acknowledged the apology. We slept in the same bed, for Christ's sake. I couldn't help thinking even the Greek economy was easier to understand than our marriage sometimes.

Every morning we played out the scene from *Angelina Ballerina* where the mischievous mouseling knocks things over by attempting pirouettes in the kitchen and ends up in big trouble. Only in Esme's case she managed to carry the whole thing off with such aplomb that instead of us getting cross and bothered about it we could only marvel at the ability of one seven-year-old to cause so much chaos.

'The milk, Esme,' I said, pointing to her cereal bowl, 'you're spilling your milk.'

'Oops,' she said with a giggle.

'It generally happens if you try to do star-jumps while pouring it,' said Will.

'What about pike-straddles?' she asked.

'I don't know. Give it a try.'

'Will,' I groaned.

'What? Like she needs encouraging.'

'How about trying yoga?' I suggested. 'You could do a nice meditation while eating your cereal.'

'Boring,' said Esme. 'I'd rather do a shoulder-stand.' She lay down on the kitchen tiles and kicked her legs up into the air, knocking over a chair which in turn knocked over the cat's water bowl.

'Mum,' groaned Will with a grin on his face. 'Now look what you've made her do.'

I pulled a face at him. Occasionally, that is what my family reduced me to. Will helped Esme mop up the mess before I sat her down firmly at the table.

'One day, young lady, we may actually resort to velcroing you to the chair.'

'Is that an actual word?' asked Will.

'I don't know. Ask Mr Hudson at school. Could you pass the milk please, Charlotte?'

Charlotte stared blankly at me.

'The milk, Charlotte, love.'

'Oh, yeah.'

She passed the jug and went back to staring blankly into space. I looked at Will. He shrugged. A second later her mobile beeped. She picked it up and held it under the table. Her hair was hanging down across her face so it was impossible to see her expression, but a second later she pushed her chair back and went to leave the table.

'Charlotte, you haven't finished,' I said. She glanced down at her plate, ran out of the room and up the stairs. I looked at Will.

'Can you get Esme ready for school please, love?'

'Sure,' he said, instantly swapping to responsible older-brother mode.

'What's wrong with Charlotte?' asked Esme.

'Big-girl stuff,' I heard Will say to her as I left the kitchen. 'Nothing for you to worry about.'

I knocked on Charlotte's bedroom door. She didn't say to come in, but nor did she shout to go away.

I went in. She was sitting on the end of her bed, tears pouring down her face, the mobile still in her hand.

'Hey.' I sat down next to her and hugged her to me, feeling her chest shake as she sobbed. I held her for a long time until the sobs subsided a little, enough for her to be able to speak.

'They've started again, haven't they?' I said.

Charlotte nodded.

'Is it the same girls?'

She nodded again.

'What would you like me to do about it?'

'I don't know. They might just stop. If I ignore the texts, I mean.'

'But you shouldn't have to ignore stuff like that. What did the text say?'

Charlotte didn't reply. I picked up the phone from the bed and clicked on the top message in her inbox. *Hey geek. Wanna shag a choirboy? Bet he won't shag u, titless freak.*

I bit my lip and looked up at the ceiling. Someone had sent this. Sent it to my daughter. Every primal instinct within me rose to the surface. If I'd had a nuclear bomb at my disposal at that point I would probably have used it.

'Oh Charlotte.' I hugged her to me again. As if she were still my little girl. As if I still had control over her world. As if protecting her from harm was as simple as applying sunscreen and putting a shade on the buggy.

'How many of these have you had?'

'A few.' I looked at her face. Wiped a tear away for her with my finger.

'Come on, honestly?'

'About a dozen.'

'Did any of them threaten you?'

'No. Just stupid stuff like that.'

'What's this ridiculous choirboy thing?' I asked.

'Just something they made up because I'm in the choir. It fits the whole geeky thing.'

I got up from the bed. Paced around the room, trying to think rationally rather than emotionally.

'Well, we can't let them do this to you. I think I should phone the Head.'

'No. Please don't. It'll only make it worse.'

'It stopped it last time.'

'Everyone knew, though. That you'd been up the school. That I'd told you who'd done it.'

I hesitated. I couldn't bear to see Charlotte hurt like this, but I also understood the importance of involving her with how this was dealt with.

'OK. So what's the alternative?'

'I ignore it. They'll get bored and go and pick on someone else.'

It didn't seem much of an alternative to me. 'I tell you what,' I said. 'Don't delete the message. Turn the phone off and leave it in your drawer. If anyone hassles you at school, you tell a teacher straight away and tonight I'll have a chat with your father about it.'

'Please don't tell Dad. He'll go off on one. He'll try and call the police or something.'

'Look, we won't do anything without consulting you. But I do have to tell him, love. This is really serious.'

Charlotte shrugged. 'OK.'

'Now, are you all right to get your face washed and get yourself to school?'

She nodded.

I went over to her, held her shoulders and kissed her

on the top of her head. 'I love you to bits and you're utterly gorgeous, you know.'

She nodded again. I wished I could record myself saying it and have it playing in a loop in her head all day long. Anything to drown out the bad words. To make sure the nasty things didn't seep through.

I hurried back down to the kitchen. Will had miraculously managed to get Esme dressed and ready for school, book bag and lunch bag in hand.

'Thanks,' I said, kissing him on the cheek. 'You are a complete and utter star and you can have that in writing if you like.'

'Can I have a tenner instead?' he asked.

I smiled at him. 'No, but it was a good try. Wait for your sister, will you? Even if it means you're a bit late. And keep an eye on her for me.'

Will nodded. I opened the front door. Esme shot out into the garden.

'Is this about the bullying?' Will asked.

'Did you know it had started up again?'

'I'm not sure it ever really stopped.'

'What do you mean by that?'

'It's just girls of that age, isn't it? They can be complete cows to each other.'

'Well I want you to look out for your sister, but no vigilante stuff, OK?'

'OK.'

I pulled on my coat, hurried outside, took Esme's hand and set off down the hill for school.

We arrived in the playground at the same time as Sam, Oscar and Zach.

'Are we early or are you late?' asked Sam, as Esme started running rings around Oscar's wheelchair.

'We're late, I'm afraid,' I replied.

'Oh well. Right, you two, have you got everything?' Zach nodded, Oscar pulled a funny face. 'Have fun,' said Sam, kissing them both before they hurtled towards the school entrance.

'You too,' I said to Esme, bending to give her a kiss. 'Love you lots.' I watched her run off after the boys, wishing for a second that I had a pause button. That it would always be as good and as simple as this. I'd never wished that before. I'd always thought it strange how some parents seemed to want to bonsai their children. For me, watching them grow up and become young adults was one of the best bits of the ride, one that I couldn't imagine ever wanting to miss. Until now, that was.

'Are you OK?' asked Sam. I realised I was still staring in the direction of the school door.

'Sorry. I'm not really with it. It's been one of those mornings.'

'What's up?'

'This bullying thing with Charlotte has started up again.'

'Oh, Anna. You poor thing. What are you going to do?'

'I don't know. Charlotte doesn't want me to go and see the Head. But we've got to do something to stop it. I can't bear the thought of her going through all that again.'

'Well, if it's any consolation, I think she's got the best mum possible to help her through it.'

'It's different though,' I said, 'when it's your own kids, I mean. All that theory and training goes out of the window and I just want to shout and scream and kick up a huge fuss like any mum would.'

'Yeah, but you don't though, do you? That's the difference.'

'Maybe. We'll see.'

'Oh,' said Sam, reaching into her bag and pulling out an envelope, 'I nearly forgot. This is for you.'

'Thank you.' I tore open the envelope and pulled out the printed card inside. It read: *'You are invited to the inaugural meeting of a new political party at Number Ten (Fountain Street, Hebden Bridge) on Sat. 2nd March at 8p.m.'*

I looked up at Sam and smiled. 'Fantastic. You can count me in.'

Sam frowned at me. 'No, it wasn't supposed to be that easy. You were supposed to say I'm crazy, ask me a hundred questions and tell me you'd think about it with a highly doubtful expression on your face.'

'You are crazy,' I said. 'Certifiable. But you happen to have caught me at the one moment when the world as it is seems crazier still.'

Sam grinned and hugged me. 'You won't regret it,' she said.

'I know,' I replied.

7

SAM

'Why can't I stay up for the meeting?' asked Oscar for the seventy-third time as he finished his spaghetti and wiped the tomato sauce on his lips all over his cheek with the back of his hand. It wasn't that he had a burning desire to talk politics for three hours, simply that he hated missing anything.

'Remember what I said, love. It's going to be a lot of talking and not very interesting for children. Plus it starts after your bedtime.'

'But it's a Saturday,' said Zach. 'People in my class stay up for *Britain's Got Talent* on a Saturday and that's not as important as running the country.'

Whilst I was pleased that Zach recognised that tonight was more important than winning a talent competition, I doubted that the G8 Summit would take place with the politicians' children in attendance. I looked at Rob as I gathered up the bowls. He gave me that look which said, 'How the hell are you going to get out of this one?'

'I tell you what,' I said, turning back to the boys. 'Why don't we have our own little meeting now instead? You boys can tell me all the really important things we can do to make the country a better place and I'll tell your ideas to Jackie and Anna.'

'OK,' said Zach, seemingly mollified. 'How about putting more ramps everywhere so children like Oscar can get around more easily?'

'Brilliant,' I said. 'And how lovely that you started by thinking of others.'

'I would like pizza and carrot sticks every night for tea though, too,' he added.

'That's fine,' I said with a smile.

'And ice cream,' said Oscar. 'I'd like ice cream every night.'

'OK. And what about something nice for other people?'

'I'd like them to have ice cream every night too,' said Oscar.

Rob snorted a laugh of approval as he scraped the plates over the compost bin.

'While we're at it, maybe we could have a chippy on every street corner as well,' he added.

'Thank you for your contribution.'

'And how about proper headphones issued with all iPods so we don't have to mess about with silly little earphones that never stay in properly.'

'I don't think you're taking this very seriously,' I said, giving him a look before I turned back to the boys.

'What about things that would make school better?'

'I know,' said Zach. 'A big telescope in the playground so we could look up at the sky. And binoculars for bird-watching.' I nodded enthusiastically and started writing their suggestions down on a piece of paper.

'A stage so I could do shows and tell jokes,' said Oscar.

'A nature trail,' said Zach.

'A banana tree, hot chocolate coming out the taps and not having to be quiet all the time.'

I smiled at Oscar and scribbled them down. I couldn't help thinking that he had the makings of a Monster Raving Loony Party candidate.

'What are you going to be called?' asked Zach. 'You'll need a name if you're going to run the country.'

'I don't know,' I smiled. 'I haven't got that far yet. You two will have to think of something for us.'

'Does it have to have party at the end?' asked Zach.

'Yeah, it does really.'

'The Cheeky Monkey Party,' said Oscar.

'Thank you, love,' I said. 'I'll write that one down too. Now, thank you both for your suggestions. I'm going to clear the tea things away while Daddy gets you ready for bed, OK?'

'Do I have to have the cough machine tonight?' asked Oscar.

I glanced over at Rob. Oscar so rarely complained that I was at a loss to know what to say when he did.

'Oh, it's not a cough machine tonight,' said Rob, wrapping his arms around Oscar. 'It's a fire-breathing dragon and you're going to be the knight. Are you up for the challenge?'

'Yeah,' roared Oscar, and set off at full speed out of the kitchen, followed by Rob.

'It's not really going to be a dragon, is it, Mummy?' asked Zach.

I ruffled his hair, wishing that sometimes he wasn't quite so worldly-wise. 'No, love. But he'll enjoy the game, won't he?'

Zach nodded, gave me a hug and headed upstairs after them.

Anna arrived first. I opened the door to find her immaculately dressed as ever and brandishing a bottle of something red.

'I wasn't sure what you're supposed to bring to the launch of a political party,' she said, 'not having been to one before. But I figured a bottle of Rioja wouldn't go amiss.'

'Thank you,' I said with a smile. 'As we're making up our own rules as we go along, I think that's a very good one to start with.'

'Oh, and I thought we'd need some sustenance, so I brought these as well.' She handed me a small brown paper carrier bag from the local deli. Inside were two tubs of olives, a pot of houmous and some organic sesame and red onion crackers.

'Thank you,' I said. 'Although this means I can no longer claim that we came from humble beginnings.'

She smiled and followed me through to the kitchen. I'd thought it was reasonably tidy until she was standing in the middle of it. Anna always made anyone and anything around her look untidy in comparison.

'Are the boys in bed?' she asked.

'Yeah. Not asleep yet, though. They both really wanted to stay up for this.'

'Esme couldn't quite get her head around the fact that I was going out on my own for the third time this year!'

'Did you tell her where you were going?'

'Yes. Didn't tell her what we were doing, though. She thinks we're just having a chinwag.'

'What about David?'

Anna hesitated. 'I didn't tell him exactly. I just said we were going to be talking politics.'

I nodded. She looked down. I poured a glass of wine for us both and one for Rob, which I put on the side for later. I sensed from Anna's response that, unlike me, she was not going to get her partner's wholehearted support over this. And I didn't want to make that any harder for her than it clearly was.

Another knock on the door.

'Hello,' said Jackie. 'I'm calling on behalf of the Three Stroppy Cows' Party. I'm wondering if we can count on your support in May?'

'You can if you come up with a better name than that.' I laughed, as I gave her a hug.

'I thought it summed us up quite well.'

'Not sure it will appeal to the voters, I'm afraid.'

'Oh well. Back to the drawing board.' Jackie clomped through to the kitchen and deposited a plastic Co-op shopping bag on the counter. 'Sorry, I couldn't run to actual champagne. I've just gone for the cheap fizzy plonk and a tube of Pringles.'

'Fabulous. Thank you.'

'Hi, Jackie,' said Anna, rising to give her a kiss on both cheeks.

'Oh,' said Jackie, gesturing to the wine and olives on the table, 'I've come to the wrong party, haven't I?'

'Not at all,' I said quickly. 'I've bought some teabags and a packet of digestive biscuits. There's room for all tastes here.'

Jackie grinned and sat down. 'So,' she said. 'Are you going to tell us your crazy plan now, or is there going to be some big fanfare and simultaneous internet launch?'

Anna sat back down and looked at me too. I realised I hadn't planned what I was going to say properly. I hadn't even come up with a decent name for the party. And these were far from salubrious surroundings. I could already see the entry in Wikipedia reading, 'The party was founded around a kitchen table in a small terraced house in West Yorkshire.' It was now or never, though. And it really didn't matter that we wouldn't have a grand beginning. What mattered was where it might end.

'OK,' I said, as I sat down and turned to the notes I had scribbled on my pad. 'It's going to be a bit of a splurge.

It might not make much sense, but please bear with me.'

Jackie and Anna nodded.

I took a deep breath. 'Our lives could all be improved by government action. Jackie wouldn't have to fret about her mum if the government made sure that social services and hospitals looked after people with Alzheimer's properly, Anna wouldn't have to worry about Charlotte being bullied if effective anti-bullying measures had been brought in years ago, and nor would she have to deal with so many screwed-up young people at work if our society cared for them properly. The hospice wouldn't have to face scaling down its respite provision if all children's hospices were fully government-funded and we wouldn't have had to raise thousands of pounds for a powerchair for Oscar if the government had prioritised giving children with disabilities better mobility above stupid things like hiring fig trees for a month for a building in Whitehall.'

Anna and Jackie were nodding.

I carried on. 'The trouble with our government and our society is that the weakest and most vulnerable are treated appallingly because they have no voice. We will give those same people a voice by putting them at the heart of everything we do. We believe that if we put that right, everything else will follow.'

I glanced at Jackie, who had a smile on her face.

'I like the way you're saying "we". You're sounding like a politician already.'

Anna, however, did not seem so convinced. 'So let's get this straight. You're actually proposing that we set up an entirely new political party from scratch and run for parliament in the general election in a couple of months' time?'

'Yep,' I said, 'That's about the sum of it.'

Anna nodded slowly. 'And what constituencies are you proposing we stand in?'

'Well,' I said, 'I've been giving it quite a bit of thought, and obviously you guys get to decide for yourselves, but my suggestion is that you do Calder Valley, Anna, as you live and work here. Jackie does Halifax because she was born and brought up there and I do Huddersfield because it's got the hospice in it. That way we'd have three adjoining constituencies.'

'That's supposing that we all got in, of course,' said Anna.

'Exactly.'

I turned to look at Jackie. She had a huge grin on her face.

'What?' I said.

'Just you,' she said. 'Being off-your-rocker crazy.'

'Do you not want to do Halifax?'

'I'd love to stand in Halifax. It's like being asked to a really wacky kid's birthday party. The one everyone wants to go to and you didn't think you'd get an invite for.'

'I hate to be the party pooper,' said Anna, 'but it will all end in tears if nobody votes for us.'

'Oh they will,' I said.

'Why are you so sure about that?'

'Because we have a secret weapon.'

'And what's that?' asked Anna.

'Mum power.'

Anna and Jackie both looked at me with somewhat bemused expressions. Clearly I was going to have to explain how it would work.

'Think about how we'd all fight to the death for our kids,' I said. 'Then multiply that strength of love by all the mums in the UK. If we can harness that power we can achieve anything.'

'She's right,' said Jackie. 'Look what happened with Shirley. And you see mums like us on the local TV news every night; fighting against knife crime because their child was stabbed or taking legal action against some drug company because of the side effects their child suffered.'

'There was a woman on last night,' said Anna, 'fighting for answers from the MoD because her son had suffered post-traumatic stress and gone AWOL in Afghanistan and instead of helping him they'd bloody imprisoned him.'

'Exactly,' I said. 'And there are women like that all over the country. We're going to get some of them to stand for our party in other constituencies and the rest to drum up support for us. On their own they're one small voice struggling to be heard. If we put them together behind a common cause they can make one hell of a racket.'

'So how exactly do you propose we do that?' asked Anna. 'Get the word out, I mean.'

I smiled at her and raised my eyebrows. 'You tell me, Ms Mummyblogger of the Year.'

'Are you serious?'

'Anna,' I said, 'you have more followers on that blog and on Twitter and Facebook than some political parties have members. It's an obvious way to spread the word and get other people involved.'

'She's right,' said Jackie. 'And it would be a hell of a lot more effective, not to mention cheaper, than advertising, because those people all feel like they know you. They trust you already.'

'As long as they don't think it's an abuse of that trust,' said Anna.

'Remember who we're doing this for,' I said, topping up Anna's wine glass. 'It's for their families as much as ours. We'd give them a real stake in it. Ask women across the country what they'd do if they were Prime Minister.'

Anna had her thinking face on. Her forefinger circled the top of the wine glass. 'I bet we'd get a fantastic response to that question,' she said.

'And we could put all their ideas in our manifesto,' said Jackie, her big hoop earrings bobbing up and down as she talked. 'It could be a mums' charter for change.

'The mummyfesto,' I said, jumping up and down at the table. 'It should be called the mummyfesto.'

Anna stared at me. I think that was the moment we got her.

Jackie finally put the Pringles down. She appeared to be physically shaking. 'Yes,' she screamed. 'That's brilliant. Absolutely brilliant. This is going to be so fucking amazing. Number Ten here we come.'

'Hey, let's not get carried away,' said Anna. 'We have to be realistic and this is in danger of entering Richard Curtis "not in real life" territory.'

'And you're going to be the uptight Kristen Scott Thomas character who always puts a damper on everything, are you?' enquired Jackie.

'If I have to be, yes. Because let's face it, Hugh Grant is not about to walk into the room, is he?'

The door opened and Rob strolled into the kitchen to be greeted by raucous laughter.

'What did I do?' he said with a shrug.

'You were a master of comic timing without realising it,' I explained.

'And you've just got a part in a Richard Curtis film,' added Jackie.

Rob shook his head. 'As long as it pays well, I don't mind.'

'There's a glass of wine on the side for you,' I said.

'Thanks.'

'Are the boys OK?'

'Fine. Oscar's all done. I think he's actually dropped off. Zach's asked for a glass of water. Says he can't sleep because he can hear you talking downstairs and he's too excited about you running the country.'

'That's really sweet,' said Anna.

'Yeah,' said Rob. 'Though I thought one potential revolutionary in the family was bad enough.' He smiled at me as he said it, poured a glass of water and picked up his wine glass. 'Anyway,' he said, 'have you lot sorted out a name for your party yet?'

'We were just going to get on to that,' I said.

'Well make it a good one,' said Rob as he headed back

upstairs. 'You don't get anywhere these days without a decent name.'

'He's right,' said Anna.

'I know,' I said. 'That's what worries me. I have a short-list, but I'm not sure that any of them are any good.'

'Go on,' said Jackie. 'Hit us with them. We'll soon tell you if they're crap.'

'OK. First one: Family Matters.'

Jackie screwed her nose up. 'Sounds like something John Major rejected before he came up with "Back to Basics".'

'Number two: The Sisterhood.'

Anna almost choked on an olive. 'Too sinister. Makes us sound like the masons.'

'Pankhurst's People.'

'Raving feminists,' said Anna. 'I do think it should say "family" more than "women", but without sounding sanctimonious or putting off women who don't have children.'

'OK. Final offering: Eve.'

Jackie sniggered. 'Isn't that the name of a sanitary towel? It should be, if it isn't. An extra absorbent one with a faint scent of the Garden of Eden.'

I started laughing. Anna almost choked on an olive. 'You're right, it does,' I said. 'I was trying to think of something which conveyed female without sounding too strident.' I sighed and crossed off all the suggestions on my shortlist. We were in danger at falling at the first hurdle. What chance had we got of winning an election if we couldn't even come up with a name that wouldn't make people snigger? Maybe that was the problem. Maybe whatever we came up with people would laugh. Because we were women and because we were trying to do something radical, and the easiest way to respond to people who do that is to laugh at them. The truth was that as much as people said they wanted a change, they only meant a small change, a change of faces at the top. Not some crazy women tearing up the rule book and trying to build something from scratch. I caught Anna's eye. I suspected that she was thinking along exactly the same lines. We were doomed.

Rob poked his head around the kitchen door and held out a folded piece of paper.

'What's that?' I asked.

'A late entry from Zach. I told him you were trying to come up with a name.'

I got up and took the piece of paper from him, unfolded it and read it. I knew as soon as I saw it that it was exactly what we needed.

'Come on,' said Jackie. 'It can't be any worse than our efforts.'

'The Lollipop Party,' I said.

'He said it was because of how you started, with saving Shirley's job,' said Rob. 'And because everyone likes lollipops.'

I looked around the room. Jackie and Anna both sat there nodding silently.

'It's bloody annoying isn't it?' said Rob, scratching his head. 'When a seven-year-old comes up with the best idea of the night.'

'What do you reckon?' I asked, turning to the others.

'It's certainly family-friendly,' said Anna. 'And it will make people smile, which is no bad thing.'

'The boy's a genius,' said Jackie. 'It's fun, it's different. And most importantly it does not sound like a sanitary towel.'

Rob looked at me quizzically.

'You had to be there,' I said. I picked up a pen and wrote '*THANK YOU. You're a star. Now get to sleep! X*' on the other side of the piece of paper and handed it back to Rob. 'Tell Zach he's hired as our campaign manager.' I smiled.

'Oh God,' said Rob. 'He'll be up all night now.'

I heard Rob go upstairs. Imagined Zach's grinning face as he told him the news. This was exactly what it should be. If we were going to give children a voice we needed to give them a say in everything.

'I think the precedent has been set,' I said. 'Jackie, I'd like Alice to design the logo.'

'Are you sure?' asked Jackie. 'It's likely to be very pink.'

'It'll be fantastic. And Anna, perhaps one of yours could come up with a slogan for us?'

'You may regret that,' said Anna. 'I'm not sure Will's even on the same planet, most of the time.'

'Well,' said Jackie, 'I think this calls for a celebration.' She picked up the bottle of sparkling wine.

'Hang on a sec,' I said. 'I haven't even asked you both if you're in.'

'I'm in,' replied Jackie.

We turned to look at Anna. 'It's probably the craziest

thing I've ever heard,' she said. 'And we really haven't thought everything out properly and there are a million and one reasons why we shouldn't do it.'

'Yes, but if you don't do it and we both get in you'll be like one of those bitter and twisted people who left the lottery syndicate just before they hit the jackpot.'

Anna sighed and shrugged. 'I guess I'm in then,' she said.

Jackie popped the cork. 'To the Lollipop Party,' she said, pouring us each a glass, although I knew she wouldn't have more than a sip of hers. 'And to Number Ten Fountain Street where it all began.'

'I'm afraid,' I said, taking a sip before putting the glass down straightaway. 'This does mean we'll have to knock the girls'-nights-out on the head for a bit. Well have campaign meeting here insteed.'

The smile momentarily disappeared from Jackie's face. 'But that was our New Year resolution.'

'I know, but so was making a difference and right now that's far more important.'

I lay awake that night, my thoughts spinning far too fast to facilitate sleep. The house was silent. The little voice of doubt in my head grew louder. I let it go. It ricocheted off the walls and came back to me, louder than ever.

Who the hell did I think I was? Some jumped-up university drop-out who'd chucked it all in to go off on some aid mission to the Romanian orphanages. Who'd come back a year later wanting to save the world and ended up covering parish fetes for the *Todmorden News*. I'd hardly covered myself in glory, had I? Hardly built up a reputation as a formidable political force. At the end of the day I'd got a handful of articles in the *Big Issue* in the North, and that was pretty much all I had to show for my campaigning efforts.

I slipped out of bed and padded across the floorboards to the sash window, peeping behind the curtain to look out. The moonlight illuminated the narrowboats moored along the towpath. At some point in my twenties I'd had this crazy idea of wanting to live on one. Permanently, not just some jolly boating holiday. I couldn't remember exactly why; like so many other things, it had never happened, but I did recall Rob taking me to meet one of his artist mates who lived on a narrowboat.

It had seen a bitterly cold January day, the canal had been frozen in places. The little curtains inside the boat were frozen to the glass. Rob's mate had explained that if the canal didn't thaw soon he'd be in serious trouble because he needed to get to the pumping station to empty the toilet in the next couple of days. Rob hadn't said anything more about it on the walk back. It wasn't his style to do so. Besides, he knew me too well to try to talk me out of anything. He was much more subtle than that.

It was lucky the visit had put me off though, narrowboats being not exactly wheelchair-friendly. That was the thing. You never knew what the future might bring. Rob had never anticipated being a painter and decorator, but when Zach had come along he knew he could no longer afford to hole himself up in an artist's studio for weeks on end in the hope of producing something that someone a lot better off than him might just be tempted to buy.

And after Oscar had been diagnosed I'd realised that there would be no going back to speculatively offering articles to the *Guardian*'s society section in the misguided belief that the odds of them accepting one must surely improve with each one they rejected.

Parenthood had forced us both to do the sensible thing. To get reliable jobs and a mortgage and put all the crazy stuff permanently on hold. And yet here I was, about to embark on the craziest thing imaginable. What on earth gave me the right to do that?

I stepped away from the window. As I turned back to the bed I saw Rob's head lifting up from the pillow.

'You OK?' he asked.

'Yeah. Couldn't sleep, that's all.'

There was a pause as I got back in bed before he squeezed my hand under the duvet and whispered, 'I'm dead proud of you, crazy woman. The boys are too.'

I squeezed his hand back. Somehow, he always knew the right thing to say.

I got up early the next morning, before anyone else woke. I tiptoed downstairs and opened up my laptop. I searched for every art gallery or restaurant or shop in Calderdale which displayed artist's work, made a note of the email addresses and composed a letter asking if they had any space to display Rob's work. I attached a couple of photos

I'd taken of his latest paintings the last time I'd gone down to his studio after he'd lugged them all around Hebden Bridge and been met with a chorus of 'We like them, but we just haven't got the space at the moment.'

Sometimes you had to fight for what you believed in. And for the people you loved. People who had crazy dreams of their own.

8

JACKIE

'You're not serious?' Sheila looked at me over the top of her glasses. I lowered my voice, the possibility that the Head had bugged the staffroom was something I had not yet discounted.

'I couldn't be more serious.'

'But what will Frodo say?'

'I don't give a toss what he says. All the campaigning will be done in my spare time, I won't name the school in my election leaflet and anyway, I'm not even going to stand in this constituency.'

'Are you sure there's nothing in your contract to stop you doing it?' asked Sheila, pushing her large, rectangular glasses further up her nose.

'I'm sure. As long as I don't bring the school's name into disrepute, I'll be fine.'

Sheila shook her head and blew out.

'Well, rather you than me,' she said. I tried hard not to smile. Sheila had been at this school for twenty years. She was not exactly renowned for throwing caution to the winds.

'It will make a refreshing change to spend my time slagging off the government instead of Frodo,' I said.

'You'd miss it terribly though, wouldn't you? If you got in, I mean.'

It was only when she asked the question that I realised it hadn't even occurred to me until that moment. Becoming an MP still seemed such a preposterous idea that I had given no thought at all to the prospect of giving up teaching. And Sheila was right, of course. Because while the likes of Frodo and Gove did my head in, I still loved teaching. And the idea of not doing it actually made me feel quite bereft.

'Yes, but just think how much better I could make it for you guys. Scrapping the National Curriculum and shaking up Ofsted. I'd be the pin-up girl of staffrooms up and down the country. You'd be telling people at the NUT conference that you used to work with me.'

Sheila smiled. 'Come to think of it, I might just come door-knocking for your campaign.'

'That's the spirit,' I said. 'Now, drink up and go and knock the Year Nines into shape.'

I sat at the back of the drama studio, a big notebook on my lap, pen poised to scribble notes. It was the last run-through the Year Elevens were going to do before their mock GCSE.

They were a good group of students: enthusiastic, innovative, bold. There were several who stood out, but only one capable of taking your breath away with the maturity of his performance. Will hadn't been sure he could do detached and brooding, let alone the Deep South American drawl that the part of Brick in *Cat on a Hot Tin Roof* required. I'd asked him to give it a go and joked with him that at least having hung out in the park in Hebden Bridge he would be able to do alcoholic.

Leanne strutted on to the set as Maggie. She may not have had the presence of Elizabeth Taylor, but she could shout and whine with the best of them. A minute later Will emerged from behind the door of our pretend bathroom. Only it wasn't the chirpy, having-a-laugh, gangly Will who always had a witty riposte. It was someone else entirely. Someone who was everything he had been asked to be with a bit more thrown in for good measure. I sat and watched as the two of them sparred with each other, spitting hurt and resentment. It should have been Maggie's scene, and Leanne gave it a bloody good shot, but Will somehow managed to edge it without looking as if he were even trying.

'Wooh,' I yelled, whistling and giving them both a standing ovation as they ended the scene with Brick reluctantly putting down the chair he had been brandishing above his head. 'Fantastic stuff. Taylor and Newman eat your hearts out.'

Leanne grinned and gave me her best Liz Taylor pout. Will immediately tried to ruffle his mop of brown hair, which had been slicked down for the part, back to life.

'It's not nice to speak ill of the dead, Miss,' he said.

'I didn't say they were bad, simply that you were better.'

'Well, at least unlike Newman I won't end up with my face on a jar of pasta sauce.'

'So where will you end up?' I asked, walking over to him as Leanne headed off to get changed.

Will knew what I was getting at. I'd given him enough prompts about doing something with his immense talent.

'Probably face down in the park, pissed or out of my head on something.'

'I'm being serious,' I said.

'So am I. That's what happens to everyone else around here.'

I hesitated, but decided this was not a time for tiptoeing around the edges. 'The kids that happens to, Will, they don't think they've got a choice, do they? And do you know what? Some of them are probably right. There are no jobs for them. There are no opportunities. *You* have a choice. You can choose a different life for yourself. They'd never admit it to you, but your mates would give their right arm to be half as talented as you.'

'Try telling my dad that.'

'Hey, I bet he's dead proud of you.'

'He would be if I was good at maths or science, but this. . .' Will waved his arm around the drama studio and shook his head.

'Well, your mum's proud of you. I know that for a fact.'

Will shrugged. It must be awkward, your mum being friends with one of your teachers. There'd been so many times when I'd thought he was holding back, not saying what he wanted to because he suspected it would get back to his mum. I also sensed that having Anna's entirely unconditional love wasn't enough. And if it was paternal approval he was looking for, that was going to be a harder nut to crack. I suspected he was right. David would have been happier had he his sights set on a career in banking or the legal profession. I remembered when I'd first met him at a parents' evening, I'd got the distinct impression that the drama teacher was the person David wanted to fit in while all the other more important teachers were busy.

'What about you?' I asked. 'What do you want?'

He shrugged. 'I dunno.'

'Don't try to fit in with the crowd, Will. Step up to the bar. And not that sort of bar.'

Will rolled his eyes.

'Am I sounding too much like a teacher?'

He managed a half smile. 'Did I really whup Paul Newman's arse?'

'Yes. And don't you dare suggest that I could play Big Mama in the next scene, OK?'

Will grinned and did an over-exaggerated impression of the sixteen-year-old boy swagger as he headed out of the studio.

'Thank you, Mr Bain,' I said, a smile spreading across my face. I busied myself tidying up in the studio. Hoping I hadn't overstepped the mark. And wishing David could see the same Will that I did.

*   *   *

We arrived at the clinic as an obviously pregnant woman was heading out. Paul held the door open for her. She smiled and said thank you. I tried hard to smile back. It wasn't her fault, of course. They should have separate entrances. Front one for those trying to conceive, back door for those who have been successful, and never the twain shall meet.

'Are you OK?' asked Paul, taking my hand as we walked down the corridor. I nodded. It was the kind of question men probably felt they had to ask. And one that women probably didn't answer truthfully.

We sat down in the waiting room. The woman across from us got up to go to the water-cooler. The glugging noise which came as the water was dispensed sounded like a rather crude impersonation of my stomach. I remembered the last time we'd been here. I couldn't help think the whole process was unnecessarily cruel: like forcing failed A-level students to have their results read to them in person by the examiner and then having to rub shoulders with those who had passed on the way out.

'Mr and Mrs Crabtree?' Paul and I rose in unison as the young woman smiled at us. 'Mr Kemp is ready for you now.'

We followed the woman's clickety heels along the corridor until she stopped outside a door and opened it for us. The man sitting at the desk looked up at us as we stepped inside. He was the smiling assassin. I knew it instantly. If you had good news to impart there would be no need to look over-the-top jolly about it. He was about to pull a hidden gun and kill us at point-blank range. And the stupid thing about it was that we were supposed to smile back at him while he did it.

'Thanks for coming back to see us,' he started. It was as if we had been transported to the land of stupid things to say. We were hardly going to go through all these tests just for kicks and then not come back for the results. 'I'll go through each test result in turn and then we'll have a chat about the implications.'

He was going to keep us talking until he pulled the trigger. Bastard.

'The semen sample you gave, Mr Crabtree, was entirely within the normal range of someone of your age.' He handed a piece of paper to Paul who nodded and smiled the best one could when you have been saved from the firing squad but your wife has taken your place.

'Mrs Crabtree, the AMH hormone sample again came back well within the normal range for someone of your age group.'

'What does that mean?' I asked, tired of the politeness of it all.

'It means you've got less eggs than you had ten years ago, but pretty much the same as any other forty-year-old would.'

I nodded. 'And what about the ultrasound?'

'That came back entirely clear as well. No sign of fibroids or polycystic ovaries and clear evidence that you had ovulated.'

'So you're saying that there's no medical reason why we haven't conceived?'

'None that we've found so far. And obviously the fact that you already have a child is also in your favour. The only other medical factor which we need to rule out is a blockage in your Fallopian tubes.'

'So why didn't you perform that test before?' asked Paul, who clearly hadn't looked at all the websites I had, or read the 'So you want to have a baby?' books.

'We always complete the other tests first as the tubal patency check involves an injection of radioactive dye and X-rays.'

'Is it painful?' asked Paul.

I looked at him and smiled. 'What do you think?' I asked.

'Sorry,' he said, grinning at me and Mr Kemp in turn. 'I guess I meant to ask how painful. Would she need an anaesthetic?'

'No, just painkillers and antibiotics. It's a day case procedure and I'm told patients suffer only mild discomfort.'

I looked at him with a raised eyebrow and resisted the temptation to ask what his definition of mild discomfort was based on. 'How soon could I have it?' I asked.

'We should be able to fit you in within the next couple of weeks.'

'That's fine. We'd like to go ahead.' Paul looked at me. A 'hey, hang on a minute' look. Mr Kemp clearly saw it too.

'There's no need to commit yourselves now,' he said. 'Have a chat about it and give my secretary a ring in the morning if you do want to go ahead. I've got some information for you about the procedure.' He handed me several sheets of paper, which I folded and put into my handbag.

'Thank you,' I said, standing up to go. I'd won a stay of execution. I was well aware that was all it was. Certainly not a cause for celebration.

Paul took my hand again as we walked back down the corridor. Fortunately I didn't see any pregnant women on the way out.

Alice was still up when I got back home after checking on Mum later. She was sitting at the kitchen table in her pyjamas, her blonde hair brushed and loose ready for bed, her felt-tips spread out across the table. Paul was unloading the dishwasher.

'Mummy,' said Alice, jumping up and rushing to give me a hug, 'would you like to see what I've drawn for you?'

'I'd love to,' I said, stroking her hair. Alice held up her picture proudly for me to see. There was a large purple lollipop on a stick with a pink spiral swirl running through it.

'It's your lego,' she said. 'The one for your party.'

'Our logo.' I smiled. 'Alice, it's fantastic, I love it. Thank you. Did you do this all by yourself?'

'The lollipop was my idea, but my first one was really tiny so Daddy said to do it bigger so it showed up better. Is it going to be on posters?'

'Yes, it is. Even if we can only afford one poster we'll make sure it's in Hebden Bridge where you can see it.'

Alice grinned and tidied away her felt-tips without being asked.

'I suppose there's no going back now' said Paul. It was a rhetorical question, I was aware of that. But I couldn't help feeling that he was still waiting for me to announce that the whole thing had been a huge wind-up.

'No,' I said. 'And I'm in it to win it.' Paul smiled at me. Although I suspected that was because he still hadn't really grasped quite how serious I was about this.

'Will you be as important as the Queen if you win?' Alice asked.

'No. I'm afraid not.'

'What about like a carnival queen?'

'Yeah,' I said laughing. 'That's probably a bit more like it.'

'Right,' said Paul, bending down to Alice and scooping her up in his arms. 'It's up to bed for you now, Missy.'

'Can we finish *Charlotte's Web* tonight?' she asked. 'We've only got two chapters to go?'

'We can if you go straightaway,' said Paul, putting her back down again. 'I'll read you a chapter, then Mummy will be up to read the last one.'

'Yay,' said Alice, heading straight upstairs. Paul put his hands on my hips as he squeezed past.

'Was your mum OK?' he asked.

'Yeah. She was in the house, at least, and she'd been fed and watered.' It was ridiculous really. How you ended up talking about your own mother as if she were the family pet.

Alice called down for him.

'I'd better see what she's up to,' he said. 'We'll talk later, OK?'

I nodded. We had gone to the hospital in separate cars so I could go straight to Mum's house and Paul could pick Alice up from Sam's. We needed to talk. Though I really didn't know what there was to say. I was going to have the tube test done whether Paul wanted me to or not – and I suspected it was not. I couldn't stop now. I needed answers. And there were still too many questions in my head.

I snuggled with Alice under the duvet when I'd finished reading the last chapter of *Charlotte's Web*. I loved the smell of her, her warm body next to mine, her little legs scrabbling around, trying to get curled in as tight to me as she could.

'Wouldn't it have been good if you'd made an egg-sac like Charlotte, when you had me?' said Alice. 'Then I would have loads of brothers and sisters to play with.'

I stroked her hair, relieved that I'd turned the bedside lamp off so she couldn't see my face. 'Yes, sweetheart,' I whispered, kissing the top of her head. 'It certainly would.'

9

ANNA

'So what's the question today?' asked Will buttering his third piece of toast as I closed the lid of my laptop. I asked a question every Wednesday on the blog. Big ones usually, the sort of thing they asked in those Sunday newspaper supplement questionnaires: What's your biggest regret? What keeps you awake at night? What would your epitaph be? It had taken off in a pretty big way, fuelled by Twitter and Facebook, of course. Today's question was a bit different to the usual ones though. I was rather apprehensive about how people were going to respond out there in the blogosphere. But not half as apprehensive as I was about how my family were going to respond when I told them what it was and why I was asking it.

'What would you do if you were Prime Minister for a day?' I said, pouring myself another cup of tea.

'Easy,' said Will. 'Ban school uniform and homework.'

'I'd cover the world in glitter,' chipped in Esme. 'And make a lot of noise because no one could tell me off.' Charlotte smiled, but made no attempt to add anything. I had a feeling I knew what hers might be though.

David looked at me over his copy of the *Independent* and raised an eyebrow. 'That's hardly the usual sort of question, is it? What happened to the on-the-psychiatrist's-couch stuff?'

'We're shelving it for a bit. We're getting a campaign going, actually.'

'What sort of campaign?' asked David.

I suspected my attempts to soften the ground for what I was about to say had been far too subtle for any member of my family to notice. I prepared for the inevitable fall-out from the imminent nuclear explosion.

'We're forming a new political party. Me, Sam and Jackie. I'm going to stand in the general election.'

David laughed. He actually had a very attractive laugh. I remembered thinking that when I first met him. But on this occasion the shards of laughter cut me as they fell.

'Very droll,' he said. There was a silence. Everyone looked at me. Will realised first why I wasn't laughing.

'Mum wasn't joking,' he said. David put the newspaper down and waited for me to deny it.

'He's right,' I said. 'I wasn't.'

David stared at me. A cloud of bafflement and bemusement masked his features. I was waiting for him to ask me if I was going through some kind of mid-life crisis, as if this were the thinking woman's equivalent of doing a Shirley Valentine.

Esme finally broke the silence. 'Are we going to have another protest where I can shout as loud as I like?'

'Not exactly, sweetheart,' I said. 'Mummy's going to be knocking on doors asking people to vote for me.'

'Please tell me this isn't true,' said David.

'Why?' I replied.

'Because if it is, you're clearly out of your mind.'

I fished my herbal tea bag out of my mug while I waited for my anger to subside and the hurt to sting a little less.

'What's so ridiculous about me standing?' I asked. 'You stood in the local elections.'

'Yes, but that was entirely different.'

'Why?'

'Because I was a longstanding member of the Liberal Democrats and I'd been to every party conference for thirteen years. You can't just set up a party one day and stand as an MP the next. It doesn't work like that.'

'Who says it doesn't? Anyway, we don't believe in having to serve your time and work your way up. It doesn't tend to favour women who have families to care for.'

David put his mug down heavily on the table. Will, Charlotte and Esme were still staring at me. I realised we were having a domestic in front of them. I wished I'd done this differently. Told David one night when the children were in bed. If I was honest, really honest, I knew I should have discussed it with him first, like Sam and Jackie had with their partners. Although he was giving a very impressive demonstration of the reason I hadn't done that.

'So what do you believe in? Your party.'

I decided to ignore the patronising tone in his voice. 'Putting families first. Speaking up for those who haven't got a voice. Making this country a fairer, more caring place to live.'

'We all believe in that. How are you going to achieve it?'

'We don't know yet. That's why we're asking people for their ideas.'

David rolled his eyes and looked up at the ceiling.

'Well, I think it rocks,' said Will. 'It's the most exciting thing anyone in this family's ever done.'

'Thank you, Will,' said David, getting up from his chair and taking his cereal bowl and mug over to the sink.

'At least they're asking people for their views and taking notice of what they say. It's more than this poxy government have done.'

I glanced at Will's face. He genuinely seemed to enjoy baiting his father like this, knowing how difficult he found it to be one of Cameron's bedfellows.

'It's all very well asking people for their crazy ideas,' said David, still with his back to us, 'but some of us have to live in the real world.'

My skin prickled. Although the comment had been directed at Will it was clear there was another intended recipient. I wanted to fire a salvo back, but I knew that doing so would demonstrate that he had got under my defences and I didn't want to give him that satisfaction. I also knew that I had an able and willing first lieutenant in Will, who wouldn't have any such reservations.

'What, you mean like make promises in your manifesto and then ditch them all as soon as you get a sniff of power?' said Will.

I took a sip of my tea, mainly so David couldn't see the smile on my face as he turned around.

He looked at me long and hard. 'I'm off to work,' he said, 'in the vain hope that when I step outside the door I'll discover that this whole thing has been a bad dream, rather like one of Edmund Blackadder's, and the world will revert to normal. Not fantastically interesting, I'll admit. But normal.'

'Wow,' said Will as the front door slammed shut. 'That was better than watching Jeremy Kyle.'

'He'll come round,' I said. 'I think it was simply a bit of a shock.'

'Why are you doing it then?' asked Charlotte. I smiled at her, recognising that the peace-keeper in the family was clearly ruffled by this.

'Because I believe in it, love,' I said. 'I don't like the priorities this country has and I really do want to do something to make things better, particularly for children and young people.'

'Can we help?' asked Esme.

'That would be fantastic. I've got a job for you all actually. To come up with a slogan for our party.'

'What's it called?' asked Will.

'The Lollipop Party.'

Will stuck two fingers in his mouth, pretending to gag.

'It was Zach's idea,' I explained. 'And actually it's better than anything we managed to come up with. We want it to be family-friendly, you see, without it sounding boring.'

'I think it sounds great,' said Esme. 'Will there be games and party bags as well as lollipops?'

'It's really not that sort of party,' I smiled. 'It's a party where we come up with ideas about how we're going to make things better.'

'You're not even going to have ice cream?' she asked.

'If one of us wins the election, we'll have ice cream,' I said.

'Chocolate?' asked Esme.

'Double choc chip.'

Esme's face brightened visibly.

'Is there a prize for coming up with the best slogan?' asked Will, finishing off his last piece of toast.

'Why did I guess you'd be looking for monetary reward?'

'You pay peanuts, you get monkeys,' Will grinned.

'We're offering an internship working for our party in the summer, actually.'

'Sorry, I've got plans.'

'That's the first I've heard of them,' I said, starting to clear the breakfast table.

'That's because they're top secret at the moment. Anyway, I was thinking more along the lines of an iTunes voucher.'

'Oh, you were, were you?'

'Twenty pounds would be nice.'

'Wouldn't it? I'll run to ten.'

'Fifteen, and that's a bargain.'

'I tell you what,' I said. 'Fifteen, as long as whoever wins shares it equally with the other two.'

'But you don't get anything extra for winning then,' said Will.

'Oh you do,' I said. 'You get the glory.' Will smiled. 'Everyone agreed then?' I asked. Charlotte and Esme nodded.

'I guess so,' said Will.

'I want some good slogans, mind, in return for my investment. And I want you two to help Esme, OK?'

They all nodded.

'Right,' I said, glancing up at the clock. 'Time for school.'

'Is Daddy going to be allowed to enter?' asked Esme, following me out into the hall.

'He's allowed, love. But I don't think he will.'

'Why not?'

Will and Charlotte looked at me. I hesitated before replying. 'He's just not interested in iTunes,' I said.

On Wednesdays I got to wear my other hat. The nutritionist's one. People were always amazed when I told them I had three jobs and three children. Words like 'superwoman' were banded around. Personally, I didn't see it as anything out of the ordinary. I knew plenty of Mummybloggers who juggled far more than that and had far more stressful lives. Besides, I only had to look at Sam and Jackie to realise how easy I had it.

I worked for a GP practice in Halifax. It had been my decision. I was well aware that Hebden Bridge was a bubble; you couldn't live and work there and claim that you had your finger on the pulse of the nation. And the reason I wanted to keep practising as a nutritionist was that I wanted to help people who really needed it.

And as I watched the procession of people entering my room that morning there was certainly no doubt that they needed help. A cruel commentator might have said that it looked like an audition for a fat-camp reality TV show. In truth, a trawl of any high street in towns up and down the land could have produced similar results.

A man called Keith sat before me, the overspill on the chair suggesting that we really ought to invest in a bigger one in order to meet our clients' needs. He was the sort of guy you wouldn't want to sit next to on a bus. To be honest, you wouldn't have been able to sit next to him, even if you had wanted to.

He, like all my clients, had been asked to produce a list of everything he had eaten over the past three days. I read through it: the usual catalogue of processed ready meals, fast-food takeaways and sugary snacks.

'Do you ever eat fruit or vegetables, Keith?' I enquired.

'Oh yeah, quite a lot.'

'What sort of things?'

'I sometimes have a Hawaiian pizza, with the pineapple on, like, as one of my five a day. And I always ask for extra tomato ketchup in my burgers.'

I nodded, trying hard to keep my expression neutral. 'Do you cook at all for yourself, Keith?'

'Oh yeah. I'm a real whiz with a microwave.'

I resisted the temptation to bang my head on the table. It wasn't Keith's fault he lived in a society that seemed intent on covering the high streets of the lands with fast-food restaurants and where the only things you learned to cook in school were pizzas and Victoria sponge sandwich cakes. You couldn't survive on that. Well, you could; you just ended up like Keith.

I went through my usual spiel, trying to find some healthy foods which he might like and handing him some supermarket shopping lists and very basic recipes that he might like to try.

'I'll maybe give one or two of them a go,' he said. 'I suppose it's like drugs, you have to wean your body off the bad stuff gradually so you don't get withdrawal symptoms from lack of sugar and fat, like.'

'Er, no Keith. It's not like that at all. You'll be absolutely fine. You may enjoy fast food but it's not clinically adictive. Your body does not need sugar or processed food to survive.'

Keith frowned at me and scratched his balding head. He'd be having a good laugh about that in the pub later. The rubbish that this fancy-food woman had come out with. And probably folding the recipe sheet up to put under the wobbly table his pint was on.

Sometimes, if the weather was horrendous, I'd drive straight to school to pick Esme up. But it was an unusually mild day for March, the sun was out, I had time to kill and, most of all, I needed a walk to clear my head. Which was why I parked outside the house then took a steady walk down the hill.

The air smelt of spring, there were pockets of green all around, pushing back the last vestiges of a long, cold winter. But inside me the coldness lingered on, throwing a damp, icy blanket over the hope and excitement which had tried so hard to push through.

I hadn't expected David to embrace my newly politicised self, but neither had I expected him to be quite so brutal in his dismissal of it. Another layer of scar tissue had formed inside since this morning. The trouble with scar tissue was that it was much harder to get rid of than it was to form.

I ached for a softness within. A warmth. Dare I say a glow? But all I had were embers of something which had once burned there but had gone out a long time ago.

Maybe I expected too much of everyone: of David, the government, of people like Keith. Or maybe I was simply tired of expecting too little.

Despite the walk, I was still the first parent to arrive. I stood at the edge of the playground and got my phone out of my handbag. I'd been so busy at work I hadn't had a chance to go online since I posted the question. I went to my blog first and scrolled down to the bottom. I started to read the answers, some of them funny, some serious. But none of them questioning my sanity for asking the question in the first place. I scrolled down further. The comments kept on coming: making public toilets free, toy manufacturers who produced pink and blue versions of the same product publicly named and shamed, hospital car parking to be free, models under a size eight banned, the list went on. And on and on. I flicked on to Twitter. I'd used the hashtag #mummyfesto. When I searched on it, a whole list of tweets and retweets came up. Some of them were from my regular mummyblogger friends and followers, but many were from people I'd never heard of before. People all over the place. All over the world even. My hands were shaking as I scrolled down. I came to the end of the page, but there were older entries and new entries were coming in all the time.

'How's tricks?'

I looked up, startled. It was Jackie. I noticed that the playground behind her was rapidly filling up. I glanced down at the phone in my hand, struggling to form anything coherent to say.

'Look,' I said instead, thrusting the phone into her hand. 'Scroll down, scroll up, scroll any way you like.'

I watched Jackie's face as she started to read. Saw the smile spread across her face as she scrolled further down.

'When did you put the question on?' she asked.

'This morning.'

'Fucking hell.'

For once, Jackie's language could be excused. She looked up and threw her arms around me. I was surprised at how good it felt, being hugged by a crazy woman jumping up and down in platform shoes.

'Hey, what's this?' asked Sam, hurrying through the gate. 'Can anyone join in?' Before I could answer Jackie grabbed hold of Sam and pulled her in between us.

'It's a Teletubbies-style big hug,' said Jackie. 'Anna here, who is really – which one had the aerial on its head?'

'Tinky Winky,' said Sam.

'Anna here, who is really Tinky Winky, has got ideas for the mummyfesto coming in from all over the bloody world.'

Sam looked at me. I nodded.

'My blog and Twitter have gone crazy with it. I haven't even had a chance to look at Facebook yet.'

Sam's features did the facial equivalent of turning up the radio and dancing around the living room. 'This thing's got legs,' she said. 'It's really going to run.'

'It's Usain bloody Bolt,' said Jackie.

'Better make it a distance runner,' said Sam. 'The election's a marathon not a sprint.'

'Paula Radcliffe,' said Jackie. 'She's the only one I know. Although didn't she end up blubbing at the side of the road?'

'Forget the running analogy,' said Sam. 'The fact is people are interested. People want to get involved. It's a fantastic platform to build on. Are you both still on for Friday?'

Jackie and I nodded.

'Good. Anna can you put all the suggestions together in a file? Even the silly ones, it doesn't matter. We'll go through them all, start to put the mummyfesto together. How are you getting on with your own ones?'

'Mine are a bit ranty,' said Jackie. 'But I've got lots of them.'

Sam looked at me.

'I haven't had much chance yet,' I replied, 'but they're all in my head.'

'Fantastic,' said Sam. 'How's David taken to the idea?'

My face must have indicated that this was an awkward question.

'You have told him, haven't you?' asked Sam.

'Yeah. This morning.'

'And?'

'He'll just need a bit of time to get his head around it,' I said.

'Right,' said Sam. 'Well tell him we'd be very grateful for any expertise he can offer. Being as he's the only person I know who's actually won an election.'

I nodded. Although I was in no doubt about the response I would get if I asked.

'I've got you a slogan,' said Will, when he arrived home shortly before teatime.

'Great,' I said, adding some more stock to the risotto. 'Hit me with it then.'

'Rip it up and start again,' said Will. 'It's a line from a song by Orange Juice.'

I smiled at him. 'I know, I did the eighties first time around, remember?'

'Oh yeah.'

'Anyway, I like it. Bit alternative.'

'So when are you going to decide?'

'I'll put all the suggestions to our meeting on Friday.'

'You haven't got any others. You may as well just give me the prize now.'

'Thank you, Will. I'm sure your sisters will come up with something.'

'I doubt it.'

'That's not very nice.'

'It's true, though. Esme may come up with something, but it will be sparkly and totally unsuitable. And I don't suppose Charlotte's going to bother.'

'Why do you say that?'

'She's got other stuff on her mind at the moment.'

'Like what?' I asked, putting the wooden spoon down and turning to face Will.

'Oh, it doesn't matter.'

'Yes, it does. Why did you say that?' Will shuffled his feet and looked down at his trainers. He had always been absolutely hopeless at keeping stuff to himself.

'It's all started up again at school.'

'The texts?'

Will shook his head. 'It's Facebook as well now.'

'What are they saying?'

'You wouldn't want to know, Mum.'

'I'm asking you, aren't I?'

'Stupid stuff. About her being a virgin. Saying she's frigid. Crap like that.'

'So being a virgin's a crime now is it? At thirteen.'

'You have to play the game, Mum. Cover it up, put on a bit of a show, act like you're something you're not.'

'Why do you have to do that?'

'To survive.'

I shook my head. 'These kids on Facebook, why doesn't she just block them?'

'It's not one or two any more. It's a whole load of kids. And they're posting all over. Not just on her wall.'

'Why hasn't she told me this?'

Will shrugged. 'I guess she's just trying to deal with it her way.'

'Which is what?'

'Sticking her head in the sand and hoping it will go away, from what I can make out.'

'Why didn't you tell me before?'

Will avoided my gaze. 'She asked me not to. Said she didn't want to worry you.'

I handed Will the wooden spoon. 'Keep an eye on that, please,' I said, pointing to the pan. 'Esme's watching CBBC. If she asks for a biscuit, say no, OK?'

Will nodded. I went straight upstairs to Charlottes's room. She'd been in there since she'd got home from school. I'd thought I was giving her space, privacy. It turned out I was doing nothing of the sort.

I knocked on the door. 'Charlotte, it's me. Have you got a minute?' There was a muffled sound from within. I went straight in. She was lying on her bed surrounded by an assortment of textbooks. I could tell by her puffy eyes that she'd been crying.

'I know what's been going on,' I said. Charlotte sighed and rolled her eyes. 'It's not Will's fault,' I said. 'I made him tell me.' I sat down on the corner of her bed. 'By the way, mums are supposed to worry. It's part of the job description. We only end up worrying that we don't know what's going on if we've got nothing to worry about.'

Charlotte sighed and looked up at the ceiling. 'I thought if I just ignored them it would stop,' she said.

'It hasn't though, has it?' She shook her head. 'We need to do something, Charlotte. We can't simply let it carry on like this.'

Her bottom lip started to tremble. I leant over and hugged her to me. Hating what they had done to her. Thinking how much easier it was when your children were toddlers, when you could simply pick them up out of harm's way.

'I don't understand why,' she said. 'What's so wrong with me that they do this?'

I took a soggy strand of her long dark hair and tucked it back behind her ear.

'There is nothing wrong with you, sweetheart. They're the ones who have got something wrong with them. Bullies are usually deeply insecure. It's easy to be one of the crowd, isn't it? But it's not so easy to be yourself.'

Charlotte sat staring at the bedroom wall. Her face devoid of any hope.

'I'd like to go and see the Head about this,' I said. Charlotte groaned. 'I don't have any choice, love. I can't let them do this to you. I love you far too much for that.'

The tears fell again. She wiped them away with her sleeve.

'At the risk of sounding like a counsellor,' I said, 'there are websites you can go on, they have mentors your sort of age who have been through this type of thing. And there are helplines you can ring. It might be good to talk it through with someone other than me. I'll do you a list of the websites and numbers, if you like.'

Charlotte shrugged. I took it as a yes.

'You have to promise me one thing, though,' I said. 'Please keep talking to me about this. I will worry far more if you don't talk to me, OK?' She nodded. 'Now, let's dry those eyes. Tea will be ready in about ten minutes.'

She nodded again. I kissed her on the forehead, wishing for a second that I was Glinda the Good Witch of the South and could leave a mark there that would somehow protect her from harm. I got up and walked towards the door.

'Mum,' she said, 'I think you'll make a really good MP.'

'Thank you,' I said. 'And please try to come up with a good slogan. We'll never hear the end of it if Will wins.'

10

SAM

The smell of the evening's curry hung heavily over the kitchen. Fresh coriander, ginger, a hint of coconut. The room smelt more like the local takeaway than the headquarters of a political party. Although having said that, I wasn't sure what the headquarters of a political party would smell like. A little musty, maybe? Or simply the pungent whiff of hypocrisy hanging in the air.

I lit the tea-light underneath the aromatherapy oil-burner. Rosemary for clarity, peppermint as a mental stimulant and frankincense for courage. I bet no one in the Number Ten policy unit did that. Not unless their latest focus group had been drawn from Hebden Bridge.

The sound of the Cough Assist machine upstairs stopped. Rob would be suctioning Oscar now before lifting him into bed. Stroking his forehead, watching his eyelids droop ever lower as he read to him. Something by Oliver Jeffers, if Rob had anything to do with it. Certainly not the Disney-story treasury which he always pushed to the back of the bookcase.

Zach would be gazing skywards through his telescope, having negotiated an extra half hour before bedtime in return for leaving me in peace downstairs.

I was tired. Oscar had woken several times the previous night and I'd had a day of fraught meetings at work regarding the state of the hospice's finances. But fortunately from beneath the blanket of tiredness came a whacking great kick of adrenalin. This was what I'd been waiting for. The moment when I stopped being a passenger on a ride I didn't want to go on and jumped into the driving seat of a runaway car which had, as yet, no track or route map but promised to be the most exhilarating ride of my life.

There was a rap on the door. As soon as I opened it to see Anna's face staring up at me, seemingly unsure whether to say good evening in a prime ministerial tone or squeal in excitement, I realised she felt it too.

'Welcome to the Lollipop Party HQ,' I said. 'The fun starts here.'

Anna smiled and was about to say something when there was a shout and we looked up to see Jackie racing over the bridge.

'Don't start without me,' she said. 'I want to say I was there at the beginning. It will sound good in my auto-biography.'

I shook my head, gave them both a hug and led them through to the kitchen.

'I've been somewhat more cultured this time,' Jackie said, handing me a brown paper bag, 'and brought Perrier, brie and crackers.'

Anna started laughing. 'Don't tell me,' said Jackie. 'You've gone downmarket and brought cheap plonk and Pringles.'

'Not quite,' said Anna, emptying her bag to reveal wine, brie and crackers.

'Never mind,' said Jackie. 'If this doesn't work out we can always set up a stall in one of those French markets.'

'Or if it does work out we could invite President Sarkozy over for the evening,' I said. Anna cringed. 'Sorry, I forgot.'

'Forgot what?' asked Jackie.

'Anna has a thing about Sarkozy.' Jackie raised her eyebrows.

'No, not that sort of thing,' said Anna. 'A "he makes my skin crawl and I can't work out what the hell Carla Bruni was thinking of", kind of thing.'

'Right,' said Jackie. 'Glad we've cleared that one up. Does rule you out of being Foreign Secretary though, I'm afraid.'

'You're only saying that because you want the job,' I said. 'Keen to be the new Jackie O, are we?'

'Piss off,' she replied.

'So you're not denying it?'

'What? That if Mr Obama walked in now and offered to carry me off to the White House I wouldn't put up any resistance? You show me a woman who would.'

'Fair point,' I admitted.

'Whereas if Sarkozy turned up, I'd be straight out of the back door,' said Anna.

'Which is a shame really,' said Jackie. 'Because you'd be much better suited in height than that Carla woman.'

Anna appeared suitably squashed. Jackie winced, obviously realising it was not exactly a compliment.

'Right,' I said, opening the wine and Perrier and pouring three large glasses. 'So we've established that should we get into government you've both ruled yourselves out of being Foreign Secretary.'

'Hang on a minute,' said Jackie. 'Don't think you've got it all sewn up. How do we know that you haven't got something to declare in the "strong or inappropriate feelings for a foreigner" department?'

I thought hard for a moment. 'No. nothing. Unless you count the massive crush I had on Rolf Harris when I was twelve.' Jackie had to run to the sink to splurt her wine out.

'Well that knocks our two right out of the water,' she said.

'What? He's not even a world leader. I'm hardly going to be accused of causing a diplomatic crisis, am I?'

'No but we can't have a Foreign Secretary with a fondness for the wobble board and the man who sang "Two Little Boys". We've got our credibility to think about.'

'It was his art,' I said. 'It was an infatuation born out of respect for his artistic ability.'

'I'm sorry,' said Jackie. 'We simply can't risk any accusations of poor judgement. It appears we've all been disqual-ified. It's not a very good start, is it?'

'Perhaps,' said Anna, 'we should just get on with the business of drawing up the manifesto for fighting our seats and leave the squabbling about who gets what job until the unlikely event that we get to Downing Street.'

'You're right,' I said.

'I think you're going to be the sensible one who can always be relied upon to put the others in their place at the Cabinet table,' said Jackie.

'Or, in this case, the kitchen table.' Anna smiled.

We sat down, Jackie got out a notebook and pile of papers. Anna and I opened up our laptops.

'OK,' said Jackie. 'So I'm a Luddite. That doesn't preclude me from public office does it?'

'No,' I said, reaching for the cheeseboard, 'and on the positive side it means you're the only one who hasn't got to worry about getting greasy fingerprints on your laptop.'

'What's that doing here?' asked Anna, pointing to my micro tape recorder on the table. 'This is not going to be used against us in some future court case, is it?'

'I think she's actually an undercover reporter for one of the Sunday papers,' said Jackie. 'This whole thing has probably been set up to see if they could find anyone gullible enough to go along with her crazy ideas.'

'It's just for the minutes,' I said. 'It saves me scribbling down everything you say.'

'You mean your shorthand's gone to pot since your jour-nalism days,' said Jackie.

'Yeah, that as well. Anyway,' I said, pressing the record button, 'let's get down to business.'

'I found something on the internet about writing a manifesto,' said Anna. 'It's very tongue-in-cheek, but I thought it might amuse you. It says to start with the word "today", write a short sentence, then a shorter one, throw in a couple of one-word sentences, add a really long sentence about our overarching themes, then end by summing up in a word that makes no sense at all. Like kumquat.'

'Job done then,' said Jackie. 'Though I'd go for pomegranate myself.'

'I think,' I said, 'that the whole point of this party should be about throwing out all the usual crap in manifestos. People don't believe them and I refuse to sound smug and condescending just because everyone else does. I think we should start with an admission that we don't have all the answers but we do have lots of ideas and we can call on a whole load of people who have an amazing amount of knowledge between them.'

'Can we?' asked Jackie.

'Yes. Well, we've got you two for a start. I imagine a teacher and a trained nutritionist and counsellor can muster up a fair amount of expertise. And then just think of all those women who have posted on Anna's blog and tweeted their ideas. I bet we've got doctors, nurses, midwives, police officers, lawyers and goodness knows what else.'

'I've actually got a mortician and a nuclear physicist following me,' said Anna.

'There you go,' said Jackie. 'If someone's about to press the red button we'll be extremely well placed to handle it.'

I laughed and passed her the cheeseboard. 'It's true, though,' I continued. 'If you put everybody's skills together that would be one hell of a CV.'

'We could still do with a bit more gravitas,' said Anna. 'I can imagine some men being very sceptical about letting a bunch of women run the country.'

'If we can get six children to school on time, OK, maybe not always on time in your case, Sam,' smiled Jackie, 'and then get ourselves to work in the face of cat sick, dog poo, teenage hormones, elderly relatives, lost socks and book bags and the lure of CBBC, then personally I think running the country would be a doddle.'

'Jackie's right,' I said. 'But I think we should also work very closely with all sorts of organisations: charities, think-tanks, unions, academia. If anyone's got some research to put forward or proposals to make things better, we should listen to them. And if they've got great ideas that promise to improve people's lives we should implement them. How often do you see these reports and research come out highlighting an appalling loophole in the law or some national scandal and everyone agrees that it's shocking and then completely forgets about it?'

'Yeah,' said Jackie. 'One of our NUT members died a few months ago from mesothelioma, a cancer caused by asbestos, which she was exposed to in a school she used to teach in. I looked it up on the internet and 140 teachers have died from it in the past ten years in Britain. We have the highest number of cases of it in the world; twice as many people die from asbestos-related deaths in Britain than are killed on the roads. An all-party parliamentary group published a report on it saying it was a national scandal and still nothing has been done about it.'

'That's outrageous,' said Anna. 'And if it's killing the teachers just think what it's doing to the children. It's a time-bomb.'

'We should put it in our mummyfesto,' Jackie said. 'We'll bloody do something about it if no one else will.'

'It's in,' I said.

'Shouldn't we vote on it, or something?' asked Anna.

'No need. Too many things that need doing and not enough time. If we think something's wrong we try to put it right, simple as that. We are guided always by our core beliefs.'

Anna nodded though she still didn't seem sure. It wasn't surprising really. She was married to a man who was steeped in the kind of political minutiae that stifled the prospect of any chance of radical reform. If it wasn't debated for an eternity at committee level, clauses and sub-clauses added to the point where whatever it was had been watered down to such an extent you could no longer taste it and then passed to the full council for approval, it wasn't really considered politics.

What we were proposing here was to tear up the rule book and not even bother to write a new one. We were going to work on gut feeling as to whether something was right or wrong. The same gut feeling that parents the world over relied on when they were trying to decide what was best for their child. Sure, occasionally they might get it wrong, but as long as they had been motivated by love, by an honest intention to do the best by their child, then nobody could ask for more than that.

'OK, so what are our core beliefs exactly?' asked Anna, spreading some Brie on a cracker and nibbling it in such a delicate fashion that I wanted to replay it in slow motion so I could marvel at it all over again.

'Children,' I said. 'I'm proposing we adopt article 3 of the UN Convention on the Right of the Child which says, "Everything we do must have the child's best interest at heart." I also want to put in the thing I said before, about our society treating children, young people, the elderly and those with disabilities appallingly. And about us putting that right as one of our priorities.'

'OK,' said Anna, seemingly warming to the idea a little. 'I'm happy to go along with that.' Jackie nodded.

'Thank you,' I said. 'Your turn, Jackie.'

'OK,' she said. 'At the risk of sounding like some leftie revolutionary, I'd like to pledge that we create a fairer society where wealth and power are more evenly distributed. A Robin Hood tax, the living wage, that sort of thing.'

'That won't go down well with big business,' said Anna.

'Maybe not, but we're a party for people, not big business. People hate bankers,' Jackie said with a shrug. 'It's the one thing which unites the electorate. There is one other thing,' she said. 'I'm aware that this whole mani-festo—'

'Mummyfesto,' I corrected.

'OK, this whole mummyfesto is in danger of sounding a bit worthy and dull. I think we need to lighten it up a bit. Show that we can laugh at ourselves too.'

'And how do you propose we do that?' I asked.

'Skipping,' she said.

'I'm sorry?'

'I think we should call for skipping to be actively encour-aged.'

'Skipping as in with a rope?'

'No,' said Jackie. 'Skipping along the road in gaiety, if we can still use that word.'

'You mean for children?' asked Anna.

'Oh no. Children do it anyway. Alice skips all over the place. I bet Esme does too.' Anna nodded. 'Well, I want adults to do it too. I hate the thought of Alice growing up and losing that wonderful expression of joy she has on her face when she skips. And I think it would wipe off the miserable look on people's faces when they arrive at work on a Monday morning.' Jackie looked at me, waiting for a response.

'I think it's up there with David Icke being the son of God,' I said.

'That's because you've forgotten the joy of skipping.'

'I haven't.'

'Prove it,' said Jackie.

'How?'

'Come with me now. We'll skip down to Market Street, round the block and back again. All of us.'

'You're crazy,' I said.

'Certifiable,' added Anna.

'And you're both too chicken to do it,' replied Jackie.

I looked at Anna, she looked at me. Neither of us found it easy to resist a challenge. We both shrugged and stood up at the same time.

'Come on,' said Jackie. 'Shoes on. You won't need your coats. Skipping is great for getting the circulation going.'

Anna and I followed Jackie to the front door. I pulled my Doc Martens on and started to do up the laces. Anna slipped on her court shoes.

'Right,' said Jackie. 'I'll be the leader, please try to keep up. It's best done at a brisk pace. It's all about getting a rhythm going. No walking or running allowed. Ready?'

'For public humiliation?' I said. 'Oh yes, count me in, anytime.'

'Come on then, stop your whingeing. Let's go.'

Jackie set off at a brisk pace, down Fountain Street, over the bridge and across the cobbles, her earrings swinging wildly, her bangles jangling, her shoes clattering across the cobbles. She made me think of a morris dancer on acid – not that I'd ever seen one – but in my imagination, at least. I followed behind, unsure whether to laugh hysterically or hang my head in shame. After a few moments a strange feeling started filtering through from my toes; a pleasant feeling, something akin to eating warm buttered toast and dancing barefoot on freshly cut grass rolled into one. It was joy. Sheer unadulterated joy. I glanced over my shoulder. The look on her face indicated that Anna was feeling it too.

'Wooh,' Jackie shouted as we made it to Market Street. My rush of exhilaration was immediately tempered by the realisation that people were looking at us. I briefly contemplated pretending to be drunk to justify my behaviour, but thought better of it. This wasn't alcohol-fuelled merriment. It was something much purer than that.

We carried on down the street. 'Hey,' I called out to Jackie as we passed the shoeshop, 'is that the first time you've ever gone past Ruby Shoesday without stopping to have a look in the window?'

Jackie snorted a laugh back to me and gave a little kick of her platform shoes. A middle-aged couple on the other side of the road stopped and stared, the woman pointing at us. They were obviously not locals. I caught sight of our reflection in the Turkish restaurant window as we skipped past. We looked like something out of *Little House on the Prairie*. Girlishly innocent and naïve. Several of the diners stopped with their forks in mid-air to look at us. I waved. Laughing as I did so.

By the time we made it back over the bridge to Fountain Street we were all breathing heavily. Actually, that was a lie. It was more like panting. We collapsed on the front gate. I was the first one to get my breath back.

'Skipping,' I said, 'is in the mummyfesto.'

'It's bloody brilliant, isn't it?' replied Jackie.

'It took about twenty years off me,' said Anna.

'And if I did it every day, it would take about twenty pounds off me,' said Jackie. 'Which is brilliant as it means it can be in on both physical and mental health grounds. They should bloody prescribe it on the NHS. Would be a damn sight better than antidepressants.'

'If we do ever get to Number Ten,' I said, 'the Downing Street one, not this one, you've both got to promise me you'll skip up the road to the door.'

'Promise,' smiled Anna.

'You're on,' agreed Jackie.

It was only at this point that we looked up and noticed Rob standing in the doorway staring at us.

'That was really weird,' he said. 'I thought I heard the front door shut so I looked out of the window and saw these three fully-grown women skipping down the street like lunatics. And five minutes later they skipped back again.'

'It's the latest fitness craze,' said Jackie, grinning.

'Came over from America, did it?' he asked.

'No, born and bred in Hebden Bridge,' I replied.

'And this skipping thing,' Rob said. 'I take it it's entirely unrelated to your political ambitions.'

'Oh no,' said Jackie. 'It's one of our core beliefs.'

'It's a sort of pillar of wisdom, actually,' Anna added.

'You haven't even had much to drink, have you?' he asked.

'Nope,' I said.

'Jeez. If there was a pill of whatever you guys are on, you'd make a fucking fortune.'

'Remember that when I'm asking you to shove election leaflets through letterboxes.' I smiled.

Rob scratched his head. 'I'm going to pour myself a glass of wine and go back upstairs,' he said. 'If I'm ever asked publicly about this incident I'll pretend for your sakes that it never happened.'

'I bet you he tries it himself when there's no one around,' Jackie whispered.

'No,' I replied, 'I think he'll remain firmly in the skipping sceptic camp.'

We settled ourselves down again at the table and Jackie cut herself a particularly large wedge of Brie.

'Well, I deserve it after that,' she said, when she caught us both looking at her.

'So, Anna,' I said, 'have you got anything for us that can top that?'

'Nothing as much fun,' she said. 'But I do have something pretty controversial.'

'Controversial is always good,' said Jackie.

'Go on,' I said.

Anna took another sip of wine. 'It's about London,' she said.

'Horrible, big, dirty place down south, isn't it?' asked Jackie.

'I don't think the government should be based there.'

'Right,' I said.

'I think we should propose a dozen video-linked mini-parliaments in cities across the UK. It would mean that no one would have to uproot their family or live away from them to become an MP, which would open politics up to loads of parents, especially mums.

'It would also put an end to the ridiculous yah-boo politics we have now. All the parliaments would have people sitting in circular chambers so they would be more likely to discuss things in a civilised fashion instead of shouting at the people opposite.'

'We could use the Corn Exchange building in Leeds,' said Jackie, leaning forward in her chair 'and the Rotunda in Birmingham. They're both brilliantly positioned for shopping too.'

Anna and I both gave her a look.

'Well everyone needs a lunch-hour, don't they?'

'Anyway,' said Anna, 'the whole thing would make the government less London-centric and mean MPs were truly in touch with people across the UK because they would actually be living in their constituencies. I mean, if Salford's good enough for the BBC, why not the government?' Anna paused and looked at us. 'That actually sounded crazier than the skipping, didn't it?'

'Only marginally so,' I said. 'It's certainly radical, but we want to be radical and why bother tinkering around with things when actually what we need to do is rip up the whole system and start again.'

'That's Will's slogan suggestion,' said Anna. 'Rip it up and start again.'

'Really? Well I like it.'

'Me too,' said Jackie.

'In the interests of fairness,' said Anna. 'I should tell

you that Esme's was "Making everything sparkly and boingy".'

I smiled. 'Sweet though it is, I don't think it would quite cut it with Jeremy Paxman. What about Charlotte's?'

'Putting people before politics.'

Anna looked at me. I looked at Jackie. We all nodded at the same time.

'Brilliant,' I said. 'Tell her she's a complete star and if she fancies getting some work experience with us we'd love to have her.'

'I will,' said Anna, looking down at her hands. I sensed all was not well on the Charlotte front, but didn't want to undo the mood-enhancing benefits of skipping so soon by delving further.

'Oh, we've got a logo as well,' said Jackie rummaging in her bag and holding up a brightly coloured purple-and-pink lollipop.

'Fantastic,' I said. 'I'll get it scanned and Rob said he'd do the lettering for us. We'll need to use it on our website and campaign leaflets and the mummyfesto and every-thing.'

Even as I said it I was hit by how daunting the whole thing sounded. There were three of us. And between us we had six children. How the hell were we going to do this? Come to that, how the hell were we going to be able to afford it?

'We need to get some funding, don't we?' said Anna, who had clearly been thinking along the same lines.

'We should launch a membership scheme,' said Jackie.

'Let's say £20.30 to join – that's a week's child benefit. What better investment could you make for your child's future?'

'Brilliant,' I said. 'You can be membership secretary.'

'And I'll write to lots of companies asking for sponsorship,' said Anna. 'Small, child-friendly companies, not big high-street names.'

'Fantastic,' I said. 'I think you've just got yourself the job of treasurer. Now, on with the mummyfesto. So, so far, we're selling off the Houses of Parliament in favour of a network of mini regional parliaments.'

'I didn't say anything about selling them off,' said Anna.

'It's either that or blowing them up,' said Jackie. 'And though I accept it would be headline-grabbing, I'm not sure I want to be tossed on to a bonfire with Guy Fawkes.'

'We'd need to fund the regional parliaments from the sale,' I said. 'And the money left over could go into affordable housing for all. And we'd make it a stipulation that whoever bought the Houses of Parliament kept them open as a tourist attraction to show future generations the anachronistic system we used to have in this country.'

'So I take it you think we should get rid of the House of Lords as well?' asked Anna.

'Oh God, yes.'

'What will we replace it with?' she asked.

'I know,' said Jackie. 'Mumsnet. A hell of a lot cheaper and more in touch with the people. They could scrutinise our legislation to make sure it was in the best interests of children.'

'To be honest,' said Anna, 'that's actually not any more ridiculous than the current system.'

'OK,' I said. 'So those are our core beliefs. Now, let's do our top five mummyfesto ideas each and then we'll listen to everything that's come in through Anna's blog and Twitter. Jackie, do you want to go first?'

'Sure. I'm proposing a big investment in treating dementia, including specialist training and care, and I'd like us to pledge more support for carers, including regular respite breaks and an annual free holiday – I was thinking Chequers could be turned into a spa retreat for carers, that way it will benefit those who save this country billions instead of a bunch of toffs who want to play croquet at the tax-payers' expense.'

'So where will foreign leaders stay when they visit the UK?' asked Anna.

'My place,' said Anna, with a wink. 'If they're American, that is. The French ones can stay at yours.'

Anna groaned. 'Right,' I said. 'Let's move on.'

'OK,' said Jackie. 'I think we could offer full employment to the under twenty-fives.'

'How?' asked Anna.

'Instead of paying those who aren't in work or training dole money we'd pay them the living wage to do really useful jobs in their communities, like being park wardens and litter-picking, running youth groups, helping to insulate old people's homes and installing and checking smoke alarms for them, driving elderly and disabled people to where they need to go, that sort of stuff.'

'It would give them a real sense of being part of their community too,' said Anna.

'I like it,' I said. 'What else?'

'All roads and road signs should be colour-coded,' said Jackie. 'So if you want to go from Leeds to Manchester you just follow the purple line along the road.'

'Now that's up there with skipping,' I said.

'But the whole road system has been designed by men. That's why women like me get lost all the time. It's not our fault. It's men's brains that are wired differently.'

'I have to say,' said Anna, 'that I fear we might be ridiculed for that one.'

'Only by Jeremy Clarkson, and if he says anything we'll suggest that *Top Gear* becomes pay per view with all proceeds to fund public-sector pensions.'

Anna and I smiled and shook our heads.

'And my final one,' said Jackie, 'is more public toilets and the right to a free wee. All public toilets and train-station toilets to be free.'

'It's a vote-winner,' I said. 'Right, what have you got for us, Anna?'

'A massive anti-bullying campaign with independently appointed children's champions at every school and specially trained play workers and child-behaviour special-ists on duty at break and lunchtimes.'

I nodded, knowing how important that one was to Anna.

'A national network of food kiosks and shops selling healthy food and smoothies to help counteract the choco-late, crisps and Coke culture out there.'

'They could be run by the former unemployed young people,' said Jackie.

'See,' I said. 'We've got joined-up thinking already.'

'I'd also like to get Jamie Oliver to do for hospital food what he did for school meals. Plus introduce free natural health centres across the UK, so people have the option of complementary therapies and counselling, which would take some of the pressure off GP surgeries and cut drug bills.

'Next, free parenting skills classes for all,' said Anna, 'with drop-in parenting centres in schools and super-markets and parenting mentors.'

'Aren't we going to get accused of being the nanny state?' asked Jackie. 'Or rather the super-nanny state.'

'It's the most important job in the world,' said Anna. 'It's ridiculous that people aren't trained for it. It wouldn't be about telling people they're doing it wrong, it would be about showing them different strategies parents can use for different situations and helping them to find solutions which may benefit their families.'

'Sounds fair enough,' I said.

'And finally,' said Anna, 'all parents to get up to ten days off work a year for sports days, nativities and parents' assemblies, with time to be made up during the year.'

'You can't get much more family-friendly than that,' I said.

'Come on then, Sam,' said Jackie, topping up her glass. 'Tell us what you've got.'

'OK. I'd like all hospices to be fully funded by the government. And no children's hospitals having to resort to tin-rattling.'

'Seconded,' said Jackie.

'I'd also like to make Terry Wogan redundant.'

'Sorry?' said Anna.

'That whole *Children in Need* thing is so embarrassing.'

'What, him with some young blonde presenter on his arm, you mean?' asked Jackie.

'Well, yes, that too,' I said. 'But what I mean is that people shouldn't have to beg for money for essential projects for needy children like that. And we shouldn't have to sit there bawling our eyes out watching them do it. What does that say about our society's priorities?'

'I quite agree,' said Anna, 'but how are we going to pay for it? They'll want figures, you know.'

'Well, we can start by scrapping the plans to replace Trident and privatising the Royal Family,' I said.

Jackie started laughing, then stopped when she saw my face. 'You're serious aren't you?'

'Yep. The money we save will be used to fund hospices and children's charities who run those sort of projects.'

'OK,' said Anna. 'Two things. I'm no royalist but a lot of people are and won't like it. And even if we did want to do it, how exactly would we go about the process of getting rid of them?'

'But that's just it,' I said. 'We're not getting rid of them. If people still want to camp out overnight and wave a Union Jack at whichever one of them gets married next, they can do. The only difference is that we won't be stumping up the cash for it because the Queen will no longer be the head of state.

'So she can stay in Buck House if she wants to and keep all her castles?' asked Jackie.

'Absolutely, as long as her family raise enough cash to keep them going.'

'Whose head will we have on stamps?' asked Anna.

'We won't have anyone's head. We'll have pictures painted by kids.'

'I think you might be sent to the Tower,' said Jackie.

'I'd like to see them try and get past Zach and Oscar to do that.'

Anna and Jackie grinned at me. I took that as a yes. I wasn't going to stop there, though. I was on a roll now.

'I'd also like us to become secular, like France, and not have any state-funded church schools. I resent the fact that although only about 7 per cent of the UK population are practising Christians, the Church controls about a third of our primary schools and even if you choose for your child to attend a non-church school they still have to do Christian worship in assembly and have vicars coming in to preach at them. Where's the choice in that?

'There are about the same number of vegetarians in this country, but we don't get to run a third of schools and go in to spout our beliefs to impressionable school-children, even though they've got proven health benefits. And yet our children come home from school believing God created the world and we're paying for that. It's obscene, it really is.'

I paused for breath and looked at Anna and Jackie who were staring at me as if I'd lost the plot.

'So you basically want to take on the Church, the state and the monarchy,' said Anna.

'Yep. That's about right,' I said. Anna nodded slowly. She didn't have to say anything: her expression said it for her.

'Look,' I said, 'I know it's ambitious and controversial and will probably lose us some votes, but if we're going to do this we need to believe in what we're fighting for and we need to fight for what we believe in.'

'There you go electioneering again,' said Jackie. 'I've told you, you've already got my vote.'

'And you'd back the secular bit?'

'Yeah, with one caveat. We still allow harvest festival assemblies because if we didn't have them, my cupboards would be full of out-of-date tins and free samples that I don't want but aren't going to chuck away.'

'OK,' I grinned, 'we can have a harvest assembly tins amnesty.'

'So what's your last suggestion?' asked Anna. 'And please tell me you're not going to sell Cliff Richard off or something.'

'Is he ours to sell?' asked Jackie.

'If we're going to get rid of the monarchy we'll need a new national anthem,' I said. 'I was thinking a medley of 'All You Need is Love', 'The Green Green Grass of Home', 'I Will Walk 500 Miles' and 'Teenage Kicks'. That way we represent all the countries in the UK and everyone will know the words.'

Jackie looked as if were in danger of falling off her chair laughing. Anna appeared to be in shock.

'The *Daily Mail* is going to hate us,' said Anna eventually.

'I know,' I replied. 'Won't it be fantastic?'

The gallery phoned on Monday morning, just after I'd dropped the boys off at school. The woman's name was Rebecca. She had what Rob called a posh London accent. It wouldn't bother him this time, though. Wouldn't bother him at all.

I drove straight to the road where he was working. It was dry today so he was painting the front door of a big house up on Birchcliffe. Pillar-box red he'd said they wanted it. Something to brighten the stonework up a bit.

I pulled up on the corner of the road and started walking down. Rob looked up and saw me, his brow furrowed for a second.

'Everything all right?' he asked. I recognised the tone in his voice and wished for a second that I'd phoned to tell him, anything to stop him panicking like that. I smiled, a big, obviously not fake, smile, so that he would know it was OK.

'Yes. I just wanted to let you know the good news.'

'Cameron's resigned and handed the keys of Number Ten to you?'

'No. Your good news.'

'Me? But I don't even do the lottery any more.'

'You're going to have an exhibition,' I said, grinning.

Rob put the paint pot down and stared at me. 'Where?'

'Linden Mill. Sorry it's not the Tate, but from little acorns and all that.'

'What have you been up to?'

'Just reminding some people of what a brilliant artist you are. Sending them a few photos. You'll have to get your act together, mind. You've only got a couple of weeks.'

A smile spread over Rob's face. He looked down at the paint on his hands and overalls. 'I'd give you a hug,' he said, 'only you might not appreciate it at the moment.'

'It's OK,' I said, giving him a kiss. 'Save it for later.'

'Thank you,' said Rob. 'For not giving up on me, I mean.'

'That's all right. Thank you for not having me sectioned.'

Rob grinned.

'Anyway, I'd better dash. I'll give you all the details later. They want you to pop by later this week with your stuff.'

Rob nodded. I started to walk back to the car. Just as I reached the corner, Rob called me. I turned around. He'd written 'I Love You' in red paint on the front door. I smiled, remembering how he'd painted it all over the walls of our first house when we'd moved in together.

'You too,' I called back.

11

JACKIE

I clearly wasn't cut out to be an undercover agent. My first thought as to how to disguise myself for my visit to the Labour Party pre-election meeting in Halifax had been to get one of those Tony Blair masks off eBay.

Sam had pointed out that I didn't actually need to go incognito because (a) I wasn't famous and (b) no one outside my immediate family and friends knew what we were about to do. But I still couldn't help feeling that it was somehow traitorous. I was obviously on a mailing list as a Labour Party voter; they'd been good enough to invite me to their pre-election shindig and yet I hadn't had the decency to inform them that I was about to announce my intention to stand against them in the constituency.

In the end I opted to wear a hat. I wasn't sure what it was about sporting a red beret that somehow rendered me invisible, but it was the best I could come up with.

I parked in King Street. It was still the only car park in Halifax I knew my way to despite having lived there for most of my life. Paul often joked that instead of having a girl in every port I had a car park space in every town and city. It just didn't make sense to me, having found a route I knew into somewhere, to go to the bother of getting lost again by trying a different way.

There was a sign in the foyer of the central library saying 'Labour Party meeting' and an arrow pointing down the stairs. It was as near as I was going to get to an underground political gathering. I stepped quietly down the stairs, half expecting a Labour Party henchman to jump out and bar my way at any point. As I got to the bottom of the stairs I realised that any attempt to disguise myself short of hiring a Mrs Doubtfire fancy-dress outfit would have been futile. There appeared to be no one in the queue in front of me under sixty. Perhaps that was what you got if you held a public meeting at 10 a.m. on a Saturday morning. Anyone under thirty was hungover and still in bed, those in their thirties and forties were busy ferrying children to Baby Ballet or Soccer Tots and those in their fifties were presumably enjoying the novelty of not having to get up to ferry their children somewhere because they were now teenagers and consequently still in bed. It was only the sixty-plus age group it seemed, for whom an invitation to a political meeting on a Saturday morning had proved irresistible. And me – who it must now be obvious to everyone had an ulterior reason for being there.

The elderly lady in front of me, who was sporting a red

mac and one of those clear plastic rain-hats, which she'd either forgotten to take off or considered to be a fashion statement, turned around and fixed me with a stare.

'Are you one of them?' she asked.

'Er, one of them what?'

'One of them who's come up from London.'

'Oh no,' I said. 'I'm not with Labour Party.'

'Oh,' she said, obviously disappointed, 'I were hoping to meet someone from London. Do you think Mr Miliband will be here?'

'I doubt it,' I said. 'I expect he's a bit busy at moment.'

'Never mind,' she said. 'To be honest, I liked his brother better anyway.'

The doors of the meeting room opened. A young man with short gelled hair and wearing a slick suit poked his head out. I saw the look of disappointment on his face as he surveyed what looked more like a bus-stop queue than the attendees of a top-flight political meeting. And I watched him recompose his features into something more favourable as he moved effortlessly into smooth PR mode.

'Good morning everyone. Thank you so much for coming,' he said. 'Please do come in. We'd appreciate it if you could leave your contact details on our list so that we can keep in touch with you during the election campaign.'

We shuffled forward. The rain-hat woman smiled up at the young man when she got to him.

'Are you from London?' she asked.

'No, Wakefield actually.' She sighed and made her way into the room.

The first thing I noticed when I looked down at the contact details list was that the people in front of me had left postal addresses. Email addresses and mobile numbers were conspicuous by their absence.

'Not exactly at the cutting edge of new technology are we?' I said to the young man. He smiled awkwardly, but said nothing. I suspected he was beginning to wish they hadn't bothered.

We took our seats. Judging from the number of empty ones, they'd been hoping for a bigger turnout. At least no one had put on 'Things Can Only Get Better'.

The PR man stood at the front of the room and waxed lyrical about how people like us were what the Labour Party was all about. I resisted the temptation to ask him if he meant clapped-out and having seen better days. Then, with something approaching a fanfare, he introduced the special guest speakers, shadow Home Secretary Yvette Cooper and the prospective Labour Party candidate for Halifax (the current Labour MP was standing down at the next election), a man who, rather incongruously, was called Jack Daniels. I thought they missed a trick by not playing 'Whiskey in My Jar' as he made his entrance wearing one of those shiny suits that ought never to be let out of a wardrobe, except to be given to a charity shop.

Yvette Cooper, on the other hand, was smart and businesslike. I'd always thought she was attractive on TV, but she was actually even more attractive in the flesh. But what most impressed me was that despite everything she managed to look as if she was actually pleased to be there.

The PR man did a little spiel about them both. He tried to sell Jack Daniels as a Yorkshireman, but he was actually from Harrogate, which didn't really count as it was posh Yorkshire as far as Halifax was concerned. I made a mental note to play the 'born and bred in Halifax' card on my election leaflet.

Finally, Yvette Cooper got to her feet. 'Thank you so much for coming here today,' she said. 'This is part of a series of events we're holding across the country to meet with our supporters in order that we can take on board your concerns and priorities as we go into the election campaign.'

'I don't know what she sees in that Balls fellow,' said the rain-hat lady, turning around from her seat in the second row and speaking in a voice which was a little too loud for comfort. 'Pretty little thing like that could have done much better for herself.'

'So this is where we throw it open to you,' Yvette Cooper continued. 'What are your priorities and what are the big issues you'd like to see us talking about during the election campaign?'

An elderly lady with a Tesco shopping bag sitting in the front row stood up. 'Me husband's got arthritis,' she said. 'And can I get a jacket for him with buttons big enough for him to do up by himself? I think government should force clothing manufacturers to do summat about it.' She sat down, having said her piece. Yvette Cooper nodded sympathetically and made a note of something. Things, it seemed, could indeed only get better.

I popped the painkillers into my mouth, took a big gulp of water and swallowed. There was something odd about taking painkillers for a pain that was yet to come. It made you feel a bit like a junkie. I could hear the voice in my head saying, 'if you know this is coming, why don't you avoid it, instead of chucking pills down your throat?'

The answer of course was that some pain couldn't be avoided. Some pain was necessary. I wished I was one of those women who had a particularly high pain threshold. The sort who went through labour without drugs because they thought nice thoughts about a wooded valley with a stream running through it. I'd screamed the bloody maternity unit down, if I remembered rightly. And yet here I was, desperate to go through it all again.

'How are you feeling?' asked Paul as we got into the car. It was a stupid question, but the expression on his face prevented me from saying so.

'Ask me again in a couple of hours,' I said with as big a smile as I could muster. He nodded. I thought he was going to say something, but if he had been he stopped himself. We talked about stuff and nonsense on the way to the hospital. Anything apart from what was about to happen and what the outcome might be. What I really wanted was an answer. A reason why. On that level I didn't mind having the dye injected. If you could see something on the screen, a barrier of some kind, then at least you had an idea of what you were up against.

We took our seats in the waiting room. I was starting to feel like a regular now. Almost expected to see my name on the back of the chair. I thumbed through a magazine. I couldn't even have told you which one it was. My hands were turning the pages, but my eyes were not really seeing.

'Mrs Crabtree?' The nurse was smiling at me. It was time to go. Time to get my answer.

It was weird, watching on screen as they squirted the blue dye into me. Like watching a dry river bed filling up inside you. I waited for it to come up against a dam. It didn't though. It kept on flowing. Right out into the sea. I looked up at the consultant, unsure whether I'd seen what I thought I'd seen.

He nodded. 'Your Fallopian tubes are clear,' he said.

'What do you mean clear?' I asked.

'Look, here,' he said, pointing to the screen. 'You can see where the dye has run through into your cervix. There are no blockages. Nothing to prevent your eggs from reaching your womb.'

I looked at Paul. He didn't seem to know whether it was good news or not. I turned back to the consultant.

'So what happens now? Is there another test?'

He shook his head. 'We've excluded all the possible medical problems. I'm afraid in these situations the diagnosis, as such, is that of unexplained infertility.'

I stared at him. How could that be a diagnosis? Anything

that had the word 'unexplained' in it couldn't be final in any way. Scientists didn't produce research papers saying they hadn't discovered anything but couldn't be bothered to go on looking.

'But you can't just stop there,' I said. 'There must be something else you can do.'

'I'm afraid not, Mrs Crabtree. We really have exhausted every avenue.'

'So what are we supposed to do now?' I asked.

'Some couples find it actually takes the pressure off. Occasionally they even get pregnant straightaway afterwards. The mysteries of the female reproductive system never cease to amaze us.'

'Can't we be referred for IVF?'

'Jackie.' The tone in Paul's voice took me by surprise.

'I have to ask, don't I?'

'Look,' said the consultant. 'Why don't you take some time to think about things? Now's not the best time to be making decisions.'

'I'm not making decisions,' I said. 'I'm simply asking for information. Might IVF work for us?'

'For someone of your age,' he said, 'we're only talking about a 2 per cent success rate per cycle and you would have to pay for that yourselves, I'm afraid.'

'Well a 2 per cent chance is still 2 per cent better than nothing.'

'As I said, take some time to think things over,' repeated the consultant. 'There's a leaflet here with all the information you need.' He handed it to Paul, as if he somehow thought it wasn't safe to give to me, that I wasn't in the right mental state to handle it.

'Thank you,' said Paul, standing up. The consultant stood too and shook his hand. They both turned to look at me. I got up reluctantly and headed for the door, my head bowed so he couldn't see the tears welling up in my eyes.

'I know you're upset,' said Paul, as we got in the car, 'but there were no need to be rude to him.'

'Well, what do you expect? The guy's just told me he's given up on us.'

'He didn't say that.'

'Maybe we should think about going private. I bet they'd be able to offer another test. There has to be a reason.'

Paul rested his forehead on the steering wheel. 'There doesn't, love,' he said. 'Sometimes life's like that. Things just aren't meant to be.'

I turned to look at him, a frown creasing my forehead. 'What do you mean, not meant to be?' I was aware that my voice had risen an octave.

Paul sighed and turned to me. 'Maybe we should start trying to get our heads around the idea that it just might not happen.'

'You've given up too, haven't you?'

'It's not a case of giving up. I just don't like to see you putting yourself through this. It were bad enough what happened today, let alone having them pumping you full of drugs for IVF.'

'Well, if that's the only way, that's what I've got to do.'

Paul reached out for my hand. 'You haven't got to do anything. We can simply decide to leave it there and let nature take its course.'

'Sometimes,' I said, pulling my hand away, 'I'm not sure you want another baby.'

'You know I do, but not at any cost. And I certainly don't want it if it means you being stressed up to your eyeballs like this and we become so obsessed with it that we stop enjoying what we've got.'

'Who said I were obsessed with it?'

Paul sighed and turned to look out of the driver's window. 'Look at what it's doing to us,' he said. 'I could understand it if we didn't have Alice, but at end of day, we've got a daughter. Some people never have that. Sometimes I think we've forgotten how lucky we are.'

I looked down at my shaking hands and waited until the lump in my throat cleared. 'I'm doing this for Alice,' I said.

'Are you?'

'What's that supposed to mean?'

'Maybe you're more bothered about it than she is.'

'How can you say that?'

'Because I think it might be true,' he said, turning back to face me. I fiddled with my wedding ring, unable to speak and determined not to cry in the middle of a car park. Paul reached out again for my hand.

'Alice loves you because you're a brilliant mum. The last thing she needs is you putting yourself through hell to try to give her something that just isn't as important as you being happy and well.'

I squeezed his hand. He was saying this for all the right reasons, I knew that. But it still didn't make it any easier to hear.

'I mean it's not as if you haven't got enough on your plate,' he went on, 'what with your mum and now this election business.'

'You don't think I should stand, do you?'

'I didn't say that. I just think you've taken on too much. It's like you're trying to be superwoman or summat.'

'I'm just trying to make things better,' I said. 'For everyone.'

'It don't feel better at moment,' he said. 'Not from where I'm sitting.'

'Well I can't back out now,' I said. 'The others are relying on me.'

Paul stared straight ahead out of the windscreen. He didn't say anything, but I knew exactly what he was thinking. I could pretty much have written the thought bubble above his head.

'Look,' I said. 'I know this is going to be tough on you and please don't think I take you for granted because I don't, but this is something I really want to do. All those motions we put forward to NUT conference, all those petitions we sign about this, that and the other, at end of day, we're pissing in the wind, aren't we?'

Paul shrugged. 'But this,' I went on, waving my arms around as if I were talking about the hospital car park, which I wasn't, 'this Lollipop Party thing is something which really could make a difference. I feel like we could change the world and I haven't felt like that since I were a student. I like it and I don't want to stop now.'

'I don't want you to stop either,' said Paul, 'but I do want you to think about consequences.'

'What do you mean by that?'

'I'm saying I want you to realise how difficult this is going to be for you and our family. Summat has to go. You've got too much on and I'm not going to stand by and watch you run yourself into ground. If you're determined to go ahead with Lollipop Party thing then we should wait until after election before we make any decision on IVF. It makes sense not to rush into it. It'll give us time to think about it properly.'

'I'm not going to change my mind, you know.'

'Fine. Let's just give ourselves a bit of a breather.'

'I still want to go on trying.'

Paul sighed. I knew what he was thinking. That there was no point. That I was in denial. Maybe I was, but the alternative was far too scary to contemplate.

'OK,' he said. 'Well I'm hardly going to complain about that, am I?' He turned to smile at me. I managed one back. 'Now, can we go home, please,' he said, 'before I have to put another couple of quid in parking machine.'

'In the mummyfesto,' I said, 'all hospital car parks are going to be free.'

Paul smiled and shook his head. 'I should bloody hope so,' he said.

12

ANNA

There was something about sitting outside the Head's office that always made you regress to your schooldays. Although it had to be said that in my case it wasn't that it brought back memories of getting into trouble – the only time I could remember being sent to the Headmaster was for good work and behaviour in primary school. He gave me a set of two crayons as a reward – a gold and a green one. At the time I'd been delighted and had passed them around for my friends to admire. I couldn't help but think how unimpressed kids would be with them today.

I wished I wasn't on my own. I knew all too well how good Mr Freeman was at belittling people and brushing off their grievances, both from my own experience and from Jackie. David hadn't been able to get the time off work. He had seemed genuinely upset when I'd told him about the latest bullying incidents. But that hadn't seemed to translate into a determination to get something done about it. Maybe I should have taken it as a compliment: that he trusted me to be able to sort it out myself. But for some reason it didn't feel like a compliment. It felt like a dereliction of his duties.

The school secretary came out of her office on the other side of the corridor, bringing the whiff of hairspray with her.

'Mr Freeman is ready for you now,' she said. I nodded. They annoyed me, men who were too high up the scale to be able to open their own office door.

I knocked and entered as commanded. Freeman stood up and offered his hand.

'Sorry to keep you, Mrs Sugden,' he said. Tempted as I was to correct him on the Mrs, I decided to let it go. There were bigger battles to be won and I didn't want to get off to a bad start.

'That's OK,' I said, shaking his hand firmly.

'Now, thank you for your letter and for bringing this matter to my attention. As you know, we at Hebden High take any allegations of bullying very seriously, but it does appear from your letter that none of these incidents took place in school.'

'The texts and messages were all sent by pupils at this school.'

'Well that may or may not be the case, but I'm sure you understand that we can't be held responsible for things that happen outside the school premises.'

'Some of these texts were probably sent from school premises.'

'May I remind you that we have a ban on mobile phones being used on site.'

'With the greatest of respect, that doesn't mean to say that they're not used.'

'Are you suggesting that we are not in control of our pupils?'

There was a note of challenge in his voice and in the expression on his face. I sat up straight, determined not to be intimidated.

'I'm simply saying that sometimes things happen that shouldn't. In our case, our daughter is being bullied by pupils at this school. As her parents, we're really not bothered what side of the school gates the messages are sent from. The effect on Charlotte is the same.'

'Well the obvious solution is to take away her mobile phone and stop her using Facebook and the like.'

'She's no longer on Facebook and she's switched off her mobile. The problem is that many of the pupils at this school are on Facebook and have seen what has been posted about her. And a minority of them are continuing to make offensive and abusive comments about her on the site.'

'Perhaps you should take that up with Facebook.'

'These are your school's pupils, Mr Freeman.'

'And this is your daughter we're talking about. Perhaps there are things you as parents could do to offer her greater protection.'

'And what do you suggest?'

'You could encourage her to integrate more with her peers in order to help her to become more accepted.'

'Yes, you're right. We should encourage her to have underage sex, wear make-up and concentrate on getting a boyfriend instead of studying hard for her GCSEs.'

'There's no need to be facetious, Mrs Sugden.'

'It's Ms, actually,' I said, no longer caring about rubbing him up the wrong way. 'And I was simply pointing out that if you have a student who is different to their peers, suggesting that they should adapt to become more accepted is not a particularly inclusive policy.'

Freeman looked down his nose at me. Any pretence that he welcomed the opportunity to discuss this matter had gone. I got the distinct impression that he was trying to think of the fastest way of getting me out of his office.

'I can only reiterate, Ms Sugden, that we do not tolerate bullying of any kind at this school and I can assure you that none takes place on our premises. What your daughter and her friends get up to out of school is really a matter which you need to resolve with the parents concerned.'

'You're well aware, Mr Freeman, that there's a history of bullying in my daughter's case. The school has a duty to safeguard its pupils. I don't believe you're taking that duty seriously enough.'

'Should you have any evidence that your daughter is being bullied on school premises, please do let me know and I assure you it will be dealt with appropriately. In the meantime, as I've made clear, I'm afraid it really is an external matter.'

He nodded at me and stood up. Charlotte was right. It had been a waste of time. He clearly didn't want the hassle and had somehow managed to make me think that I was to blame.

'I'm an adolescent counsellor, Mr Freeman,' I said, as I stood up. 'I spend my time trying to repair the damage caused by this sort of thing. It would be nice to think that schools were genuinely interested in the well-being of their pupils, because whether things happen inside or outside the school gates, that child's education is still affected.'

I walked out of his office and down the corridor, propelled by indignation and anger. My instinct was to find Charlotte, drag her out of the classroom and take her home with me. I didn't want her to be here any more. I wanted her to be loved and valued for who she was. Most of all I wanted her to be protected.

I knew I couldn't do that, though. Knew she would never forgive me and it would only make things worse. But I still hated leaving her there. Still brushed away the tears as I walked out of the gates. Still wished I was bringing her home from hospital, wrapped snugly in a blanket, David at my side, with a look on his face which proclaimed that he was going to look after us both and protect us from harm. No matter what.

'Esme, no handstands indoors, please,' I said, glancing through the open kitchen door to the hall where her upside-down face was turning pinker by the second.

'Ohhhh,' she said coming down straightaway, but

knocking a pot plant off the hall table as she did so. 'Ooopps.'

'Come and get the dustpan and brush please,' I called out.

'Do I have to?'

'Yes. We clear up after ourselves in this house, thank you.'

Esme bounded into the kitchen, grabbed the dustpan and brush and danced out again, her ability to bounce back from such mishaps was the one positive thing about it all.

I glanced at Charlotte who was sitting at the kitchen table with a history textbook in front of her and a faraway look in her eyes. I hadn't had the chance to tell her about my visit to Mr Freeman since she'd come home. Or maybe it was more that I'd been putting it off. The thought of telling her that her school had washed its hands of its responsibilities didn't exactly appeal to me.

'I'll run you down to choir practice, if you like,' I said, 'being as it's tipping down.'

'I'm not going,' she said, without looking up from the book.

'Why?' I knew why, of course. I guess I'd been half expecting it. I'd seen it so many times in the teenagers I worked with. But I still wanted to hear how she dealt with the question.

'I just can't seem to fit it in any more,' she said. 'Not with all my school work.' It was a predictable answer, if not an entirely honest one.

'I'm sure we could make time for it,' I said. 'You've always enjoyed choir so much. It would be a shame to waste that beautiful voice.'

Charlotte closed her textbook. Her hair was hanging down in front of her face, but I could still see her eyes welling with tears. I walked over to her and wrapped my arms around her.

'Don't let them win, love,' I said. 'Don't stop doing the things you love, being the person you are.'

'I just need to get them off my back,' she said, her voice quavering.

'Then be yourself,' I said. 'Be proud of how special you are. I know it's hard, but every time they say something which hurts you, try to remember that it's not going to last forever. And that you'll so regret it when you're older if you let them change who you are and who you're going to become.'

Charlotte sniffed and wiped her nose with the back of her hand. 'I can't go now,' she said. 'My face is a mess. I'll go next week.'

I nodded and squeezed her shoulders. Scared that by next week there'd be another excuse but knowing I had to stay with her. That she had to have someone who believed in her.

'How did you get on at the school?' asked David later, when they were all in bed.

'Not good,' I said. 'It was pretty much what I expected.

Freeman basically said if it's not happening on school premises they don't want to know.'

'That's ridiculous.'

'I know. That's what I told him.'

David put his mug down on the coffee table, took off his glasses and rubbed his eyes. 'So what happens now?' he asked.

I shrugged. 'We pull her out of school.'

'We can't do that.'

'We can't leave her there either. There'll be nothing left of her soon. That's why she didn't go to choir practice this evening. Because it's something else they take the piss out of.'

'Did she say that?'

'She didn't have to.'

'Are you sure you're not reading too much into this? I mean all teenagers go through phases don't they? Falling out with each other. Especially girls of that age.'

'David, these girls weren't even her friends to start with.'

'Has she got any friends?' I stared at him. It appeared to be a genuine question.

'Well, Emily, obviously. But she's no use to her at a different school, is she?'

'Can't we get Lotte into her school?'

'It's a grammar school, David.'

He nodded and sighed. 'I always said she should have done the eleven plus.'

'Oh cheers.'

'What?'

'Well that makes it sound as if the whole thing is my fault.'

'I'm simply saying that the argument about this school being part of the community and having a creative curriculum doesn't seem so strong right now.'

I stared at the far wall. He was saying it was my fault. The argument he was talking about had been mine. The grammar school had seemed formal and stuffy when we'd looked around. David hadn't thought so, but then he'd gone to a very similar school himself. The worst thing about it was that he was probably right. Maybe she would have been happier there. And maybe I should have seen that. Maybe I'd failed her.

'We can't change the past now,' I said, switching to counselling mode to avoid beating myself up. 'All we can do is try to work out a way forward.'

'Well, if it's not a school matter we should get the police involved.'

'No. Charlotte would never forgive us. I don't want to lose her trust.'

'So what do you suggest?'

'Like I said, we pull her out of school. We could home educate.'

'And how are you going to have the time to do that?'

I didn't know what was worse. The fact that he'd said it or the fact that judging from the look on his face he had no idea what was wrong with what he'd said.

'Who said it was going to be me?' I said it quietly, more

out of disappointment than anything. David looked across at me as if I'd said something utterly ridiculous.

'Well I can't give up my job, can I?'

'And you think I can?'

'You're the one who suggested home-educating.'

'I was thinking we could maybe do it between us.' David made a soft snorting sound. 'What's that supposed to mean?'

'Have you forgotten that you're about to stand as a candidate in the general election? Where exactly do you propose you'll fit in home education?'

'I don't know. I haven't got that far yet. But I'd find a way.'

'The only way would be to forget the whole idea of standing.'

I stared straight ahead again, unable to look David in the eye. 'And you think that's what I should do?'

'I think I've made my views on the subject quite clear, Anna.'

I wanted to say, 'Is it b'coz I is a woman?' in Will's fake Ali G voice. I didn't think David would appreciate it though.

'That's not how I'd have reacted if you were standing, is it?'

'No, but that would be entirely different. I've been active in politics all my life.'

'So have I. Life is politics.'

David rolled his eyes. 'It's not as if it's actually going to achieve anything.'

'How do you know that?'

'You've got no supporter base. You'll just be one of these novelty candidates.'

I waited to hear him say we were on a level with the Monster Raving Loony Party. I suspected he had been, but the natural instinct for self-preservation must have kicked in because he stopped himself.

'I'm not doing this for a giggle, David. This is serious. I'm fighting for things I believe in. We all are.'

'And what about fighting for your family?'

I jumped up from the sofa like a cat who'd had its tail sat on. 'Who was at the school today? Who took time off work to do that?' I was aware that my finger was jabbing in the direction of David's face. He was lucky I didn't have my claws out.

'Yes and I appreciate that,' said David, adopting a deep, measured tone, presumably in order to highlight the screechy nature of my voice. 'But the fact remains that our daughter is being bullied at school and our son appears to prefer hanging out with some dubious characters in the park, rather than applying himself to his revision. And when you look at which one of us has the qualifications and experience to deal with those issues, it appears very much to fall to you.'

I stared at him. Desperately searching his face for any hint of the man I'd fallen in love with. A man who, yes, had always had a rather serious demeanour and whose formidable intellect had sometimes allowed him to stray into patronising territory without realising it, but a man who'd also had a heart and soul.

I wanted to say something, but there was nothing I could say. I was empty inside. I picked up my mug and walked towards the door. He didn't say anything. Just picked up the remote and turned *Newsnight* on.

I was the first to arrive at Sam's house. Rob let me in.

'She'll be down in a minute,' he said. 'Oscar's pulling the "but it's your turn to read a story" string.'

I smiled and nodded. 'How's work going?'

'Oh, you know. Just about paying the mortgage.'

'No, I meant your painting. Your art work.'

'Oh,' said Rob, grinning. 'People don't usually class that as proper work.'

'You've got a degree in it, haven't you? It's what you love doing.'

'Yeah. It's just not exactly lucrative. Unless you're David Hockney or Damien Hirst that is.'

'You need to be more controversial then,' I said.

'Oh believe me, I'm trying. I've got an exhibition opening at Linden Mill of nude pensioners.'

I started laughing. 'Sorry,' I said. 'I'm imagining strategically placed bus passes.'

'Damn, I wish I'd thought of that. I can assure you that it's all tastefully done though.'

'I bet the sittings were fun.'

'They were. Never let it be said that an octogenarian isn't capable of flaunting her wares.'

'What's all the hilarity about?' asked Sam, entering the kitchen as I was bent double laughing.

'Rob tells me you've been letting him consort with disreputable ladies of a certain age.'

'And disreputable men, too,' Sam said. 'You should go and have a look, get an insight into what we've got to look forward to in thirty years' time. You could take David. Get Charlotte or Will to babysit and go for a meal afterwards. Make a night of it.'

I smiled at her. How could I possibly begin to explain that the thought of spending an evening alone with David at the moment did not exactly fill me with joy? She couldn't possibly understand. She had Rob. She had a soulmate.

'Right. I'd better go and get Oscar sorted out,' said Rob, smiling at me. 'See you all later when you've put the world to rights.'

'Any more policy suggestions?' Sam asked.

'A better deal for pensioners,' he said. 'They are a force to be reckoned with and you need them on your side. Preferably clothed, of course.'

He left the room. Some of his warmth stayed behind, though. I could see it forming a Ready-brek-style glow around Sam. I pulled my sleeves down, suddenly feeling the cold.

'So, how's you?' Sam asked.

It was tempting sometimes to tell her. Until, that is, I remembered what she had to cope with with Oscar. At which point my problems appeared so small that they hardly seemed worth mentioning.

'Fine, thanks,' I said.

She put the kettle down and looked at me. Maybe there'd been a tell-tale quaver in my voice.

'Any progress with Charlotte?' she asked.

'No. The school don't want to know.'

'That's appalling,' she said.

'I know. If it was down to me I'd pull her out.'

'Does David think she should stick it out then?'

'Yeah,' I said. 'Something like that.' I was saved from having to say anything more by Jackie's arrival. She was one of those people who never made a quiet entrance. On this occasion, I was very glad of it.

'Sorry guys. Mum had been doing other people's gardening again. I had to stop her from deadheading next door's still-blooming daffodils and Alice was having a meltdown because her tooth is wobbly and she thinks she's going to swallow it in her sleep and miss out on a Tooth Fairy visit. Apart from that, everything's fine and dandy. How about you two?' She looked at both of us in turn.

'Fine, thanks,' I said.

'How did you get on with Freeman?'

'Not good. They've washed their hands of it, basically. Our problem, not theirs.'

Jackie shook her head. 'I'm sorry,' she said. 'It's so bloody typical that the person who denies there's any bullying going on at our school should be the biggest bully of all.'

'I can quite believe it,' I said.

'Look, if there's anything I can do. If you want me to have a word with the girls involved I'm happy to do so.'

'Thanks. We're going to have to work out where we go from here.'

'Well obviously I'll keep an eye on Charlotte as much as I can, but I only see her in class once a week, and like you said, they're far too savvy to do anything in front of a teacher these days.'

'I know. But thanks anyway.'

'Will keeps an eye out for her, doesn't he?'

'Yeah. Best he can in the circumstances, anyway.'

Jackie turned back to Sam. 'And how's things with you?'

'Pretty good,' said Sam. 'Oscar saw the physio again today and she said he's still maintaining the same range of movement as six months ago.'

'That is good,' said Jackie.

I nodded, though I knew that it was simply a case of holding the deterioration off for as long as possible. The one thing that wasn't in doubt was that he would never get better.

'Right,' said Sam, 'we'd better get started. We've got loads to get through if we're actually going to be ready for next week.'

'I've booked Eureka for the launch,' I said. 'Though I'm still not sure it's such a good idea.'

'Of course it is,' said Sam. 'If we're putting children and families at the heart of this then we need to show that right from the beginning. And what better place than a children's museum?'

'You'll regret that when there's a kid having a tantrum outside during the press conference,' said Jackie.

'It's OK, it's after closing time,' I said.

'And the good news is the *Times* has already confirmed they'll be there,' added Sam. She actually managed to keep a straight face for a second afterwards until Jackie elbowed her. 'Well, OK,' she said. 'It's the *Hebden Bridge Times*, but you've got to start somewhere, haven't you?'

We sat down at the table. Sam held up a wodge of A4 paper. 'Right,' she said, 'I have here, drumroll please, the draft mummyfesto.'

Jackie whooped and clapped.

'Tell me it doesn't read as ridiculously idealistic as I fear,' I said.

'It reads brilliantly,' said Sam. 'The words radical, reforming and revolutionary spring to mind.'

'Don't tell me this is going to be the Hebden Bridge spring,' groaned Jackie.

'Well, we're not far from Bradford, maybe it's heading our way.'

'As long as Galloway isn't heading our way with it,' Jackie said, grimacing. 'I still gag every time I see a cat lapping milk.'

'Anyway,' said Sam. 'Back to the mummyfesto. I'll run through what's in from all the Twitter suggestions. We've got OAP playgrounds in parks, term-time school hours working available to all, boarding schools to be banned for children under thirteen on the grounds that a child is for life not just for the cute toddler bits, we stop putting the clocks back in autumn on the grounds that children are more important than farmers, all school playgrounds to be covered with that spongy stuff they use under the swings in parks, in order to cut A & E bills, breast-feeding to be recognised with national awards screened live on TV and badges saying 'I did my best so don't give me dirty looks' given to all mums who tried but have now stopped, and last, but by no means least, children's party bags replaced with 'thank you for coming and just be grateful you were invited' stickers in order to teach them about the true meaning of friendship and to cut down the amount of plastic tat ending up in landfills.'

Sam paused for breath and looked up. 'All those in favour?'

Jackie and I both raised our hands.

'So what's out, then?' asked Jackie.

'Well, I'm afraid we aren't going to be calling for the monkey translator, as used to broadcast unspoken thoughts in *Cloudy with a Chance of Meatballs*, to be fitted to all men.'

'Damn shame,' said Jackie.

'And heavily subsidising all sanitary products with the proceeds from a menstrual lottery which men will be too embarrassed to buy a ticket for – that didn't make it either, I'm afraid.'

'Another big loss, if you ask me,' said Jackie.

'But necessary if we want to look credible,' I added. 'I'm still concerned we're a bit lightweight in some areas.'

'What do you mean?' asked Sam.

'Well, "don't start any wars" is hardly a comprehensive defence policy, is it?'

'It would keep us out of trouble, though,' said Jackie. 'And save the country a hell of a lot of money.'

'And what about the foreign policy?' I asked. 'Remind us what it says, Sam.'

Sam flicked through the pages and read, '*Apply the playground mantra for foreign affairs: play nicely with everyone and if someone isn't playing nicely report them to the teacher and go and play with someone else.*'

'Do you really think that's going to stand up to scrutiny?' I asked.

'I don't see why it has to be any more complicated than that,' replied Sam. 'It should be about getting on with everyone, and if we didn't let religion and the male quest for world domination get in the way we'd all be a hell of a lot better off.'

I smiled at her. She had a wonderful knack of being able to convince you that her somewhat simplistic way of looking at the world was actually the right one. And while I loved her to bits for it, I also knew that it lay us open to accusations from people like David that we were not a serious party.

'OK. Well I still think we should concentrate on domestic policy, that's clearly where our strength lies.'

'Anything we should add to it?' asked Sam.

'I think it should be a living mummyfesto,' I said.

'What do you mean by that?' asked Sam.

'We launch it with this next week, but it's just a starting point. It keeps on growing throughout the election campaign as people suggest things to us. Essentially it's like a tree and we can keep on adding branches and leaves to it as it grows.'

'I love it,' said Sam.

'Me too,' said Jackie. 'For a Londoner, you can be very Hebden Bridge sometimes.'

'I'll take that as a compliment,' I said.

'Right then,' said Sam. 'Let's go through all the arrangements for the launch and make sure we've got all the admin stuff sorted out for the party. Everything properly registered and all forms completed and signed. And Anna can show us the fabby website.'

'After that,' said Jackie, 'does anyone fancy going out for a skip?'

13

SAM

'Were they all too poor to buy clothes, Daddy?' asked Oscar. 'Like the Africa children on the news.'

I glanced at Rob, unable to suppress a smile. Trying to explain about his rather avant-garde approach to art clearly wasn't going to be easy.

'No, they've got clothes,' said Rob, crouching down to Oscar's level. 'I just asked them to take them off before I painted them.'

'Isn't that a bit rude?' asked Zach.

'Not if they were happy to do it, which they were,' explained Rob. 'They'd all volunteered, you see.'

'Is there anyone we know?' asked Oscar, manoeuvring his powerchair to get a closer look, as if he might recognise someone's wrinkled left buttock.

'No, love,' I said. 'Daddy didn't know any of them.'

'So they were all strangers who you asked to take their

clothes off?' asked Zach, who was clearly perturbed by the overfamiliarity of it all.

'Yep,' said Rob. 'Sometimes if people don't know you, they're more natural when they're sitting for you.'

'*He* wasn't sitting,' said Oscar, pointing to one of the paintings. 'He was standing up and you could see his willy.'

'Er, yes,' said Rob, scratching his head.

'And that lady's showing you her boobies,' Oscar added for good measure.

'Anyway,' I said, sensing that the conversation might be about to veer into even more awkward territory. 'We'd better be getting back.'

'I'll be a little while yet,' said Rob. 'I've got some more sorting out to do here to get everything ready for later.'

'You do remember I've got my hair appointment at two?' I said.

'Have you?'

'Yeah, I told you. You said you'd be OK looking after the boys.'

'Did I? How long's it going to take? Will you be done by half past?'

'No. Sorry. It's a proper cut.' By that I meant I was going to the most expensive hairdressers in town. You got a bloody good cut, but most of the time I couldn't justify the expense. I'd agreed with Rob that I would go there once a year and have a couple of cheap rubbish haircuts elsewhere in between. It wasn't that he'd said I couldn't go to the expensive one any more than that, simply that I knew I would feel too guilty if I did.

'OK, then,' said Rob.

I suspected it wasn't OK, though. 'It's just that it's too late to cancel it now,' I said. 'I'll ask them to be as quick as they can.' I didn't want to mention the fact that I also wanted to make myself look half presentable before the Lollipop Party launch. It was bad enough thinking it, let alone saying it out loud.

'Right,' said Rob. 'But I'll need to come back here directly afterwards.'

'I know. That's fine.' It wasn't really fine. I had stacks of work to do on the launch, and work from the hospice that I'd ended up bringing home with me.

'OK then, you two,' said Rob, looking at the boys. 'What do you fancy doing for an hour or so?'

'Cinema,' Oscar shrieked.

'The pirates' film is on,' said Zach. 'I saw it on the board when we came past.' Rob looked at me. I knew exactly what he was thinking. We couldn't afford it. And it was going to last longer than an hour.

'Take them,' I said, knowing I would disappear under a tidal wave of guilt if I said no. 'I'll come straight to the cinema when I'm done. We'll ask if they'll let me take over your ticket when you go.'

Rob looked at me doubtfully. I tried to think of the last time we had been to the cinema together, all four of us. I couldn't actually think of one. Having said that I couldn't think of the last time Rob and I had been to the cinema alone – or anywhere else for that matter. I delved into my bag and managed to find a couple of chewy bars and packets of raisins amongst the debris.

'Save having to buy popcorn,' I whispered as I handed them to Rob.

I sat in the hairdressers looking at my watch every five minutes and feeling guilty about how much this was costing when we were denying the boys popcorn. I actually put one pound a week from my wages away for it in a special pot at home, like I was some kid saving for something special that I'd been gazing at longingly in a shop window.

'OK, so it's looking a bit wild,' said the hairdresser, running her fingers through my mass of thick red curls as she smiled out from under her immaculate bob.

'I know, good haircuts come but once a year and all that.'

'What would you like me to do with it?'

'Just a really good cut, something that will last. Quite a bit shorter. I'm in danger of starting to look like Rebekah Brooks.' She smiled and led me over to the washbasins.

I edged my way down the cinema aisle in the dark, my eyes still trying to adjust from the bright sunlight outside. I could just make out Oscar's powerchair at the end of the aisle in the front row.

'I'm here,' I whispered, tapping Rob on the shoulder. 'They've said it's OK to swap.' He nodded, rummaged around on the floor for his bag, said goodbye to Oscar and Zach, and crept out down the aisle. I sunk quickly into the still-warm seat, trying not to think about how ridiculous it was that this was as close as I seemed to get to Rob at the moment.

Zach immediately took hold of my hand and snuggled into me. Oscar was far too busy staring at the screen even to notice my arrival. The film pretty much washed over me. I had far too much to think about to be able to concentrate properly. I was vaguely aware of Hugh Grant's voice, and I did have to try to explain at one point who Charles Darwin was, but I couldn't have told you much about the plot except that it involved a dodo.

We headed out of the fire-exit doors and down the side alleyway, meeting the rest of the audience as they came down the steps at the front.

'When I grow up,' said Zach, 'I want to be like Charles Darwin, discovering things about the world.'

'That's fantastic,' I said. 'You'd make a great discoverer.'

'When I grow up,' said Oscar, 'I want to be a pirate. Can I be a pirate, Mummy? Do they have pirates in wheelchairs?'

I looked down at him, his normal exuberance dented for a moment by the doubts.

'Of course they do,' I said. 'You can be anything you like.'

My parents arrived shortly before teatime. Actually it was shortly before the time I'd told them we would be having tea. In truth I'd not even made a start on anything food-related, having been waylaid by the need – and Oscar insisted it was a need – to build a pirate ship out of re-cycling containers and vegetable crates in the backyard.

'Grandma and Grandad ahoy!' shouted Oscar, looking through the rolled-up newspaper telescope I'd made him. It still felt weird hearing them described as such, even almost eight years on. I suspected they felt the same; they hadn't even been keen on being called Mum and Dad, encouraging me to call them by their first names once I'd reached my teenage years. I'd never really taken to it though, and had reverted to Mum and Dad by the time I'd hit my twenties. It was weird enough when Rob called them Julian and Carole now. And I'd been adamant that my own children weren't going to follow suit.

Zach put down his treasure chest and ran over to greet them, throwing himself against my mum's legs.

'Hello, gorgeous boy,' she said, bending down to give him a hug. 'What's this you've built?'

'It's a pirate ship,' shouted Oscar in a voice which suggested he couldn't believe she hadn't worked it out for herself.

'Yes, of course,' she said, letting Zach lead her up for a closer look and to give Oscar a kiss.

'Hi, Dad,' I said, walking over to give him a hug. He was in his sixties now, but it didn't seem like it. Which was just as well, as otherwise Rob would have thought to ask him to sit for him for his nude-pensioner thing. And I had a horrible feeling Dad would have said yes.

'Hello, love,' he said, brushing his unruly mass of grey hair back from his face. 'How's things?'

'Oh, mad as ever, you know.'

He nodded. 'When's your launch?'

'Wednesday.'

'Bloody great timing,' he said. 'You couldn't get a country more disillusioned with politics than we are right now.'

'I know,' I said. 'That's what's so scary. It feels like quite a responsibility.'

'You'll do a great job,' he said. 'You're standing up for what you believe in. That's what'll set you apart.'

'Thank you.' I smiled at him, knowing I was lucky to have such supportive parents. Last I'd known, Anna hadn't even told hers yet.

'I'm hungry,' called out Oscar. 'What's for tea?'

'Pirate stew, if you carry on being that cheeky,' I replied.

'Why don't I go in and give Mummy a hand?' suggested Mum. 'I'm sure you can find someone else to walk the plank.'

'Grandad,' shouted Oscar, 'come and be fed to the crocodiles.'

'He seems on good form,' said Mum, as we made our way into the kitchen.

'Yeah, as ever. I swear he runs on Duracell batteries sometimes.'

'Only Zach's the one with the copper-coloured top,' she said.

I smiled and started rooting around in the kitchen cupboard for the big lasagne dish. Mum put the washing-up gloves on and ran water into the bowl. She was good like that. Just got on and did stuff without being asked.

'And how are you?'

'Fine,' I said. 'Well, crazy fine – you know how it is.' She nodded slowly as she scrubbed one of the pans.

'Are you sure you're not taking too much on with this election thing?'

'You sound like Rob.'

'We care about you, that's all. And I guess we both know that you're already flat-out, just with work and the boys.'

'I need to do it,' I said. 'Someone's got to stand up for what's right.'

'But why should it be you?'

'Said the woman who singlehandedly keeps Amnesty, Greenpeace and Friends of the Earth going.'

Mum turned to smile at me and put the pan she was washing back in the bowl.

'Unlike you,' she said, 'I don't have a job and two young children, one of whom needs an extraordinary amount of care.'

'I'll make sure Oscar doesn't suffer because of this.'

'I know you will, love. But in doing that you're going to put even more strain on yourself.'

'I'm OK. I can deal with it. It's not a problem.' The lasagne dish slipped through my hands and fell onto the quarry tiles. It smashed clean in half. I burst into tears. Big, proper tears. Mum took the washing-up gloves off and wrapped her arms around me. And for just a minute I wished I was a kid again. Wished she could make it all go away. That I had nothing more to worry about than a grazed knee.

'It's all right,' she said. 'Let it all out. It needs to come out.'

'I'm sorry,' I sniffed. 'Most of the time I'm OK and then some stupid little thing happens and . . .' my voice trailed off.

'You cope with so much,' said Mum, stroking my hair. 'And all the time you've got this smile on your face and I know there must be times when you don't feel like smiling.'

'Sometimes I want to shout and scream at people, "You don't know what it's like to have a child with SMA." Only I don't because it would be rude. And because I'm glad they don't know what it's like. I wouldn't wish it on anyone.'

'You need to talk to someone, love.'

'Who? I can't talk to the staff at the hospice because they're dealing with children who are far sicker than Oscar. Children who might not even see the week out. And it's stupid because the one person I could talk to, who knows exactly what it's like is Rob, only he doesn't want to talk about it.'

'Have you tried telling him how you feel?'

'I can't. He's got his own way of coping with it which is to stick his head in the sand and pretend there's nothing wrong with Oscar. That he really is just like any other kid. And if I tell him how I feel that will remind him that Oscar's not like any other kid and I'm not sure he's strong enough to cope with that.'

'So you'll both go on suffering in silence?'

'I can't see any other way. I can't destroy Rob's coping mechanism just so I can get things off my chest.'

'Maybe you'd be doing him a favour. In the long run I mean.' Mum looked down. She didn't have to say anything more. I knew what she meant.

'I've thought that sometimes, too. But I still can't be sure it's the right thing to do. What if he's right? What if it's best to just enjoy the here and now instead of worrying all the time like I do?'

Mum nodded and walked a few paces away to look out of the window where Oscar could be seen commanding the pirate ship and doing a very passable Captain Hook impression.

'It's daft isn't it?' she said. 'Sometimes, just listening to him, it's hard to believe there's anything wrong with him.'

'I know.'

'Why don't you try to get some respite care?' said Mum. 'Even if it's only for a night or two. I'm sure it would do you all the power of good.'

I shook my head. 'There are so many families worse off than us, Mum. Families who really need those places. We're OK. It's tough but we can get through this.'

'What about you and Rob? About the strain this must be putting on you.'

I shrugged. 'We'll be all right.'

'You still need to be a couple as well, you know. Instead of always being Oscar and Zach's mum and dad.'

'I know. And I really appreciate tonight.' I glanced up at the clock then looked down at the broken lasagne dish which was still lying on the floor. I felt like crying again. My face must have shown it.

'We'll do spaghetti,' Mum said, picking the pieces up and putting them on the kitchen counter. 'The boys love it and it'll be ready in ten minutes.'

'Thanks,' I said, rummaging in the cupboard for a jar of pasta sauce and wondering how the hell I was going to stand for parliament when I couldn't even manage to get a decent meal ready on time. 'Sorry about all this.'

Mum turned to face me. 'No one will remember the lasagne you didn't cook,' she said. 'What they'll remember is the love you always showed them.'

I'd quite forgotten how good Rob looked in a suit. Well, not a suit exactly, he had a pathological aversion to ties, but a smart shirt and trousers at least.

'Hey,' I said, sidling up to him before the guests arrived. 'You scrubbed up pretty well. I can't even see any paint in your hair.'

'Cheers,' grinned Rob. 'You don't look too bad yourself.'

I glanced down. I had my one posh frock on: a brown-and-gold silk number from Monsoon. I'd got it for a wedding years ago and had only worn it half a dozen times since.

'Why, thank you. Had to make an effort to look my best, didn't I? What with all the female flesh on show tonight.'

Rob smiled as we gazed around us at the array of nudes

on display. His paintings gracing the walls of the gallery, ready to be admired by the guests.

'They look OK, don't they?' asked Rob.

'No,' I said. 'They look absolutely awesome.'

'Thank you,' said Rob. 'For all of this, I mean.'

'Just make sure this is the first of many,' I said.

There were voices in the corridor. The first of the guests walked through to the gallery, glass of wine in her hand, silver-grey hair blow-dried to within an inch of its life.

'She looks familiar,' I whispered.

'Third portrait along on the left,' Rob whispered back. 'I almost didn't recognise her with her clothes on.'

I crept into Oscar's room when Rob and I got back later that night. Although I'd taught Mum how to use all the machines I still had to see for myself that everything was fine. I switched the bedside lamp on so I could check the night-time ventilator was secured properly. He always looked so little under it, as if somehow it was deflating him as he slept, instead of helping him breathe. I kissed him on the forehead. 'Night-night, Pirate Oscar,' I whispered.

I tiptoed across the landing to open Zach's door a crack. Unlike Oscar, Zach was a light sleeper. It was as if he never totally switched off. A pirate in the crow's nest, always on the alert for danger.

'Night-night, Mummy,' came a voice from within.

'You should be asleep, sweetheart,' I said, bending to stroke his hair.

'I heard you come home,' he said. 'Did lots of people go to Daddy's exhibition?'

'Yes, love.'

'And did they all love his paintings?'

'Absolutely. Everybody said they were brilliant and he's sold two already.'

'So are there two gaps where the paintings used to be?'

'No, love. The people who bought them won't take them home until the exhibition has finished.'

'That's OK then,' said Zach. 'As long as they haven't spoiled Daddy's exhibition.'

I shook my head in the dark. I loved him and worried for him in equal measure. 'Let's get some sleep now,' I said, kissing him on the cheek.

'Have Grandma and Grandad gone home?'

'Yes.'

'Is Oscar asleep?'

'Yes.'

'OK. Night-night, Mummy.'

I shut the door and went into the bathroom. I imagined Zach listening to every sound. He was a parent way before his time, unable to rest until everyone in the household was safe and sound in their bed. I padded barefoot into our room, still a little light-headed from the wine. Rob was already in bed. Eyes wide open and staring at the ceiling though. And looking utterly wired.

'Today Linden Mill, tomorrow the world,' I said, undressing and climbing into bed next to him.

'I wish,' he said, putting his arm around me.

'Well, why not?' I asked.

'How long have you got?'

'I don't see any reason why you couldn't do it.'

'That's because you don't see any barriers to anything.'

'And that's a bad thing?'

'No. Just so long as you understand other people might not share your optimism and might be a bit more grounded.'

'You still think I'm crazy, don't you?'

'Yes, but I wouldn't want you any other way. And as long as I continue to be a raging pessimist we make a good team.'

I looked up and smiled at him, kissed him on the lips. 'It was good tonight. I was dead proud of you.'

'Thanks. The way I see it, that'll pay for new shoes, wellies and trainers for both of them and leave a bit towards the gas bill.'

'Hey, come on. I meant I was proud of your pictures, not how much money you made.'

'I know. But it's not going to go amiss is it?' He was right, of course. I was actually glad he hadn't commented on my hair now. It would only make me feel even worse.

'I'm going to get the money for the election deposit back,' I said. 'Anna's going to approach some people for sponsorship. She's got a proper fundraising plan. It involves spreadsheets. This really isn't going to cost us a penny. We'll make sure of it.'

'I told you. As long as you win I don't care how much it costs. Just so long as there's a nice little cubbyhole somewhere in Downing Street which will do for a studio.' I smiled and stretched my arm further across his chest.

'Oh, I'll do better than that,' I said. 'I'll get you an exhibition at the Tate. I'm sure I'll be able to pull some strings if I'm PM.'

Rob shook his head. 'See,' he said, 'it's true what they say. Power corrupts and all that.'

I kissed him again on the mouth to shut him up. Rubbed my foot up and down his leg.

'Hey,' said Rob. 'Are you sure we've got time for this? Don't you have a speech to write or something?'

'Shut up and make the most of it.' I smiled. 'But keep the noise down because Zach's probably still awake.'

14

JACKIE

I drove past her without even realising. It was only the flash of pink in my rear-view mirror which set off some kind of alert in my brain. I pulled over sharply, bumped up the kerb and parked at an awkward angle. I could see her in my wing mirror now. An elderly lady with unkempt grey hair, wearing a long pink nightdress and red carpet slippers. Shuffling along the pavement, secateurs in hand and seemingly oblivious to anything around her.

I jumped out of the car. 'Mum,' I called. She didn't turn around, of course. Just kept on shuffling. I started running down the road, running as best I could, that was, in a pair of high platforms and a too-tight skirt. I couldn't imagine Cameron taking a detour like this on his way to the Tories' election campaign launch. You just didn't see it: a top politician arriving breathlessly in front of the assembled media and apologising that his mother had escaped, armed with secateurs and he'd had to give chase down the street.

I slowed down as I drew nearer. I didn't want to startle her. And I wasn't sure she'd even know who I was.

'Hello, Mum,' I said, gently taking her arm. 'We need to get you back indoors.'

She turned to stare at me. I waited for the flicker of recognition. It didn't come.

'Roses need pruning,' she said.

'Not now they don't. I'm going to get you inside. You're not even dressed.'

She glanced down at her nightdress then looked back up at me, a frown creasing her brow. 'Do I know you?' she asked.

I nodded, unable to speak for a second. 'I'm your daughter,' I managed, eventually.

'Deborah?'

I shut my eyes for a moment. 'No. Jackie.'

'I can't find me roses,' she repeated, her voice increasing in volume. I tried to turn her around and steer her in the right direction.

'Get your hands off me,' she shouted, pulling her arm out of mine.

I swallowed hard, feeling the mercury rising inside me. I realised I was going to have to grab her, to manhandle her into her own house. 'Come on,' I said, taking hold of her arm again and turning her around to face the right direction. 'We'll go and see your roses. They're in your back garden. I'll show you the way.'

'Let go of me,' she shrieked, struggling some more.

My grip on her arm tightened. I was aware of a couple of passers-by looking at me. I smiled weakly at them, hoping they were local and would recognise Mum, or at the very least see the family resemblance between us. 'Come on now,' I said. 'We're almost there.' I took the secateurs from her, more for her own safety than anything.

'Help!' she screamed. 'She's going to hurt me. She's come to steal me roses. Get her off me.'

A middle-aged man walking his Labrador crossed over from the other side of the road. 'Are you OK, love?' he asked. He was talking to Mum. He wasn't even looking at me.

'She's come to steal me roses,' Mum repeated. The man looked at me. The Labrador was sniffing Mum's slippers.

'She's my mum,' I said, trying to hold myself together. 'She's got Alzheimer's. She went for a wander and I'm just getting her back home.' He looked again at Mum, who remained silent, before nodding at me.

'Sorry,' he said.

'No, not at all. Thank you for stopping and checking. I appreciate it. I'd have done the same myself. Really.'

'Do you need any help?' he asked. I shook my head.

'Thanks. But it's probably better I do it.' He nodded and crossed back to the other side of the road. Went on his way. Maybe he'd tell his wife about it later. The crazy, shrieking woman and her daughter. Perhaps he'd even think about it lying in bed at night. Worrying in case the same fate befell him or his wife.

I took Mum's arm firmly and hurried her towards the front door. It was only as I neared it that I realised she'd left it open. Wide open. I swore under my breath. As soon as we stepped inside she quietened down. She didn't even mention the roses. She went straight through to the living room. I helped lower her into the armchair. She didn't put up any fight this time. Even patted my hand. 'Thank you, love,' she said. 'Cup of tea wouldn't go amiss.'

I nodded and went out into the kitchen, grateful for the opportunity to try to compose myself. I had no idea whether she knew who I was now. She may have thought I was one of the council carers. All I did know was that I couldn't leave her like this, but that I had to go. I looked at my watch. The launch was due to start in half an hour. I couldn't call Paul because he was looking after Zach and Oscar, as well as Alice. For a fleeting moment I considered taking Mum with me, but I realised it would be dismissed as some kind of cheap PR stunt, added to which I didn't want to run the risk of her accusing me of kidnapping her in front of the assembled press. I was going to have to ask Pauline across the road. I couldn't think of anything else. I poured Mum's tea and took it in to her.

'I just need to pop to my car to get something,' I said. 'I won't be a minute.'

I hurried over the road and knocked on Pauline's door. It felt ridiculously cheeky to be asking, but I didn't have an option. I waited a minute and rang the bell. Still no reply. She must be out. I racked my brain to think of any other neighbours, but it had all changed since I'd lived there and short of knocking on doors up and down the street until I found someone I recognised, I was stuck.

I looked at my watch. The others would be there by now. Wondering where the hell I was. You couldn't be late to your own political party's launch. You just couldn't. I ran back to Mum's. There was no point ringing the council. The word 'immediately' did not feature in their vocabulary and I couldn't really claim this was an emergency anyway. It was simply inconvenient. Damned inconvenient. The option of locking her in her own home entered my head. It was probably the safest thing to do, but I was also aware that it was morally reprehensible. I couldn't sit in a press conference talking about giving elderly people dignity and respect when I had just locked my own mother in her house. What I needed was a babysitter, or rather a grannysitter. And that was when it came to me. I'd do what hard-pressed mums everywhere did in a crisis when they needed an hour or so to get something done. I'd put on a DVD. I knew just the one as well: *Hello Dolly*. It had always been one of Mum's favourite films. We'd got it for her birthday a couple of years ago after she'd told me how she used to watch it with Deborah and me when we were little.

'Let's put something nice on for you to watch, shall we?' I said, rifling through the TV cabinet. I got the DVD out and checked the back of the case for the running time. Two hours twenty-five minutes. Even better. I put it in the machine and stood there tapping my fingers on the case until it got to the bit where I could skip the trailers. Eventually I was able to press *play*.

'There,' I said. 'It's your favourite.'

Mum stared at the screen. A warm glow came over her face as the opening music came on. All I could think of was the scene in *WALL-E* where he lovingly watched the same film. Where he was happiest and safest in the confines of his own home, surrounded by his possessions and memories and away from the outside world which he found lonely, confusing and unwelcoming.

I blinked back the tears and kissed her on the cheek. 'One of your carers will be here before it's finished,' I said. 'I'll pop back later this evening to check you're OK.'

She didn't say anything. She didn't even acknowledge me. But she was fine and I was convinced enough that she wouldn't stray from her armchair while the film was on.

It was only as I pulled the door shut behind me and ran to the car that I realised I hadn't even got her dressed. I couldn't go back now though. I was late enough as it was. I grabbed the mobile from my bag and rang Sam, counting the rings in my head before she answered.

'Where the hell are you?' she said.

'Family crisis. I'm just leaving Mum's. I'll get there as soon as I can. I'm really sorry.'

I threw the phone down without even waiting for a reply, pulled my seat belt on and started the engine.

The first thing I noticed when I arrived in the Eureka car park was the BBC television van. Parked next to the Yorkshire TV van.

'Fuck,' I muttered, as I ran up the yellow brick road to the front door, aware that I was out of breath, dishevelled and very late.

I burst through the main doors and hurried up to the reception desk.

'I'm here for the Lollipop Party launch,' I said.

'They're in the town square,' the young receptionist said. 'Just around the corner to your right.' I realised she thought I was one of the guests, not one of those presenting it.

'Thank you,' I said, holding out my hand for the dinosaur stamp I always got when I came here with Alice. The receptionist looked at me, clearly trying to stifle a giggle.

'Just testing,' I said, laughing awkwardly. I pushed through the turnstile. It was weird being here after closing time. The complete lack of children was unnerving, as was the quietness and stillness of it all. Like stumbling on to the set of *Justin's House* when everyone had gone home for the night. I took a deep breath before rounding the corner, but I still wasn't prepared for the sight which greeted me. There were two television cameras set up with lights glaring, a couple of dozen journalists holding copies of the mummyfesto and assorted microphones on the table at which Sam and Anna were sitting.

'Sorry,' I mouthed to them. They both gave rather strained smiles. I sat down heavily next to Sam, feeling awful for letting them down and thinking what a shame it was that my fifteen minutes of fame should come at a time when I probably looked like some bag lady they'd dragged in off the streets.

'Apologies again for the unavoidable delay, folks,' said Sam. 'Thank you all for your patience. I hope you've had a chance to look through our mummyfesto. We're now ready to begin.'

She paused for a second and glanced at Jackie and me in turn. I could see it on her face. Exactly what I was feeling inside. A rush of adrenalin that this was actually happening, that we were going public and there was no going back now, coupled with a cramping feeling in the stomach as the enormity of it all sank in. We weren't sitting around Sam's kitchen table, winding each other up and stuffing our faces with Pringles any more. This was real. I nodded at Sam. She nodded back and turned to face the media.

'We decided to launch the Lollipop Party because we, like many people, were so disillusioned with what the mainstream political parties had to offer. In particular, we wanted to give a voice to the weakest and most vulnerable people in society: the children, young people, elderly people and those with disabilities who successive governments have treated with scant regard. Our mission is to put those people at the heart of everything we do.

'We are not in this because of our egos, or because we're on some power-kick or simply to line our own pockets. I can assure you that none of us have any intention of buying a duck-house or getting a moat installed, accepting money to ask questions in parliament or charging anyone two hundred and fifty thousand pounds to come round to our place for dinner.'

There were a few smiles from the assembled journalists. I glanced across at Sam, who hadn't appeared to notice. She was on a roll now. And she was sounding bloody good.

'The reason we're doing this is because it's time the public were offered an alternative to the Oxbridge men in suits who lead the mainstream political parties. Women are woefully under-represented in parliament and we aim to put that right by introducing a radically different system that doesn't discriminate against women, or any parents for that matter.

'Setting up mini regional parliaments across the UK will make government more family-friendly, will reconnect MPs with their constituents and end the London-centric political set-up.'

I stared out at the journalists who were either busily scribbling it all down in shorthand or staring at Sam with stunned and rather bemused expressions on their faces. Maybe the world wasn't ready for this. Maybe what had sounded radical to us around Sam's kitchen table was coming over as stark-raving mad out here in the real world.

Sam stopped and looked at me. I'd prepared my speech as instructed, but decided on the spur of the moment to ditch it and attempt to address the doubts which were clearly out there.

'We're the first to admit that we don't have all the answers,' I said. 'That's one of the things that makes us so refreshing. Our mummyfesto has been built with the help of women of all sorts of political persuasions all over the country. We've also pulled together lots of great ideas which various charities and pressure groups have put forward over recent years.

'We make no apologies for the fact that we want to revolutionise politics in this country. We aim to create a fairer society where wealth and power are more evenly distributed and where our most vulnerable citizens, rather than wealthy fat-cats, are our priority.'

I looked down the line at Anna. She grinned at me, ready to take up the baton.

'Our mummyfesto is also a living thing,' said Anna. 'What we'd like now is for people to get in touch with us through our website, Twitter and Facebook and tell us their ideas about how we can make the UK a better place for our children to grow up in.

'We're starting small with just the three of us, but we aim to grow organically. We want to hear from ordinary people who would like to stand for our party in the constituency they live in.

'We started out by successfully fighting to save the lollipop lady at our children's school. We know that there are hundreds, maybe thousands, of other women out there fighting for justice and what's right for their children, their families and their communities. We'd like them to join us and together we can make a real difference.'

Anna smiled and clasped her hands as she finished. I looked out at the faces of the journalists. The words dazed and bewildered came to mind. They didn't have a clue what to make of us. I couldn't help but smile too.

'Now,' said Sam, 'we're very happy to answer any questions you have.'

There was a slight pause before the first hand was raised.

'Michelle Wilson, *Huddersfield Examiner*. You have no political experience whatsoever. Why do you expect people to vote for you?'

I nudged Sam, keen to take this one. She nodded.

'Look at the mess the professional politicians with years of experience have made of it,' I said. 'All three main parties have had a go in recent years and they have all screwed up. People have nothing to lose in giving us a chance.'

'John Anderson, Radio Leeds. Are any men allowed to join your party?'

I looked at Sam and Anna. We all appeared to be sporting the same awkward expression. We'd never even discussed it. I felt so bloody stupid. I kicked Sam under the table, confident that she'd say the right thing.

'Of course,' she said. 'We're not excluding men from this at all; we're hoping lots of them will vote for us. And if any of them would like to support our campaign or stand as an MP we'd be delighted to hear from them.'

'Virginia Mason, *Halifax Courier*. I see you've got plans to privatise the Royal Family. How do you think the Queen is going to respond to that?'

Sam was straight in. 'Hopefully she'll see it as a way of increasing her income, without having to justify every penny she spends to the taxpayer. And her children have already demonstrated their entrepreneurial skills: Prince Charles charges more than three quid for a packet of his organic biscuits, and if they get stuck Prince Edward could start a *Royalty's Got Talent* TV show.'

There were a few more smiles from the hacks. I sensed we were winning them over.

'Aiden Kielty, Calendar News. Perhaps you'd like to explain why you intend to actively encourage skipping?'

'I'd be delighted to,' I said. 'Would you like to step this way?' Everyone turned to face Mr Kielty, who I knew from watching the programme was game for anything. Sure enough he stepped forward, albeit somewhat gingerly.

'OK,' I said, 'just follow me. We'll go three times around the fountain. Don't look so worried. It'll make great television.' The main thought that crossed my mind as we skipped merrily around the fountain was that I wished I'd worn a sports bra for the occasion. Not that I had a sports bra because the only exercise I did was swimming, but I made a mental note to pick one up the next time I was in M & S.

We were given a round of applause at the end. Mr Kielty took a bow. I did my best with a curtsey.

'See,' I said. 'Our policies are guaranteed to put a smile on everyone's faces. And what other political party can say that?'

It was getting dark by the time I got back to Mum's. The curtains were drawn, which meant a carer must have been. She never did them herself now. I let myself in and called out, 'Hello, Mum. It's me, Jackie.' There was no reply. I hurried through to the living room. She was sitting in her armchair, still in her nightie. I suspected the carer had decided it wasn't worth dressing her and had simply left her in it.

'Have you had your supper?' I asked.

Mum frowned. 'I don't know,' she said. I popped through to the kitchen to check. There was a plate and knife and fork on the draining board. The carer had at least washed up after her.

'It's OK,' I said, going back in to her. 'You've had it.'

'What were it?' she asked.

'I don't know, Mum.'

Her face crumpled. I thought for a moment she was going to cry.

'Did you enjoy film?' I asked.

'What film?'

'*Hello Dolly*. I left you watching it this afternoon.'

'No,' she said, shaking her head. 'I haven't watched that since Deborah were little.'

I nodded, walked over to the TV, pressed eject on the recorder and put the DVD back in its case without saying another word.

15

ANNA

It was surreal, watching it all on TV later; as if I were having some kind of out-of-body experience, hovering above someone who looked like me and sounded like me but couldn't possibly actually be me.

Only the presence of my children, piled on to the sofa next to me and shouting in turn, 'Mummy's on the telly', 'Oh my God' and 'Get in', indicated that it was indeed me we were all watching.

We saw it on Calendar first, complete with Jackie's skipping, then turned over to see it all again on *Look North*, minus the skipping, of course, as they clearly didn't want to showcase their rival reporter's star turn. I was still getting my breath back and trying to take it all in when my mobile rang. Sam's number was on the display. Although, to be fair, 'screaming, hysterical woman' would have been more accurate.

'Turn back to ITV,' she shouted, above a cacophony at her end. 'We're going to be on the national news.'

She put the phone down before I could say anything. I reached for the remote and pressed 3.

'What are you doing?' David asked. He had been standing quietly in the doorway all this time, seemingly interested enough to want to watch, but not supportive enough to join the rest of us on the sofa.

'That was Sam,' I said. 'It's going to be on the national news as well. She said they trailed it at the beginning.'

David looked at me as if I had been caught in flagrante with Nick Clegg. I wasn't sure whether it was me he was disgusted at, or simply a world where people could graft hard all their life and never get any further than first base, not because they weren't any good but because they didn't have whatever it took to capture the media's attention.

I shrugged. What did he expect? I could hardly offer an apology. He remained in the doorway, resolutely refusing to join us, but equally unwilling or unable to go the other way. An old-school Liberal Democrat if ever there was one.

We were the 'And Finally' piece on ITN. The introduction was bordering on the patronising and they didn't mention many of our most serious policies, but I was past caring. We were out there. Our policies were out there. And raising a few eyebrows too, no doubt.

'Are you famous now?' Esme asked, when it had finished.

I smiled and hesitated before answering, aware that David was in earshot.

'Being on the news once doesn't make you famous, love.'

'But you weren't on once,' said Esme. 'You were on three times in a row.'

'And one of those was the national news,' chipped in Charlotte, who despite being thirteen, couldn't disguise the fact that she was more than a little impressed with her mother's performance. 'Everyone in the country saw this one.'

'What, even the Queen?' asked Esme.

'Yes, she might have.' I smiled. 'Although I suspect she watches the BBC news. I don't think she'd like the adverts.'

'But if she did, she won't be very happy because Mum's going to abolish her,' said Will, his legs sprawled over the arm of the sofa. 'She'll probably send her to the Tower.'

'Will,' I said.

'The Blackpool tower?' asked Esme.

'No, love. Don't worry about it, Will was only joking.'

'Wait till Esme finds out you're ditching party bags too,' Will whispered into my left ear, 'then you really will be for it.'

I smiled at him and got up to go into the kitchen.

'Any chance of getting some tea tonight then?' asked David. 'Or is that not included in your manifesto?' He said it with a half-smile on his face which meant I had to treat it as an attempt at humour rather than being patronising.

'The enchiladas will be about five minutes,' I said. 'It's called multi-tasking and yes, it's in the mummyfesto.' I said it with a half-smile on my face too. So he couldn't accuse me of sarcasm.

My laptop was still on the kitchen table. I decided to have a quick check on Twitter before I packed it away. I wanted to know if the exposure had brought in some new followers for the Lollipop Party. I was thinking maybe fifty or sixty. A hundred if we were lucky. I was not thinking 3,782. Neither was I expecting to see mummyfesto trending. I was still scrolling down all the @mummyfesto tweets five minutes later when a combination of hunger and the smell of enchiladas brought first Will, Charlotte and finally Esme into the kitchen.

'We're trending,' I said, looking up at them with barely concealed glee. 'Mummyfesto is trending on Twitter.'

'Woo-hoo,' said Will. 'My mum's bigger than Justin Bieber.'

'Who's Justin Bieber?' asked Esme, at which point I gave thanks that we lived in one of the few places in the country where a seven-year-old girl wouldn't know that.

'He's a so-called singer from Canada with rubbish hair and like, really cheesy songs who, for some unknown reason, is fancied by loads of twelve-year-old girls,' explained Charlotte. Esme looked suitably bewildered. I was pleasantly surprised to find Charlotte that opinion-ated about anything.

'And he's got twenty-odd million followers on Twitter,' I added, 'so I'm not bigger than him really.'

'But right this minute, you're trending and he's not,' said Will. 'Therefore you own him.'

David walked into the kitchen.

'Mummy's trendy and she owns Justin Bieber,' announced Esme.

David stared at me blankly.

'I'll explain later,' I said, closing the lid of the laptop. 'It's not important.'

By the time I arrived at school the next morning it had all gone seriously crazy. I was practically mobbed by parents stopping me outside the school gates and promising to vote for us. Jackie arrived with Alice a few minutes later and had to fight her way through to me. 'Quick, there,' she said, pointing to a baby in a buggy, 'you'd better start kissing them if you want to get elected.'

I smiled at her. A great big 'I can't believe this is happening to us' smile. Alice and Esme ran off together into the playground.

'We've got more than ten thousand followers on Twitter,' I said.

'That's incredible,' said Jackie. 'Actually, I have no idea if it's incredible or not but I guess you wouldn't have told me if it wasn't.'

'Well, I only set the account up on Sunday so it's not bad going in forty-eight hours. We've had five hundred people join as party members, too, so that's ten grand in the kitty. And lots of people wanting to stand for us in the election.'

'Fucking hell,' said Jackie, very quietly, of course, given our location.

'I know,' I said. 'It's more than a bit scary, isn't it?'

At that point we spotted Sam coming up the hill, or rather we spotted Oscar, who had a skull and crossbones flying from his wheelchair, was wearing a massive home-made pirate hat and shouting 'School ahoy' at the top of his voice. Zach was walking a few steps behind, brandishing a telescope. Sam herself was wearing her purple hat and scarf and sporting a smile so wide it was in danger of sprouting wings and flying off her face altogether.

'Woo-hoo,' she shouted from across the road. All the parents turned to look and started cheering. I'd never felt anything quite like it. This sense that we had been unleashed on an unsuspecting nation and anything was now possible.

'So,' said Jackie, when at last Sam reached us, 'world domination beckons, I guess.'

'What, for Pirate Oscar here?' She smiled. Oscar did a disturbingly convincing pirate laugh.

'I saw you skipping on telly,' Oscar said to Jackie, with a giggle.

'And I bet you're laughing because you think I'm a rubbish skipper and you can do better than me,' replied Jackie. She clapped her hand over her mouth as soon as she said it.

'It's OK,' said Sam.

'Yeah,' said Oscar. 'I *can* skip better than you.' He zig-zagged across the playground in his wheelchair. Zach dutifully skipping along behind. The other kids started joining it. A few minutes later half the school was skipping along behind Oscar around the playground.

'See,' said Sam. 'Now look what you've started.'

'I'm sorry,' said Jackie. 'I don't have size seven feet for nothing, you know.'

'Don't worry,' said Sam. 'I like the fact that people forget there are things he can't do. I wouldn't want it any other way.'

Jackie put her thumb up in the air as Oscar 'skipped' past.

'So, have you looked at Twitter this morning?' I asked, turning to Sam.

'Yep. This is only the start though. It can only get bigger.'

'So what do we do next?' asked Jackie.

'We need to have a meeting,' said Sam. 'How about tonight at my place?'

'Sorry,' I said. 'I can't do tonight. David's got a town council meeting.'

'You should tell him you've got bigger fish to fry,' said Jackie. She meant it jokily. I knew that. Only I couldn't think of anything particularly jokey I could say in return. I looked down at my feet.

'Tomorrow, then,' said Sam quickly. I nodded. Jackie nodded too.

'I'll chase up the companies I approached about donations,' I said. 'Maybe the publicity will spur them into action.

'Good stuff,' said Sam. 'If we've got people queuing up to stand we need to work out how many candidates we can field.'

'Are you sure this isn't going to get too big for us to handle?' I asked.

Sam looked at me as if she couldn't quite believe what

she'd heard. 'Nothing,' she said, 'is going to be too big for us to handle.'

I could tell as soon as Charlotte got home that something else had happened. It was the way she was trying to appear less miserable than usual which gave it away.

That and the fact that I noticed the smell as soon as she came into the hallway.

'Oh, that's a bit pungent,' I said. 'You'd better slip your shoes off, I think you might have trodden in something.'

Charlotte did as she was told. She also put her violin case on the doormat and tried to walk past me in a crab-like fashion so I couldn't see her face.

'Hey,' I said. 'What's up?'

She mumbled something incomprehensible.

'Sorry?'

'I said it's not my shoes.'

'Well what is it?' She nodded towards her violin case. 'How did it get on that?' I asked. I knew, of course, as soon as the question passed my lips. It hadn't got on it at all. It had been put on it.

'At lunchtime,' she said quietly. 'I must have left my locker open. They took it out without me realising. Took it into town, I guess.'

'Oh Charlotte.' I held my arms out to her, she came to me without a fight. Emptied herself into my arms. Sobbing, shaking.

'I'm sorry,' she said eventually.

'It's not your fault.'

'No, I mean they took my violin out of the case. They've basically ruined it.'

I realised my hands were trembling. My whole body was pulsating inside, trying to repel the bad smell. And feeling increasingly sick.

'Did you tell anyone?'

'Only Mrs Partington. I had to explain why I couldn't do my lesson. Well, not really explain. Make something up about dropping it, I mean. I cleaned it best I could in the girls' loos, but I still can't get rid of the smell.'

I nodded slowly. 'I'm going to get this sorted first thing tomorrow morning,' I said, my voice on the edge of breaking. 'I want you to go upstairs, love, and get a shower and then I'm going to run you down to choir practice. I don't want you to worry about anything. Esme's gone to Alice's for tea and I'll put the case in the shed before she gets back so she won't need to know what's happened. And tomorrow, I'll go to school and get this whole thing sorted once and for all and we'll get your violin replaced, OK?'

She nodded. Muttered some thanks. She didn't even have enough left in her to protest. I hugged her to me. Told her I loved her. Watched her go upstairs like a disgraced puppy with her tail between her legs and vowed silently that I would never let anything happen to her again.

Sam sat at the head of the kitchen table, seemingly unable to speak for smiling.

'Will you tell us whatever it is you've got to tell us before you burst or do yourself an injury,' said Jackie.

Sam looked at us both in turn and took a deep breath, 'We've been asked to do some media appearances,' she said.

'Go on,' I replied.

'*Newsnight.*'

'Bloody hell!' said Jackie.

'And *Question Time.*'

'You're having us on,' said Jackie.

'Nope. And an alternative leadership debate on Radio 4, just for good measure.'

Jackie whooped a little and did a series of air punches. Sam laughed and grinned some more. And I sat there trying to take it all in. The first thing that went through my head was that David was going to hate me for this, not having ever made it past the *Hebden Bridge Times*. And the second thing was that I was going to have to leave Charlotte while I went down to London.

'Are you OK?' It was Sam who was asking. I realised I had been sitting there silently while they had been staring at me.

'Me? Yes, sorry. I was miles away.'

'What's up? You don't seem very pleased.'

I sighed. I hadn't wanted to mention it, more because I couldn't trust myself to stay composed while I told them rather than a desire to keep it to myself. And I hated crying in front of Sam. Always felt so bloody ungrateful.

'It's this whole thing with Charlotte,' I said. 'She had

dog shit smeared all over her violin today. She's in a bit of a state.'

'Oh Anna,' said Sam. 'That's awful. How could anyone do that to her? I just don't understand.'

I shrugged. 'I'm not sure I do either. All I know is that it's got to stop. I'm going to see Freeman first thing in the morning.'

'Sorry,' said Jackie, looking down at her hands.

'It's not your fault.'

'It's my bloody school, though. I'm embarrassed just thinking about it. If Freeman doesn't do something about this he wants shooting.'

'He won't have any choice this time,' I said.

'Well, if there's anything I can do to help, inside information, whatever, just let me know, OK?'

I nodded.

'Are you sure you're up to doing this tonight?' asked Sam.

'Yes, absolutely. It's good to have something to take my mind off it, to be honest. And to get out of the house.'

Sam and Jackie nodded. None of us said anything for a moment.

'Anyway,' I said, 'you were saying about the TV stuff. When are they?

'*Newsnight*'s next Monday,' said Sam, 'they're having a debate about new-style politics, *Question Time*'s next Thursday and Radio 4 on the Friday morning. I say we do one each. Anyone got any preferences?'

I racked my brain, trying to remember if David had any

council meetings next week. I was pretty sure he had something on Monday. I also knew that Radio 4 would be the least conspicuous of the three. And that it would give me longer to get things sorted with Charlotte before I had to go away overnight.

'I'll do Radio 4,' I said. 'If that's OK with everyone.'

'Fine by me,' said Sam. 'Jackie, I think you'd be great on *Question Time*.'

'I think I'd be the token crazy woman with big earrings who didn't have a clue what she was talking about.'

'You'd be brilliant,' I said, backing Sam up.

'Did they say who else is going to be on?' asked Jackie.

'No. It's in Leeds, though. So I guess a few Yorkshire MPs.'

'Oh God! It'll probably be Galloway. He'll be trying to get me to tickle him under his chin.'

'And you'll eat him alive,' said Sam, 'which would be great television.'

'I'll do it as long as you both promise not to sack me if I'm an embarrassment to the Party.'

'Deal. And you won't be,' said Sam. 'You'll be fantastic.'

'So you get Paxman,' I said to Sam. 'Are you sure it's going to be OK for you to go down to London? With Oscar, I mean.'

'Yeah. Rob will be fine with him. They'll have a boys' bonding session and probably pizza for breakfast, dinner and tea, but they'll survive.'

'And Rob won't mind?' I asked.

'No. He'll be fine. He'll enjoy it, actually.'

I nodded. Wishing I felt that confident about David's reaction.

'Well,' I said, 'if we're going to be a serious Party it's a bit of luck we've got some serious funding.' The others turned to look at me. 'See, I can keep a secret too, you know.' I smiled.

'What? Who? How much?' asked Sam, jumping up and down on her chair.

'We've got fifty companies willing to sponsor a candidate which will bring in twenty-five grand. Not massive high-street chains. Smaller companies, mainly based online and mainly run by mums. A lot of them selling ethically produced children's wear or toys, cloth nappies and eco-friendly baby products, that sort of stuff. In return they get a link to their website on our website.'

Sam leapt up and flung her arms around me. 'You're a genius,' she said. 'Remind me to make you business secretary when we get in.'

'That's fantastic,' said Jackie. 'All we need now are some candidates.'

'Oh, we've got a lot of those too,' I said, opening up my laptop. 'Over eighty at the last count. All of them with something particular they want to fight for or some kind of campaign they're running. I'll email them all to you, but there's one in particular I want to read to you.'

I scrolled down to the email I'd read that morning, the one that had got me off to a weepy start to the day. 'It's from a woman in Leicester,' I said. 'Her name's Karen. This is what she said: *My son James has a serious disability and needs a major operation on his spine as the metal rods he had inserted when he was younger are now preventing him from growing properly.*

'"*We had been on the waiting list for a long time, then in January the number of children's IT beds in the unit was cut from ten to four. A date came through for his op, but it was cancelled. They rescheduled for a month later. The day before the op I received a phone call to say it was being cancelled again as a little girl who had already had her op cancelled five times needed the bed.*

'"*When I told James he turned pale and was quiet for a moment. Then he turned to me and said, 'I'm not important, am I?'*

'"*I, of course, reassured him that he was. But what he said broke my heart because I knew deep down that he was right. In this country he's not important and nor are any of the other children whose operations are cancelled every day. If they were, they wouldn't be cancelled, would they? We wouldn't put one single child through that extra trauma. It's as simple as that.*"'

My voice caught as I finished reading. I looked up. Sam had tears streaming down her face. Jackie was fumbling in her bag for a tissue to blow her nose. No one said anything for a bit.

'That's why we've got to do this,' said Sam, wiping her cheeks with the back of her hand. 'Because she's right. Children like James are important. At least they bloody well should be. I want her to stand for us. I want her to bloody get in as well.'

'Well, let's tell her she's in,' I said. 'We'll go through the rest of them later. We should probably skype everyone who looks like a contender. Make sure they're genuine and sound like they've got what it takes. Then we can sort out membership and put them in touch with other candidates in their region. Then they can support each other.'

'Good idea,' said Jackie. 'Let's tell Karen we're going to add it to the mummyfesto as well. No child should have their operation cancelled within a week of the op. And if it's cancelled before that the hospital has to guarantee that it will not be cancelled again.'

'Agreed,' said Sam. 'It's in. Who else have we got?'

I ran through the list of prospective candidates: a mum who had launched a campaign against knife crime after her son was stabbed; a woman who was fighting for better treatment for her anorexic daughter; a woman who was trying to get legal aid to take a pharmaceutical company to court over the side effects her father had suffered after taking a prescription drug. The list went on, amazing women doing amazing things on their own. And now we were going to join them together, who knew what they could achieve.

'Any blokes?' asked Jackie.

'Why are you so interested?' asked Sam.

'Because I don't want people saying we're sexist and anti-men when we're not.'

'We've got a couple,' I said. 'A guy called Chris who runs a campaign group which is calling for an end to male violence against women.'

'Great, he's on the list,' said Sam. 'Who else?'

'A chap called Boris who is calling for family cycle lanes for safer commuting in London.'

Jackie snorted a laugh. I looked up. Sam was also smiling.

'What?' I asked.

'I think you'll find that one is a wind-up,' said Jackie. 'From a Mr B. Johnson of Oxfordshire, I presume.'

I smiled and shook my head. 'Well, it's good to see we've got the opposition worried, isn't it?'

David looked up when I walked in later on.

'Oh,' he said. 'I was hoping it was Will.'

'He's still not back?'

'No. Obviously not.'

I raised my eyebrows, but stopped myself from saying anything. I went into the kitchen to check the calendar before going back to David.

'Are you OK to hold the fort next Thursday night?' I asked.

'Another meeting?'

'No. I mean all night. I've been asked to go on an alternative leadership debate on Radio 4 on Friday morning. I'll have to go down to London the night before.'

David stared at me. It was a moment or two before he spoke. 'Can't one of the others do it?'

'They're doing *Newsnight* and *Question Time*.'

'Fucking hell!'

'Do you have a problem with that?'

'Would it make any difference if I did?'

'Look, I know it's a bit sudden ...'

'Sudden? Meteoric more like. I can't believe they're all taking you seriously.'

'Thanks,' I said and walked out of the room.

I'd wanted to tell him about Charlotte. To share the pain of what was happening to our daughter. To ask him what he thought we should do. But he wasn't there for me. He hadn't been for a long time. I was to all intents and purposes a single mother who just happened to live with the father of her children.

I heard the key in the door. I went out into the hall. I could smell cigarettes on Will's clothes. At least I hoped it was just cigarettes.

'Did you know about what happened today with Charlotte?'

He appeared surprised to be challenged about something to do with his sister rather than the time he'd chosen to roll home and the company he'd been keeping.

'No,' he said. 'What have they done now?'

'Dipped her violin in dog's mess, smeared it over her case.'

Will's eyes grew darker, his jaw set hard. 'They are bang out of order,' he said. 'If I had my way—'

'I don't want you to touch them,' I said. 'I'm going to see the Head tomorrow morning to put a stop to it, but I'd like you to keep an eye on her for me, at least at break and lunchtime. And if anyone still finds it amusing I hope you'll find a suitable riposte to wipe the smile off their faces.'

'Sure,' he said. 'Leave it with me.'

*   *   *

'Mrs Sugden, I don't think you've got an appointment,' Freeman's secretary said, as I strode past her towards his office.

'It's OK,' I said. 'I don't need one, thank you. This won't take long at all.'

I went straight in without knocking. Freeman was on his computer. I couldn't see the screen, but I guessed from the expression on his face that it was probably something he shouldn't have been looking at.

'What the hell is going on?'

'That's exactly what I was going to ask, Mr Freeman. Because my daughter came home in tears yesterday having had her violin and its case smeared in dog faeces by some of your pupils. They stole it from her locker and took it off the premises at lunchtime. Here are the girls' names,' I said, handing him a piece of paper from my trenchcoat pocket.

Freeman looked up at me. 'And you have evidence of this, do you?'

'Oh yes,' I said, plonking the bin bag containing Charlotte's violin and case, on his desk. 'This is exhibit one and I'm sure you'll find plenty of pictures of the culprits on your CCTV pictures, and probably those on the high street as well.

'Now, obviously you could take strong immediate action against those concerned or we can simply go straight to the police with this matter. I'm sure you'll make the right decision, Mr Freeman. And if you don't, I feel it's only fair to let you know that I and my colleagues in the Lollipop

Party will be appearing on Radio 4, *Newsnight* and *Question Time* in the coming week and will have no hesitation in raising the issue of bullying at this school at a national level.

'Oh, and we expect Charlotte's violin and case to be replaced by the school by Friday. Whether that's paid for by the culprits' parents or the school is up to you.

'Finally, by the time we come back to school after the Easter break, I expect to see the anti-bullying strategy actually being implemented across the whole school. Thank you, I'll see myself out.'

I turned on my heel and strode out of his office and past his secretary, who still appeared to be in a state of shock. The adrenalin was still surging through me, my primeval desire to protect my offspring flashing red. I wished I hadn't needed to do it, wished Charlotte hadn't had to suffer the indignity of the previous day, but maybe sometimes things needed to get worse before they could get better.

16

SAM

Millie from next door stood forlornly at our front gate. She was six going on sixty. This, coupled with the fact that she spoke in a broad west Yorkshire accent and her knee-high school socks were invariably around her ankles, always made me think she should have been an extra on *Last of the Summer Wine*.

'Mummy's run over Easter bunny so there'll be no eggs this year.'

'Oh,' I said, trying hard not to laugh. 'That's a shame.' I couldn't help thinking Millie's mum, Caz, could teach the government a lesson or two about how to dress up the cutbacks as a tragic accident. 'I tell you what,' I continued. 'We'll be having a little Easter egg hunt next weekend. Why don't you come and join in that?'

'Will they be real eggs?'

'No, little chocolate ones wrapped in foil.'

'Yeah, I will then if they're chocolate. I don't like real eggs. Not unless they're in cakes.'

I nodded and smiled. 'Would you like to come in and play with Oscar?'

'What's he doing?' she asked, watching him intently as he chalked on the easel in the garden.

'I'm drawing a picture of Jesus dying on the cross,' he replied, very matter of fact as he added what appeared to be spurts of blood flying out everywhere. Clearly the school's efforts to relate the Easter story had left a lasting impression.

Millie turned to me with a solemn expression on her face. 'There's summat I want to know about Jesus and the cross,' she said.

'OK,' I replied, bracing myself for an awkward question.

'Well, where did they get all the nails from?'

I tried very hard to keep a straight face. Clearly this had been troubling her. I was glad Rob was at the studio because I was quite sure he would have told her 'B & Q'.

'That's a good question, Millie,' I said. 'Only I'm afraid I don't know the answer. Maybe you should ask your teacher at school.'

Millie looked at me with a frown, seemingly disappointed that I should have reached adulthood without knowing the answer to such questions.

'It's only a story anyway,' said Zach, who until that point had been sitting quietly on the front step with his head in an astronomy book. 'Jesus wasn't real. Like God isn't real.'

'What makes you say that, love?' I asked.

'Well, you and Daddy don't believe in God.'

'No. But we've always told you that you're to make your own mind up about what you believe in.'

'And I have,' said Zach.

'Can I go and play indoors with Millie?' asked Oscar, cleared bored with the philosophical nature of the debate.

'Of course you can, love. If that's OK with Millie.'

'Yeah. May as well. Nowt to do out here,' she said.

Oscar manoeuvred his chair to the foot of the ramp.

'How many buses are you jumping over this time?' I asked.

'Twenty-five,' he replied. 'It'll be a new world record.'

Oscar managed to get himself to the top and I stood behind him to watch him over the drop.

'Woo-hoo,' I said. 'Didn't even touch them.' Millie, who had seen it all before countless times, followed him in.

Zach sat back down on the step again with his book. He opened it then shut it again and looked up at me. 'I know there's not a God,' he said, 'because if there was one, Oscar's muscles would work properly, wouldn't they?'

I sat down on the step next to him and gave him a hug. Letting his pain seep into me and join mine.

'If it's a birthday party, does that mean there's going to be cake?' asked Oscar.

'Let's wait and see,' I replied as we pulled off the cobbles on to the main road.

'You must know,' said Zach, 'you helped to organise it.' You really couldn't get anything past him.

'OK, there's going to be a huge great birthday cake in the shape of a number two with icing and everything.'

'Can I blow the candle out?' asked Oscar.

'Sorry, love, we've already chosen a little girl to do that. Her name's Amelia. It's her birthday today as well, you see. And she's also going to be two.'

'Is she going to die soon?' asked Oscar.

He wasn't being nasty. He understood what the hospice was about. 'She's got liver disease, love. She needs a new liver because her own one doesn't work properly. She's on the list for a transplant. That means if someone else dies and their family donates the liver, Amelia could have it put into her and get well again.'

I could almost hear the cogs going around in Oscar's head. The fault-lines had appeared in my heart before he even said it.

'They don't do leg transplants, do they?' he asked.

'No, love,' I said, trying hard to stop my voice from cracking. 'I'm afraid not.' I glanced over at Rob. He pretended to be concentrating on driving, but I knew he wasn't. I knew he was hurting every bit as much as I was. I only wished he could find some way to show it.

It was only the third time he'd been to the hospice. He usually found some reason to get out of it, but he knew how much today meant to me. Besides which Oscar had insisted he come because it was 'a family day out' and he was part of the family.

The roads were quiet, even the Ainley Top roundabout, suggesting lots of people had already got away for the

Easter holidays. When we pulled into the car park in Huddersfield we were clearly amongst the first ones there.

Rob went around to the back of the people carrier, opened the door and started unclipping the various belts which secured Oscar's chair. Zach climbed down from his seat next to Oscar and ran around the back to help me with the ramp and the winch.

'Ready for take-off,' shouted Oscar.

'Chocks away,' I replied.

It was a well-rehearsed routine, but fortunately one that Oscar never tired of. Nor did he tire of coming here. The way he gazed around at the specially adapted playground in awe made me wonder what he'd be like if we ever saved up enough money to take him to EuroDisney.

'Can I have a go on the roundabout before we go in?' Oscar asked.

'Go on then,' I said. 'Zach will come with you.' He didn't need asking either. He was already running over to the roundabout. I watched them. My boys playing together at a playground. Taking turns, arguing over what to go on next. Like brothers should. Only it was all too rare to see it.

'Are you OK?' I asked Rob.

'Yeah, fine. Bit big for the swings, that's all.'

'They like it here.'

'Yeah. I can see that.'

'It's good for Zach, too. When they can play together like this.'

He nodded.

'It'll be fine, you know. Inside I mean. It's a party, remember. Everyone's going to be happy.'

'I know.'

'I appreciate you coming, anyway.'

He nodded. Managed a bit of a smile. 'Not often we get the chance to spend an afternoon together, is it?' he said.

'No, I guess not. Anyway, look, I'd better go in and see if there's anything I can do to help. You can let them play for a while longer if you like. It doesn't start until two.'

'OK. We'll see you in there.'

I waved to Oscar and Zach as I made my way across the courtyard and into the main building. Simon was wandering around in the foyer smiling at nothing in particular and fiddling with the buttons on his suit.

'Nibbles,' I said.

'Sorry?'

'You could always put the nibbles out if you're stuck for something to do.'

'Er, right, yes. Thanks, Sam. Actually, I'd better go and run through my speech again.'

I smiled at him. Simon didn't do practical. But at least I'd stopped him wearing the floor out.

I walked along the corridor to Marie's office and stuck my head around the door. 'Oi, you,' I said, catching sight of her at the computer. 'This is a party, you're not supposed to be working.'

'Rotas won't wait for owt,' she said.

'Well at least come down for the cake-cutting,' I said.

'I think Simon's going to need a bit of moral support for the speech.'

'OK, but I shan't stop long. You know parties aren't my thing.' I nodded. I suspected she didn't even approve of the party taking place, what with finances being so tight.

'It'll be good for everyone, you know, to be reminded of how much we've done. Why we're all here. Why no one should try and take a single penny away from us.'

'Yeah, I guess so,' she said, still sounding unconvinced.

'Right, well I'd better go and do my meet-and-greet bit. See you for the cake.'

I made my way back down to the foyer, someone had put the nibbles out. It was a safe bet it wasn't Simon.

It was only as I stood amongst the assembled guests later, waiting for Simon's speech that the enormity of it all hit me. All these people whose stories I knew, some with their children, some whose children were no longer here, but all of them a part of this place. Not just because of their children's names carved in glass bricks in the memorial wall, but because of the love which had cemented the whole thing together. The love that supported people, held them up when they were in danger of falling and propelled them through the next second, minute, hour of a day they hadn't thought they would be able to bear.

I swallowed hard. It was impossible to believe that just over two years ago this place hadn't even existed. Had all these people really come through our doors only in the past twenty-four months? So many precious moments: of a step forward, a breath taken, a smile to be remembered. And it begged the question what would they have done without us? And what would the next round of parents do if we were no longer here?

I glanced down at Zach and Oscar who were deep in conversation about the exact size of the piece of cake they would be having. I felt it more keenly than ever. The fact that I was lucky to have them. I was so aware that although this was a celebration of Sunbeams' first two years, there were many people here today who would find it difficult to celebrate. Who would smile and raise a glass for us, but who inside were still full of hurt and loss and grief.

Simon stepped up onto a small podium and called for hush. 'I can't tell you how good it is to see so many friends here today,' he began. Despite his nerves he was a good speaker. His words were full of warmth and comfort, shared hopes and shared heartache. I let them wash over me, tuning out at the parts which I knew would push me close to the edge, allowing them to penetrate again only when I was sure I was strong enough to hear them.

I glanced at Rob. He was staring very hard at a picture on the far wall. His face expressionless. Perhaps not realising how much that gave away to me.

'When are we going to have the cake?' Oscar whispered.

'Very soon,' I said. 'You're doing really well.'

At the end of the speech the cake was brought out and Amelia's father carried her forward in his arms. Clearly she was no longer strong enough to be able to walk. A cheer went up as her father helped her cut the first slice.

I caught Rob's eye as I turned around. He tried very hard to smile, but he simply couldn't.

It turned out *Newsnight* didn't need me to go down to London, only to the BBC studio in Leeds. Which was just as well, as Zach had been particularly clingy since the hospice party. And whilst I was disappointed not to get the chance to meet Paxman in person, it at least got me out of having to tell the boys I wouldn't be there in the morning. I'd never actually spent a night away from them. Quite a few people seemed to think that was weird – although admittedly most of those people didn't have a child with a disability to care for. The fact was if I went away and anything happened to Oscar I would never forgive myself. And I wasn't sure Zach would forgive me either. So I stayed.

The taxi arrived at the end of the road. I half expected Jackie to be outside taking a photo, she'd been that excited when I told her they were sending a cab for me.

'Right, I'd better be off then,' I said. I bent down and kissed Zach, who had been given special permission to stay up late to say goodbye.

'Don't forget to tell them I came up with the name the Lollipop Party.'

'I'll do my best.' I smiled.

'And see if you can sell him one of my pictures or at least mention the name of my exhibition while you're at it,' said Rob with a smile. I pulled a suitable face.

'Text me afterwards and let me know if I came over like a blithering idiot, OK?'

'I will, but you won't,' he said. 'An opinionated, unhinged woman from Hebden Bridge maybe, but not a blithering idiot.'

'Thank you,' I said, kissing him. 'Although I'm not sure what for.'

I sat in the reception area at the BBC studio wondering if that was the description of me they'd put up under my name on the screen 'opinionated, unhinged woman from Hebden Bridge'.

When I'd spoken to the researcher on the phone he'd given me a Paxmanesque grilling, I presume to try to establish whether I was a complete fruitloop or actually had something useful to contribute. I hoped the fact that I was here meant it was the latter, but I still wasn't entirely sure.

I looked up at the large TV screen. The ten o'clock news was just about to finish. I didn't understand why they hadn't come to get me. Maybe they'd forgotten all about me. I'd go down in the history as the 'nearly woman', the one who would have been elected had she not been left sitting in a foyer with a cup of coffee while the big debate took place without her.

'Hi.' The bubbly young woman who had got me the coffee poked her head back round the door. 'Do you want to come through now?'

I was ushered into what could only be described as a large cupboard. In it were a stool, a television camera and a rail of jazzy ties.

'They're the weatherman's,' the woman (whose name was Lisa or Laura, I couldn't quite remember) said. 'This is where he usually does his weather reports.'

'Right,' I said, perching myself rather precariously on the stool. I remembered Jackie saying that such things were designed for men with small arses and made a mental note to add '*stools for women*' to the mummyfesto.

I looked around for a TV monitor but couldn't find one. 'How do I see what's going on?' I asked.

'We've found it's best not to have a monitor,' she said. 'It's too distracting for the guests. If you just look directly into the camera that'll be great.'

I nodded. So although to the nation I'd be taking part in a television debate, actually I'd be playing blind man's buff in a glorified broom cupboard. I understood now why the people in the link-ups on *Newsnight* always looked so dazed and confused. They also tended to have a live TV feed of some iconic national monument behind them. Presumably to make the viewer think, 'Ah, the Acropolis, it must be Athens.' I wondered if they'd have live pictures of someone throwing up outside a Leeds nightclub behind me.

'I'll just fix the earpiece in. They can be a bit fiddly, but try not to touch it once it's on, it doesn't look good on screen.' I now had a vision of myself blind and partially deaf going into battle with Paxman. I half expected them to give me a gobstopper as well, just for good measure.

I glanced up and caught her looking at my nose-stud. Presumably they didn't have many of those on *Newsnight*.

For a second I thought she was going to ask me to take it out in case in interfered with the sound quality.

'OK,' she said. 'You're all set. The producer will speak to you in a moment just to check the sound levels and when the red light comes on we're on air.'

I nodded and sat there, probably looking as if I were about to go to the gallows, as that was what I felt like. The producer did indeed speak into my ear, telling me they were going to have the main story of the day from the Leveson Inquiry and then come to the 'Is there an alternative to mainstream politics?' debate, which is when Jeremy would come to me.

I sat there rigid as Paxman introduced us. I wasn't sure whether to smile, do that nodding acknowledgement thing or stare straight ahead and try to look serious and intelligent. I tried a combination of all three and suspected I looked as if I had something wrong with me.

The Health Secretary was in the studio, representing the government and mainstream politics, they also had a young man from UK Uncut, whom they introduced only by his first name – he being clearly too radical to have a surname – as well as a professor of politics from Warwick University. And me, the token northerner, sitting in a glorified broom cupboard awaiting public humiliation on national TV.

'Is mainstream politics already dead or merely in need of lifesaving surgery?' I heard Paxman ask in my earpiece. I panicked. I had no idea if he was talking to me or not. For all I knew my face could be live on screen, the nation waiting with baited breath for me to open my mouth and say something. Ideally something mildly intelligent.

'I think it's already—' I started. But before I could go any further I heard them cut me off straight away and the politics professor answered instead. They hadn't been waiting for me at all. Which meant they now thought I was some jibbering idiot, butting in when it wasn't her turn, as well as a token crazy, nose-studded woman.

I listened as the debate in the studio intensified, not daring to say anything in case I was cut off again.

Finally, Paxman brought me in. 'So, Sam Farnell, why the hell should anyone take the Lollipop Party seriously?' The intonation in his voice as he said the 'Lollipop Party' made it sound like something out of an Enid Blyton story.

'Because we are the only party who put children and families at the heart of everything we do, hence the name, which, incidentally, was chosen by my seven-year-old son, Zach. We don't just pay lip-service to the putting-children-first thing, you see, we actually practise what we preach.'

'But with policies which include selling off the Houses of Parliament to set up some tin-pot regional parliaments across the UK, and letting a bunch of online mums who are more used to debating potty-training scrutinise government policy, you're clearly not going to be seen as a credible political force, are you?'

'Not compared with a London-centric system in which women are woefully under-represented and which excludes MPs from outside the capital from being with their children during the week, you mean. And where a bunch of unelected peers gets to veto the wishes of the electorate. Compared to that, I think we look damn credible, to be honest.'

'But how can you seriously expect people to vote for you when you've got no political experience whatsoever?'

'For that very reason,' I said. 'How often do you hear people say that all politicians are as bad as each other? There are forty-six million registered voters in the UK, you know and yet only twenty-six million of them voted for one of the three main parties at the last general election. That tells me that twenty million people out there are sick of politicians. Well, we're not politicians, that's the whole point. We are normal people who care about the same things they do and we're not in it for greed, or ego, or personal gain. We're simply doing it to try to make this country a better place for our families. For everyone's families.'

'It's all very well saying that,' said Paxman, 'but the reason normal people aren't running the country is because they don't have the expertise. What are your economic credentials for example?'

'Our households are all solvent,' I said. 'Despite the difficult economic climate, we are not in debt. Whereas successive governments have been.'

'She's got a point, hasn't she?' Paxman said, addressing the Health Secretary. 'The current system of government is anachronistic, out of touch with the modern electorate and regarded by them as a downright failure.'

'What we have in this country,' he replied, 'is a

democratic system that has served us well for centuries. If it ain't broke, why fix it?'

The guy from UK Uncut proceeded to tell Paxman exactly why the current system was broken. Even the politics professor admitted I had a point. I could tell by the tone in the Health Secretary's voice that he was clearly getting rattled.

'It's all very well coming up with radical reforms and crazy policies, but in the real world someone's got to pay for them and we happen to have been left with a huge amount of debt and a financial mess to clean up. We're taking the responsible course of action by making that our priority. That's real politics not playground politics.'

'Oh it's real politics,' I said, not even waiting to be brought in. 'And the victims of real politics are real children. Children like a little boy called James whose mum wrote to us this week. His major operation was cancelled with less than twenty-four hours' notice because beds in the IT unit he was in have been cut from ten to four since you got in. Do you know what James said when his mum told him? He said "I'm not important, am I?" And he's right you know. In your government's Britain he's not important. And nor are the children who come into the hospice where I work. Less than five per cent of our funding comes from your government and you're still going to cut our grant next year. That's why we came into politics and that's why we won't stop until things change. Because I can tell you that nothing is more important than a poorly or dying child. Absolutely nothing.'

There was a stunned silence at the other end of my earpiece. I put my arm down, realising I must have been jabbing my finger. I had an overwhelming sense that the Lollipop Party was not going to be belittled and ridiculed again.

The young woman was smiling as she took my earpiece off at the end.

'Was I OK?' I asked.

'No,' she said. 'You were bloody brilliant. I would have paid to watch that. I really would.'

'Thank you,' I said easing myself down from the stool, 'please make sure you vote for us then.'

'Do you know what?' she said. 'I think I will.'

I turned my phone on in the taxi on the way home. Jackie had texted me to say I had 'whipped their arses' and Anna to say that both I and the Lollipop Party were trending on Twitter.

Rob grinned at me as I let myself in. 'Well, turned out the crazy nose-studded, Hebden Bridge woman wasn't so crazy after all.'

I smiled at him. 'I'm just relieved to have survived, to be honest.'

'There is one thing I need to pick you up on, though. I'm afraid our household isn't actually solvent. We've gone a hundred quid overdrawn today. You're all right though, I won't tell the papers.'

I smiled at him again. A tired, apologetic smile this time. 'We'll be all right,' I said. 'I'm sure we'll be able to get straight after the election.'

'When we move to Downing Street, you mean?' It was the way Rob said it which took me back. And the way he looked at me with such a serious face.

'What do you mean by that?'

'I'm just concerned that your head is in cloud cuckoo land and at some point you're going to come crashing back down to earth with a bump.' I looked at him and shook my head.

'No,' I said. 'This is massive. And I think it's going to get even bigger.'

'Bit like our overdraft,' he replied.

'I can't stop this now. Even if I wanted to.'

Rob shrugged, as if he were already resigned to that fact. 'I know,' he said. 'That's what worries me.'

17

JACKIE

I stared down at the darkish-red discharge and felt the familiar wrenching and tearing deep inside me. It was stupid really. We'd just had a diagnosis of unexplained infertility after four years of trying and failing to conceive and yet for some reason I was still left inconsolable by the arrival of my next period. I wondered if there would ever be a time when it didn't have that effect on me, when its coming would be as predictable and unemotional as the passing of the seasons signalling another month crossed off on the calendar. Nothing more and nothing less than the relentless passage of time. Somehow, I doubted it ever would. Far more likely, I suspected, was that the monthly sense of loss would be with me right up to the point where there was no next period. When the loss was no longer temporary but a permanent ache, a constant grief that I would carry with me for the rest of my days.

I crept back into the bedroom. Paul had his eyes shut. I didn't think for a minute he had gone back to sleep though. I thought he had chosen to shut them to avoid the situation. He would have guessed from the length of time I was in the bathroom. That and the inbuilt copy of my menstrual calendar which he no doubt carried around with him. He knew he was on a loser if he so much as opened his mouth. He didn't feel it the way I did. We'd had the conversation enough times to establish that. And because he didn't feel it that way there was nothing he could say or do to make it better or make me feel he understood, because he didn't. I didn't hate him for it. It wasn't his fault. But sometimes I resented the fact that he got away so lightly. And it was hard to be OK about everything when you were resentful.

I slid back under the duvet next to him, knowing it would be only a matter of time before Alice woke and we were freed from this impasse.

'I meant what I said. I think we should wait,' said Paul, still with his eyes closed.

'Wait for what?' I asked, my eyes still fixed on the ceiling.

'I think we shouldn't make a decision about IVF until after election. It's a massive decision. Standing in a general election is a massive thing to do too. And situation with your mum is getting harder day by day. We do one thing at a time. Get election out of way first. See how we both feel after that. No promises, mind. I still don't want you to put yourself through it. I'm just saying let's not make a decision now when so much is up in air.'

I lay there, still staring at the ceiling, hardly daring to breathe. He wasn't saying yes, but neither was he saying no. Maybe it was just a delaying tactic. Maybe he was stalling for time. But the only thing that was worse than a tiny bit of hope was having no hope at all.

'OK,' I said. Paul opened one eye and turned his head to look at me.

'What do you mean "OK"?'

'Exactly that.'

'Bloody hell,' said Paul, throwing the duvet back and swinging his legs out of bed.

'What are you doing?'

'Going to get diary to write it in: "Won argument without Jackie saying a word t'other way."'

I smiled as he disappeared into the bathroom and stretched out on to his side of the bed, luxuriating in the extra space and starting to work out in my head exactly which day I was likely to be ovulating.

It was safe to say I was not a fan of board games. Actually, that was not true. Proper board games were fine: Scrabble, Monopoly and that thing called Coppit I played when I was a kid were of the first order. It was whoever had invented these ridiculous children's games that it took longer to set up than to actually play that I had it in for. Take Mouse Trap, for example. Where the hell was the fun in that? You needed a degree in engineering and patience to set it up and within a few seconds of doing so, some cocky sod – usually Paul – got to flush a pretend toilet and knock part of it down again. There was not an ounce of cunning or strategy involved. Just a quest for a poxy piece of plastic cheese. This probably explained why Mouse Trap was right at the bottom of the toy box in an 'Oh, what a shame we haven't got time to get to it tonight' position. Buckaroo, however, had somehow inexorably worked its way towards an accessible corner and into Alice's line of vision.

'Buckaroo,' she squealed, making a grab for it before I could move anything to cover the box. 'We haven't played this for ages.'

Paul appeared suitably amused. 'Great,' he said. 'Mummy will put it together for you. She really likes this one.'

I gave him the look he deserved, took the lid off the box and started trying to get the bucking bronco's hindlegs set down into the starting position. Five minutes later Paul, still with a smug grin on his face, asked if I wanted any help.

'It's OK,' I said. 'There's a knack to it. It's just fiddly, that's all.' I turned it round so the base was facing me and tried to do it from a different angle, bending my face down closer to it as I tried to force the legs into place.

'Please don't break it, Mummy,' said Alice. A second later the legs snapped in and the mule bucked, propelling the base into my face at point-blank range. I screamed as the pain shot through me and instinctively threw my hands up to cover my eyes.

Alice, who was never one to take such things calmly in her stride, screamed too and started shrieking, 'It's kicked Mummy's eye out. Quick, Daddy, do something.'

I heard Paul jump up and dash out of the room, returning a minute or two later. 'Here,' he said, 'I've got a warm flannel for you.' Quite how that would have helped if the mule really had kicked my eye out I wasn't sure, but at least he was trying. All I was thinking was, 'Please God, don't let me have to go to A & E.' If I needed stitches or my nose was broken I would end up on one of those lists they do of the top ten most stupid or embarrassing injuries people presented themselves with at A & E. My Buckaroo injury would be up there with men who'd had eye-watering accidents with their flies and kids who'd got their heads stuck in buckets. I was afraid to take my hand away in case there was blood – Alice was not at all good with blood – but she was shrieking so hysterically by now that I realised that unless I showed her otherwise, she really would think it had kicked my eye out. Gingerly, I lowered my hands and blinked open my eyes.

'It's all right, love. I'm OK,' I said, trying hard to smile at Alice, although I suspect it came out as more of a squint.

'No blood,' said Paul, bending down to take a closer look. 'And I don't think your nose is broken. You'd be screaming blue murder if it was.'

I breathed a sigh of relief that I would be spared the embarrassment of a hospital visit.

'It does look pretty nasty though and I expect you're going to have a shiner tomorrow.'

'Oh great,' I groaned, as the reality of a far greater embarrassment hit me. 'That's going to look wonderful on *Question Time*, isn't it?'

Paul put his head down and started laughing. I wanted to tell him he was a bastard, but I couldn't with Alice there.

'Why's Daddy laughing?' she asked.

'Mummy's going to be on television again tomorrow,' I said, 'and I expect I'll have a great big bruise on my face from playing Buckaroo.'

Alice smiled and started laughing too, I suspected more out of relief than anything.

'You'll have to tell them the donkey kicked you,' she said. 'He's a very naughty donkey, isn't he?'

'Yes,' I said, cursing the fact that he hadn't gone to the great donkey sanctuary in the sky, otherwise known as the Oxfam shop, a long time ago. 'A very naughty donkey indeed.'

'Fuck,' I said, sitting bolt upright in bed.

'What?' asked Paul, opening his eyes with a start.

'The Tooth Fairy,' I hissed. 'I haven't done the bloody Tooth Fairy.' I looked at the alarm clock. It was 7.30. Alice would wake up at any minute, she was like an alarm clock herself.

'Bloody hell. I thought it were summat serious,' Paul said with a yawn. 'Can't you say she got held up in traffic, or summat?'

'That,' I said as I leapt out of bed and threw on my dressing gown, 'is exactly why there wouldn't be a Father Christmas, Easter bunny or Tooth Fairy if men were left in charge.'

I raced downstairs, missing out the two creaking steps as I went, and started rummaging in my purse for a 50p piece. There wasn't one, of course. Nor was there one in Paul's wallet. The Tooth Fairy always left a 50p piece. She never asked for change and neither did she deposit a collection of silver and coppers. It just wasn't Tooth Fairy. In desperation I raided Alice's piggy bank and found one. I took it, feeling like the kind of sicko who steals charity collection boxes. It was no use replacing it with loose change, it was the 50p she got from the Tooth Fairy last time. And Alice was the sort of girl who knew exactly what she had in her piggy bank.

I then had to rummage around in the wrapping paper bag for some shiny gold paper and a piece of red ribbon, cursing Anna as I did so. It was she who had started all this fairy-scroll business. Esme, who'd been the first of Alice's friends to lose a tooth, had come to school proudly brandishing a beautiful miniature scroll with the neatest fairy-sized writing imaginable, thanking her for her tooth and telling stories of the far-off fairy kingdom she had come from. Sam and I had looked at Anna with a mixture of awe and loathing as we realised that such souvenirs would now be expected by our offspring for years to come. I'd managed five so far, none as impressive as Anna's, it had to be said, but all at least passable as fairy missives.

This was clearly going to be the exception.

Dear Alice, thanks for the tooth. Must fly, your Tooth Fairy. x

All of it written in the sort of slapdash handwriting that made it look like her particular Tooth Fairy had been on the alcopops all night.

Unable to find any ribbon, I tied it with an elastic band, ran back upstairs, crept into Alice's room and began the task of trying to remove Alice's tooth from under her pillow without waking her. It had long been a mystery to me why the MoD didn't target mums of seven-year-olds for their bomb-disposal work. If they were looking for a steady hand, precision timing and nerves of steel, we had it in bucketloads.

Alice, of course, was lying protectively over the very corner of the pillow she had slipped her tooth under, as if guarding it with her life. It was bad enough doing this at 11.30 at night when I knew she should be in a deep sleep; doing it at 7.40 in the morning, when I knew she would wake up at any second, was asking for trouble.

I had just managed to place the 50p and the scroll under her pillow when she stirred. Instinctively I dropped to the floor. I heard her rummaging about under the pillow and then the squeal. I knew what was coming next and there was only one solution. I slid myself under her bed, grateful that we had decided against the under-bed storage drawer. I saw her legs flip down and her footsteps shooting out of the bedroom as she shouted, 'She's been, Tooth Fairy's been.' I scrambled out from under the bed and tiptoed into the bathroom on the landing, flushed the toilet and strolled as casually as possible back into our bedroom.

'Mummy, look what Tooth Fairy has left' Alice smiled, holding up the 50p piece.

'That's great. Did she leave you a scroll too?'

'Yes, but it's not a very good one. And she forgot the fairydust.'

Paul gave me a suitably reproachful look as I walked around to climb back into bed. It was only now the emergency was over that I realised how sore my face was. Alice started giggling.

'What?' I said.

'Your face looks funny.' I glanced in the mirror on the chest of drawers and groaned as I saw the extent of the Buckaroo injury. And that was in the dim light of morning. It didn't bear thinking about what TV studio lights would do to it. David Dimbleby had no idea what he was letting himself in for.

The very fact that I was a panellist alongside Ed Balls, Baroness Warsi, Sir Patrick Stewart and Baroness Shirley Williams was surreal to say the least.

Two baronesses, a knight who was better known as Captain Jean-Luc Picard and a man named Balls who had been the former PM's right-hand man. It was a lot to get my head around. I suspected they had looked at the list of panellists and thought, 'Who the fuck is Jackie Crabtree?' Or a slightly more polite version of that, maybe. I could only presume George Galloway had been unavailable (perhaps a case of cat flu) as the token minority party representative, which was why it was me being shown into a side room in Bradford Cathedral and smiling awkwardly as I was introduced to the other panellists and David Dimblely himself. I wasn't sure if they smiled at me because they were being genuinely friendly or because they couldn't keep a straight face when they saw the state of mine. There was only so much that make-up could cover – and a whacking great bump on my nose and bruise under my eye were not among those things.

'I had an argument with a mule,' I said feebly. Dimbleby raised his eyebrows at me.

'Well I hope he came off worse,' said Balls.

'Let's just say he won't be bothering anyone again.'

Balls laughed. The rest of them nodded and turned away.

'We're just waiting for Sir Patrick,' said the assistant producer who had introduced me. I resisted the temptation to ask if the starship *Enterprise* had developed engine problems. Sam's last instructions to me had been not to make any *Star Trek* jokes.

'If you need the toilets you'll find them at the back of the cathedral. We'll be going on set in about ten minutes.'

I nodded and headed off in the direction of the loos, more to avoid any more embarrassing small talk with my fellow panellists than anything. It was only as I deposited my tampon in the bin provided and started rummaging around in my handbag for a replacement that it started to dawn on me that there may not be a spare one. I didn't usually use this bag, and despite the fact that you'd think someone nearing their fortieth birthday would be able to manage their own menstrual cycle, clearly it hadn't yet happened in my case.

'Shit,' I said out loud, at which point I worried that I would now be struck down from on high for blaspheming in the house of God. I stuck my head out of the cubicle and checked the walls for tampon machines. Nothing. Obviously the congregation were the type who were either too old to need them or were organised enough to bring their own. I briefly contemplated delving into the sanitary bin to try to fish my used one out before thinking better of it. Clearly there wasn't time to dash to the shops. There was nothing else for it, I was going to have to ask someone.

I walked back into the side room where I had been waiting. All the BBC people in the room were men. The only other women were Baroness Williams and Baroness Warsi. And I couldn't ask a Tory: Paul would never forgive me, even if I could forgive myself.

'Excuse me,' I whispered in Shirley Williams' ear. 'I'm very sorry to bother you with this but I'm having a bit of an emergency. You don't happen to have a spare tampon on you, do you?'

She looked at me over the top of her glasses, a bemused expression on her face. 'I'd love to help you, my dear, but I'm afraid when you get past eighty you don't tend to carry them about with you.'

I shut my eyes and waited for a hole to appear beneath my feet which would swallow me up and save me from the humiliation I had just brought on myself. It didn't.

'No, no, of course you wouldn't. I'm so sorry. I'm clearly not thinking straight. I do apologise.'

She smiled affably and I turned and shuffled away from her. There was nothing for it, I was going to have to ask the chair of the Tory Party for a tampon. She was at least a woman. And I was pretty sure she wasn't much older than me.

I tapped her on the shoulder and whispered into her ear. She looked at me with a mixture of pity and contempt.

'Let me have a look,' she said. A moment later she produced something from her bag and slipped it discreetly into my hand.

'Thank you,' I said. 'Thank you so much and I'm very sorry to have had to ask.' I was about to tell her I took back everything I'd ever said about the Tories, but I decided not to get myself into any more trouble. I dashed back to the toilets. She used a different brand to mine. For a second I wondered if the warning about toxic shock syndrome on all the leaflets might actually turn out to be Tory shock syndrome in my case and my body might reject it, as if it were an organ donated by an alien species. I took a deep breath and inserted it. We were it seemed, all the same on the inside after all.

Patrick Stewart had arrived by the time I got back and we were all hurried through on to the set. The audience clapped, more for him than anyone else I suspected.

I was going through the questions over and over in my head. My answers sounded fine to me, but I couldn't help thinking that once they left my mouth they would turn into utter drivel. I tried not to think about Anna and Sam watching at home, sure that they would both have made a better job of this than me. I did up and undid the button on my jacket twice before deciding to leave it open in case it looked as if it were pulling a bit. There was nothing worse than a woman stuffed into something a size too small for her. I was glad it was top half only and they couldn't see how tight my trousers were. Although it was a shame they were missing out on my shoes. They were bloody nice shoes.

I was pretty uncontroversial on the first couple of questions, which were about the economy and the euro. And then we got on to the one I'd been waiting for. The one about the youth unemployment figures.

'Jackie Crabtree,' said Dimbleby. 'How can we give our young people hope of finding a job in the current economic climate?'

'Well, the Lollipop Party would offer full employment to the under-twenty-fives,' I said. 'We'd create thousands of jobs by investing in public transport, manufacturing, green industries, more NHS staff, more social workers and more teachers. And for those who still didn't have a job we'd offer paid employment as community workers on the living wage rather than job seeker's allowance.

'It is a national scandal that so many people are essentially written off in the job market at such a young age and this government should be ashamed of its record.'

There was a loud round of applause from the audience. Even a few whoops. I tried not to look at Baroness Warsi, scared she might ask for her tampon back for insulting her party. She didn't. I relaxed a little, though not so much that my trouser button would pop.

I felt myself growing in confidence with each question. I even managed to forget about my face a little. At least until there was a question about domestic violence.

'I think I should make it clear at this point that my facial injuries were caused by an overenthusiastic game of Buckaroo last night. But for many people watching this, that will not be the case. Domestic violence has long been treated as a minority issue. Politicians pay lip-service to it, but nothing changes. The Lollipop Party will fund women's refuges throughout the country. We will also fund a national charity, based in the Calder Valley constituency, called the White Ribbon Campaign, which is working with boys and young men to bring about an end to male violence against women. We will pay for anti-domestic violence education at every school in the UK and we will not stop until it is eradicated. No other political party can match that because no other political party puts women and children first.'

My earrings were still swinging wildly as I finished speaking. There was a massive round of applause from the audience. When it finally died down Patrick Stewart reached across the table to shake my hand.

'I've waited for a long time to hear a politician say that,' he said. 'I don't know about anyone else, but I'm voting Lollipop.'

'May the force be with you.' I grinned. And regretted

it immediately when I realised it was from the wrong film.

'I told you not to mention *Star Trek*,' said Sam, when she phoned me on my mobile on the way home in the taxi.

'I know, but you said nothing about *Star Wars*.'

'Did you know about his background? That he was a supporter of Refuge and that? I had no idea.'

'Nor did I till I did some research.'

'Wow, so you actually did some homework?'

'Teachers do the best kind of homework. The "read Wikipedia in two minutes to know everything you need to know" variety. Anyway, I didn't say it just to get him onside. I said it because it's what we believe in.'

'Well the good news is the "I'm voting Lollipop" hashtag started trending on Twitter within a couple of minutes. Followed shortly afterwards by '*Star Trek* v. *Star Wars*.'

'So even Anna's pleased with me, then?'

'Of course she is. Although she's probably wondering how the hell she's going to follow that on Radio 4.'

'Don't worry,' I said. 'I'll tell her she can boldly go where no woman has been before.'

'So you do know the right line.'

'Yep. Brain just wasn't functioning properly. I blame Baroness Warsi's tampon. I think it may have been drugged.'

'What on earth are you on about?'

'It's a long story. I'll tell you in the playground tomorrow. Beam me up, Scottie.'

18

ANNA

I thought it must be an April fool. The first poll since the general election was called had us in third place, above the Lib Dems, at 15 per cent. I put the copy of the *Independent* down, my hands still shaking, and logged on to my laptop.

If it was an April fool the BBC news website was doing the same one. As was the *Guardian*.

David came into the kitchen. I hoped he wouldn't think I had left the paper deliberately on his table mat like that. I saw him glance at the headline then do a double-take and go back and look at it again more carefully.

'I thought it was an April fool myself,' I said. 'It seems not.'

I was careful not to smile as I said it, or to give any indication of the multi-million-pound firework display which was going off inside me.

'Happened to Clegg last time,' he said. 'Massive peak after the first leadership debate. Then the tabloids started getting at him. That's as good as it gets, I'm afraid. It's downhill all the way from here.'

I nodded, deciding not to rise to the bait. Although inside I was sure this wasn't some flash in the pan. We had the momentum now. And if the response on Twitter of the past few days was anything to go by, we could only get bigger.

'I was thinking of going out about eleven, once the kids are up,' I said, as I filled the kettle. 'With the leaflets I mean.'

David shrugged. 'Sure, that's fine by me. I've got plenty to be getting on with.' I put the kettle down heavily on its stand.

'You're not coming with us?'

David laughed. 'Of course not. Why would I do that?'

'Er, because I'm your wife, perhaps?'

'I think you're forgetting that I'm also a Liberal Democrat councillor.'

'And that's more important, is it?'

'I can hardly campaign for the opposition, can I? There are rules against that sort of thing. They'd throw me out. Surely you realised that?'

I turned back to the kettle, the colour rising in my cheeks. Of course he couldn't. I should have realised. It didn't stop it hurting though.

'Yes, of course. I don't think the kids will understand that, though. They were looking forward to us all going out together.'

'Well I'm sure you can explain it to them. It will be a good exercise in democracy, won't it? The fact that every person has the right to their own opinion. To vote the way they see fit. Regardless of what those around them are saying or doing.'

Put like that he made it sound as if I were the one who was being unreasonable. Maybe I was. Maybe I had a bloody cheek to expect my husband to offer any kind of support when I was standing against the party he'd supported and worked hard for all his adult life. And when I was adding insult to injury by achieving more in a few weeks than he had in twenty-odd years.

'Yeah, you're right,' I said. 'I'm sure it'll be fine.'

'I still can't believe Dad's not coming,' said Will, as we set off down the road armed with rucksacks full of leaflets.

'I told you, it's against party rules.'

'What about family rules?'

'There aren't any,' I replied.

'Yes there are,' said Esme. 'Lights off at eight o'clock, no talking with your mouth full. There are lots of them.'

'I wasn't talking about those sorts of rules, love. I was simply explaining that just because Daddy isn't coming leafleting with us, it doesn't mean he isn't supporting us.'

Even as I said it I realised it sounded pathetic. Will gave me his best 'Yeah right, whatever' look. Clearly he thought so too.

'So is he campaigning against you?' asked Charlotte,

who until that point had appeared to be engrossed in whatever was on her iPod and not paying any attention at all.

'Not this afternoon he isn't, no.'

'But on other days is he? Is he leafleting for Laura whatever her name is?'

'Jenkins. I suppose so. I don't know for sure. I haven't asked.'

It was Charlotte's turn to give me a look. One that involved raised eyebrows. Any other time I'd have been happy to have sparked a response in her, seen a bit of an appetite for a fight. Unfortunately, I hadn't really wanted it to be against her father.

'Right,' I said, as we reached the bottom of the road. 'We'll start here. Will, if you and Charlotte do the other side of the road, I'll do this side with Esme. One leaflet in each letterbox. If anyone comes out to ask a question give me a shout and I'll come over.'

'Why can't we knock on the doors?' Esme asked.

'Because people don't like being bothered by politicians, especially not on a bank holiday Monday.'

'But I want to tell them to vote for you.'

'We don't tell them, sweetheart. We ask them. And if anyone comes out to talk to us, that's what we'll do.'

Esme nodded. She looked resplendent in her purple jacket, which she now called her lollipop jacket, and her Lollipop Party sticker. Will and Charlotte had been more reluctant to wear theirs. Until I'd mentioned the extra pocket money for doing a good job, that was.

The first house on our side had a 'beware of the dog' sign, so I told Esme to wait at the gate. The offending creature tore the leaflet from me as soon as I poked it through the letter box. I imagined it lying in shreds on the mat. I supposed it was a political rite of passage, up there with kissing babies, although I was quite sure I would draw the line at that.

'We can't do that one, Mummy,' said Esme, pointing to the next house. 'They've got a different colour poster up.' I eyed the 'Vote Lib Dem' poster in the window, wondering if it was someone David knew.

'It's OK,' I said. 'We can still put our leaflet through. That's how you get people to change their mind, or at least see another point of view.'

'They might like our colours better too,' said Esme, taking a leaflet from me and popping it through the letterbox. 'I don't like the yellowy one. It looks a bit like cat sick.'

I smiled quietly to myself.

By Wednesday afternoon, when I walked down the road to the station, cat-sick yellow was no longer the prevalent colour. There was purple. Lots of it. The Lollipop Party poster from the back of our leaflets. It made it seem real, somehow; convinced me that this wasn't some fantasy I was playing out in my head. People were actually planning to vote for us. They believed in what we believed. I was tempted to do a little dance in the street. Only my pull-a-long overnight case stopped me – and the worry that someone might look out of their window and change their mind.

The whole Radio 4 thing didn't seem quite so daunting any more. We were there on merit. We were doing better in the polls than any of the other minor parties. Better than all of them put together, to be honest. Some people were even saying we should be invited to the real leadership debates, not just Radio 4's alternative one. We wouldn't be, of course. But it was still nice that they were saying it.

There were some things about London I missed. The anonymity, for one. While part of me liked the fact that everyone knew everyone else in Hebden Bridge, another part of me craved the idea of walking down the street and seeing a sea of unfamiliar faces. You could lose yourself here, if you wanted to. And there was something to be said for that.

I missed the noise too. The chance to let it blot everything else from your thoughts, to allow it to carry you along the street to wherever it was you were going next. You couldn't do that in Yorkshire. At first I'd thought that was a good thing, but now I wasn't so sure.

Returning to London was a little like running into an ex-boyfriend. There was a lurching feeling in your stomach as you remembered the things you liked, the things you missed, the things you couldn't seem to get from anywhere else. It was a bit of a thrill, being reminded of all the great times you'd had. But tempting as it was to give it another try, you knew it was a bad idea. Because whatever it was that had made you leave was probably still there. And if you looked hard enough you'd surely find it again.

I stepped off the train at King's Cross station. Even that was a bit of a disappointment. I could still remember the time when you could slam the train door shut behind you. They hadn't yet invented anything which gave as satisfying a feeling as that and I doubted they ever would.

I made my way towards the snack shop near the departure boards. David had always teased me about the fact that I was the only woman he knew who was unable to walk past a health food shop or stall without going in. It wasn't there, though. Everything had changed. The arrivals side of the concourse was empty and a notice pointed to the shiny new departure area on the other side.

I went down to the tube station and was again reminded of how long I'd been away. There were those with Oyster cards and there were those without. And I was in the without camp. Not having one gave you a tiny inkling of what it might be like to arrive in this country as a refugee. I joined the queue of mainly foreign visitors and stood tapping my fingers on the handle of my case as the official Londoners whizzed past me, fast-tracked through the system. Some of them hadn't even been born here and yet they were now more London than me. I wondered if they had any idea how fragile their status as Londoners actually was that if they went away for only a short time the city would move on relentlessly without them and they would find themselves craving acceptance on their return.

I shuffled forward, everyone else in the queue seemed to be speaking in a foreign language. Maybe that explained why when I finally got to the counter the man behind spoke very slowly and in a loud, deliberate voice.

'It's OK,' I said, 'I'm from London. I moved away, but I do still understand the language, even a south London accent.'

He raised his eyebrows and said something like 'hummpphh' before handing me the appropriate form. Some time later, and after more form-filling than I suspected you needed for a passport application, I came away with a smart Oyster card wallet. It was only when I opened it up to look at the card that I saw they'd given me a commemorative Jubilee one. My first thought was to take it back. Sam would surely kick me out of the party for disloyalty to the republican cause, but one look at the queue changed my mind. I'd just have to destroy it once north of Watford again.

At least my parents' house could be relied upon to stand still in time. Everything was as it had always been. It was only the fact that my father was now rather stooped and that my mother's sleek dark hair had been replaced by a sleek grey bun that reassured me I had not emerged from the tube station into some kind of timewarp.

'Hello, Anna, lovely to see you,' my mother said, kissing me on both cheeks. Her obvious pleasure at seeing me only succeeded in making me feel bad about how little I visited. How little we all visited, come to that.

I don't think she'd ever got over me leaving. Our family was not the type that had sprawled out all over the country. My brother, Charlie, and his family were less than a mile away. I don't think they could understand why London hadn't been enough for me. Most of all I don't think my mother had understood why I'd taken Will and Charlotte away from her. It hadn't been too bad when they were small: we used to make the effort to come down to see them a lot more and both of the children would chatter away happily to her on the phone. But we didn't get down nearly as often these days, and Will and Charlotte were both pretty monosyllabic on the rare occasions I could get them to the phone. Esme still talked to her, of course. It was difficult to shut her up. But I suspected my mother felt that to all intents and purpose she had lost the older two.

I kissed my father, feeling the frailness of his body as I held him. Fortunately his mind still had a youthful energy; he may have retired from lecturing now, but he was mentally as sharp as ever. Which was a huge relief really, as it was the one thing I couldn't bear to think of: him losing his faculties in the way Jackie's mother had. I don't think my father could have coped with it. I suspected he'd gladly lose the use of a limb or two in return for keeping his brain intact.

I followed them through to the lounge, my mother's piano still taking pride of place. I ran my fingers along the closed lid, remembering the hours I'd sat at it as a child.

'You're welcome to play, Anna,' Mum said.

I smiled and shook my head. 'It's been a long time.'

'You never play at home?'

'I never seem to get the chance these days.'

'Of course,' she said. 'I imagine this campaign is taking up rather a lot of your time.'

'The polls are looking good,' Dad said. 'Extraordinarily good, to be honest.'

'I know. I could hardly believe it myself. Whether it will last, we'll just have to see.'

'I expect the children are very excited about it,' Mum said, plumping a cushion on the sofa for me.

'Yes. Yes they are,' I replied.

'And David must be an enormous help,' she added, 'what with all his political experience.'

I smiled and nodded. Remembering now why we came down so rarely.

Arriving at the BBC was like going to a rather bizarre job interview where all the other applicants just happened to be leaders of political parties. Except, of course, we were well aware that the top three candidates for the big job were being interviewed on another day, we were merely the warm-up act.

I gave my name at the reception desk and clipped on my visitor's pass while the receptionist called up to let them know I'd arrived.

'Someone will be down for you in a minute.' She smiled. 'Do take a seat.'

I perched myself on the edge of a trendy purple sofa and straightened the collar of the crisp white shirt I had put on that morning. I'd gone for a black suit with a crop jacket and a long straight skirt. Businesslike, I thought, was the order of the day.

I had just picked up a copy of the *Guardian* from the coffee table when I heard a voice enquire 'Anna?'

I looked up, the speaker was a man around my age, maybe a couple of years younger, with dark hair which, though cut very stylishly, still managed to look slightly messy.

'Gavin Joyce, assistant producer,' he said, holding out his hand.

'Anna Sugden,' I said, standing up and shaking it. 'Thanks for inviting me.'

'Not at all. I trust you're impressed that we've got sofas in your party's colours. I hope the others don't notice otherwise we'll have fresh allegations of BBC bias on our hands.'

I smiled, not knowing what to be more impressed with: the fact that he knew the Lollipop Party's colours or that he was capable of humour before seven in the morning.

He swiped us through the security area and into a lift.

'You're the first here, actually,' he said. 'Which is probably a good thing as it will give me a chance to go through everything with you before all hell breaks loose.'

I nodded and followed him out at the second floor and

through to the studio area. Looking into the glass studio I could see John Humphrys' head poking out from behind various pieces of equipment. Around the other side of the table six microphones were placed a small distance apart from each other. Six chairs crammed in around the desk.

'It's going to be a bit of a squeeze, I'm afraid,' Gavin said. 'We only had five people last time, but you guys have rather forced your way into the frame.'

'Yeah,' I smiled, 'I guess we have.'

Gavin leant in close to me. 'I'm probably not supposed to say this, but your party is an absolute breath of fresh air. All those tired old arguments and then you come along with a radically different agenda and turn everything on its head.'

'Most people just think we're crazy,' I said. 'Especially men.'

'Oh, you're crazy all right, but you're clever with it. And when you're running a topical-news programme, crazy and clever are exactly what you need.'

I smiled again, conscious of the colour rising in my cheeks. I wasn't used to this. Being out there. Having political conversations with men I didn't know. Having any type of conversation with men I didn't know, come to that.

'I don't suppose you think we can actually win, though,' I said.

Gavin looked up from a pile of papers he had been flicking through on his desk.

'Why not?'

'Convention. Money. Hundreds of years of tradition. The fact that at this very moment the editors of the tabloids are probably thinking of ways to annihilate us.'

Gavin smiled. 'Ah, don't let the little things put you off. I'd say you're worth a tenner as an outside bet. You can still get bloody good odds on you.'

'Well, thank you for your conviction,' I replied. 'I hope you enjoy your winnings.'

Gavin's phone buzzed. 'Right, you'll have to excuse me,' he said, 'Galloway's arrived. If you don't mind pouring a saucer of milk while I get him, I'm sure it would be much appreciated.'

Half an hour later I was in the studio, positioned only a few feet away from George Galloway and still not daring to look at him in case I started laughing about what Gavin had said.

We were positioned boy, girl, boy, girl, boy, girl, around the table in what I suspected might be a prank on Gavin's behalf. If you'd told me three months ago I'd ever end up sandwiched between George Galloway and Alex Salmond on Radio 4, I would have laughed you out of the room.

Caroline Lucas smiled at me in what I suspected was sisterly support. Sam, who appeared to regard her as nothing short of the green goddess of alternative politics, had actually suggested I ask her to defect to our party. Jackie, of course, had merely asked if I could find out how she kept her eyebrows so well maintained.

The format of the leadership debate had been explained to us quite clearly in advance. We had three minutes each to make an opening statement, after which Humphrys would be asking us questions, some of which had been suggested by Radio 4 listeners.

I had my speech typed out in front of me. I had practised it so many times I suspected I wouldn't even need to look at it, but it was there anyway as a sort of grown-up comfort blanket.

Alex Salmond went first, sounding rather, well, Scottish really. He was followed by Nigel Farrage, who, until I'd told Jackie otherwise, she'd thought had actually died in that helicopter crash before the last election.

And then it was me. Broadcasting to the nation. And loving it. Loving every second. So much so that I didn't want my three minutes to end. When it did, I looked up to find the men were all staring at me, as if realising that I wasn't there to make up the numbers at all. And that softly spoken mothers-of-three in suits from Jigsaw could actually have something interesting and powerful to say.

I glanced out through the glass to where Gavin was sitting at his desk, headphones on and a suitably impressed expression on his face. And I felt good. For the first time in a long, long time, I felt good about myself.

The debate started with a question about the economy. I put forward our views about creating jobs and introducing the living wage. At the end of it both Caroline Lucas and George Galloway said, 'I agree with Anna,' at exactly the same moment. I almost fell off the chair. It was my own 'I agree with Nick' moment. Only as soon as I thought of that it worried me. If you googled Nick Clegg the suggestions it came up with were Nick Clegg looking sad and Nick Clegg jokes. I didn't want to go there. I thought of David listening at home. If indeed he was listening. And wondered if he agreed with anything I'd said. Strangely, I didn't even know any more.

'Was I OK?' I asked Gavin quietly when we emerged from the studio, forty minutes later.

'No,' he said. I must have looked worried because he broke into a smile straight away. He leant closer to me. 'If I'd been scoring points, which I wasn't, of course, I'd say you won by a country mile. I think I shall put a bet on for you to win your seat on the strength of that.'

I grinned at him. 'I hope you know what you're doing.'

'No. I hope you know what you're doing,' he replied. 'Because you could end up running the country.'

I spent most of the journey home on the train catching up on the response to the debate on Twitter and the BBC news website, where the general consensus seemed to be that I had acquitted myself pretty well. And being con-gratulated by Sam, of course, who called from the school playground, with Jackie whooping in the background, to say what a fantastic job I'd done.

By the time I got to Leeds the Lollipop Party was up to thirty thousand followers on Twitter. It was hard to keep up with them all, but I followed back as many as I could. Caroline Lucas was one of them. And Gavin from Radio 4. It was not surprising really. When I looked at his profile he followed pretty much every politician on Twitter. I sent him a message when I followed him back. 'Good to meet you. Thanks again for having me on. Hope you're not wasting your money.'

The reply came almost instantly. 'No worries. Good to meet you too. It's much more fun to back the dark horse.'

19

SAM

'The father of your children is a depraved sicko.' Rob came in the back way through to the kitchen with a huge grin on his face when he said it, which was why I didn't take it seriously at first.

'What makes you say that?' I asked, looking up at him from the packed lunches I was making for Zach and Oscar.

'It's not me, who says it. It's the *Daily Express*.' He slapped a copy of the newspaper, which he had cunningly hidden inside the *Guardian*, on to the kitchen counter. The front-page story was something about benefit cheats. But there was a panel across the top which read, '*Lollipop Party Leader's Boyfriend in Nude OAP Shame*'.

I looked up at Rob. 'I don't believe it. This is about you.'

'Yep. If you turn to page five you get the whole story. The one where they call me depraved for painting shocking pictures of naked pensioners' genitalia.'

'But this is ridiculous,' I said. 'What the hell has this got to do with the election?'

'Nothing. It's called muck-raking. They get to publish pictures of naked people and stir up a whole hoo-ha about nothing in an effort to besmirch your good name.'

I turned to page five. They had indeed used pictures of two of Rob's paintings. They'd even slapped a 'censored' banner over one of them.

'Oh, this is outrageous.'

'I don't know,' said Rob. 'It's incredible exposure for my work. I'll probably sell a shedload of them after this.'

'Come on,' I said. 'I'm being serious.'

'So am I.'

'What about your models?' I asked. 'I can't imagine they'll be happy about having their wobbly bits plastered all over a national newspaper.'

'I'm going to call them in a minute. But knowing Betty and Norman I imagine they'll think it's quite a giggle.'

'But that's not the point is it? They shouldn't be allowed to get away with it.' I realised I was gesticulating wildly with the vegetable knife and promptly put it down.

'Hey, chill out,' said Rob, taking hold of my shoulders. 'Do you honestly think anyone's going to decide not to vote for you because your partner paints pictures of elderly people without their clothes on?'

'I'm not saying that. What I'm saying is we should complain. Where the hell did they get the photo of you from, anyway?'

'From the exhibition brochure.'

'And what about the paintings?'

'Rebecca from the Mill rang me yesterday and told me she'd caught someone taking photos. She asked them to leave, but didn't really think any more of it.'

'Why didn't you tell me?'

'I didn't want to worry you. Anyway, you said yourself the tabloids would be taking potshots at you now. If this is the best they can do it's bloody hilarious, if you ask me.'

I heard Zach's footsteps coming down the stairs. 'Put it away,' I said. 'I don't want the boys to see it.'

'Why not? They saw the exhibition.'

'Just put it away,' I repeated sharply.

Zach came into the kitchen in his rocket pyjamas, still yawning and rubbing his eyes.

'Morning, sweetheart,' I said. 'Toast or cornflakes?'

'Have you got marmalade?'

'Yes.'

'Toast with marmalade then, please.'

'OK. Daddy will do it for you while I go and get your brother sorted. Is he awake?'

'No. I haven't heard him at all.'

I hurried upstairs and into Oscar's room. It wasn't unusual to have to wake him up for school, but it did tend to make him grumpy for his morning routine. I drew the curtains back, letting the light pour into the room. I sat on the edge of the bed and stroked his arm. I always liked to touch him before I took the night ventilator off. I didn't like the first human contact he received in the morning to be essentially a medical one.

Oscar's eyelids flickered open then closed again.

'Morning, love,' I said, nuzzling his face and kissing him on the cheek.

'I need a drink,' he said. 'My throat's sore.'

I sat up immediately. 'When did this start?'

'Just now. When I woke up.'

'It wasn't sore last night?'

'No.'

I nodded, trying to keep a neutral expression on my face. A sore throat wasn't some little thing for Oscar. A sore throat could lead to a cough or a cold, which could lead to all sorts of complications. Complications I didn't even want to think about.

'I'll get you some water,' I said. When I returned I helped Oscar to sit up and he drank it straight down.

'That's better,' he said.

Maybe it was nothing. Maybe had had simply been thirsty. I took his temperature. It was within the normal range. I let out a deep sigh of relief. Managed a proper smile.

'Right then, mister,' I said. 'Let's get you up and ready.' I swivelled him around so his legs were hanging over the side of the bed. I hated seeing him sitting like that. His stick-like legs devoid of any muscle hanging limply down. He reminded me of Pinocchio. And what I wanted more than anything else in the world was for him to be a real boy. To wake up one day and find that he did have proper legs after all and to leap up and dance around the bedroom singing 'I've Got No Strings'. That wasn't ever going to happen, though. Because we didn't have a blue fairy. And real life wasn't a Disney film.

I lifted Oscar up, careful to keep my back straight as the occupational therapist had shown me, and headed towards the bathroom. As we got there he sneezed over my left shoulder. I stopped, feeling the vibrations of the sneeze going through my entire body. My stomach tightened. Everything tightened. And I knew it would stay that way until the next sneeze. Whenever that would be.

The three of us were sitting round my kitchen table that evening.

'I think it's hilarious,' said Jackie, wiping her eyes and smudging her mascara as she looked at the headline in the *Daily Express* for the tenth time. 'All that digging for sleaze and the best they can come up with is Rob's painting of some old boy with his todger out. I mean it's hardly Profumo is it?'

'They're calling it wrinklywillygate on Twitter. It's backfired on them massively. People seem to think it's pathetic of them to try to turn this into a scandal.'

I looked at them and nodded. I knew they were right. This wasn't going to do us any harm at all. In fact it would probably do us some good. I suspected our poll ratings would go up even further. And throughout the day Rob had been inundated with enquiries about his work. I guessed it was a case of every cloud and all that. But I still couldn't help being unnerved by the whole thing. Clearly we were now seen as a legitimate target. And not just the three of us, but our families too. And if they so much as printed a word about any of our children. Well, I daren't think what I'd do.

'I know,' I said. 'But I still think we need to be very much on our guard. Have our wits about us at all times.'

'But if there's no dirt for them to find,' said Jackie, 'then we haven't got anything to worry about. You're obviously so squeaky clean that this was the best they could do. I've got such a boring past that they'll struggle to come up with anything more exciting than me once snogging my English teacher under the mistletoe.'

'You never!' I said.

'I was in the sixth form at the time and I did it for a bet. There were no tongues or anything. And as for Anna, well you've only got to look at her to know she's as pure as the driven snow.'

Anna smiled and looked down at her laptop.

'I guess so,' I said. 'Although it's our friends and family I worry about. It's only a matter of time before they discover I live next door to a couple of lesbians.'

'Sue and Caz wouldn't mind,' said Jackie. 'They'd probably think it was a great laugh.'

'It's not them I'm worried about. It's Millie. Well, all of our children, to be honest.'

'Let's hope they've learnt their lesson from this,' said Anna. 'With any luck having been made to look pretty stupid with this one they'll leave us all alone.'

I smiled and nodded at her. I was too distracted by the

sound of the Cough Assist machine upstairs to concentrate properly, to be honest.

Oscar had been sneezy at school and his nose had started running a bit too by home time. The noise of the machine stopped. I heard footsteps coming down the stairs and then Rob popped his head around the door.

'Hey,' said Jackie, 'it's the pensioner pervert from the paper.'

Rob took a bow, but I could tell by the fact that he didn't come up with a witty riposte that all was not well.

'Sorry to interrupt. Have you got a minute?' he said to me.

'Back in a sec,' I said to the others, following him out of the kitchen.

'What's the matter?' I asked, as soon as we were out of earshot.

'There's a lot of stuff come out in the Cough Assist,' he said. 'It's not looking too healthy.'

I went through to Oscar's bedroom. He was lying on the bed, Rob had lowered the upper half for him so his head was below his body, as we always did if he was a bit chesty. I sat down on the edge of the bed. Oscar looked tired. The usual cheeky grin was notably absent.

'How are you feeling, love?' I asked, stroking his brow.

'The monster sucked a lot of yucky stuff out of me.'

'I know, sweetheart. Daddy told me. Did it feel a bit sore?'

'Yeah.' I nodded. Oscar rarely complained or admitted that anything was sore.

'At least we've got all the nasties out now. Hopefully you'll be able to get a good night's sleep. Daddy'll give you some medicine and then he'll put your mask on and sit with you until you drop off, OK?'

Oscar nodded. I bent and kissed him on the forehead.

'Night-night sweetie. Mummy and Daddy love you lots.'

I went over to the Cough Assist machine and discreetly glanced at the contents in the bowl. I turned to look at Rob. I didn't say anything. I didn't have to.

'We'll take him to the doctor first thing in the morning' I said quietly. Rob nodded. 'Call me if you need anything, OK?' Rob nodded again. I went back downstairs.

'Everything OK?' asked Jackie as I sat back at the table.

'Yeah. Oscar's just got a bit of a cold.' They both looked at me, their faces immediately filling with a mixture of concern and sympathy. They knew the score. When Oscar had started school I'd had to send all his classmates' parents a letter, explaining his condition and politely requesting that they keep their child off school if they had a cough or cold. I'd hated doing it. I hadn't wanted Oscar to be different and for his condition to inconvenience other parents. But given the choice of that or Oscar facing a spell in hospital with a respiratory infection, I knew which I'd prefer.

'Oh no, poor little thing,' said Anna. 'When did this start?'

'Only today. It's nothing serious at the moment. I'm going to take him to the doctor first thing in the morning, get them to check him over.'

'Are you sure you're OK to carry on?' asked Jackie. 'I mean, if you need to give Rob a hand.'

'No, he's fine thanks.'

'If you need us to have Zach at all just let us know,' said Jackie.

'I will do. Thanks. Now someone tell me some brilliant news to take my mind off it.'

'Well, as it happens,' said Anna, 'I might just be able to help you out there.'

'Oh,' I said, watching the smile spread slowly over her face and suspecting she'd been keeping something to herself for a while.

'I figured, why should we stop at Sir Patrick Stewart? I mean if celebrities are going to vote for us, it would be very good to know about it and be able to use it in our publicity. So, I emailed some people to see if they would be prepared to publicly endorse us. And, a few of them were.'

'Like who?' asked Jackie.

'Oh, no one much. Just Davina McCall and Jamie Oliver.'

'You're having us on,' I said.

'Nope,' she replied. 'They're following us on Twitter and they've even offered to come out on the campaign trail with our candidates in their constituencies.'

'Oh my God.' Jackie pretended to fall off her chair. 'That's bloody brilliant. You're wasted on us, Anna. You should be out there getting Obama re-elected or something.'

Anna smiled. I still couldn't speak I was that choked, so I went over to her and gave her an enormous hug instead.

'And you,' I said, turning to Jackie, 'can stop giving her fancy ideas.'

'Don't worry,' said Anna. 'I'm not going anywhere. Unless they offer me a massive salary, of course.'

'Here, have a Hob Nob,' I said, passing her the plate. 'It's the best we can offer, I'm afraid.'

'Fortunately,' said Anna, taking one, 'I'm rather partial to Hob Nobs.'

'Right then,' I said. 'So when can we break this news to the world?'

'Tomorrow, if you like,' said Anna. 'I suggest we just post it on Twitter. Hopefully they'll both retweet it and within a few hours half the world will know.'

'Do you think running the country will be as easy as this?' asked Jackie.

'Probably not,' I said. 'But I'm not sure it will be any harder than running our own lives.'

Unfortunately, Oscar didn't have a good night's sleep. Neither did Rob or I, come to that. We took turns to do the Cough Assist machine and sit up with him, operating on a one hour on, one hour off basis, which in hindsight was probably stupid as it meant we were both knackered the next morning.

I finally got him back to sleep just after seven in the morning. It reminded me of those groggy newborn days when I only ever seemed to get to sleep just as everyone else was getting up.

When I was sure he was sound asleep, I crept out of

Oscar's room. Zach was just getting up, although he too looked as if he hadn't had much sleep.

'Sorry, love,' I said, ruffling his hair. 'Did the machine wake you up in the night?'

Zach nodded. He didn't complain though. 'Is Oscar poorly?' he asked.

'He's got a cold and a bit of a cough, love.'

'Will he have to go to hospital?' He clearly remembered what had happened last time. Even though he'd only been four at the time.

I took him by the hand and sat down on his bed next to him. 'We don't know yet, love. I'm going to take him to the doctor this morning. Hopefully, he'll get over it in a few days. Let's hope so, eh?'

Zach nodded. 'Are we still going to do Lollipop Party things today?' I'd said we would go over to Huddersfield to do some campaigning. Zach had really been looking forward to it.

'Not today, I'm afraid. Maybe later in the week.'

Zach nodded in a rather resigned way, as if he knew that was unlikely to happen. 'But if you don't do campaigning, you might not win the election.'

I smiled at him. Not wanting to admit he had a point.

'It's OK,' I said. 'We've got plenty of other people to help out. Oscar's the most important thing, right now. Let's get him better first. There's still a month to the election. We've got plenty of time to win some votes.'

'If you win, Mummy, and if you get to run the country,

are you still going to be here in the mornings or if Oscar needs you in the night?'

I pulled him closer to me. 'Of course I will, sweetie. You and Oscar are the most important things in the world to me. You know that, don't you?'

Zach nodded.

'Now, let's creep downstairs and make marmalade on toast.'

Zach managed a smile. 'Can we still have marmalade on toast when you're Prime Minister?' he asked.

'I should think so.'

'Good. Because I don't want anything to change. I want everything to stay exactly the way it is. Except I want Oscar to get better.'

I smiled and hugged him to me. Loving the smell of strawberry shampoo on his hair.

20

JACKIE

As soon as I saw the front door wide open, I knew. I pulled up sharply, took my seat belt off and looked up and down the street. There were no flashes of pink this time, no little old lady shuffling along in her slippers. She was nowhere to be seen.

I sighed, cursing the fact that I had Alice with me. That there was no way I was going to be able to hide this from her. I turned around to Alice, trying hard to keep my voice measured and calm, although I wasn't feeling that way inside.

'Now,' I said. 'It looks as if Grandma might have gone for a little wander. She does this sometimes and she usually finds her way back just fine.'

'Why has she left the door open?' asked Alice, her voice full of the sense of panic I had tried to disguise in mine.

'You know how forgetful she is, love. She might even

have gone back inside and left it open. Let's go in and have a look first, shall we?'

Alice nodded. Although she didn't seem at all sure about it. I took her hand and hurried into the house. We went to each room in turn, calling out as we did so. I even checked the bathroom and bedroom in case she'd got confused again about what time of day it was. The house was empty. It was more than empty. It was deserted. Bereft even. Because its owner had gone AWOL and there was nothing I could do about it.

Alice gripped my hand tightly. I could see the set of her jaw. She was trying very hard not to cry.

'What we're going to do,' I said, 'is call Daddy and ask him to come and take you back home while I look for Grandma.'

'But I want to stay and help find Grandma.'

'I know, love. But I'm going to have to walk quite a long way and I'm going to have to go fast. And I'm sure Daddy will find something much more fun to do with you.'

'But Daddy's working.'

We'd left Paul marking and doing some lesson plans. I was conscious that with all the campaigning, this was the first chance he'd had to do a full day's work in the holidays. And it was going out of the window.

'I know, love. But he won't mind stopping to look after you.' I stopped short of saying, 'because it's an emergency'. Alice was looking worried enough as it was.

'Hi, love,' I said when Paul answered. 'Would you mind

coming over to get Alice. I just need to go and find Mum.'

Paul saw straight through the bright and breezy voice I'd put on. 'I'll be straight there,' he said.

'Right,' I said to Alice. 'While we're waiting for Daddy we'll go and ask a couple of neighbours. They might have seen Grandma, you see. They might know which direction she went.'

I tried Pauline across the road first. She came to the door, looked at my face and looked down at Alice.

'Hello, sweetheart,' she said. 'Everything OK?'

'I just wondered if you'd seen Mum at all today,' I said, a forced smile on my face.

'No, sorry, love. I've been out back all morning doing garden. Was door open?'

I nodded.

'Why don't you ask Bill at Number Thirty-two? He usually cleans his car on a Friday. He might have seen her.'

'Thank you,' I said. 'I'll do that.'

'Let me know if I can help at all, won't you, love?'

'Yeah. I'm sure it'll be fine. She's probably on her way back now.' I said it more for Alice's benefit than anything. Pauline smiled as if she understood that.

Bill hadn't seen Mum. Although he admitted he might not have noticed her, he'd been that intent on getting a nice shine on his bonnet. We tried a few more doors with no luck. I felt the urge to start screaming. Or to swear out loud at the very least. We walked up and down the street for a bit. I tried to turn it into a game, pretending Grandma was playing hide-and-seek. I wasn't sure Alice bought it but at least it kept her occupied. We went as far as the corner shop and back again. Twice. Until finally Paul arrived.

Alice started crying the second he did so. 'I don't want to go home. I want to help find Grandma.'

Paul glanced at me and appeared to sense that I was not in a fit state to deal with it. 'I know, love, but Mummy'll find her quicker on her own. Anyway, I'm taking you to Upsy Daisy's. How about that?'

Alice hovered for a moment between tears and excitement. Fortunately, the latter won out.

'Is there owt I can do to help?' Paul asked, as Alice bounced into his car.

I shook my head. 'Just keep her occupied. I'll call you as soon as I find her.'

Paul nodded and squeezed my hand. 'Love you,' he said. 'I'm sure she's fine. Probably just looking at the roses somewhere.'

I nodded and watched as they drove off. As soon as they disappeared around the corner I started running, wishing for the 931st time in my life that I'd put some sensible shoes on. I went down every terraced street in turn, asking anyone I saw on the way. None of them had seen anything. It was as if she had disappeared off the face of the earth.

I rang social services, although I wasn't quite sure what I expected them to do about it. They told me that a carer had been that morning. That they'd dressed Mum and that she'd appeared to be fine. The carer had left shortly before 9.30. I looked at my watch. It was 11.30 now. She could be anywhere.

I jumped into my car and started driving. I had no idea where I was going, it was simply a matter of trying to cover every square inch of road. I went as slowly as I could, looking both sides and checking in my mirrors. Every time I saw a flash of pink out of the corner of my eye I slowed down or stopped. Every time it was some little girl skipping along the street or splashing in the puddles in her pink wellies.

I arrived back outside Mum's house. I went in again and had another look in case she'd come back while I'd been driving around. I checked in the bowl by the front door. Her keys were still in there. But I looked in every room again anyway, in case I'd missed anything first time around. I looked under the bed, in the wardrobe, in the cupboard under the stairs. Stupid places I hadn't looked when Alice was with me because I hadn't wanted to worry her. She wasn't there. The house reeked of that fact. I sat down heavily at the foot of the stairs. I knew what I had to do next. I called the hospital.

'Hello,' I said. 'My elderly mother's gone missing. She has Alzheimer's. She might not even remember her own name. I'm trying to check if anyone of her description has been brought in.'

I gave her name and description, right down to the hole in the left arm of her pink cardigan. The receptionist was very helpful. She went through her list on the computer; she even rang through to A & E to double-check. Nothing.

'Have you reported her missing to the police?' she asked.

I felt stupid. I should have done it right away. Well, as soon as Alice had gone, anyway. But I'd been so sure I'd find her. So positive she'd wander around the corner any moment.

'No,' I said. 'I didn't want to bother them.'

'Perhaps it's time you should.'

I thanked her and put the phone down. She was right, of course. I couldn't spend the entire day going up and down the same streets. She wasn't here. I didn't know where she was and I certainly didn't know if she'd be able to find her way home.

I dialled the general number for reporting crimes in Halifax: it felt less extreme than calling 999. I still didn't want to accept that it was an emergency. Wanted to believe that I'd be apologising for bothering them in a minute when she appeared at the window.

The man who answered went through a whole load of questions with me. He seemed to be taking it pretty seriously. Which, far from making me feel better, actually made me more concerned.

He told me Mum's details would go out to all officers immediately. That he'd send a patrol car round within the next fifteen minutes.

'Fuck,' I said as I put the phone down. And for the first time that day, I started to cry.

They sent a PC and a WPC, who was one of those sympathetic liaison officer types. I showed them through to the front room and offered them a cup of tea. I talked incoherently at them. All the usual things you do in a crisis.

'Can you think of any places she might have gone?' the female officer asked. 'Favourite spots, friends' houses, a park?'

I shook my head. 'She really doesn't go far afield. She used to go to Ackroyd Park and Shroggs Park when we were younger, but we haven't been for years.'

'What about family?' asked the WPC.

'She's a widow. The only brother she's still got alive is in Scarborough. And me and my husband. That's it.'

The male officer spoke for the first time. 'I think in the circumstances it would be sensible to put this out to the media. Local radio, evening rag, local TV, that sort of thing.' I shut my eyes and looked up at the ceiling.

'Hopefully it will all be sorted within the hour,' said the WPC. 'But the media can be very important in this type of case. Thousands of extra pairs of eyes, you see.'

I nodded. I didn't see how I could say no. Even though I knew the media would probably twig who I was and it would end up as headline news by teatime. The male officer got up and left the room. A couple of seconds later I heard him talking on his radio in the hallway. The WPC came and sat next to me on the sofa.

'Do you have a recent photograph?' she asked. I thought for a moment then pointed to the small framed photograph of Mum on her seventieth birthday on the mantel-piece.

'You can have that one. It's a couple of years ago, but it's probably the best we've got.'

She nodded, took the photo out of the frame and went out to give it to her colleague.

'Right,' she said. 'If it's OK with you, PC Sullivan is going to wait here in case your mum comes home, while someone shoots over to copy that photo and get it out to the media. In the meantime I'm going to go for a drive around in the patrol car. Would you like to stay here or come with me?'

I opted to go with her. I thought she'd be better company for a start. And I knew I'd feel better actually doing something rather than sitting around waiting. I got in the police car. Pauline across the road was looking out. I gave her a little wave, trying to pretend that everything was fine, or at least let her know that no news was good news.

The policewoman's name, which I'd forgotten when she'd first introduced herself, was WPC King, but she said to call her Jenny. She was probably ten years younger than me, but for some reason seemed a hell of a lot more sensible and grown-up at that moment.

'We'll do all the local streets first,' she said, 'then fan outwards from there. We'll probably find her sitting on a park bench somewhere, having lost complete track of time, really we will.' She gave me a reassuring smile. I didn't like to tell her that Mum had no idea what century it was, let alone what time it was.

We criss-crossed the lattice of terraced streets around Mum's home. Streets I had grown up playing in. Streets it turned out I still knew well enough to be able to direct her this way and that.

'We've sent people to check out the parks,' she said, when we'd drawn a blank. 'So maybe we'll just do a run up and down the main road next, if you think that's a good idea?'

I shrugged. It was pointless asking me. I had no idea where she was at all. My stomach rumbled, reminding me of the fact that I hadn't had any lunch. Although as I didn't think I'd be able to stomach anything right now, it would have to go unheeded. I looked at my watch. It was nearly three o'clock already. I just hoped we'd find her before nightfall. The thought of her being out all night was almost more than I could bear.

It was the second time we went up the main street that I saw it. A tiny flash of pink the other side of the thick steel school railings.

'Stop,' I said. Jenny pulled up sharply on the kerb. I pointed to a figure slumped on the ground around the other side of the railings, by the front gate. 'I think that's her.'

I flung open the passenger door.

'I'll come with you,' said Jenny.

I bit my lower lip and blinked hard as I hurried across the grass as fast as I could in my heels. Rawson Junior and Infant School was where Deborah and I had gone. The building hadn't changed much. It was just the railings which were unfamiliar. I'd often tutted as I'd driven past, hating the fact that it looked more like a secure training establishment. Paul has said it was just the way things were nowadays. That local authorities were more concerned about safety than aesthetics.

As I rounded the corner I saw her move. It was the first time I knew for certain that she was alive. She was sitting on a low wall rocking back and forth hugging her legs.

'Mum,' I called.

She turned around. I noticed her red puffy eyes, a solitary tear still visible amongst the wrinkles on her face.

'What are you doing here?' I asked.

'I'm waiting for Deborah,' she said. 'It's about time she came out, but I've not had sight nor sound of them. I tried gates but they're locked. Do you think she's all right, our Deborah?'

I stopped in my tracks and screwed up my eyes.

'Who's Deborah?' whispered Jenny in my ear.

I hesitated for a second before I answered. 'She was my sister. She was killed in a road accident just over there,' I said, nodding back towards the main road. 'When I was seven.'

Jenny nodded. 'Take as much time as you need,' she said. She walked back towards the car. I heard her voice talking into the radio. Telling them it was all over now. For them, at least.

I sat down on the step next to Mum, put my arms around her and pulled her to me. Just as she'd done with me all those years ago. And I rocked with her. Stroking her hair, letting my tears run into hers. Lil Webster. A tough old bird. Or at least she had been, until that day.

We sat for a long time. Until the rocking had stilled somewhat. And I finally felt able to speak. 'It's the Easter holidays,' I said. 'None of the children are here today. That's why the gates are locked.'

She looked up at me, her face visibly brightening. 'Of course,' she said. 'I'm a silly old bugger, aren't I?'

'Come on,' I said, helping her to her feet. 'Let's get you home.'

The police had, of course, notified the media about Mum being missing before I found her. They'd given them her name and photo and all the details. Which meant they had to tell them she'd been found safely too. And give them some brief details about the circumstances. It didn't take them long after that. By the time the local news came on that evening, they'd pieced it all together.

'*Tonight, the Secret Heartache of Lollipop Party Candidate's Family*,' was the headline. I'd declined their offer to be interviewed. Just issued a statement saying I was relieved Mum had been found safe and well and thanking those who'd helped. And asking that we now be left in peace. They filled in the gaps themselves. They even found archive footage of the court case when the drink-driver had been sentenced to just five years for ending Deborah's life. And the reaction to the news that he had two previous convictions for drink-driving.

I sat and watched it in Mum's living room with tears rolling down my cheeks. I'd never even seen it myself. It felt unreal, watching my father read out a statement, his voice cracking, barely able to conceal his anger. And my mother, standing forlornly next to him, her face deathly pale, clinging on to his arm as if she might not be able to stand without him.

The same mother who was asleep upstairs now, the day's exertions having proved too much for her. But who, for all I knew, had waited outside the school gates for Deborah on other days. And had returned home never quite understanding why she didn't come out.

21

ANNA

I suppose I should have anticipated it. Bad luck comes in threes and all that. Or simply realised that I was next in line. Having taken potshots at the other two, it was only to be expected that they'd reload and come back for me. I suppose I'd naïvely believed that there would be a period of grace after Jackie. I wasn't to know that at the very time the rest of us were sharing in her heartache, wringing our hands over how much she and her mother had suffered, the parasites were already lining up their next target. And it was me.

The ammunition had actually been provided by Will, albeit unwittingly. One of his so-called friends had tagged him on a photo on Facebook. Unfortunately the photo showed him sitting in the park with a joint in one hand and a can of Special Brew in the other. Short of a having a heroin needle stuck in his leg, it couldn't really have been much worse.

I was alerted to this fact by a phone call from a reporter from the *Sun on Sunday*. Clearly they'd just 'come across it' on Facebook. It wasn't part of a systemic campaign to sabotage the Lollipop Party's attempts to get elected. No, no. She even made it sound as if she were doing me a favour by alerting me to my son's misdemeanours. As if the *Sun* were now the arbiter of moral standards and simply whispering some gentle advice in my ear rather than maliciously trying to get some dirt on my teenage children without any regard for the impact that would have on them.

'We wanted to give you the opportunity to make a comment,' the reporter said. 'We could turn the story around and do a first-person piece from you on the pitfalls of being a parent, if you like. Something along the lines of how even middle-class professional people's children can go off the rails. It might sound better coming from you like that.'

I wasn't stupid. I was well aware they would twist whatever I said to suit their needs. I said I'd get back to them when I'd had a chance to see the photograph and talk to my family. She said she would email it through to me so I could look at it.

I stared at the photo on my screen. Struggling to reconcile the youth in the picture with the son I knew to be so much more than that. Unfortunately, within twenty-four hours that was how the rest of the country would know him. Because whether I liked it or not they were going to print the photo. And there was nothing I could do about it.

To be honest, I didn't know what I could say. The photo pretty much said it all. I couldn't deny it was my son. I couldn't deny that he'd done those things. And if I tried to say he wasn't like that normally, that I'd no idea what had been going on, people would simply conclude that I would say that, wouldn't I? Because I was his mother.

I phoned Sam. 'Hi. Is it OK for me to pop round in five minutes. I need to ask your advice.'

'Yes. Yes, of course. Is everything OK?'

'No, not really. I'll explain when I see you.'

'Sure,' said Sam, her voice full of concern. 'Come right over.'

'Are you sure it's convenient with Oscar and everything?'

'Yeah, Rob's here. The doctor's already been this morning. It's fine. Honestly.'

'Thanks. I'll see you in a bit.'

I packed my laptop away and poked my head around the door of the study. David was stuffing envelopes with Liberal Democrat leaflets. He stopped as soon as he saw me. Tried to cover them up with some papers. Under normal circumstances I'd probably have had a big scene with him about why exactly he was not only not supporting my campaign but now actively campaigning against me. It wasn't normal circumstances, though. I had far more important things on my mind.

'Are you OK to hold the fort for half an hour? I need to pop to Sam's.'

'Yeah. Sure,' he said, seemingly perplexed by the fact I hadn't said anything about the leaflets.

'Esme's doing some colouring at the table. If Will or Charlotte do emerge from their rooms, they can get their own breakfasts.'

'Fine. No problem.' He smiled at me. A guilty, awkward smile. I knew I should tell him about the photo, but I didn't want to say anything before I had spoken to Sam. I knew already what his reaction would be. Which was maybe why I wanted to tell someone more supportive first.

'Hi,' I said, when Sam opened the door. 'Sorry about this. Are you sure it's OK?'

'Yes. Stop apologising and come in and tell me what's going on.'

I followed her into the kitchen, put my laptop down on the table and opened it up. 'I've had a call,' I said. 'From *The Sun on Sunday*. They got this picture from Facebook. They're going to use it tomorrow.' I turned the screen around to show her.

She looked, then dropped her head down to her chest. It was a moment or two before she said anything. 'Oh Anna. I'm so sorry.'

'It's not your fault.'

'I feel responsible. This whole bloody thing was my idea.'

'You weren't to know it would end up like this. Besides, it's not your fault that my son's been up to no good.'

'I just can't believe it,' she said, shaking her head. 'Not so soon after Jackie.'

'How is she?' I asked. 'I've left a couple of messages and texted her.'

'She stayed the night at her mum's. I spoke to her very

briefly this morning. She sounded pretty cut up by the whole thing.'

'You knew, didn't you?' I said.

Sam nodded. 'I knew her sister had been killed in a road accident. I didn't know all the details. She finds it really hard to talk about it. She'd hardly told anyone else.'

'And now the whole bloody world knows,' I said. I looked back at the screen. Tomorrow, the whole world would know about Will, as well.

'What do you want to do about it?' asked Sam.

I shrugged. 'What can I do? I can't deny it. I don't know if I'm supposed to apologise or try to explain it away, or what.'

'I think,' said Sam. 'That you ought to say that your son is not standing in this election. That he's sixteen years old. He's made a mistake. Clearly one he's going to pay a heavy price for. And he should be allowed to make his mistakes in private, the way other teenagers do.'

'The thing is, it doesn't really matter what I say, does it? They're clearly going to castigate me, and I have to say I don't blame them. I've set myself up for this, haven't I? I'm an adolescent counsellor and nutritionist, for Christ's sake. A mummyblogger who writes on parenting issues. Not to mention a parliamentary candidate who's standing on a family-friendly ticket. It's an absolute joke.'

Sam gave me a hug. 'You've never claimed your children were perfect,' she said. 'And you've never claimed to be a perfect parent. There's no such thing, anyway. I read it on your blog once.'

I managed a smile. Albeit a thin one.

'That may be so, but they're still going to have a field day with this.

'What does David say?'

I looked down at my hands. 'I haven't told him yet.'

Sam nodded slowly. The sort of nod that suggested she thought I should have.

'I just wanted to speak to you first,' I explained. 'And I needed to get out of the house to try to get my head straight.'

'I take it Will doesn't know either, then.'

'He wasn't even up when I left.'

Sam walked over to the kitchen window and gazed out for a moment or two before turning back to face me. 'Look, why don't I email you a draft response? Have a look when you get home and see what you think. Obviously, it's up to you what you say. You need to feel comfortable with it. I accept it's only damage limitation, but I do think you need to stress that a sixteen-year-old lad who hasn't got anything to do with this is not fair game.'

I nodded. I heard a bout of coughing from upstairs.

'How is he?' I asked.

'Still no better. The doctor said we're doing everything right. It's just a matter of waiting and hoping he turns the corner.'

I noticed the dark circles under her eyes and realised that if you scraped back her current concerned expression there'd be a far more worried one underneath.

'Poor thing. Give him a hug from me. We're happy to

have Zach any time, you know. If it helps, I mean. Just give me a shout.'

'Thank you,' she said.

'Anyway. I'd better go back. I guess I've got to face it sometime.'

'You're a brilliant mum,' she said, giving me another hug. 'Just you remember that.'

I nodded. Although I didn't really believe it inside.

Will still hadn't emerged from his bedroom when I got home. Esme was entertaining Charlotte in the kitchen with what appeared to be a re-enactment of *The Sound of Music*.

'Morning, love,' I said. 'Where's your father?'

'Working. In the study. He left me in charge.'

'Right,' I said, wondering how long exactly he'd actually spent with either of them. 'How about you do me a favour and take Esme down to the park so she can get rid of some of that excess energy?'

Charlotte looked at me, a slight frown on her forehead, as Esme squealed in delight.

'I don't have any choice in the matter, do I?'

'No,' I said, rubbing her shoulder, 'but I am very grateful.'

'Is something up?' Charlotte whispered in my ear, as she waited for Esme to get her shoes on.

'Just need to have a chat about something with your brother. After I've had a chat about the same thing with your father.'

'So Will's screwed up,' said Charlotte.

'I'll fill you in later,' I said. She shrugged and opened the door for Esme. I waited until they were halfway down the street before I picked up my laptop and ventured into the study. David had put the election leaflets out of sight, perhaps hoping I'd somehow forgotten all about them in the intervening period.

'I need to talk to you,' I said, shutting the door behind me. I saw him straighten slightly, bracing himself for the inevitable onslaught. 'It's about Will.' He stopped short, the defence he had obviously prepared put on hold.

'Oh,' he managed to sound both relieved and concerned at the same time.

'I thought I'd better show you this.' I put the laptop down on his desk and brought up the photo.

David stared at it a long time before he said anything. 'Where did you get this?' he asked finally.

'I was sent it by one of the Sunday newspapers. They'd got it off Facebook. They're going to publish it tomorrow.'

David looked up at the ceiling and shook his head. 'Fucking hell, Anna. Where is this all going to end?' I'd thought he'd be mad at Will, but he wasn't. He was mad at me.

'I didn't do this.'

'You brought it on us by standing. I told you they'd all be out to get you, but you didn't listen.'

'This photo was posted months ago. It's not as if the campaign has turned Will to drink and drugs. He was obviously managing quite well on his own.'

'But it wouldn't be in the bloody papers if you hadn't stood, would it? We'd probably never even have known about it.'

'Well, we do know about it now. The question is, what do we do about it?'

'You pull out of the bloody election, that's what.'

'Excuse me?'

'That's the only way this whole thing will end. You bow out in disgrace and we hope that within a couple of months we can all get back to normal.'

'I meant what do we do about Will?'

'Don't ask me. You're the adolescent-behaviour expert.'

'There's no need to be like that.'

'You're not going to tell me you're surprised? What did you think he was up to in the park? Playing Ring-o-Ring of Roses?'

I stared at him and shook my head. Any tiny shred of hope I'd had of getting some support from him, of having some sense that he took equal responsibility for Will's behaviour, had now disappeared in a puff of facetious-ness.

'I'll talk to him then, shall I?' I said, staring up at the ceiling.

'I'm not sure what good that's going to do.'

'Well I can't not talk to him, can I?'

'We could ground him. Stop his pocket money.'

'He's sixteen years old, David. He'll probably have a summer job in a few weeks.'

'Then I'll leave it with you. I'm sure you know best.'

We stood there looking at each other. I wondered whether he was thinking what I was thinking. Somehow I doubted it though.

'So you don't mind what I say to the press?'

'I told you what to say. You tell them you're pulling out.'

'And if I don't want to?'

He gathered some things from his desk and stuffed them into his rucksack. The election leaflets were among them. 'Then you'd better think very carefully about what's more important to you: your family or this bloody campaign.'

He pushed past me to the door. A few seconds later I heard the front door slam shut behind him.

I walked out into the hallway, shaking my head.

'What's up with him?' Will called from the landing.

'You'd better come down,' I said. 'We need to have a chat.'

I sat across the kitchen table from Will. I'd made a mug of tea for both of us. It seemed a very English thing to do in a crisis.

'You'd better look at this,' I said, opening up the laptop.

His mouth gaped open. 'Where did you get this?' he asked.

'A friend of yours posted it on Facebook.'

Will shook his head. 'I can't believe Connor could be such a twat.'

'I don't really care who posted it, Will. That's not what I wanted to talk about.'

He stared at me. The cogs were clearly going round in his head. 'How come you were looking at Connor's Facebook page?'

'I wasn't,' I said, sighing. 'I got a phone call from a newspaper.'

Will stared at me even harder. He really wasn't prepared for all of this. For the first time in ages he seemed a hell of a lot younger than sixteen.

'I'm sorry,' I said to him. 'It's the downside of having a mum who's running in the general election. There's no such thing as a private life any more.'

'They're going to publish it?'

'Yeah. Tomorrow.'

'Jeez.' Will put his head in his hands. For a moment I thought he might actually start to cry.

'They've asked me to make a statement, Will. I need to know how often this happened. Whether it was a one-off, whether you were caught out in some way. Or whether it was just another Friday night at the park for you.'

He hesitated for a moment. 'I didn't smoke any joints until I was sixteen.'

I nodded. 'And is it just joints or do you ever have anything stronger?'

'Just joints. I only started because of the exams. It was the only way I could wind down.'

'I see. And what about the alcohol?'

'Same thing. I have a can or two. I don't get off my face like the rest of them.'

'There are other ways, Will,' I said. 'If you were stressed

out with the exams you should have told me. Was it school putting pressure on you?'

'Yeah, a bit. And Dad.'

'What did he say to you?'

'Nothing. He doesn't have to say anything, does he?'

I looked down at my hands. Took a sip of tea, even though it was much too hot for me. 'I want you to stop going down the park in the evenings,' I said. 'To be honest, I think you can find much better mates than that.'

'It's not my fault Sol got a girlfriend, is it?'

'No, but you could still make better choices. Like stop smoking the joints. And yes, before you ask, I did smoke a couple myself at uni, but I also saw what they could lead on to and that's why I decided not to have any more. And as for the alcohol, well, at least find something bloody better to drink than Special Brew. You can have a decent glass of wine at home, if you like.'

Will almost managed a smile before he looked back at the screen and sighed. 'No wonder Dad's gone ape.'

'He's not mad at you, if that's what you're worried about.'

'So who is he mad at? I heard all the shouting.'

'He's mad at me for standing in the first place. For bringing this all upon us.'

'But that's ridiculous.'

'I don't know. Maybe he's got a point. Maybe I should accept that you can't be a politician and have a private family life at the same time. He wants me to choose between our family and the election.'

'So what are you going to do?'

I shrugged. 'Pull out, I guess.'

Will stood up and pushed the chair away behind him, shaking his head at me.

'What?' I asked.

'Why do you always have to be so fucking reasonable?'

The headline next morning was particularly damning. '*Put Your Own House in Order First*' it screamed, above the picture of Will. Followed by what was essentially an assassination attempt on me, albeit with words rather than bullets. I felt grateful that at least this wasn't America.

The gist of it was that before I started pontificating about how the rest of the country should be raising their children and what the government needed to do to become more child-friendly, I should make sure I knew what my teenage son was up to on a Friday night.

To be honest, you couldn't really argue with that. I went with Sam's suggested comments, but I knew it was only damage-limitation. The question was, how much damage had it already done? To the party and to my family.

I logged on to Twitter. My timeline was full of messages of support: people sending their love, telling me to stay strong, saying their teenagers had done far worse things.

I checked my direct messages. Some fellow mummy-bloggers asking if I were OK, saying they were around if I needed to talk. And one message from Gavin from Radio 4, saying simply, 'Don't let the bastards get you down. I've got ten quid riding on you, remember?'

22

SAM

It had turned into the week from hell. The phrase 'it's all gone pear-shaped' didn't even begin to describe it. I suppose on one level I should have been grateful that I had something to take my mind off Oscar's cold. Maybe if I'd had a bit more sleep I'd have been up to going on some kind of offensive. As it was, I arrived at Monday morning a physical, emotional and nervous wreck.

I rang work to tell them I wouldn't be able to come in because of Oscar.

Marie answered. 'You sound like you need some respite yourself,' she said.

'We'll be fine. We've been here before.'

'No, I mean it. Why don't you all come in? We could take care of Oscar while you guys got a bit of a break.'

It was incredibly tempting. But I hated the thought of taking up a room when I knew how precious they were.

And how some families needed them far more than we did. Besides, I knew Rob wouldn't want to go.

'Thanks,' I said. 'But we'll manage. Hopefully he's over the worst of it now. The doctor said he hadn't got any worse last night.

'OK,' said Marie. 'But if you change your mind you only have to call.'

I came off the phone to find Zach loitering in the hallway, still only half-dressed for school and looking decidedly glum.

'Hey, what's up?' I said, crouching down to him.

'I don't like going on my own when Oscar's poorly.'

I smiled and hugged him to me. 'I know, love. But you still need to go in. And there's really not much you can do at home.'

'I could read to him again, or something,' Zach said.

'You've been a brilliant helper,' I said. 'But the doctor said the thing he really needs right now is rest. And he'll get more of that if you're at school. You know what he's like. He'll be trying to tell you jokes all the time or wanting to do magic tricks if you're here.'

'I guess so,' he said.

'How about you come and read to him when you get home? I'm sure he'd like that.'

'OK.'

'Right,' I said, standing back up again. 'You get yourself ready in super-quick time. Paul will be here for you in a minute.'

'Why isn't Jackie taking Alice to school?' he asked.

'Jackie's mum needs looking after at the moment, love.'

He nodded. I was worried some of the older kids at school might talk about what had been in the papers. I still wasn't going to tell him myself, though. He already had the weight of Oscar's illness on his shoulders. If I gave him anything more to worry about he might just keel over.

A few minutes later Paul knocked on the door.

'How's she doing?' I asked quietly while Alice was stroking the cat.

'It's brought a whole load of stuff back for her, I think. She still hasn't really talked about it properly, though. She's at her mum's today, they're trying to sort out a new care plan.'

'Tell her if she can't make it over tonight I'll completely understand.'

'She says she still wants to come. To be honest I think it will be good for her. To be with you guys, I mean. Think she could do with some female company.'

'Of course,' I said. 'Whatever she thinks best.'

I poked my head around Oscar's door.

'Mummy,' he said.

The brightness in his voice lifted me. Maybe he was over the worst. Maybe we were going to be all right.

'He's not long woken up,' said Rob, glancing up from his chair at the side of the bed. He sounded shattered. He looked it too.

'I'll take over now. You can go and get some rest,' I said.

Rob shook his head. 'Can't do, I'm afraid. I promised the woman in Hangingroyd Lane I'd get her kitchen painted by tomorrow.'

'Right. Well, I'll do the night shift myself then. I don't want you running yourself into the ground.'

Rob smiled at me, although I suspected he would contest it later. He gave me a quick kiss as we swapped over.

'Grab yourself some breakfast on the way out,' I said. I knew he wouldn't though. He'd probably just take a banana for later.

'Right, mister,' I said to Oscar. 'Time for the cough machine. Then I think the suction dragon's going to come and get you.'

Oscar barely raised a smile.

'You've been so brave, love,' I said stroking his forehead. 'Hopefully we'll be back to normal soon.'

'Can I go back to school then?'

'Yes,' I said, glad that he was keen to see his friends again. 'Of course you can.'

I'd seen happier faces at wakes. Jackie and Anna looked as if they were barely holding it together when I opened the door that evening.

'Come here,' I said, giving them a group hug on the doorstep.

'I feel like I'm attending a meeting of parliamentary candidates anonymous,' said Jackie.

'You'd better come in then,' I said. 'Before anyone sees you.'

They followed me through to the kitchen.

'How's he doing?' asked Anna, gesturing up towards the sound of Oscar's cough machine.

'Hard to tell. He seemed to rally a bit this morning, the doctor still said there was no need for him to go to hospital. But this whole routine with the machines and suctioning leaves him so drained. He's dipped a bit again now.'

'Poor you,' said Jackie.

I shrugged. 'I guess none of us have had a particularly good week.'

We stood there, seemingly all lost in our own thoughts.

'Anyone for wine?' I asked.

'Actually,' said Jackie. 'I could murder a cup of tea.'

I looked at Anna and she nodded. I put the kettle on.

'How's your mum, Jackie?' asked Anna.

'She's OK, thanks. I suppose the one blessing is that she's been pretty oblivious to the whole thing. She didn't even bat an eyelid about getting a ride home in the police car.'

'I'm sorry,' Anna said. 'About your sister, I mean. I had no idea.'

Jackie nodded. I saw her swallow hard.

'Have you got anywhere with the carers?' I asked.

'They're doing a couple of extra visits a day,' she said. 'But they've made it very clear it can only be a short-term measure. They're suggesting we look at getting her into a care home.'

'Do you think she'd go for that?'

'I don't know. I think she'd find it very upsetting. There

aren't really any other options, though. We've talked about having her live with us, but it's not as if that would be much better, not with both of us being out all day. She needs to be somewhere safe. Somewhere she can be watched over twenty-four hours a day.'

I nodded. We were quiet again for a moment. I poured the tea. We sat there, staring into our mugs.

'How's Will?' Jackie asked, turning to Anna.

'Hard to tell really,' she said. 'He was doing the old bravado bit this morning, but I suspect he had a rough ride at school today. He was a bit quiet at teatime. I think Charlotte talked more than he did.'

'You've heard then,' said Jackie. 'About the girls being suspended.'

'Yeah,' Anna said. 'Charlotte's really pleased. It's only a temporary solution, of course, and I know they weren't the only offenders, but maybe it will make the others think twice about it.

'It's daft though, I haven't even had a chance to feel relieved about it, what with this whole business with Will. It's bloody ridiculous, isn't it? If it's not one, it's the other.'

'I remember when they did it to Tony Blair's son,' said Jackie. 'They shouldn't be allowed to get away with it. I bet some of their teenagers are up to far worse.'

'I'm just hoping it doesn't affect his exams,' said Anna. 'It couldn't be worse timing, really.'

'I'm sure he'll do fine,' said Jackie. 'His drama pieces are looking really good.'

'That's if they let him stay in school. I could hardly complain if they suspended him, could I? Not after all the fuss I made about Charlotte. I bet Freeman would love to put me in my place.'

We sat there in gloomy silence for a while. Presumably none of us was able to think of something suitably positive to say.

'Right,' I said, eventually, 'I guess we'd better get down to business.' I turned around to get my laptop.

'There's something I need to tell you.'

I turned back, unsure for a second which one of them had said it. It was only as I saw them staring at each other that I realised they'd both said it. At exactly the same time. I had a clenching feeling in my stomach. I sensed I was bracing myself for more bad news.

'You go first,' said Jackie, as if grateful for the opportunity to stall for a moment.

Anna looked at me and let out a big sigh. 'I'm really sorry,' she said, 'but I think I'm going to have to pull out.'

The clenching in my stomach got tighter. I should have guessed this was coming. 'But Anna, you've worked so hard. And you've been so bloody brilliant. We wouldn't be in the position we are now without you.'

'David gave me an ultimatum. He said I need to choose between the campaign and my family.'

'Jeez,' I said. 'He can't do that.'

Anna appeared flustered. 'Well, he did. And do you know what? I can understand where he's coming from. Our son has had a picture of him drinking and smoking a joint plastered all over the media. He's sixteen, for Christ's sake, and I feel bad that I brought that on him. I'm supposed to be there to protect him, not put him in the firing line. I can't risk hurting my children like this. It could be Charlotte next and I'm not sure she's strong enough to take it.'

I glanced across at Jackie. She was looking down at her hands. 'You're going to quit too, aren't you?' I said quietly.

She nodded. 'I'm sorry. I just can't do this at the same time as looking after Mum. It's not like I'm in a job where I can take time off work. They gave me today off because it was an emergency, but I'm going to have to spend a lot more time with Mum now, when I'm not working. And then there's the whole business about my sister being dragged up.' She paused for a second as her voice started to falter. 'Even if mentally I felt able to get back out there campaigning, I'm just not going to physically be able to spare the time.'

I nodded. The three of us sat in silence, apart from the occasional whirr of my laptop.

'Look, I know you've both had a tough week,' I said. 'And I feel awful, absolutely awful, about what's happened to you and your families and I totally understand your reasons for feeling like this. But this is exactly what the media wanted to happen. They wanted to bring us down and they knew damn well that the way to do that was to get at our families.'

'And they were right,' said Anna. 'This whole thing started because we were trying to protect our families, remember. I passionately believe in what we're doing and I lay awake most of last night unable to sleep because I felt so bad about it. But it's a mother's instinct to protect her family, isn't it? And that's what I've got to do.'

'For what it's worth, I feel like a complete cow too,' said Jackie. 'I know you've put in more hours that anyone else on this and I am totally in awe of your ability to keep going when Oscar's poorly too, but I know that I would never forgive myself if I was out campaigning and Mum wandered off again and something happened to her. It's lousy timing and all that, but I have to put her first.'

We drank some more tea. I offered the plate of biscuits. They both shook their heads. All I could think of was all those people out there whom we had touched with our campaign. All those other mums who were making similar sacrifices to stand for us. I'd got to know a lot of them over the internet during the past few weeks and was now on first-name terms with Val in Blackburn and Sally in Dorset, amongst many others. Women, and a handful of men, spread across the UK, who had come together because of us. I knew how passionate they were about what we stood for. How they were running themselves into the ground to try to make a difference. And I knew from their daily reports that the momentum really had spread across the country. That we were within touching distance of doing something truly remarkable.

'Will you give it one more week?' I said. 'I'm not asking you to keep campaigning. You don't have to do a thing. All I'm asking is that you don't withdraw just yet. The deadline isn't until the sixteenth. A lot can happen in a week. We all know that.

'If you pull out now it would send totally the wrong signal to the voters and I think there's a chance it could frighten some of our candidates off as well. Make them think we're not as serious as we claim to be.

'If you still feel the same in a week's time then go ahead and pull out. I will understand that completely. But let's all try to get back on our feet and see how we feel then. What do you say?'

I looked at each of them in turn. Anna looked up at the ceiling and bit her lip. Jackie nodded. I looked back at Anna.

'OK,' she said finally. 'I'll tell David I'm withdrawing on the sixteenth. I'm supposed to be doing that hustings at the town hall on Wednesday, so I'll go through with that, but it will be the last thing.'

'Thank you,' I said. My balloon had burst, but there was at least a tiny bit of air left in it. A week was indeed a long time in politics.

It was only about ten minutes after they'd left when Rob shouted down to me. I knew straightaway that something was wrong. Very wrong. I ran upstairs. Rob had the ventilator mask over Oscar's face.

'He started wheezing, he was struggling to breathe,' he said. 'We need to call an ambulance. Now.'

I ran into our bedroom and dialled 999. I could barely get out the word 'ambulance' to the operator. I got myself together enough to give our address when they put me through.

'Our son's got spinal muscular atrophy type 2,' I told them. 'He's got a cold and he's just started struggling to breathe. We've got a ventilator on, but we need to get him to hospital.'

I phoned my mum straight afterwards. 'Can you come round to look after Zach,' I said. 'We've got to take Oscar to hospital, he's struggling with his breathing.'

'Oh Sam. I'll be straight round.' I heard something in her voice which I recognised. It was fear. Fear that had finally been realised.

I put the phone down and turned around. Zach was standing in the doorway in his pyjamas. His eyes far too knowing for someone of his age. 'Oscar's going to hospital, isn't he?'

I bent down and gathered him up in my arms, feeling him crumple against me. 'Yes, sweetheart. He's finding it tricky to breathe right now because of his cold. The doctors will help him. They have all the best equipment for him at hospital.'

Zach nodded, his jaw set. He was trying so hard not to cry.

'Grandma's whizzing straight round to look after you,' I said. 'She'll get you to school in the morning if we're not back.'

'I want to go with Oscar,' he said. 'I want to go to the hospital with him.'

'I know, love, but the doctors and nurses are going to be really busy and we won't be able to look after you properly because we'll be with Oscar. We'll phone Grandma to let you know how he's doing. I promise.'

Zach nodded some more. I wished he wouldn't be so brave. I wished he would just cry. 'You get yourself tucked back up in bed,' I said. 'I'll get Grandma to come straight in to see you as soon as she gets here, OK?'

I kissed him on the forehead. He wouldn't get much sleep tonight. I knew that. He could worry for England. And I knew full well where he got it from.

I whizzed around our bedroom throwing things into an overnight bag. It was something I'd rehearsed so many times in my head and yet now it was here I had no idea what to take, what I needed, even how to feel.

I went back in to Oscar. Knelt down beside the bed next to him and held his hand. His face looked grey, his eyes startled.

'It's OK, sweetheart. We're going to get you to hospital. They'll be able to help you there.' His little hand gripped mine. I stroked his forehead with my other hand. It felt clammy. I glanced across at Rob. He nodded. He was thinking exactly what I was thinking.

There was a knock on the door. Rob ran down to let the paramedics in. I heard him talking to them as they came up the stairs. Filling them in on Oscar's condition. Telling them what they needed to do. They practically ran into the room.

'Hello, little man,' one of them said to Oscar, as he knelt down beside him. 'I'm going to quickly check you over, we'll put you on our nice big ventilator and then you're going to get a ride in an ambulance. We'll even get the siren going and the lights flashing. How about that?'

I smiled at him gratefully. He had kids, I was sure of it. Only parents could work out a way to make something bad sound like huge fun to children. I watched as he ran through the tests, relieved it wasn't up to us any more. That we didn't have to worry about whether we were doing the right thing.

'Right, he's OK, but his oxygen levels are a bit low. We're going to get him on our ventilator.'

I held Oscar's hand while they took off the mask and quickly secured the new one. It made him look unfamiliar. He didn't look like our Oscar any longer. He looked like a little boy who was very poorly.

'OK,' the paramedic said. 'If one of you can carry him downstairs, I'll carry the machine and then we'll get him on to the stretcher.'

I looked up and realised Zach was standing in the doorway, tears streaming down his face.

'Hey,' I said, hurrying over to hold him. 'It's all right. They're going to help Oscar now. They're going to try to get him better.'

A few moments later I felt a hand on my shoulder and mum's voice in my ear. I hadn't even heard her come up the stairs.

'I'll take him now, love. I'll sit with him until he gets to sleep.'

I nodded, I had never been more grateful to see her. 'Thank you,' I whispered, delivering Zach into her arms. 'We'll ring Grandma as soon as we can,' I told him. 'Love you lots.'

I picked up the overnight bags and nodded to Rob, who bent to gently lift Oscar.

'Don't forget his chair,' said Zach. 'He'll need his chair for when he comes home.'

'Yes,' I said. 'Yes, of course.'

I held Oscar's hand all the way in the ambulance. I wished he was still attached to me by his umbilical cord. Wished I could pump oxygen into him and take all the bad stuff away.

Rob followed behind in the car. He'd put Oscar's chair in it just as Zach had asked. I imagined Rob trying not to look in his mirror to avoid seeing it empty and playing his Stone Roses CD very loudly to cover up the fact that Oscar wasn't there to provide the usual running commentary.

We must have met up in the hospital car park though I didn't even register it happening at the time. All I knew was that Rob and I arrived at A & E together with Oscar.

Everything went into overdrive. People in white coats were running. I tried to tell a nurse that Oscar had SMA. She wasn't listening to me. I started to go after her.

Rob took hold of my arm. 'It's OK, they know,' he said. 'They all know. It's on his notes.'

I nodded and swallowed hard. Rob ran his fingers down my arm and took hold of my hand.

'I feel so bloody helpless,' I said.

'Me too.'

We stood at the end of Oscar's trolley. I took hold of his foot. It was about the only part of his body I could get to. I kept craning my head to see through the doctors and nurses, trying to make eye contact with him. To let him know we were still here.

When the bodies finally parted enough for me to see him, he was hooked up to a drip. Oscar. Our Oscar.

Before I could say anything a doctor took us to one side. 'We're going to take him straight down to intensive care. We're getting some antibiotics into him. We won't know for certain until the test results come back, but I'm afraid we're pretty certain it's pneumonia.'

His mouth continued opening and closing, but I didn't hear the rest of the words. I'd heard the only one that mattered. The one we'd dreaded ever since he'd been diagnosed. And which neither of us had dared speak.

23

JACKIE

It was the time of the month. Not that time. The other time. The time when we should be 'trying'. It was a horrible word. Our failure to conceive suggested that we weren't 'trying' hard enough. But I also knew Paul thought we were 'trying' too hard. And that maybe there was no point 'trying' at all, as it simply wasn't going to happen.

But still I couldn't let the window of opportunity pass without, well, trying. Which explained why I had put on a camisole and some French knickers and was attempting to slither between the sheets in something approach a seductive manner when, to be honest, I felt more like sticking on my pyjamas, taking a hot-water bottle to bed with me, curling up in a ball and going into hibernation in the hope that when I woke up in a few months time everything would be looking considerably brighter.

Paul slid his arm around my shoulders. He knew. He was like a male animal who waited for the female of his species to perform some colourful, elaborate mating ritual to alert him to the fact that the time was right. Only in my case it was simply sticking on something black and slinky instead of my pyjamas.

It was all pre-programmed from here on in. He'd slip one of the spaghetti straps of my camisole off my shoulder, give me a little nuzzle. I'd kiss him on the mouth, run my foot up and down his leg. And so it went on. One thing I'd learnt about spontaneity – it doesn't sit comfortably with menstrual calendars.

Paul slipped one of the spaghetti straps of my camisole off my shoulder. I tried. I tried really hard to get everything out of my head. To clear out the jumble of emotions which appeared to have taken up residence there. But I'd told Paul often enough over the years; if I was troubled or tired or fretting about something, it was pointless, absolutely pointless, trying anything. Because if my head was elsewhere, the rest of me was, to all intents and purposes, absent too. And at that moment it really wouldn't have mattered if George Clooney had been lying there next to me. Because I was so not up for it.

A big fat tear plopped off the end of my nose on to Paul's chest.

'Hey,' he said, lifting up my chin with his finger. 'Come here.' And that was it, the floodgates opened and Paul was nearly washed away downstream. Some women cried beautifully. I knew, I'd seen them, it wasn't just in films.

I didn't. I did big, bawl-your-eyes out crying. The sort that left you puffy-eyed and red-nosed.

It was a long time before I was able to say anything. I needed to empty myself first. And whenever I thought I had, when I tried to draw a breath in order to speak, another snivel came instead. So I waited. Waited while the gaps between the sobs grew longer and longer. Until finally there were words there when I opened my mouth.

'I'm sorry, I just can't. It's nothing to do with you, it's all this crap going on in my head. I feel such a cow about pulling out of the election and I hate what I just did to Sam. I know I had to do it but now I have, I still don't know if I can look after Mum properly and I don't know what the hell to do about putting her into a home and I feel so bad because I can't remember the last time I spent a day with Alice, just with Alice, with nothing else getting in the way. And now I feel bad because I know we should be trying and it's not fair on you to put you through all this and then not be up for it myself, but I can't. I just can't.'

I managed to snort some snot over Paul's shoulder. Not something that's really encouraged in the 'How to drive your man crazy with desire' articles in *Cosmo*. He wiped it off with a corner of the duvet. That's what I liked about Yorkshire men. They were practical to the end.

'You need to stop apologising,' said Paul. 'I'm surprised you're still capable of speech, let alone owt else, after all you've been through.'

'I feel so pathetic,' I said. 'Sam's managing to cope with

Oscar being poorly and all the stuff that goes with looking after him and yet Mum goes walkabout once and I'm in pieces.'

'It's not about that, though is it?'

'What do you mean?'

'It's this whole business with your sister. That's what it's all brought up.'

I was quiet for a moment. I wiped my eyes with the back of my hand. I hadn't really talked about Deborah to Paul. It was all too painful. As far as he was concerned she was simply the girl next to me in the pictures in the photo album. The girl who disappeared from the pages when I was seven, leaving only a shadow behind. A shadow which was sometimes visible, sometimes not, but was always there.

'It were my fault,' I said.

'How can it have been your fault?'

'I wanted to go to sweet shop,' I said. 'That's why we crossed over main road. There were no need to cross it, Mum were always telling us that. That's why she let Deborah walk me home from school. Because there were only a couple of little roads to cross. Only on that particular day, greedy guts here decided she wanted to get some sweets on way home. If it hadn't been for me . . .'

'You can't say that. The guy were twice over limit. He's one what knocked her down.'

'You don't think like that when you're seven years old, though,' I said, 'and when you're growing up without a sister you loved more than anyone in world.'

The tears came again. Slow, silent ones this time, scoring a path down my cheeks. Paul pulled me to him, stroking my hair, kissing the top of my head. Doing his best to do what he always tried to do – to take the pain away. Only this pain ran so deep, I had no idea if it were possible even to reach it.

'I know you're hurting, love, but you can't let this ruin your entire life. You need to put it to rest.'

'What do you mean?'

'It's why you're so desperate for another baby, isn't it? You're trying to give Alice the sibling you had taken away.'

'No, it's not about that at all,' I said, pulling away from him slightly.

'I'm not saying it as a criticism,' he said, stroking my hair again. 'It's perfectly understandable, given what you went through. But the thing is, love, you don't miss what you've never had. It didn't happen to Alice. It happened to you. And you can't make it better by giving her a brother or sister. Because she's not the one who's hurting.'

And as he said it, I knew it was true. That every time I looked at Alice I saw myself. And that all these years, I'd been fighting to prevent something that wasn't going to happen to her. Because she wasn't me.

The tears came again. Dredged up from somewhere I had never dared to go. Tears so old I could practically taste my seven-year-old self on them.

'It's OK,' I whispered to her. 'You can let go now.'

Paul held me and stroked my hair for a long time. Until I was ready to speak again.

'Alice is so precious,' I said. 'It scares the hell out of me sometimes.'

'I know. Me too.'

'What if something happened to her?' I said. 'We'd be left with nothing. I'm not sure I could cope. Mum always used to say I was the thing that kept her going afterwards. That she had to cope because she had me to look after.'

'Nothing's going to happen to Alice,' said Paul, taking my head in his hands.

'Me and you and Alice are just fine together. We're a family. And as much as I'd love another child too, if it doesn't happen it's not going to stop us being a family. It can't take away what we already have. Not unless you let it.'

I nodded and wiped my nose on the pillowcase. Paul smiled. I smiled back. The heaviness inside my head lifted for a second. Enough for me to be able to take residence inside my body again. It was OK. My skin fitted. It was forty-years old and scored with stretch marks and cellulite, but for the first time in years it felt comfortable. It felt like I could live in it. I kissed Paul on the lips. A little kiss. Followed by a bigger one. Wrapping my arms around him. Drinking him in. Easing myself on top of him. He looked at me with one eyebrow raised slightly.

'It's OK,' I said. 'This isn't trying. This is something entirely different. Something I'm doing because I want to. Because I want you.'

It was only when I switched my mobile on the next

morning that I got Sam's text: '*At hospital with Oscar. He's got pneumonia.*'

I screwed my eyes up. I didn't want to see it. I didn't want to know. But when I opened them the message was still there. I called Sam. It went straight to answer phone. I opened my mouth to say something, but realised I couldn't think of anything anywhere near adequate. I called back and tried again.

'Sam, it's Jackie. I'm so sorry. If there's anything I can do. Absolutely anything, please let me know. Or just if you need to talk. I'm here. We're thinking of you all and sending a great big hug to Oscar.'

I went out to the landing and stuck my head around Alice's door, which she always insisted on leaving open a little at night-time. She was still fast asleep, her fingers curled tightly around the Peter Rabbit Mum had given her soon after she was born. I felt very, very lucky.

Will was waiting outside in the corridor for me as I came out of the drama studio at break-time. He looked a bit awkward, peering out at me from under his mass of thick dark hair. I realised that he hadn't seen me since all the stuff had been in the papers and that he might be worried I was going to lay into him like everyone else had.

'Hi. Good to see you,' I said. 'How's tricks, or shouldn't I ask?'

'Been better,' he said, managing a hint of a smile. 'I'm sorry. I should have listened to you. It might have stopped me from behaving like such a dickhead.'

I smiled at him. 'Parents and teachers are there to be ignored,' I said. 'It's part of our job description. But what's more important is that when people make mistakes we help them pick themselves up and move on.'

'Good,' he said, visibly brightening. 'Because that's why I've come to see you. I want to do something about bullying. Put on a play for the whole school, something like, raw and hard-hitting. Something they won't easily forget. I need you to help me though.'

His face was serious, as serious as I'd ever seen it. If I didn't know better I'd say there was a hint of humility there as well. He was clearly feeling this every bit as much as Anna.

'OK,' I said. 'That's a great idea. Fancy helping me put it together, you and some of the other Year Elevens doing some improv?'

'Yeah,' he said. 'I'd like that.'

'Come down here at 12.30 then. Bring some of your mates and we'll see what we can come up with.'

'What about Freeman?'

'What about him?'

'He might not let us do it.'

'He might not have any choice,' I said with a smile.

24

ANNA

I wondered if it would be obvious to everyone that I was simply going through the motions. Mentally I'd already withdrawn from the election. I was only doing this because I'd made a promise to Sam. And as I'd tried to explain to David, right now, the last thing I wanted to do was to break a promise to her.

I'd spoken to Sam twice on the phone since Monday night. She'd sounded tired, which was not surprising seeing as she hadn't been home. And distant. As if this had transported her to an entirely different world. A world where the minutiae of day-to-day life did not even register. She said Oscar was hanging on in there. Which I guessed was shorthand for fighting for his life.

It was only after I'd put the phone down that I realised it was the first time in months she hadn't mentioned the campaign. And I wished to God that it hadn't happened like this. That the whole thing had fallen apart due to some internal squabbles or the fact we weren't even registering in the polls not because we'd discovered the hard way that some things were far more important than politics.

'You nervous?' asked Will, who was walking down with me to the town hall. David had announced that he wouldn't be attending to support his Liberal Democrat colleague in order not to embarrass me publicly. Will had said it was big of him. I wasn't sure whether David had picked up the sarcastic tone in his voice.

'Not really,' I said. 'It's not as if it matters any more. Not like it did before, anyway.'

'I still can't believe you're going to pull out,' Will said, shaking his head.

'Well, one day when you're older you'll realise that sometimes you have to make sacrifices for people you love.' Will pulled a face. I realised I must sound like some housewife from the fifties.

'People you love, or people who tell you what you can and can't do with your life?'

I hesitated. I knew full well what he was getting at. But if there was one thing I'd learnt in this election campaign it was how to wriggle out of an awkward direct question.

'I did it for you, Will,' I said, turning to face him. 'You and Charlotte and Esme.'

'I don't know why. None of us asked you to.'

He had a point. Though to be honest Charlotte didn't seem to be bothered either. She'd chosen to shut herself in her bedroom listening to Ed Sheeran rather than come with me to the hustings tonight. Though I suspected it was more because she was at that age where being seen out in public with your mum was just generally embarrassing, rather than specific lack of interest in the campaign.

Esme was still sporting the Lollipop Party sticker on her coat, but seemed to have cooled a bit on the whole idea because her favourite colour was now red.

'You know why I did it, Will.'

'Yeah,' he said, giving me a sideways look. 'I do.'

We climbed up the stone steps to the town hall and made our way through to the room where the hustings were being held. Some people had already arrived and staked their claim to front-row seats. A middle-aged man had bagged a seat near the back.

'I bet he's the heckler,' Will whispered.

I glanced across to the far end of the room where the other candidates had gathered: two women, Lib Dem and Green, and two men, the Labour guy and the sitting Tory MP. They turned to look in our direction. I felt instantly protective of Will. They could think and say anything they liked about me. I didn't want Will brought into it. The Liberal Democrat woman nodded at me. Her name was Laura Jenkins. I knew her from way back when she'd sat on the town council with David. She was tall and slim. Reedy, I suppose, was the word. Probably a few years older than me, but very stylish. I nodded back. I even managed a weak smile.

'Right,' I said, turning back to Will. 'I'd better go and join the rest of them. Are you sure you're OK about this? I mean, I don't think anyone will mention the stuff in the papers but if they do—'

'I know you'll give them hell on my behalf,' smiled Will.

'Something like that,' I said.

It was all fairly gentle at first. We made our opening speeches. The Tory MP tried to distance himself from the Lib Dems, Laura, the Lib Dem woman, tried to distance herself from the Tories, the Labour guy claimed it wasn't his party who had caused the recession and the Green woman banged on about needing a sustainable public transport system. All standard political fare really.

And then the middle-aged man near the back stood up and asked whether, in light of recent newspaper revelations, I was a fit candidate to represent the Calder Valley.

There was an awkward silence for a moment. The Green candidate looked down at her hands. The Labour guy shuffled his feet.

It was Laura who started talking. 'Personally, I don't think the children of parliamentary candidates should be subjected to this type of press intrusion.'

I started nodding, thinking she was going to be supportive.

And then she carried on. 'However, I do feel that people who put themselves forward as parliamentary candidates, particularly those standing on a family-friendly ticket, should be honest with the electorate about their own drug use. And to hear someone who used to smoke marijuana herself, talk about the dangers of drug-taking, is nothing if not hypocritical.'

A hush descended on the room. I stared at Laura. She didn't even have the guts to look me in the eye. I was aware that everyone was looking at me. Waiting for a response. And yet all I could think was 'How the hell did she know that?'

Because I knew there were only two people it could have come from. David or Will. I looked down into the audience and found Will. I could see the veins on his neck bulging. The colour rushing to his cheeks. He looked me in the eye and slowly shook his head. And I knew he was telling the truth.

'I didn't tell anyone,' said Will, afterwards as we made our way quickly down the steps of the town hall and away from the staring faces, 'not even any of my mates.'

'I know,' I said.

'So who told her?'

I didn't answer.

'You don't think?'

'I don't know what to think right now, Will.'

'Jeez, this is a mess.' I looked at him, my sixteen-year-old son, pronouncing on the shambles that my life had become. It would have been funny had it not been so painful.

'Did I do OK? Apart from being outed as a pot-smoking student, I mean.'

Will managed a smile.

'You were good. Made her look bad for mentioning it. And you wiped the floor with them on the other stuff. Shame it doesn't really matter now.'

I looked at him. For a moment I had forgotten about pulling out.

'Yeah,' I said. 'I guess it is.'

The house was quiet when we got back. Esme was asleep. Charlotte was still shut in her room with Ed Sheeran. David was in his study. I was going to wait until after Will had gone to bed to talk to him. But Will clearly had other ideas. He opened the study door without knocking and went it. I had no choice but to follow.

'What did you tell that Lib Dem woman about Mum?'

David looked up from his desk. He appeared genuinely startled.

'What on earth are you talking about?'

'Don't play dumb,' said Will, 'it doesn't suit you.' His jaw was set. He was jabbing his finger in the air. I had never seen him so wound up before. 'You did it to make her look bad, didn't you? To make sure she pulled out. All because you can't cope with her being more successful than you.'

David stood up. His eyes were dark. Darker than I'd ever seen them before. And they were boring into Will.

'I don't know what the hell is going on, but you'd better be very careful, young man. I have not done anything to harm your mother's campaign. I think you've made a very good job of that yourself.'

Will lunged towards David. I managed to get in between them, to pull Will away.

'Stop it,' I shouted. 'Stop it both of you.'

David was visibly shaken. Will still hadn't taken his eyes off him. It was like that game they used to play when he was younger, when Will dared him to see who would blink first. I could see the perspiration forming on David's top lip. The study was far too small for three of us.

'Look, I have no idea what went on tonight, but I can tell you that I have said and done nothing which would harm your mother's campaign. I don't know what you think of me, Will, clearly not very much, but I can tell you that I would not do that. I would not stoop that low.'

I looked him in the eye. He was telling the truth. I felt awful for having doubted him. For putting the very idea in Will's head. Maybe the tabloids had been digging dirt again. Maybe someone knew someone who used to know me back then – one of the psychology students at St Andrews.

'I'm sorry,' I said, turning to David. 'I'm really sorry. Everything got a bit heated in there tonight.'

'You said no one else knew,' said Will, turning on me. 'That the only people who knew were me and Dad. And I didn't tell anyone.'

'I'm not accusing you, Will.'

'You must be if you're saying it wasn't him.'

'Would someone mind telling me exactly what we're talking about?' asked David.

'Laura said it was hypocritical of me to talk about the dangers of drugs when I had smoked dope at uni.'

David stared at me, his brow furrowed slightly and then the colour dropped out of his face.

'You said you didn't say anything,' I said.

David shook his head slowly. 'I didn't. Not now. Not during the campaign.'

'When did you say something?'

He sighed deeply. 'Years ago. twelve or thirteen years ago.'

'Why would you have told her that about me years ago?'

'It came up one day,' he said, 'when we were talking.'

'But you don't just drop that sort of thing in a conversation, do you? Not personal stuff about your wife to some woman you hardly know.'

David hung his head.

'Oh Christ,' I said, realising straightaway.

'What?' said Will. 'What's going on?'

'Will, can you give us five minutes please? There's something we need to talk about.' Will tutted and shook his head, the sense of rage and frustration still palpable after he had left the room. I waited a moment, trying to compose myself. I wanted to sound strong when I spoke. Stronger than I was feeling, anyway. I also wanted David to have to sweat it out for a bit.

'How long did it last?' I asked finally.

'Just over a year.'

I nodded, trying to give no indication of how deeply the knife was cutting. 'Did you love her?'

David was still staring at the floor. 'No, not really. Not

like I . . .' his voice trailed off. He held his head in his hands.

'Why then?' I asked.

'Does anyone ever know why?'

'I don't know, David. I've never done it myself.'

He sighed. Took a long time before answering. 'I was lonely. You were always busy with the children. I missed having proper adult time with you.'

'Sex, you mean?'

'No. Not sex. Talking. Talking politics or art or music. Anything other than whether Will had just done a poo or whether I could remember if you'd made puréed butternut squash or sweet potato for Charlotte the previous night.'

His words slapped me around the face leaving me with red marks on my cheeks.

'Having two children under three wasn't easy, you know. It wasn't really conducive to intellectual debates.'

'I'm not blaming you.'

'That's good to hear.'

'I broke it off myself. I couldn't deal with the guilt.'

'She's clearly never forgiven you. Or forgiven me for winning you back without even realising it, maybe.'

David looked up at me for the first time. 'I'm sorry. I had no idea she'd even remembered what I said, let alone that she would be bitter and twisted enough to use it against you.'

'And the affair?' I asked. 'Are you sorry for that?'

'Yes. Yes, of course I am. I wouldn't have ended it other-wise.'

'But you never thought to tell me.'

'I didn't want to hurt you. I thought it was better you didn't know.'

'Better for whom? You or me?'

'Like I said, I'm sorry.'

'Were there others?' I asked. He shook his head.

'No.'

I believed him. Whether I forgave him, of course, was another matter. All those years I'd lived in an empty marriage because I didn't want to hurt David or the children. All the times I'd wondered about the other life I could have had. The one where I didn't lie awake at night aching for the touch of someone who was my soulmate. Who was there for me, emotionally and physically.

'I'm going to need some time to think,' I said.

'Yes, yes of course.'

'Perhaps you could sleep on the sofa tonight.' I realised as soon as I said it that I was doing that thing again. Being, as Will would put it, 'fucking reasonable'.

'Sure,' David said. 'I'll go and get the spare bedding.' He was heading back downstairs with it a few minutes later when Will came out of the kitchen. I'd thought he was angry earlier. But that was nothing compared to this. He looked at the bedding and at me then back to David.

'You cheated on her didn't you?'

'Will, really. This has nothing to do with you,' said David.

'Well that's where you're wrong. Because if you were cheating on Mum you were cheating on the rest of us too.

Mum might be too nice to tell you what she thinks of you, but I'm not.'

'Will, leave it,' I said.

'No, I won't leave it. Because someone has to tell him that you do not treat people like that. You do not walk all over them, say sorry, kip on the sofa for a couple of nights and expect everything to be OK.'

He turned to David. His finger started jabbing again. 'She deserves so much better than you. She really fucking does.'

He pushed past David and ran upstairs to his room, slamming the door behind him. Somewhere in the explosion of emotions which had just taken place inside of me was a strand of pure maternal pride.

When I came downstairs the next morning there was a note on the kitchen table. I knew as soon as I saw it that I didn't need to check the lounge. He would be gone.

I unfolded the piece of paper and read it.

'Will's right, you know. You do deserve better. You all do. I'm very sorry. I'll stop by this evening, about seven, to pick up some clothes. I'd appreciate it if the children weren't there. I don't want a big scene.'

So that was it. He wouldn't be home at 6.01 in the evening any more. And I was to stop being Mrs Banks. I stood for a moment, trying to work out how I felt about that, and then filled the kettle to make a cup of tea.

25

SAM

I sat at his bedside and watched Oscar breathe. Every breath as precious as his first. I could still remember it. Holding him in my arms for the first time. Kneeling in the birthing pool as the midwife passed him to me. Cradling his warm body. Marvelling at his tiny fingers and toes. Grinning at Rob who, unlike with Zach's birth, was not still in shock at the length of the umbilical cord.

'He's perfect,' Rob said. 'Absolutely perfect.' Except of course he hadn't been. Although we'd had no way of knowing that then. I often tried to recall, after we'd got the diagnosis, whether he hadn't kicked in my womb as much as Zach had. Whether they'd been anything in those first few months which could have alerted us to the fact that there was something wrong. Because that was the cruellest thing about this disease. The fact that it allowed you to have your perfect baby. To build those dreams for the future. To be lulled into thinking that you would hold your child's hand as he took his first tentative steps, like other parents do. And go on to see them walk and skip and run like other children do. And only then, when it had allowed you to relax entirely, safe in the knowledge that your child was ticking off their early milestones, did it reach in and wrench those hopes and dreams from you. Turning some invisible wheel on your child's back, so that their progress slowed. Slowed to the point of stopping entirely. Regressing even. And you were suddenly confronted with the stark realisation that there would be no first steps. Because your child wasn't normal after all. It had just taken nine months for you to find out.

Rob put two plastic cups of tea on the bedside table and sat back down next to me. He didn't say anything. He hadn't said anything much at all in the past four days. I'd tried to talk, to break through the shutters which had come down. But I didn't want to push too hard because I suspected he had put them down for a reason. Because it was the only way he could get through this.

I reached out and squeezed his hand. He squeezed mine back. It was the best we could do for the moment.

And all the time Oscar lay there. His face covered with a ventilation mask, which, as far as I could see, was sucking the life out of him, not into him. Because Oscar without words, Oscar without a cheeky grin, Oscar without a constant stream of jokes was just not Oscar at all. Sometimes, during the bits and pieces of sleep I managed to get on the put-you-up at night-times, I dreamt that our

Oscar was still at home. Still exactly the same as before. It was interesting because even in my dreams, I didn't imagine him not having SMA, just not having pneumonia. I wasn't greedy. I didn't want it all. I simply wanted back what I'd had up until a couple of weeks ago: a little boy with an incurable disease but not a life-threatening illness.

It was only when I brought myself back to the present and looked afresh at Oscar that I noticed his lips appeared to have gone a bluish colour. The machine that measured Oscar's oxygen levels bleeped. I called a nurse. Rob called too. Within seconds nurses and doctors were rushing to his bedside. Somewhere amongst the commotion I heard myself crying out 'no'. A second later my head was against Rob's T-shirt as he pulled me to his chest as if trying to muffle the sounds of my sobbing so he didn't have to hear it. So it didn't break through his defences. And just for a moment I wanted him to let me in to wherever it was he was. A place where this wasn't happening. Where I too could shut it all out.

When I looked up finally, everything appeared to be under control again. Oscar was still there. He was clearly still breathing. But the look on the doctor's face told me all I needed to know.

We were ushered into a side room. You are only ushered into a side room for one reason. I knew that. We sat down. I looked at Rob. His eyes were still vacant. I wanted to slap him around the face in order to bring him back to me. Because I needed him right now. I needed him so much.

'I won't beat about the bush,' the doctor said, peering

at us over the top of his glasses. 'Oscar's oxygen levels have fallen again. As we suspected, his body is not responding to the antibiotics. And as I explained before, because of his SMA, the muscles in his respiratory system are exceptionally weak and quite unable to fight pneumonia. He's done incredibly well to get this far, but I'm afraid there's nothing more we can do that we're not doing already. I feel I should warn you that his condition will only deteriorate from this point onwards. I'm very sorry, but he may only have a matter of days to live.'

All the times I had thought about this moment over the years, I'd imagined myself shouting, screaming hysterically, beating my fists on the walls. But actually, when it came, it was a quiet moment. The world stopped. I was aware of the ticking of the clock on the wall, but I knew that time was only progressing in the other world, the one I had just stepped out of. Our world was still and flat and silent. My eyes were hot with tears. I could feel a huge chasm opening up inside me. And I knew at that moment that what I needed to do was to get Oscar out of there. Get him to a place he could be at peace.

'So there's absolutely no chance . . .' The doctor shook his head.

'I'm so sorry,' he said again. 'We will do everything we can to make sure he's not in pain.'

'I'd like him to go to the children's hospice,' I said. 'It's nothing personal. I work there. It's where I want him to be.'

The doctor nodded. 'I understand. We can arrange that

for you if you're sure that's what you want.' He looked at Rob, who still hadn't said anything. Rob shrugged. The doctor got to his feet. 'I expect you need some time alone. Take as long as you need.' He left the room, pulling the door shut quietly behind him. I wished he'd slammed it. Anything to break through the silence which enveloped us. Rob stared straight ahead at the wall, expressionless. I stood up and walked over to him. Stroked his head, screwed up my eyes and started to cry.

'It's OK,' Rob said, clutching my hand.

'No,' I replied, shaking my head. 'It's not OK. Did you hear what he said? Oscar's going to die.'

'We don't know that for certain,' said Rob. 'Doctors can get it wrong. They often do. Maybe it's just going to take longer for the antibiotics to work on him. Maybe they need to give him more time.'

'Rob, you're not listening. There's nothing more they can do.'

He looked up at me sharply. 'And you're just going to accept that? You're the one who goes on about fighting for what's right, for what you believe in.'

'I've fought,' I said, wiping my eyes with the back of my hand. 'I've fought so long and so hard for him since the day he was diagnosed, but all that's left to fight for now is where he dies. And I am not having him dying here, surrounded by machines in a cold, sterile hospital.

'There's only one place I want him to be. Because if he goes to the hospice, we can all be there together and we can have time and space and privacy, but we can also have love and support, all the support we need, that Zach will need. We might just be able to get through it there. Here, I don't think we stand a chance.'

I sat down on Rob's lap to stop my body shaking, wiped my nose on my sleeve because I didn't have a tissue. It was then I realised it wasn't my body shaking at all. I put my arms around Rob's neck. Pressed my face next to his.

'I'm so scared,' he whispered. 'I'm so fucking scared.'

'I know,' I replied, shutting my eyes. 'Me too.'

I sat with Oscar. Tracing the veins in his arm with my finger. Trying not to think about the blood running through them. And the day when it would stop running. His eyes were open, although how much he was able to take in, what with his fever and the drugs he was on, I wasn't sure. I needed to tell him, though. I needed to let him prepare.

'We're going to take you somewhere you'll like tomorrow, love. We're taking you to Sunbeams. They're going to look after you there. We'll all be going, even Zach. They're going to take good care of you there, love. Very good care.'

For a second I thought I saw him smile. Not a big smile like he used to do, but a tiny little upturn at each corner of his mouth. Maybe I didn't. But maybe I did.

He understood what it meant. I was sure of that. He'd always understood a hell of a lot more than people gave him credit for. I missed him. I missed him already. I couldn't begin to imagine how much I'd miss him when he was actually gone.

I took Zach to the bench on the canal to tell him. I hadn't wanted to do it in an enclosed space. I wanted him to be outdoors. To have the sound of the wind and the stillness of the water to cushion him and fresh air to fill his lungs when he needed to take a big gasp. As it turned out, I didn't even have to tell him. He already knew.

'Oscar's going to die, isn't he?' His eyes were wide, his face open as he looked at me. I brushed an auburn curl back from his forehead. He was too young, far too young to be so wise.

'Yes, love. I'm afraid he is.' He nodded. His bottom lip started to tremble. 'The doctors have done everything they can, sweetheart. It's just his muscles not being strong enough to fight it because of the SMA.'

'But can't they zap him with something to make him better? Or give him some big medicine that will make his hair fall out? I wouldn't mind if his hair fell out. At least I'd still have a brother.'

I pulled him to me, any thoughts I'd had of not crying gone in an instant. He'd always asked lots of questions about the children at the hospice. He was well versed in dying children. Too well versed, maybe.

'It's not like other diseases, sweetie. The scientists haven't worked out how they can stop it yet.'

'Well when I grow up,' said Zach, taking a huge gulp of air between sobs, 'I'm going to be a scientist and I'm going to find out how to make children like Oscar better.'

'That would be a brilliant thing to do, love. But I want you to remember that you are the best big brother anyone could ever have. And Oscar loves you to bits, OK? We all do.' Zach stared out from my arms at the canal, I could almost feel the ache inside his head as he tried to make sense of everything.

'When is he going to die?'

'We don't know exactly. But it will be soon. That's why we're taking him to Sunbeams tomorrow morning. We think that's the best place for him to be. For all of us to be.'

Zach dried his eyes on his sleeve. 'So I can come too?'

'Of course you can.'

'What about school?'

'You don't have to go this week.'

'But everyone has to go to school.'

'Normally, yes, but not this week. This week you're going to be with us. I'll phone Mrs Cuthbert on Monday morning to tell her. She'll understand.'

Zach nodded, but still didn't seem sure. It broke my heart that the boy who worried too much now had even more to worry about.

'He won't be able to go on the playground with me this time, will he?'

'No, love,' I said. 'We'll find nice things for him to do inside, though. Nice places for him to be.'

'OK,' said Zach. 'I'll go and pack my things.'

I put gel on Oscar's hair before we left the hospital. He never went to Sunbeams without sticky-up hair.

'There,' I said to him when I finished. 'You're ready now.' I wasn't ready though. I was so not ready.

I went with him in the ambulance. His body appeared to have grown smaller by the day, surrounded as it was by so many machines. His face barely visible now beneath the mask. I talked to him all the way. Silly little things, anything I could pull out of the bag marked 'memories'. The bag which would soon be all we had left of him.

We pulled up outside Sunbeams. The ambulance driver came round to help his colleague get Oscar out. He lowered his eyes as he passed me. I knew he meant it kindly, that he was trying to be sensitive, but I still wanted to shout at him, 'He's not dead yet, you know.' It felt like we were in a funeral cortège. That they were carrying a coffin instead of a little boy. And then I looked up and saw Rob and Zach standing solemn-faced next to the car. Our car. Our specially adapted wheelchair-accessible car. And I realised that we would have to sell it afterwards. Because we would not need it any more. And because I would not be able to bear to go in it once Oscar was gone.

I managed to dredge up a smile for Zach from somewhere deep inside. Albeit a rather watery one.

'Come on, sweetheart,' I said, taking his hand. 'Let's go and get Oscar comfortable.'

When we stepped inside it was instant. The love hit me like the heat does when you step off a plane into a tropical climate. It enveloped us, instantly easing the stresses and strains of a long and tiring journey. My muscles relaxed a little, the tension was sighed away. Marie came forward and hugged me, the tenderness in her welcome sand-papering the edges off the fear.

'Come and make yourselves at home,' she said. I turned to see the tears streaming down Rob's face. And I was relieved, so very relieved that at last they had found a way out. I took Rob's hand. Marie put her arm around Zach's shoulders.

'Now, I've got an important job for you,' she said. 'While Mummy and Daddy get settled and I get Oscar comfortable, could you go with Julie here and help her choose some special things for Oscar's room? She needs to know what toys and bits you think he'd like.'

Zach nodded. He went with Julie down the corridor. I squeezed Rob's hand. He was going to be OK.

I turned back to Marie.

'Would you like to be with Oscar while I take him off the ventilator?' she asked.

I nodded.

'Come through with me to his room then, and we'll do it as soon as Julie's taken Zach to play.'

Ten minutes later I was looking at a little boy lying on a bed. A boy I almost didn't recognise. There were no masks, machines or tubes. It was just him. Oscar. He'd come back to us. I felt a brief spurt of elation before the reality flooded in. The laboured breathing. His bloated abdomen sticking out below his sunken chest. The glazed look in his eyes. He would not be with us long. But while we had him, he would be made so very welcome.

26

JACKIE

I found her sitting in a crumpled heap in front of the cupboard under the stairs, her wet knickers around her ankles. Tears were seeping silently from the corners of her eyes.

'It's OK,' I said, crouching down next to her and pulling her to me. 'I'm here now. Everything's OK.'

Mum looked at me, the skin around her mouth twitching. 'I couldn't find toilet,' she said. 'I couldn't remember which door it were. I thought it were in there.' She pointed to the cupboard under the stairs. Mum had lived in this house for fifty-odd years. She had never had a downstairs toilet.

'No, it's upstairs, next to your bedroom. Never mind, let's get you cleaned up.' She nodded and shut her eyes for a moment as if she couldn't bear me to see her shame. My mother, who had no doubt had to clear up plenty of my 'accidents' in her time, now having to be cleaned up by her own daughter.

She was quiet as I helped her get changed. Quiet and thoughtful rather than quietly vacant. She looked up at me when we were finished and took hold of my hand.

'I don't know where owt is any more,' she said. 'Not even in me own home. It don't feel like me home now. Not really. It's too big for me. I'm scared, you know. Scared of getting lost in me own home.'

She looked old and frail and bewildered. She looked lost.

'How about we find you somewhere new to live?' I said. 'Somewhere you've just got one room with a little bathroom. Where you'll get your meals cooked and there'll be company for you and where there'll always be someone there to help you when you need it.'

She shrugged. She really wasn't up to making decisions any more. Life had come full circle. It was my turn to look after her. To do the right thing. Even if she didn't understand what that was.

I'd known the performance was going to be good. Actually, beyond good. But it was only when I saw Will up there on stage, playing the part of the bully, that I realised just how good it was.

The audience of Year Nines was silent, none of the usual giggling and fidgeting. They watched intently as Will chose his 'victim' and began his calculating reign of terror. Psychological, all of it. He never laid a finger on him. But he coaxed and cajoled his classmates to join in the laughter, to point the finger, to sign up to the silences.

And when, after a sustained campaign of terror and ridicule, the victim didn't come to school one morning, they watched Will sneer and gloat, crack jokes about what might have happened to him. Until they were called into assembly, that was, and told by the Head what had actually happened to him. And told in no uncertain terms that it must never happen to anyone at that school again. At which point everyone turned to look at Will and he slunk off on his own down the corridor, knowing that this was all his doing. And that nobody would ever allow him to forget it.

Charlotte was crying by the end of the performance. She wasn't the only one, though, not by a long chalk. Several of the girls in her year had tears streaming down their faces. Only theirs were tears of guilt.

The pupils broke into a spontaneous round of applause. Not the usual behaviour at the end of a PHSCE lesson, albeit a rather unconventional one. Will wasn't interested in milking the applause, though. He simply went up to Charlotte and gave her a hug. And everyone knew then that things had changed and she wasn't on her own any more.

I waited at the bottom of the road for Anna to arrive. I hadn't wanted her to come to the house. Alice would have asked too many questions about where we were going and why. Saying goodbye to people wasn't one of her strong points. She'd cried on the three or four occasions when one of her classmates had left the school. And that had been because they were moving away from the area. Not because they were dying.

Dying. I still couldn't get my head around it. Still couldn't forget the catch in Sam's voice as she told me on the phone. And the silence at my end as I'd failed miserably to find anything suitable to say. What could you say? It was a mother's worst nightmare. My own mother had worn the same haunted expression on her face for thirty-two years because of it. The thought of Sam having to go through that, of Zach having to cope with losing a sibling, was so unfair. And so bloody, bloody cruel.

Anna's silver Polo pulled up on the kerb next to me. I opened the door and got in. We looked at each other. We'd both opted for navy. One stop short of funereal black. We burst into tears at exactly the same moment.

'I can't believe this is happening,' I said as I leant over and hugged her.

'I know, I feel so utterly helpless. I'm still not even sure if we're doing the right thing by going. Maybe visitors are the last thing they need.'

'I did ask her to text me if she changed her mind. If it wasn't a good time.'

'I don't suppose there is such a thing as a good time,' replied Anna.

'No. I guess not. But I just want to be there for her. To let her know she's not on her own.'

'It sounds like Rob needs a hell of a lot of support too. Sam always said he was in denial about the whole situation. I think it's hit him hard.'

'Maybe we could ask Paul and David to help,' I suggested, 'take Rob out somewhere to get away from it all. Not now. Afterwards, I mean.'

Anna's face crumpled. The usual air of cool, calm togetherness, replaced by something altogether different.

'He's gone,' she said.

'I'm sorry?'

'David. He's left me. Well, actually Will sort of kicked him out. It's rather complicated.'

I stared at her. Not quite able to take it in. I don't think she was, either.

'Why? What happened?'

'The whole fuss at the hustings. The stuff about the dope. It came from David.'

'Jeez. You mean he told her on purpose, to smear you?'

She shook her head.

'No. He told her years ago. When he was having an affair with her.'

My mouth must have visibly gaped open. She managed a weak smile.

'Oh, Anna,' I said, 'that's awful. You poor thing.'

'Not really. Not as poor as Sam.'

'Hey, this isn't competitive misery, you know. On any normal scale this is massive.'

'Not really,' she said. 'I don't love him, you see. I haven't loved him for ages.'

She said it quietly and calmly. The way you would if you were discussing a type of cheese you'd gone off.

'Oh. I'm sorry. I had no idea.'

'I did a very good job of the whole sham marriage thing.'

'And you didn't know, about the affair I mean?'

'No. I guess I was too busy with the children. It was when Will and Charlotte were little. That's why he said it happened.'

I shook my head and blew out a short whistle. 'Women can't win, can they? They get slagged off if they're not putting their kids first and cheated on by their husbands if they are.'

Anna smiled. 'Shame that can't be in the mummyfesto,' she said. 'It's a good line.'

'Why did you stay with him so long?' I asked.

'The usual reason. I was planning to stick it out until Will and Charlotte had both left school.'

'But what about Esme?'

Anna hesitated. 'She wasn't planned. We were still having sex, although it was pretty much down to being every Friday. You know, like how some people have fish on Fridays. That sort of thing.'

I nodded. 'So when she came along it meant you had to stay that much longer.'

'I tried to make it work, but he grew more distant than ever. He just wasn't there for me emotionally. Maybe he was only staying for the same reason I was. I don't know. He never wanted to talk about our relationship. Said I should stick to counselling people at work.'

'But there must have been times when you were tempted. You know, to see another man.'

'It's surprising how easy it is to avoid eligible men if you put your mind to it,' she said. 'Especially if you counsel troubled teenagers and you work from home the rest of the time.'

'You went out of your way to avoid them?'

She shrugged. 'It was easier that way. I was far too vulnerable. It would have been so easy to fall for someone else.'

'Someone who could have made you happy.'

She shrugged again. 'Like I said, the children always came first.'

'And you still didn't throw him out when you found out about the affair?'

'Will said I was too fucking reasonable. I guess he was right. That's why he ended up doing it himself.'

I shook my head. 'So what happens now?'

'We go and see Sam and neither of us breathes a word about it, OK? I don't want her to know. Not right now. She's got enough to deal with.'

I nodded slowly and sighed. 'Considering we were planning to run the country a few weeks ago, we really are in an awful mess, aren't we?'

'Yes,' she said. 'I guess we are.'

I was dreading the visit to the hospice. I couldn't think of anywhere worse in the world than somewhere that children go to die. Of course, Sam had told me enough times that it wasn't like that at all. That a lot of children just went there for respite care. That it was actually an incredibly life-affirming place to be. I hadn't believed her though. I'd thought it was her just seeing the good in everything. And always being so bloody positive.

She was right. I realised that within a few minutes of walking through the door. The woman who greeted us was bright and welcoming. Inside it was light and airy, the sounds of music and laughter resonated along the corridor. People who walked past us were smiling. An air of calm pervaded the place. I glanced at Anna. She raised her eyebrows at me. Clearly she hadn't expected this either.

The corridor led to a communal area where a boy was sitting with his father playing chess. It was a few seconds before I realised it was Zach and Rob.

'I hope you're beating him,' I said, bending down and putting an arm around Zach's shoulder. He turned around and smiled. Not a full grin but a smile all the same.

'I've got him on the defensive,' Zach said.

'And the sad thing is I am actually trying,' added Rob.

'Where's Oscar this morning?' the woman who had shown us in asked.

'In the lights-and-bubble room,' Zach replied. She gestured to us to follow her and opened a door off the corridor we had just walked down. Oscar was lying on a water bed. His eyes were open and he was gazing up at a massive lava-lamp-style tube which ran from the floor to the ceiling. His eyes swivelled to us as we came into the room. I tried to think there was a flicker of recognition there, but I couldn't be sure. He looked very weak. Very weak indeed.

Sam was lying next to him. Her red curls lacking their usual bounce, the dark shadows under her eyes telling a different story to the smile she managed. She got up slowly and came over to us. I held out my arms and hugged her, feeling her chest expanding and contracting. Anna put her arm around her shoulder, rubbing her hand up and down her arm.

'Why don't I lie with Oscar for a bit while you catch up with your friends?' the woman who had shown us in suggested.

Sam nodded. 'He's due the cough machine and suctioning in about fifteen minutes,' she said.

'It's OK,' the woman replied with a smile. 'We won't forget.'

Sam turned back to us. 'Can we go outside? I haven't been outside for a while.'

'We can go anywhere you want,' I said. 'Only we're providing the refreshments.' I opened my bag to show her the stash of chocolate I had brought with me.

'I'll get the coffees in,' said Anna.

I followed Sam back down the corridor to a glass door which led to a small outside courtyard with several bench seats. It was a nice evening, unusually mild for a Yorkshire April. I watched her look up at the sky, drinking in the sunshine as if she were solar-powered and needed its energy to keep going. She sat herself down on the bench. I sat one side of her, Anna followed us out with the coffees and sat down on the other side.

'You were right,' I said to Sam. 'About this place, I mean.'

Sam nodded. 'I wouldn't want to be anywhere else right now. They know exactly what to do, what to say. I knew they would. I've seen them do it so many times with other people. Although I guess it's only when it's you that you really appreciate and understand what a difference it makes.'

'How's Zach?' I asked.

'Better than I thought he'd be. They're taking such good care of him. He's been getting counselling and everything. But not in an obvious way that would scare him off. They do everything they can to prepare them.'

'How's Rob bearing up?' asked Anna.

'Difficult to say. He's got so much ground to make up. All those years he wouldn't really accept what had happened. What the future might hold.'

'They'll help him here, though, won't they?' said Anna.

'Yeah,' she replied. 'He has at least admitted to me that I was right – that this is the best place to be.'

'And what about you?' I asked. 'How are you doing?'

Sam looked up at the sky again. Her hands clasped tightly in her lap.

'I'm mad as hell,' she said, 'because there is so much I wanted Oscar to do. So many places I wanted to take him. So many things I wanted him to experience. I used to think it was a bit weird, you know when we had families with children with life-limiting illnesses who traipsed halfway around the world so they could say their kid had been to Disneyland. But I understand now. Not about Disneyland, maybe, but about that need to show them new things before they go. Oscar's never been to Scotland. I wanted to take him on the ferry over to Mull. To the place where *Balamory* was filmed. He would have loved that. Or to Cornwall. He's never even seen a bloody lighthouse. How can you die without seeing a lighthouse? That's not right, is it? It can't be right.'

I pulled her in towards me, but she wasn't ready to cry just yet.

'And the other thing,' she went on. 'The other thing which really pisses me off is these God bods who go around saying that everything happens for a reason. That God has chosen him for an angel and all that crap. He's going to die because he has an incurable disease that means he can't fight pneumonia. Not because God's one short on the nativity play for fuck's sake. And if anyone so much as suggests putting angel wings on his obituary notice I'm going to hit them. I really am.'

The tears came this time. Fast and furious. Anna and I sandwiched her between us, supporting her body as it shook and heaved, taking it in turns to stroke back the damp hair from her face.

'Sorry,' sniffed Sam finally.

'Don't be daft,' said Anna. 'This is good, you know. Letting it all out. This is exactly why we came.'

Sam looked up at us, her eyes rimmed with red. 'I can't stop wanting to fight it. That's what I do. I fight things I don't agree with, things that I think are wrong. And yet somehow I'm supposed to accept this. And accept that there is absolutely nothing I can do about it.'

'But you are doing something,' said Anna. 'You're making things the best they can possibly be for your family in the circumstances. You've brought them here, surrounded by everything they need and you're going to be there for them all through this whole horrible time.'

'It's not enough, though,' said Sam. 'I want to do so much more. A couple of weeks ago we were planning a revolution. We were going to make life better for millions of families. Now I can't even make my own son better. The best I can do is to sit next to him and hold his hand while he dies. I feel so weak, so pathetic. So utterly helpless.'

We held her some more. Cried some more. Tried but probably failed to say the right things. All the time knowing that we were getting nearer and nearer to the point we were dreading. The point where we were going to have to say goodbye to Oscar.

Sam came in with us. I told her not to. I didn't want her to have to witness it, but she insisted. She lay back down on the water bed next to Oscar. I took his hand in mine, already feeling the tugging and tearing inside me.

'I love you little boy,' I whispered to him. 'You are the funniest, most gorgeous, cheekiest little chap I've ever known. And Alice thinks so too. We all do. And you've got the most brilliant mummy in the world too. But you already know that, don't you?'

I let go of his hand after one final squeeze and turned

so he wouldn't see my tears. Sam saw them, though. I wiped my eyes, annoyed with myself for not being stronger. Because whatever it was I was feeling was only a tiny fraction of the pain she must be going through. I kissed her on the cheek and gave her a huge hug.

'If you need to talk,' I said, 'any time, day or night, just call me, OK?'

She nodded. I walked from the room without daring to look back.

I waited for Anna outside the hospice. It was a long time before she came. When she did do, her face was ashen. Her gait a little unsteady. We walked silently to her car and got in.

'Have you withdrawn yet?' I asked her. 'From the election.'

She looked at me and shook her head.

'Good,' I said. 'Neither have I.'

27

ANNA

'When can I go to Daddy's new flat?' asked Esme, for the hundredth time as she bounced up and down in the kitchen. It was ironic really. All that time I'd stayed with David for the sake of the children and when we did finally split up, far from being bothered about him leaving she seemed to be positively fizzing at the idea of there being another home for her to wreck.

'Just a few minutes now and he'll be here.'

David had got a room in a large three-storey town house five minutes walk from where we were. He'd emailed me with the details the day after he left. He was very efficient like that. Always had been. In a bizarre way I thought he'd probably be a much better ex-husband than he had been a husband. He was punctual, responsible, good at practical arrangements. He wouldn't be the sort of ex who was forever cancelling plans and letting me down.

'Why aren't Charlotte and Will coming?' asked Esme.

'I told you, love, Charlotte's busy with her homework and Will's going to come and help me with the election campaign.' I wasn't lying to her. I was simply being economical with the truth about the fact that had they not been otherwise engaged they still wouldn't have wanted to see him. Charlotte had sat quietly while I'd told her. She didn't do angry or outspoken like Will, but in her own quiet, thoughtful way she'd clearly been appalled. She'd also made it very clear that she did not want to see her father. She'd come round. I was sure of that. She had my reasonable genes and was not one to bear a grudge. But she'd do it in her own time and when she did that would be fine by me. Will, on the other hand, was extremely unlikely to forgive and forget. I knew David was aware of that. Maybe that was why he'd left. Because he'd known Will would be capable of making his life a misery even if I wasn't.

The doorbell rang. Esme shot out to the hall.

'Daddy,' she cried when I opened the door. David's face went up two notches on the brightness control, no doubt relieved that at least one person in this house was still pleased to see him.

Our eyes met for a split second. He was the one who cracked and averted his gaze. I didn't get any satisfaction out of his guilt. None whatsoever.

'Best behaviour, remember,' I said to Esme, kissing the top of her head. 'She's had her tea. If you could have her back by 7.45, please. Eight at the latest.' David nodded.

'Mummy's going campaigning with Will,' said Esme. David looked at me questioningly.

'For Sam,' I said. 'We're carrying on for Sam. Oscar's at the hospice.'

'Oh,' said David, lowering his eyes.

'They've got a lights-and-bubbles room there,' said Esme. 'I'd like to go sometime.' I smiled and stroked her hair, not having the heart to tell her that it wasn't somewhere you could pay £3.50 for the pleasure of being able to dive into a ballpond.

I waved goodbye and shut the door behind them. I stood with my back against it for a few moments trying to gather my thoughts. It was only then that I noticed Will looking down from the landing.

'Has he gone?' he asked.

'Yeah,' I said. 'He has.'

It felt strange being back on the campaign trail. So much had changed since the last time I'd been out electioneering. I was a different person. We all were. But as I walked down the road, gazing at the number of purple Lollipop Party posters in the window, the one thing which I did know was that I was glad to be back.

'I can't believe how many there still are,' I said to Will.

'Well they didn't know you were going to pull out, did they?'

'No, but I thought the whole thing at the hustings might have put people off.'

Will started laughing.

'What?' I said.

'Mum, this is Hebden Bridge. People are hardly gonna decide not to vote for you because you rolled a few joints at uni, are they? Not when some of them have got cannabis plantations in their backyards. It's probably boosted your popularity, given you a bit of street cred.'

I smiled. Every politician should have a teenage boy as a special adviser. They were very skilled at cutting through the crap.

'Thank you,' I said. 'You are officially my campaign manager. Although I'm not sure I should be pleased at getting a popularity boost through revelations about my drug-taking.'

'And mine,' he said. 'That probably got the youth vote out for you.'

'Will!'

'Only joking,' he said. 'Anyway. I haven't touched the stuff since. Just so you know. I haven't even been to the park.'

'Good.'

'Actually, I'm going round Sol's place tomorrow, after school.'

'Are you? That's great, love. I'm really pleased.'

'His parents have told him to cool it with Katie a bit, until the exams are over, like.'

'So he's going to muck about with you instead?' I said smiling. 'I don't suppose that's exactly what his parents had in mind.'

'We won't be mucking about. We're working on the duologue thing for our drama exam.'

'Oh,' I said, not wanting to make my surprise too obvious, 'that's great. Good for you. Jackie told me how brilliant your performance was, by the way. In the bullying thing. Thank you. I know it meant a lot to Charlotte. It meant a lot to me, too.'

Will shrugged. 'Jackie reckons if I knuckle down to it I could get As. And if I want to get into drama college, that's what they're going to be looking for.'

'Right,' I said. He had never mentioned drama college before. I suspected Jackie had been chipping away at him. 'Well it sounds like a good plan to me.'

Will stopped walking for a moment. 'Look, I know I screwed up. But I also know that if that photo hadn't been published I would probably have screwed up even worse. In a weird way, they did me a favour.'

'In the old days,' I said, 'it was called a kick up the arse.'

Will grinned. 'Yeah. Something like that, I guess. Anyway, we'd better get these leaflets out. If you want to kick some ass, that is.'

I smiled as Will took a pile of leaflets from his rucksack.

He looked at me. 'You never really wanted to pull out, did you?' he asked.

'No,' I replied. 'I didn't. I was just trying to keep everyone happy.'

'Trying to keep Dad happy, you mean.'

'Not just that. I was worried about the media, about

what they could do to you and Charlotte and Esme. I still am, to be honest.'

Will shrugged. 'I guess it's down to us not to do stupid stuff. If we don't do stupid stuff they can't have a go at you.'

I shook my head. 'So some day I'm going to have to credit the tabloid press with keeping my children on the straight and narrow.'

Will smiled. He put a leaflet through the next letterbox and looked at me. 'I'm glad you're not pulling out,' he said. 'I'm dead proud of you. We all are.'

'Thank you,' I said. 'If it wasn't that it would embarrass the hell out of you, I would kiss you in the street.'

'Phew,' said Will. 'Lucky escape there then.'

I sat behind the table staring out at the assembled media. We had to hire a big room at the town hall to do things like this these days. There was a time when the very thought of that would have sent us giddy with excitement. It was a very long time ago now though. I glanced across at Jackie who gave me a wink. Neither of us was relishing doing this. Putting ourselves out there again. Having to be in the same room as some of the people who had caused us so much pain. It wasn't about us, though. It was about something far bigger. Which was why I was about to swallow my pride and smile and be polite to our assembled guests.

'Thank you for coming at such short notice,' I began. 'We have a statement on behalf of the Lollipop Party which we want to read to you. For reasons which will become apparent, we won't be taking questions afterwards.

'The last couple of weeks have been extremely trying for us. Our family members have been thrust into the media spotlight in a way which, rightly or wrongly, we never anticipated.

'Last week Jackie and I reluctantly decided that we would withdraw from the election campaign in order to protect our families from any further intrusion. Sam asked us to wait a week before officially withdrawing in case we changed our minds.

'Unfortunately within hours of that decision, Sam's youngest son, who, as has already been reported, suffers from spinal muscular atrophy, was taken seriously ill. We're heartbroken to say that he has now been given a matter of days to live.'

I paused as my voice caught. Jackie squeezed my knee under the table. I looked at the faces of the assembled media. Faces that were now softer than they were a few minutes ago.

'Jackie and I have decided that we will stand in the election as a tribute to Sam's passion for the Lollipop Party and her desire to make this country a better place to live for children and families.

'Sam will not, of course, be taking part in any more campaigning. But we and the other Lollipop Party candidates standing across the country will be continuing the campaign. If you believe in what she believes in, we ask you to vote for us.

'We also ask that the media respect the privacy of Sam and her family at this most difficult time. What she has discovered, and indeed what we have all discovered, is that there are some things in life more important than politics. And that is why we are standing. We are not career politicians. If we get elected our families will still come first. If you would rather vote for someone who thinks the world begins and ends at Westminster then please do so. If, however, you think it's time that ordinary people who are not in it for the money or the kudos or because of their egos, who, to be honest, would rather not be standing at all right now but are doing so because they believe so passionately in making this country a better place for everyone, then you may wish to consider voting for us.

'Most importantly, we ask you to think of Sam and her family. They aren't religious. They don't want your prayers because no amount of praying is going to change what will happen to Oscar. But what you can do for them is to think about what's important in your life and make sure it's the things that really matter. Thank you.'

My hands were still trembling as I finished. I put the piece of paper down and glanced at Jackie. She nodded. We got up and walked out together. Leaving a strangely quiet room of people behind us.

The response was instant and overwhelming. Tweets, Facebook postings, emails and messages on the blog from other mums, all of them sending their thoughts to Sam and her family. Quite a few of them from people who had lost a child or been through their own traumas and come out the other side. Several from politicians from other parties, putting aside the election rivalry for a moment to demonstrate that they were human beings too.

I had a direct message on Twitter from Gavin at Radio 4 saying simply,

Best speech I've ever heard a politician make – because it wasn't about politics. Thinking of your friend and her family. X

Perhaps in different circumstances I might have replied. Might have sat there trying to think of something suitably appreciative to say. But at that moment, it was enough to know that someone cared. That lots of people cared. That we were not on our own.

My mobile beeped. The message was from David.

Well done. Send my regards to Sam.

I shook my head and looked at the ceiling. It was too late, of course. And it wasn't going to change anything. But I was glad that the father of my children had shown some degree of humanity.

I continued scrolling down the messages. My phone beeped again. Sam's name came up. For a second I thought the worst. Until I saw the words on the screen.

Thank you. Marie made me watch it. So thank Jackie for phoning her too. I love you both to bits.

28

SAM

There was a knock at our door, Julie, our family support worker, put her head around it, saw that Oscar was sleeping and gestured to Zach.

'Are you coming, Zach?' she whispered. 'Molly and Jack are ready to play.' Zach nodded, jumped up and followed her out without so much as a backward glance. Molly and Jack were the other members of the sibling group. They had a bond. Not an obvious one, like being into Moshi monsters or something. A far deeper one than that. They each had a brother or sister who was going to die soon. In Zach's case, it would be any time now. And what I hoped more than anything was that Molly and Jack would be able to understand in a way that no one else could. And that one day, Zach would be able to understand for them.

'He'll be OK,' said Rob. He didn't mean at the group. I

knew that. We had got used to saying big things in a small way.

'I hope so.'

'I know so.'

I looked at him. 'It's surprised you, hasn't it, this place?'

Rob nodded. 'I was so scared of it for such a long time.'

'Because of what you associated it with?'

'Yeah. I didn't want to have to think about any child dying. Let alone Oscar.'

'I guess I was the other way. I wanted to immerse myself in it, as if I could build up some kind of immunity.'

'It didn't stop it happening though, did it?'

'No. But it did mean I knew to come straight here when the time came.'

We sat for a while, silently watching over Oscar, until Chris, one of the nurses came in. He stopped, realising instantly that Oscar's breathing was more laboured than it had been. Noticing that the blue-tinge on his lips was stronger than ever.

He crouched down next to us. 'I think we're very near,' he said. 'You might want to gather the people you want to be around you. Give everyone a last chance to say goodbye. I can't say how long you'll have with him, but he will be all yours.'

'Thank you,' I said. Rob put his arm around my shoulder. I turned to Marie who was standing in the doorway behind us, trying very hard to stay professional when I suspected from the look on her face that she wanted to burst into tears as much as I did.

'Can you get Zach back please?' I asked. 'And can you call my mum and dad in from the garden. Ask them to come straightaway.'

'Of course, love,' she said.

I sat down next to Oscar's bed. Stroked his clammy forehead. 'It's OK,' I whispered. 'Mummy's here. I'm going to be right here with you all the way.'

Rob sat down next to me, his face pale and drawn. His legs were stretched out under the bed. I could see his left knee shaking. I took his hand in mine.

'He looks tired,' I said. 'Oscar never does tired. Maybe it's his way of letting us know he's ready.'

There was a knock at the door. Julie came in with Zach. 'I'll be right outside if you need me,' she said.

Zach looked at me, his eyes darker and deeper than I'd ever seen them before. He was too young. Far too young to have to be dealing with this. I lifted him up and sat him on my lap, hugging him to me.

'It's time to say goodbye to Oscar, love. He's tired now. He's finding it too tricky to breathe.'

Zach nodded solemnly. 'And Daddy won't have to do the dragon monster sucking machine on him ever again, will he?'

'No, love.'

'Good. I don't think he liked that. Not really.'

I buried my face in his hair, drinking in the goodness in him. Wiping away both our tears in turn.

'Where will he go when he dies?' asked Zach. 'And please don't say he's going to be a new star in the sky because

I know all about astronomy and I know it doesn't work like that.'

I smiled again through the tears. My big boy being so grown-up. So brave.

'Marie's going to take him through to the butterfly suite for us. Remember, the place I showed you yesterday?'

'The one that felt like the fridge bit in Tesco?'

'Yes.' I smiled and stroked his hair.

'Good. He'll like it there. They've got a Mickey Mouse duvet cover. And there was an Ey eore on the bed.'

I swallowed hard. 'Do you want to go through with Julie now and get it ready for him, then? You can take his bits and pieces from here if you like.'

Zach picked up Oscar's pirate hat and home-made telescope from the bedside table. I opened the door. Julie nodded, took his hand and led him through.

I turned to Rob. He looked as if he might either collapse, fall or be sick at any moment. 'We can do this,' I said to him. 'We can get through it together.'

He stared at me. He looked lost. Empty. 'Sorry,' he said, looking down at his feet. 'I'm being totally crap at this.'

'No, you're not,' I replied, taking his hand. 'You're just hurting. And everybody hurts differently.'

Rob gazed down at Oscar. 'I don't think I can bear to let him go.'

'Don't think of it as letting go,' I said. 'Think of it as releasing him.'

Zach came back in with Julie. He sat on my lap. He was quieter, rubbing the nail of my thumb over and over again.

There was a knock on the door. Julie opened it. It was Mum. Zach ran straight over to her. She folded him into her arms. Her first-born grandson. Soon to be her only grandson. The word precious, didn't even come close. She looked up at me, her eyes glistening, and shook her head slowly. I knew exactly what she was thinking. No one should have to see their child suffer. No one at all.

Dad shuffled into the room. I hadn't even realised he'd been standing in the doorway, teetering on the edge, perhaps unsure about what to say or do. He came over and took my hand, patted it and opened and closed his mouth without saying anything, looking for all the world like an actor who'd forgotten his lines.

The truth, of course, was that there was no script. We were all having to ad lib, to improvise our way through a scene we had never wanted to be in. A play we had always hoped would not make it to this stage.

Oscar's face turned towards us for a second. I was sure he could hear us. Sure he could feel the overwhelming love in the room. His breathing quickened again.

'I'll be outside if you need me,' whispered Julie. I beckoned to Mum and Dad to come forward. Mum stroked Oscar's cheek with her trembling finger, the tears streaming down her face, before kissing him on the forehead. Dad bent and kissed him on the lips, as if in a valiant last attempt to breathe life into him. Neither of them was able to speak.

'Is it my turn now?' asked Zach.

'Yes, love,' I said, 'take as long as you need.'

'Night-night Oscar,' he said, giving him a great big slobbery kiss on the cheek. 'You were the best pirate captain ever.'

I smiled and cried at the same time. Leant over and hugged my boys to me for one last time.

'Will I have to go home when he dies?' asked Zach. 'Will one of those sad men in black coats come and get Oscar?'

'No, love,' I said, stroking his hair. 'He can stay in the butterfly room until the funeral. We'll be right there with him in the flat. We can go into his room and see him whenever we like.'

'Good,' said Zach. 'I'd like that.' And without another word he slipped down off the bed, took Mum's hand and led her out through the patio doors into the remembrance garden beyond. Dad followed them, leaning heavily on Julie.

I watched them for a moment. Saw Zach looking at the water fountain, no doubt asking Julie a dozen questions about how it worked. Saw Mum and Dad sitting next to each other on the garden bench. Their eyes on Zach. Dad's hand resting lightly on Mum's knee.

I got into bed next to Oscar. Curled myself around him, the way I used to do when he was a baby, and breathed him in as I held him in my arms.

'You have brought us nothing but joy,' I whispered. 'Joy and love and laughter. And we wouldn't have missed having you as our little boy for anything in the world. And now you're going to be the birdman of Bognor. Just like you always wanted.'

Rob broke down sobbing next to me. He leant over, his long fingers sliding through Oscar's hair.

'We'll get you some gel on that, mate, don't worry.'

Oscar laughed. His last breath was a laugh, not a wheeze. And then he slipped away.

Marie and Chris came to take Oscar through to the butterfly room. Marie didn't need to be there, but I think she wanted to.

'Are you ready?' Marie asked softly, shortly afterwards. I looked at Rob. He nodded.

Julie brought Zach in from the garden and we walked through to the butterfly suite together. The chill was actually oddly welcoming. Cooling things off, slowing them down, allowing us to steady ourselves. I looked at the things Zach had put out for Oscar and arranged on the bed.

'Thank you, sweetheart,' I said. 'What a good job you've done here. Oscar will love it.'

Chris and Marie lifted Oscar on to the bed. Zach came across and pulled the duvet over him.

'Look, it's the Mickey Mouse one,' he said. For a second I thought Oscar might reply until I remembered he couldn't. We wouldn't be hearing his voice ever again. I sat down next to the bed, pulled Zach up on to my lap and took Oscar's hand.

'Hello, sweetheart,' I said. 'Your big brother's done a fantastic job for you, getting this lovely room ready. You can rest now, love. That's why you're here.'

*   *   *

The one thing I hadn't been expecting was to get so used to it. Seeing Oscar's body lying there. Not once did I flinch when I walked into the room or feel the need to avert my gaze.

I actually found it enormously comforting, seeing him lying so serenely. My grandmother had cancelled my grandfather's cremation at the last minute after going to view his body at the morgue. I understood that now because I didn't think of it as Oscar's body at all. It was Oscar. And the mere thought of sending him to a furnace sent me cold.

There had been no question about where Oscar would be buried. It had been one of the first things I'd talked to Julie about when we'd arrived at the hospice. I'd looked the place up online about a year ago when I'd heard them talking at work about a child being buried there.

Bluebell Hill, it was called. A natural burial ground only a couple of miles from the hospice. Tucked away in one of those quiet corners of Huddersfield that it was easy to forget existed. It was green and tranquil. A place to sit and remember. A place you would want to be.

I didn't tell Rob that I had checked it out a year ago. It seemed wrong somehow to admit I had been looking at such things before Oscar had even started school. I didn't want him to think I had doubted Oscar's ability to survive. It had simply been that I'd needed to know there was somewhere nice he could go to if the worst did happen. Somewhere he'd be able to be at peace.

We were having the actual service there too. We both wanted it to be outdoors. Open to the elements. Not constrained by a building. Or religion, of course. A humanist celebrant with pink hair called Marika was leading the service. It was, as Rob had already pointed out, very Hebden Bridge.

I turned to look at Rob. He was standing by the patio doors, gazing out into the garden, as he had done on so many occasions over the past three days.

'Do you know the really weird thing?' he asked. I shook my head. 'I don't actually want to leave. If they offered us a two-year lease I'd take it right now. It's ridiculous, isn't it? Coming from someone who used to be too scared to set foot in the place.'

'We can come back as often as we like. The counselling will carry on. Zach can still go to the sibling group.'

'I know, and that's all great. But tonight we've got to go home for good. Back to our house. And Oscar isn't going to be there.'

I walked over and wrapped my arms around him. 'For what it's worth,' I said, 'it scares the hell out of me too. But we need to do it for Zach's sake. We need to create a new kind of normal. Whatever that's going to be.'

'It'll be quiet,' said Rob. 'That's the thing I'm dreading most. How quiet it will be.'

'Mealtimes,' I said. 'That's what I'm dreading. The empty place at the table. Not having to tell him about speaking with his mouth full.'

'And birthdays and Christmas and going out without him. We're going to have to sell the car, aren't we? Just get a little runabout instead.'

'Yeah, I know. I was thinking maybe we could use the money to go on holiday this summer. Cornwall would be nice. You can stay at a lighthouse, you know. I've seen them in a brochure. I'd like to take Zach to stay at a light-house. I want to sit with him and watch the waves crashing on the rocks. We can take his telescope. They sky will be so clear, he'll love it.'

Rob kissed me on the forehead. 'Silly old bean,' he said. 'That's what Oscar would have said.'

There was a knock on the door. Julie had come back with Zach.

'We've got it,' he said, holding up a tube of hair gel.

'Come on then,' smiled Rob, 'you'd better put it on for him.'

I watched as Zach squeezed some gel onto the palm of his hand, rubbed his hands together and started applying it. To describe it to anyone else, it might well sound macabre. But to me, standing there, watching him, it was the most beautiful display of brotherly love I had ever seen.

'There,' said Zach finally, stepping back to admire his handiwork. 'What do you think?'

I looked at Oscar, dressed in his favourite orange shorts and blue-and-orange stripy T-shirt, his hair gelled up at the front, just how he liked it.

'I think he looks a treat,' I said. 'Thank you.' Zach came over and let me ruffle his hair. 'Right then,' I said, looking up at Rob. 'I guess we'd better get ready too.'

I'd asked people not to wear black. There wasn't anything

black about Oscar. I'd asked for stripes instead. In as many different colours as possible. Oscar would have liked that. It would have made him laugh.

Zach came with us to get changed. He put on his rainbow striped T-shirt. Mum had been back to the house to get what we needed. She'd brought my green-and-yellow stripy knitted top and the green skirt with wavy lines on. She'd even managed to find an old stripy tie of Rob's that he didn't know he had.

'There,' I said when we'd finished. 'What do you think?'

'I think Oscar will giggle when he sees us,' said Zach, before stopping short as he realised what he'd said and looking up at me with sorrowful eyes. 'I mean he would have. In the old days.' I took him into my arms and squeezed him tight. Trying not to think about the old days.

The horse-drawn hearse had been Zach's idea. He'd seen it in a folder of photos Julie had shown us. Said he thought Oscar would have loved it. Mum and Dad had insisted on paying for it. They'd wanted to do something to help and had seemed massively relieved to be able to. The lady who ran the company had apologised about the fact that they only had black horses, but she'd got some rainbow plumes for them and had even gone to the trouble of finding a rainbow blanket for the driver's legs.

We stood and watched as Oscar's tiny bamboo coffin was carried out of the hospice and loaded into the hearse. Zach in the middle of us, clutching our hands very hard. Everyone had come out to pay their respects: staff, volunteers, other parents. The courtyard was awash with stripes. Simon had an outfit on which made him look like an ice-cream seller. It was great, though. People were actually smiling as they blinked away their tears. Oscar would have loved to know he'd left the audience with smiles on their faces.

Marie and Julie were going with us. They were taking Mum and Dad. It was only going to be a small gathering at Bluebell Hill. We'd wanted it that way.

I took Zach up to stroke the nose of one of the horses. It snorted and shook its head. I reached out too, its velvety muzzle soft against my fingers.

'Mummy says you've got to go slowly,' Zach instructed the horse, 'but I think you should go a bit fast. Just at the end. Oscar liked going fast.'

I smiled and guided Zach towards the car where Rob was waiting. He'd left the side door open for us. I was going to sit with Zach on the way in case he got upset. Oscar's powerchair was in the back of the car where we'd left it. Zach stopped for a second as he saw it. I wasn't sure where it was going to go.

'Can we give it to someone else now?' asked Zach. 'Because Oscar doesn't need it anymore.'

I nodded. Sat down next to him and helped him put on his seat belt.

As it happened, Zach was fine on the journey. Looking out of the windows, following the progress of the hearse. Asking why everyone was slowing down or stopping to let us go.

'Look,' he said, suddenly pointing. I followed the direction of his gaze. There were five houses in a row, all with Lollipop Party posters in the window. We had stepped outside our bubble. We were back in the outside world.

We rounded the corner into Bluebell Hill and came to a halt behind the hearse. A small gathering of people were waiting for us: our nearest and dearest, dressed in stripes of every colour, like a big clump of flowers, brightening up the hillside. I could see Alice in a green-and-white striped T-shirt with a big pink heart on it, clutching Jackie's hand. Esme next to her, her hair tied back off her face in a huge rainbow bow, tugging on Anna's arm, pointing to the horses.

'They all really loved Oscar, didn't they?' said Zach.

'Yes,' I said, turning to look at him. 'They did.'

29

JACKIE

'I'm going to read some of Oscar's favourite jokes,' said Zach, as Rob passed him a book from inside his jacket pocket.

'What did the policeman say to his tummy?' Zach paused for a second, looked around at the assembled mourners in case any of them were going to proffer an answer, before announcing proudly, 'You are under a vest.'

Alice giggled. Not as much as she'd giggled when Oscar had told it, but she giggled all the same.

I watched Zach as he carried on, marvelling at his ability to retain his composure while all around him were either laughing, crying or a mixture of both. He'd asked Sam if he could do it. She'd told me that. She hadn't been sure at first, had been worried it would prove too much for him. But I was so glad she'd said yes in the end, because this was helping. It was helping Zach and it was helping all of us to be able to smile again. When he'd finished there was a spontaneous round of applause. I saw Rob ruffle Zach's hair; Sam hug him to her. A plume of pride rising above there heads.

I hadn't gone to Deborah's funeral. I supposed it hadn't been considered appropriate in those days. Or maybe Mum and Dad simply hadn't thought I'd be able to cope with it. Perhaps I wouldn't have, not that sort of funeral. But this, this was different. This was lifting Zach up. And it would sustain him for years to come. Knowing he had said goodbye to his brother in such a special way.

Anna stepped forward, a copy of *The Lighthouse Under the Clouds* in her hand. She'd remembered reading it with Esme at the library and had ordered it specially from the bookshop in town.

She started to read. Her voice shaky at first, but finding its rhythm after a minute or two. Telling the story of a girl called Kate who dared to try to find out what might be above the clouds over her lighthouse. She found the sun, when all around her had doubted that a clear blue sky could exist in such a place.

I nodded at Anna as she finished reading. I gave her Esme's hand back. And let her take Alice's hand on the other side. I took my place at the end of the grave and opened up my copy of *Tell Me Something Happy Before I Go to Sleep.* There had been no doubt about what I would read when Sam had asked. There wasn't a better story about sibling love than Willoughby looking after his little sister Willa who was too scared to go to sleep in case she had a bad dream.

The tears started rolling down my face when I got to the bit about Willa's chicken slippers. By the time Willoughby had looked at the night sky with Willa and told her about all the wonderful things which were waiting for her next morning, the trickle had become a stream. I kept going though, determined that I would see this through. Conscious of Zach and Alice and Esme hanging on my every word.

Finally, when I'd finished, I closed the book. Sam mouthed 'thank you' to me. And Oscar's coffin was lowered into the grave.

I held Zach's hand as we walked back up towards the cars, leaving Sam and Rob to have some time alone at the grave.

'They'll be daffodils on it by next spring,' I told him. 'He would have liked that, wouldn't he?'

Zach nodded. He looked up at me with a solemn face. 'Mummy said your big sister died when you were seven.'

'She did, sweetheart.'

'Do you still miss her?'

'Yes,' I said. 'And you'll always miss Oscar. But you mustn't let it stop you enjoying your life. Oscar wouldn't want that, would he?'

Zach shook his head. 'Do you think he liked my jokes?'

'Liked them?' I said. 'He *loved* them. In fact, I think I can still hear him laughing.'

I walked into the press conference with Anna at my side and felt stronger, far stronger, than I had ever felt in my life.

I sat myself down at the table, shuffled the papers in my hand and promptly stood up again. 'OK,' I said. 'It's my turn and I'm angry. And when I'm angry I like to stand up.'

A couple of flashes went off. I took one quick look at my speech and put it down on the table. 'Two days ago,' I began, 'Sam Farnell's son Oscar was laid to rest. He spent his last days at the Sunbeams Children's Hospice in Huddersfield. A hospice which is currently struggling to raise enough money to offer a full range of services.

'Less than 5 per cent of its funding comes from the government. The rest of the five million pounds a year it needs to survive comes from fundraising. Ordinary people running half-marathons, doing sponsored bike rides, shaving their hair off, for Christ's sake.

'It's embarrassing. I'm embarrassed. I hope you are too. Because if there's one thing in this world everyone should be assured of, it is dignity in death. And as much as Sam is hurting over Oscar's death, what is sustaining her and her family is the knowledge that he could not have had a more loving, dignified and peaceful end to his life.

'And if anyone can think of one single thing that is more important to fund than that, I would like to hear it. I think Sam would like to hear it too.

'So today the Lollipop Party is reiterating our pledge to fully fund all hospices in the UK and to fund the building of new ones in whichever areas they are needed.

'And we are also challenging the new government,

whoever that may be, to pledge to do the same. Because it is at times like this that you realise what's important in life. And small-minded, backbiting, negative election campaigns appear crass and undignified.

'So if you want to slag us off for being crazy, being different, for daring to dream that we can make better choices, set better priorities and take better care of our people, then go ahead.

'I like to think that the people of the UK will see straight through that. Because they are not stupid. They are crying out for politicians who care about the same things they do. Who share the same priorities they do. And who are prepared to do anything, absolutely anything, to ensure children like Oscar can end their all-too-short lives surrounded by love and dignity and peace. Thank you.'

I sat down heavily on my chair at exactly the same minute that Anna stood up.

'Er, I think we're done, actually,' she whispered. 'I don't think there's anything else left to say.'

I nodded, stood up again and walked out of the room arm-in-arm with her.

Alice asked for *Tell Me Something Happy Before I Go To Sleep* again that night. I suspected it was going to be the bedtime story of choice for quite some time to come. Not that I minded. Anything that helped her to deal with it, that allowed her to talk about Oscar instead of bottling it up inside was a good thing.

'Zach's not going to die, is he, Mummy?'

'No, love. He hasn't got the disease Oscar had. He's been tested and everything.'

'Oh. Only I did like the ponies, you see,' said Alice. 'I would like to see them again if someone else dies.'

I smiled and shook my head as I turned out the bedside light, safe in the knowledge that she was going to be just fine.

The final leaders' debate had just started when I went downstairs. I sat down next to Paul on the sofa and stared at them: three Oxbridge-educated men in suits pontificating over whose fault it was that we were in such an economic mess and who was better qualified to get us out of it. I seemed to remember hearing something very similar at the last election.

'Nothing's going to change, is it?' I said.

'Don't write it off just yet. I bet they'll be running your speech on ten o'clock news later.'

'Yeah, but it feels like we're just a sideshow now. Something a bit quirky to give viewers a break from serious politics.'

'Bollocks. Last opinion poll still had you at 13 per cent.'

'I know but that's not going to win us election, is it? And besides, you know what people are like when they get to polling booth. They suddenly lose their bottle and vote for same old parties as usual.'

'I'll still vote for you. Well, not you because I can't, but Sam anyway.'

'Thank you,' I said, rubbing his shoulder. 'Let's just hope you're not only one.'

'I've found somewhere by the way. For your mum, I mean. A home I think will be just right for her. Somewhere you'll like.'

I turned to look at him. 'When did you do this?'

'Just while you've been busy. I figured it was least I could do. I've got a brochure; you can have a look through it if you want. I've been through lots of different ones. There's quite a few I wouldn't touch with a bargepole, mind. This is a good one, though.'

'Thank you,' I said. 'She'll be OK, won't she?'

'She'll be in the best place she can possibly be.'

I sat on the toilet for a long time the next morning gazing at the testing stick in my hand. There had been so many occasions when I had stared at one, willing a blue line to appear, that I still wasn't convinced it was real, rather than a figment of my imagination.

I was only a day or so late. It could be a false result. I could quite easily be in the one point whatever it was inaccurate bracket. But somehow I knew that wasn't the case.

I started crying. Soft, silent tears full of so many mixed emotions. All the times I'd imagined this moment and the one thing I'd never envisaged was that I would feel guilty. Guilty for having a new life growing inside me when Oscar's had just been extinguished. For somehow swapping places with Sam so that she was the mother-of-one and I wasn't.

I felt I'd cheated. Had run in and stolen the treasure while the other person hadn't been looking. I should give it back. It wasn't fair. It wasn't supposed to be like this.

My crying must have grown louder. There was a quiet knock on the door.

'Jackie? You all right?'

I stood up somewhat shakily. Washed my hands under the cold tap and opened the door, the test stick in my hand. 'I'm pregnant,' I said.

Paul stared at me and the test stick in turn, then back to me again. 'Are you sure?'

'Well, 99 per cent so, I guess.'

'But that's brilliant, isn't it?' he said.

'It would have been, but it feels so wrong now. The whole thing with Oscar. It's too soon.'

'Don't be ridiculous,' he said, taking hold of both arms. 'Sam'll be delighted. She'll be thrilled. You know she will.'

'But how can I tell her?' I said. 'After everything she's been through.'

'Well I'll tell her if you don't.'

'No. I just mean—'

'She's in a dark place, Jackie. But that doesn't mean she wants to be surrounded by doom and gloom. I imagine she's desperate to see some chinks of lights. It'll be the best news she's had in ages.'

'Really?' I asked. 'You don't think she'll hate me for it?'

'I'm not even going to answer that,' said Paul.

I looked at him again. I breathed for the first time in what seemed like ages. And slowly, very slowly, a smile began to creep over my face. 'I'm pregnant,' I said again, wanting to hear it this time.

'I know,' said Paul, pulling me closer. 'And I'm bloody chuffed to bits.'

'We weren't even trying,' I said, allowing the smile to develop into a full grin.

'Oh, you're always trying,' he smiled, 'believe me.'

30

ANNA

I opened my eyes, the sunlight was forcing its way through the muslin curtains into my bedroom. It took me a few moments to remember what day it was. Thursday, 2nd May had been a long time coming. A very long time indeed.

I stretched out. It was going to take some getting used to, having a double bed all to myself. I hadn't yet worked out whether I missed David or simply missed the presence of another adult in the house. It wasn't exactly something people aspired to, being a single mum. You didn't catch little girls writing it on their 'When I grow up I want to be . . .' lists. But there again, you didn't catch them saying they wanted to be in an unhappy, loveless marriage either.

And the truth was I had been lying in bed at night feeling lonely and unloved for a long time. The fact that there was no longer anyone there with me actually made it a bit easier. I had taken the first step. Or maybe I'd been pushed over the edge. Either way, I was on my own now. And the view wasn't nearly as terrifying as I had feared.

I switched the radio on. The election day coverage on Radio 4 was in full swing. I'd never expected to feel this detached about the whole thing, had assumed I'd be out there at the crack of dawn knocking on doors, monitoring the latest poll results. I hadn't known life would overtake us. And then death would overtake that too.

I ached for Oscar. And if I ached I couldn't even begin to imagine the raw pain Sam and Rob must be feeling. Oscar was gone and nothing would bring him back, and somehow they had to accept that, get used to it and get on with their lives. Anyone who said running the country was the hardest job going was wrong. Very wrong indeed.

Esme charged into the bedroom as I was drying my hair.

'It's come out,' she squealed. 'My wobbly tooth's come out. I just kind of pulled it and it came out all by itself.'

I smiled at her. 'I see,' I said. 'Well, you'd better put it somewhere safe until later. Looks like the Tooth Fairy's going to have a busy night.'

She beamed and ran back into her bedroom. I tried to recall whether I had any ribbon for the fairy scroll. Just what a parliamentary candidate needed to be worrying about on election morning. And then I stopped and looked in the mirror. And realised how lucky I was to be able to worry about such things.

*   *   *

'The latest poll's got the Lollipop Party at 15 per cent,' said Will, looking up from the toaster as I entered the kitchen. I didn't know what to be more surprised at: the fact that he was up, making toast, or that he was listening to Radio 4.

'Really?' I said.

'Yeah. And that's the national polls. You'll do miles better than that in Hebden Bridge.'

'Yes, but it's the whole valley, isn't it? And what with everything that's happened, we haven't managed to cover half of it.'

'Switch your laptop on,' Will instructed. 'I bet you anything you'll be trending on Twitter.'

I did as he said. Vote Lollipop was the top hashtag in the UK.

'Woo-hoo,' said Will, doing a top bit of air-punching.

'Has Mummy won?' asked Esme, coming into the kitchen with her cardigan buttons done up the wrong way.

'Not yet,' said Will, 'but she's going to.'

'Hey, don't get her hopes up too high,' I said.

'I'm not. I'm just saying I think you're going to win. I wish I had some money on it.'

'Not you as well,' I said.

'As well as who?' he asked.

'Nothing.' I smiled.

We left the house together for a change. Will, Charlotte and Esme all sporting 'Vote Lollipop' stickers. As I looked down the road into town, there were dots of purple all over the hillside and along the valley.

'Look, Mummy,' said Esme, 'you've turned Hebden Bridge all purple.'

And I smiled. Because we had. And because no one could have predicted that happening three months ago.

The blur of purple increased the closer we got to the school gates. The school had even put purple-and-pink bunting up along the roof and railings. The Head was standing at the gates when we arrived.

'Thank you,' I smiled, 'although I thought you weren't supposed to be political.'

'Oh, we're not,' she said. 'We just thought it was a good day to have a celebration of how brilliant our parents are. And they happened to be the only colours the local shop had in.'

She had a twinkle in her eye as she said it and hummed 'My Boy Lollipop' as she walked away. I gazed around me: virtually every child and parent was wearing a Lollipop Party sticker. I felt humbled. Very humbled. But most of all I felt proud.

I looked out past the gates and saw Jackie and Sam walking up the road together, Alice and Zach chattering away behind them. When they got to the crossing point, Shirley the lollipop lady came over and gave Zach his special hug, as she had done every day since his return to school a week ago. Maybe one day she'd manage to do it without tears in her eyes. Zach smiled when he saw her lollipop. It had 'school crossing patrol' on one side, but on the other was a great big home-made Lollipop Party rosette.

'You don't have to come with me, really,' said Sam, when she opened her door later that evening.

'No, we know that,' said Jackie, 'but we want to. You started this whole thing, remember? It's only fair that we see it through with you till the end.'

Sam's count was at Huddersfield. Jackie's and mine were both at the leisure centre in Halifax. We'd offered to stay with her for the whole night, but she'd insisted we go back for our own count which was due first. She picked up a jacket from the coat stand. Put it down and picked up another one instead.

'Are you sure you're up for it?' I asked. 'People would understand if you didn't turn up, you know.'

'No. I want to be there. I think it would be worse sitting at home, to be honest. Besides, I've got to face the world sometime. It may as well be tonight.'

I gave her a hug. Jackie kissed her cheek and then groaned and tried to wipe her lipstick mark off with a tissue.

'Get off me,' said Sam, 'you great big mumsy thing, you.' Jackie pulled a face at her.

'Is Rob coming later?' Jackie asked.

'Yeah. He's going to hang on until Zach's fast asleep, then he's going to leave him with Mum and come over.'

'How's he doing?' I asked.

'Oh, you know,' said Sam. 'One day at a time and all

that. He's been taking Zach over to the sibling group. I think it does him good to go there too.'

'And you're still planning to go back to work next week?' Jackie asked.

'Yeah. They've been great in offering me more time off, but I think if I leave it any longer I might never go back. I know it'll be tough, but in a weird way I think it might help me. There's a sense of peace there. Of calm. And a little piece of Oscar is there too.'

'Have they done the memorial brick yet for the glass wall?' I asked.

'A week on Saturday,' she said. 'We're going to have a little ceremony. Zach and Rob will be there. And Mum and Dad of course.' She hesitated and looked down. 'I'd like you guys to come too,' she said, 'but I'd totally understand if you can't make it. I know the kids have got lots of stuff on at the weekend.'

'We'll be there,' I said. 'We wouldn't miss it for the world.'

We had another group hug. I was already glad I'd opted for the waterproof mascara. Although if we continued at this rate, even that might not survive.

'Right then,' I said, 'We'd better get going.'

We walked either side of her along Fountain Street and down the steps.

Jackie stopped and held out her arm. 'Your election battle bus awaits.'

It was only then that Sam looked up and saw the purple-and-pink monstrosity which was parked on the cobbles.

'What on earth. . .?' she said, as she gazed at what had once been Jackie's Renault Scenic but was now lost under a sea of purple-and-pink Lollipop Party stickers, posters and bunting.

Jackie opened the door. She'd even put purple covers on the seats. 'I'm afraid Paul drew the line at a respray,' she said. 'Bloody spoilsport.'

Sam said nothing.

Jackie glanced across at me and grimaced before starting to speak rather rapidly. 'I did check with Rob. He said he thought it was a good idea. That you wouldn't think it was over-the-top or insensitive or anything. That Oscar would have loved it.'

'Yes,' said Sam, looking across at her and managing a small smile. 'Yes, he would have.'

We climbed into the back seat while Jackie got herself sorted in the front. 'I've left a few gaps so I can see out,' she reassured us, before turning the radio on and setting off.

'So, how are you doing?' I asked Sam.

'Middling days, bad days, well, mainly bad days actually. It's all the things I keep finding that belonged to him. Stupid things – felt-tips and what not. And I go to put them back and then remember that he won't actually be needing them. Not any more. There are stupid things I miss as well. Like the sound of his cough machine. It's daft, isn't it? How something so mundane, so unpleasant really, could become so much part of your life.'

I nodded and squeezed her hand. Unable to speak for a moment.

'And what about you?' asked Sam. 'How are you doing?'

I'd told her, a couple of days after the funeral, about David leaving. She'd been cross with me for not telling her sooner. Kept asking if there was anything she could do to help – as if she didn't have enough on her plate.

'I'm fine,' I said. 'I guess it will just take a bit of getting used to – being on my own again. The kids have been brilliant, though. Will especially. It's almost as if he sees himself as the man about the house now. He's pretty much grown up overnight.'

'Well, at least that's one thing, I guess. I had no idea, you know, that things were so bad between you.'

'I don't think I realised quite how bad they were myself,' I replied. 'It's weird, the things you find out about during an election campaign.'

We walked up the steps of Huddersfield town hall together, Jackie still talking about how many people had beeped and waved at us on the way over. I wasn't sure whether she was genuinely that excited about it or whether she was simply talking to try to take Sam's mind off what it was she was about to do.

Attending an election count was probably one of the last things she felt like doing right now. Attending an election count in which she was one of the candidates was probably *the* last thing.

'Ready?' I asked, as we paused at the top of the steps.

Sam nodded. 'Ready as I'll ever be.'

'Hang on then,' said Jackie, reaching into her bag for

a camera. 'I want to record this for posterity.' She corralled a short, balding man who had the air of a council election official about him, into leaving his post at the door to take a photo of the three of us standing there, our arms around each other, dressed head to toe in purple.

'Come on, then, my fellow musketeers,' said Jackie, when she'd put the camera back in her bag, 'all for one and one for all.' And with that we linked arms and walked into the town hall, across the foyer and pushed open the double doors to the room where the count was being held.

It wasn't like one of those surprise parties where people hide under tables and jump out cheering as soon as you enter. It was more of a ripple effect. As we walked down the side of the room, people looked up, stopped whatever they were doing and started to clap. The sound grew, gathering momentum as we made our way to the far end of the room. People of all political parties, all sorts of beliefs, religions and backgrounds, joining in the spontaneous round of applause for Sam. Applause which carried her forward without her legs really needing to move. She held on tightly to our arms, her tears splashing down onto our hands, and the sound of applause, of respect and sympathy and admiration, ringing in our ears.

It was gone eleven by the time Jackie and I got back to Halifax, having left Sam at the Huddersfield count with Rob. North Bridge leisure centre didn't exactly look like a place to stage a political revolution. It didn't even look like much of a place to have a game of badminton, to be honest. But if we were going to put the Lollipop Party on the political map, it was probably quite apt that we should do so at the most unlikely of venues.

The counting was well underway when we got inside and Will was running up and down the sidelines like something demented.

'How's it going?' I asked, managing to keep him still for a second.

'It looks like you're up there with the big guys, both of you.'

'Really?'

'Yes, really. Look at those piles of votes. And look at the faces of those miserable-looking gits from the other parties.'

Jackie and I went up for a closer look. Will was right. It did indeed appear that we were in with a fighting chance.

'Bloody hell,' whispered Jackie. 'I haven't written a speech or anything.'

'Don't get too carried away,' I said. 'It's early days, remember. They're not expecting to declare until four in the morning.'

'Yeah, but still.'

I knew exactly what she meant. I could feel it too. The sense that we were on the verge of something extraordinary here. There was a shout from Will. He was pointing up at the large TV screen hanging on one wall.

'Look,' he said. 'The first result's in. We got 13 per cent of the vote in Sunderland south. And that's a Labour stronghold. The Dimbleby guy said so. It's happening. What they said in the exit poll is happening. You're gonna get a massive chunk of the vote.'

I stared at Jackie. She stared at me. And we both did the really uncool thing of jumping up and down in delight.

And so it went on. Result after result with the Lollipop Party coming second or third. Our purple-clad candidates grinning from the rostrums, looking elated but slightly dazed by what they had achieved.

By the early hours of the morning, things were starting to become clearer. It looked as if there were going to be a new government, for a start. The electorate, as Jackie had so delicately put it, had given the Prime Minister a massive kick in the balls.

It wasn't clear yet whether Labour would win enough seats to get in or whether they too would need to form some kind of coalition. But the story of the night, as David Dimbleby kept telling everyone, was the meteoric rise of a party which hadn't even existed three months ago. Whenever they broke off to go to Emily Maitliss for a look at the big picture, her graphs and charts told the same story: the Lollipop Party were consistently polling around 15 per cent of the vote and picking up second and third places across the UK.

And still they counted in Halifax. I didn't think that many people lived in the Calder Valley, let alone voted. The view from the deck was that Jackie appeared to be involved in a three-way fight with Labour and the Tories in Halifax, while I was in a similar situation in the Calder

Valley. The Liberal Democrats had disappeared off the electoral map.

There was a whiff of expensive perfume in the air. Laura Jenkins, the Lib Dem candidate, squeezed past behind me. Her metaphorical tail between her legs. I felt my body stiffen. Will opened his mouth to say something.

'Don't,' I said. 'It's not worth it. We're not going to stoop to her level. We're going to hold our heads up high and let our votes do our talking for us.'

Will sighed. 'You're no fun, you are,' he said. 'No fun at all.'

'Well I'm hardly going to let you pick a fight with her, am I?'

'Permission to air-punch if she loses her deposit?'

'OK.' I smiled. 'Permission granted.'

Jackie's result came first. I stood, tapping my feet on the floor as the returning officer went through all the preliminaries. I fixed her with a stare, trying to work out from her expression what the outcome was. But she simply kept smiling down at me. The sort of smile which gave nothing away at all.

The returning officer finally got to the interesting bit. 'The number of votes cast in Halifax are as follows: Michael Blenkinsopp, Conservative Party, 9,162; Roger Carstairs, Liberal Democrat Party, 4,069; Jackie Crabtree, Lollipop Party, 12,793.'

A roar went up from our supporters gathered in the hall, led by Will, and with me as a very able first lieutenant. We hadn't had the Labour vote yet, though.

The returning officer waited for a hush to descend on the hall again. 'Duncan Fairweather, Labour Party, 14,658.'

I shut my eyes and groaned, but when I opened them a moment later Jackie was still smiling. A great big, 'the girl done good' grin across her face.

Barely fifteen minutes later I stood on the same rostrum, my face running through a variety of expressions in the hope of finding one which would fit. I'd always thought how weird it was that the candidates were told the results first and then had to pretend not to know. But now I was in that situation I was relieved that was how it worked. I needed the extra time to try to regain my composure and figure out how I felt about it all as the returning officer started to read out the results.

'Laura Jenkins, Liberal Democrat Party, 3,577.'

I saw Will do an air-punch. She may not have lost her deposit, but it was still a pretty appalling result. I was relieved David had chosen not to come to the count tonight. It would have been difficult for all of us.

'Anna Sugden, Lollipop Party, 14,321.

It was hard to tell who whooped louder this time, Jackie or Will. A faint smile settled on my face as the returning officer continued.

'Jerry Broadhurst, Conservative Party, 11,890; Martin Simpson, Labour Party, 12,468. I hereby declare—'

But we never did hear what he declared. My name was lost in the huge roar that rose up from floor. And I stood there, the Lollipop Party's first MP, still struggling to take it all in.

I stepped forward to make my speech. My legs were wobbly, my hands trembling, but my voice was firm and strong. 'Three months ago, Sam Farnell had a dream. A dream to create a different kind of political party, one that put the most vulnerable people in our society first. One that reflected the priorities of ordinary people, that spoke for those who would not otherwise have a voice.

'Today, across the country, millions of people have voted for that party. They have sent a message to the Westminster establishment, a message that their days are numbered. It's time for a new kind of politics, a politics which puts children and families first. And that's why I dedicate my victory tonight to Oscar Farnell, who lost his own brave battle for life, but who has left a lasting legacy, a promise of a better future for all our children.'

'Jeez,' said Will as he hugged me a few moments later. 'My mum's gone all Martin Luther King on me.'

'I still can't quite believe it,' I said. 'I never in a million years thought this would happen.'

'Well, it has. You whipped their arses.'

'And that's the official political analysis, is it?' I said.

'So what happens now?' he asked.

'I don't know,' I said. 'To be honest I'm not even sure I can do it.'

'What do you mean?'

'Well, I'll either have to live in London five days a week

and never see you, or we'd all have to move down, and I'm not sure it's fair to disrupt you all like that.'

Will stared at me and shook his head.

'What?' I said.

'So our father's walked out, I'm about to finish school and need to get away from this place and find a drama college and Charlotte's being bullied at school and is desperate to make a fresh start somewhere new. And the rest of your family live in London. It's a complete no-brainer.'

Put like that, I had to admit he had a point. 'What about Esme?'

'She won't care where she is. You could drop her on Mars and she'd be happy, as long as she could find some-where to do cartwheels.'

'Do you know what?' I said. 'I still wouldn't mind having you as my special adviser.'

'Depends what you're offering,' smiled Will, 'us actor types need a bit of easy money while we're resting.'

Jackie finally managed to fight her way through the crowds of well-wishers and media. 'Woo-hoo,' she shouted, throwing her arms around me. 'How's it feel to be the Lollipop Party's first MP?'

'Good,' I said. 'Very good indeed. I'm only sorry you didn't beat me to it.'

'No worries,' she said, her eyes glistening. 'I guess it wasn't the right time for me anyway. I don't think the electorate would have been very impressed if I'd gone off on maternity leave in seven months' time.'

I stared at her.

She nodded.

'Congratulations, that's fantastic,' I said hugging her. 'Have you told Sam?'

'Not yet,' she said. 'I'll do it after her count.'

When I finally made it through to the relative quiet of the ladies I switched my phone back on and checked my direct messages on Twitter. Gavin's was top of the list.

How about we get the first studio interview with the country's brightest new MP? Might even buy you a drink on my winnings while you're down here!

I smiled to myself. London was going to be just fine.

31

SAM

Somewhere in the midst of it all I was aware that I had come very close. That the numbers involved had been less than one hundred. That people had patted me on the back and said better luck next time.

None of it really mattered. It wasn't about me. Had never been about me. And especially not now. Hearing Anna's result had been all I needed. The Lollipop Party had made history tonight, confounded the critics, ensured that our voice would be heard in the corridors of power, that we had a platform from which to go forward.

I did my interviews, without really being aware of what I'd said, packed my things away, thanked all the people who needed thanking, took Rob's hand and walked out of the hall, down the steps and across the road to the car park. The dawn already breaking; a new day about to begin.

'Let's go home,' I said. 'Zach will be waking up soon.'

We drove in silence back to Hebden Bridge. Not an angry silence, a contemplative, peaceful one. The radio was on in the background, confirming what I already knew. That something amazing was happening across the UK. Something which had been started by two little boys who hadn't wanted a lollipop lady to lose her job.

Anna and Jackie were already there when we got back. As was a whole army of reporters and photographers, thronging the narrow street and towpath beyond and making the whole thing feel decidedly surreal.

'We're thrilled,' I said, when a dozen microphones were thrust in front of my face. 'Thrilled that so many people have voted for us in such great numbers. That our beliefs and our policies have been vindicated in this way.'

I didn't sound thrilled, of course. I sounded numb with it all. And, for once, I actually think they understood that.

I was submerged by hugs and kisses as soon as I got in the door. Anna and Jackie were in tears and so was Mum. Dad simply stood there at the end of the hallway, a look of utter pride on his face.

I kissed them all in turn, accepted the platitudes and commiserations which were proffered to me and went through to our tiny lounge where the television was in the corner, the volume turned low so as not to wake Zach.

'I'll put the kettle on,' said Mum. Dad and Rob went with her. Leaving the three of us staring at a television screen showing a lot of red, some blue, a bit of yellow. And one tiny dot of purple.

'I'm so proud of you,' I said, turning to Anna and smiling.

'Don't be daft. You're the one who should be proud.'

'I am. I'm proud of all of us. I just can't quite get my head around the fact that you're going to be an MP.'

'We're going to move back to London,' Anna said. 'Will reckons it will be good for all of us.'

'What about David?' I asked.

'He might go back himself. If not, we'll be up some weekends and during the holidays. Whenever you'll have us, really.'

'You'll have to get somewhere as a constituency office,' Jackie said. 'Somewhere with a flat above where you could stay. Or a canal boat – that would be very Hebden Bridge.'

Anna smiled and looked back at Jackie. 'Are you going to tell her now?' she asked.

'Tell me what?'

'That I'm pregnant,' Jackie said. 'Only six weeks or so, it's very early days yet. But I'm pregnant.'

I threw my arms around her, a fresh flood of tears coming, followed by a smile so big you could have seen the rainbow from the other end of town.

'That's brilliant,' I said. 'That's the best thing I've heard in ages.'

'See,' said Anna. 'I told you she'd be thrilled.'

I looked at Jackie. She looked down at her feet. 'It felt a bit soon, that's all.'

'Do you know what?' I said. 'It couldn't have come soon enough.'

'Good,' said Jackie, wiping her eyes, 'because we want you to be godmother or whatever the non-religious, politically correct version is.'

'Guardian.' I smiled. 'And thank you. 'I'd be delighted.'

Anna's phone rang. She slipped into the hallway, speaking in hushed tones. David Dimbleby was still going strong.

'I don't know about you,' said Jackie, letting out a deep sigh, 'but I'll have what he's having.'

Anna came back in. A look of thinly veiled elation on her face.

'Who was it?' I asked.

'Oh, only the next Prime Minister, asking if I'd help form a coalition and offering to fully fund all hospices.'

'I hope you said yes,' I told her.

'No, I asked him for proper dementia care and to introduce a national anti-bullying strategy. Then, when he agreed to that, I said yes.'

The room was quiet for a second. Only a second, mind, before it exploded in a riot of shrieks and screams and tears.

'We did it,' I said. 'We changed the world, well the country at least. We made a difference, in just a few months as it turned out. Just think what we'll be able to do in a year.'

It was Zach's face I saw first when it all calmed down. Leaning down over the top of the banisters. 'Did you win?' he called out.

I went to the foot of the stairs and caught him as he flew down them and emptied himself into my arms.

'Mummy didn't win. Not quite. But Anna did. And the new Prime Minister wants her to help him run the country. He's going to fund all the hospices, including Sunbeams.'

Zach grinned at me, the beginning of a tear welling in his eye, and nodded. 'Oscar would have been really pleased about that, wouldn't he?'

'Yes,' I said, squeezing him tightly. 'Yes, he would.'

It was another half an hour or so before we got ourselves together enough to go outside and face the press.

I was vaguely aware of how bizarre it was, seeing the nation's media camped outside our front gate. Caz from next door was already out there, offering everyone coffees. Which meant that some guy from the *Daily Mail* was about to drink from an 'Everyone loves a lesbian' mug. The world had indeed been turned on its head.

We stood side by side in the front yard as they jostled for positon. I glanced up to where Zach was leaning out of his bedroom window with Rob, his telescope trained down on us. And then I started speaking.

'Last night,' I said, 'politics changed. It changed for the better. It changed because people wanted it to.

'The Lollipop Party has been asked to help form a coalition government. In return, the new Prime Minister has pledged to fully fund all hospices in the UK and to implement national dementia care and anti-bullying strategies.

'It is only a start and we will go on campaigning for

everything we believe in. And who knows, maybe one day we will have a regional parliament here in Yorkshire and others across the UK, and maybe children's operations won't be cancelled five times any more and maybe we'll even have free public toilets.

'Because three months ago people thought none of this would ever happen. People thought we were crazy. Because what people in this country had done was to stop believing. Believing that one person could make a difference. And that if they joined with another person, and another, they could make an even bigger difference.

'So this morning we pay tribute to all those who dared to dream. The candidates across the UK who put their lives on hold to go out and campaign for us, and the people who voted for us, even though they were repeatedly told it would be a wasted vote. Change takes courage, change takes a leap of faith, change doesn't necessarily take a long time.'

I paused for a moment and looked up at Zach and Rob again. Zach had put Oscar's pirate hat on the windowledge where I could see it.

'And the one thing I've learnt more than anything during this election campaign is never to stop fighting for what you believe in. Because my son Oscar taught me there is no such word as "can't". And he also taught me something else: that there are some things in life far more important than politics.

'Which is why we are all going to go home now and have breakfast with our families.'

'Shit,' cried Anna. I spun around to see a look of sheer terror on her face.

'The Tooth Fairy,' she shrieked. 'I've forgotten the bloody Tooth Fairy.' And with that she pushed past the crowd of photographers and legged it down the road.

'Don't forget the fairy scroll,' Jackie called out after her. 'And skip for goodness sake.'

And with that we turned around, hugged each other, and went back inside Number Ten Fountain Street.

ABOUT THIS BOOK

Like many people, I watched the leadership debates during the 2010 general election campaign with an increasing sense of disillusionment with mainstream politics and the men in suits who were leading it. Where were the women? Where were the radical ideas? Where were the policies which would really improve the lives of ordinary families?

I bored my husband silly talking about where the major parties were going wrong and how a bunch of mums could make a better job of it. One night, desperate for some sleep, my husband suggested that instead of attempting a one-woman political coup, I should write a novel about someone else doing it. The ploy worked; he got to sleep, I began plotting a fictional revolution.

I started to write a synopsis about three mums who, having led a campaign to save a lollipop lady, are asked by a TV presenter if they fancied standing in the general election. I worked on the backgrounds of my central characters, Sam, Jackie and Anna, friends who had busy, stressful lives trying to juggle work and family commitments, whether it be caring for a child with a disability, dealing with teenage children in crisis, or struggling with an elderly mother who had Alzheimer's.

They all had a reason to want to make things better and despite all the obstacles in their way, the passion and determination to make it succeed. All they needed was a cause they could believe in – something which would resonate with other mums across the UK. Something which had the potential to change the face of politics forever.

I began putting together a Mummyfesto, allowing each character to devise policies which they felt passionately about. Some were serious; the government to fully fund children's hospices, a dementia care plan, tough anti-bullying measures. Others were not quite so serious; privatising the royal family, The House of Lords replaced by Mumsnet, Chequers turned into a spa retreat for carers and the active encouragement of skipping for all.

Some policies never made the final cut; the introduction of a menstrual lottery which most men would be too embarrassed to buy a ticket for, and the monkey translator, which broadcasts unspoken thoughts in the film *Cloudy With a Chance of Meatballs* to be fitted to all men. But eventually my characters had a Mummyfesto which they were ready to go to the country with.

What I needed at that point was a publisher who

believed in the book as much as I did and that was where Quercus stepped in and, to use horrible management speak, picked up the ball and ran with it.

I got down to the task of researching. Probably the most difficult week I had was the one spent researching a whole host of awful childhood illnesses and diseases to find the one which Sam's son Oscar had. I can't hear Coldplay's 'Fix You' now without remembering some of the heart-breaking videos I watched on You Tube.

Eventually, I settled on Spinal Muscular Atrophy, an inherited neuromuscular condition causing weakness of the muscles. It affects approximately 1 in 6,000-10,000 babies born. There are four main types of SMA, babies with type 1 do not usually survive past 2 years old but those with the other types can survive into adulthood or even have a normal lifespan. About 1 in 40-60 of us carries the faulty gene copy which causes it. When both parents carry a faulty copy of the disease gene, there is a 1 in 4 chance in each pregnancy of the baby being affected by SMA. At present there is no known cure.

I also researched Alzheimer's Disease extensively and spent a lot of time researching children's hospices (Sam works in a fictional one). I had visited a children's hospice in my former life as a journalist and was keen to high-light the amazing work they do.

There are approximately 23,500 children who are not expected to reach adulthood in the UK. All children's hospices provide their services for free to the children and families that use them but on average only fifteen per cent of each hospice's £2.6million per year running costs are funded by the government.

With my research, the Mummyfesto and character studies complete I was ready to start writing. And so the Lollipop Party was formed around Sam's kitchen table at number ten Fountain Street in Hebden Bridge, West Yorkshire. The battle for number ten Downing Street was about to begin. It really would be the mother of all battles, both personally and politically for my characters. I laughed and cried in equal measure as I accompanied them on their journey. And at least I can now say that I was instrumental in starting a revolution – even if it was a fictional one.

There are two charities which were an enormous help to me in my research. I will be making a donation from the royalties of this book to each of them but if you have been moved by this story and would also like to make a donation, I know they would be enormously grateful. Thank you in advance.

'The Jennifer Trust for Spinal Muscular Atrophy is a national charity dedicated to supporting people affected by SMA, and promoting essential research into causes, treatments and eventually a cure for the disease. For more details and to make a donation please go to their website www.jtsma.org.uk or call 01789 267520.

The Forget Me Not Children's Hospice in Huddersfield, West Yorkshire supports children with life-limiting conditions and their families. It costs £2.5million a year to run and the vast majority of its funding comes from charitable donations. For more information and to make a donation please go to www.forgetmenotchild.co.uk or call 01484 411 040.

Writing this book moved me immensely and I know the characters will stay with me always. Thank you for reading it and please do get in touch via my website www.linda-green.com or by Facebook (Fans of Author Linda Green) or Twitter (@lindagreenisms).

ACKNOWLEDGEMENTS

Warmest thanks to the following people: my editor Jo Dickinson for believing in this book and being everything an author could want in an editor; the fantastic team at Quercus, especially Bethan, Margot, Caroline, Mark, Iain and Kathryn, for their hard work, energy and enthusiasm; my agent Anthony Goff for his expertise and support; Marigold and everyone at David Higham Associates, my Quercus stable-mate Dorothy Koomson, without whom this book might never have seen the light of day; Keris Stainton and her fellow We Should Be Writing group members and Emily Barr for their feedback and enthusiasm, Michael Tatterton for showing me around the Forget Me Not Children's Hospice in Huddersfield and providing invaluable research information and feedback; Tilly Griffiths, whose wonderful book *Tilly Smiles* showed me what children with Spinal Muscular Atrophy type 2 CAN do; The

Jennifer Trust for Spinal Muscular Atrophy, The SMA Trust, Smash SMA, Together for Short Lives and the Alzheimer's Society, who all helped with my research; Lance Little for my great website; James for lending his story and for being, like all children, very, very important; my Facebook followers Anna Ruth Yates and Sammy Joe for lending their names; my Twitter friends for providing a welcome (sometimes too welcome!) distraction; my family and friends for their on-going support and encouragement; my wonderful son Rohan for his ideas, coming up with the best lines for the children in the book, caring so much about them and regularly saying 'haven't you finished it yet, Mummy?'; my husband Ian for pointing out that it would be easier to write a novel about women who start a political revolution than actually doing it myself, and who, really annoyingly, came up with the title in five seconds flat when I had been trying for weeks. And you, my readers, without whom it wouldn't be half as much fun and whose comments and feedback on previous novels kept me going through the slog barrier of 30,000 words; Thank you all!